I0746322

THE TOY COLLECTOR

COLLECTOR

—THE RUSSO MAFIA—

-B. Lybaek

The Toy Collector Copyright © 2025 by B. Lybaek

Paperback ISBN: 978-1-917740-09-8
Hardback ISBN: 978-1-917740-10-4
eBook ASIN: B0F6M4QBFS

Follow

B. Cybaek

While I've done my best to list all the tropes and themes my team and I picked up on, everyone views content differently. Please read responsibly, and remember—your mental health always comes first.

Alpha-hole MMC | CNC | Coercion
Difficult family relationships | Drugs
Drugging of characters | Dub-con
Electronic surveillance | Emotional neglect
Explicit sexual content & kinks | Forced proximity
Kinks | Mafia | Manipulation | Non-con Power imbalance
Rape (Not H & h) | Sexual coercion | Somnophilia | Stalker
Touch her and die | Trauma | Unaliving | Violence

If you still love playing games, especially the ones that end with you aching, breathless, and begging for more…

If you read the rules and still beg to be broken by them…

If you like your games dark, your strings tangled, and your endings filthy, twisted, and absolutely earned…

Then this is for you.

The late August sun is relentless, baking the pavement as Lena and I walk across the quad, bags slung over our shoulders, cold drinks in hand. Campus is alive with first-day energy—students reuniting after the summer, freshmen looking lost, and professors checking their watches as they head to class. It's our final year of grad school, but the excitement of being back still lingers, that rush of new schedules, new classes, new possibilities.

"God, did we ever look that young and scared?" she giggles, nodding toward a group of freshmen.

"Us? We've never looked young, Lee," I laugh back. "I swear I had crow's feet at eighteen. And I think I found my first gray hair the day of my final high school exam."

I take a sip of my iced coffee—whipped cream, caramel drizzle, borderline dessert but absolutely necessary—Lena cradles her iced chai tea like it's holy. She eyes my drink with disapproval but wisely doesn't comment on my drink choice. As my best friend, her word is law in many areas of my life, just not the calorie goodness that is this drink.

"This is the year, Pipes," she says, confident as ever. "We own this shit."

"Damn right," I mutter.

"We need to manifest good energy. Straight A's, zero drama, and a thriving social life."

I snort, licking whipped cream off my straw. "Yes, cause nothing says thriving social life like being a political student." I mock good-naturedly.

Sighing, she slashes her hand through the air in a dramatic gesture. "Hey, it's your birthday today, bitch. I don't want to talk about capstone, internships, or anything else. We're celebrating this weekend, right?"

Shrugging one shoulder, I avert my gaze. "Umm… what did you have in mind?"

While we make our way across the quad and into the office building, Lee lists off suggestions, each one involving copious amounts of alcohol. I try to keep my facial expression neutral, pretending to consider the options.

It's not that I don't like alcohol. But cocktail bars are more my scene than the loud clubs she's prattling on about. Seriously, I don't get the point of those places since you have to scream if you want to have a conversation.

"Give it up," Lena laughs, hip bumping me as we stop outside the career center where I have a meeting with my advisor. "I know you hate going out. But seriously, Pipes. This is not just our last first-day. It's your birthday, and our last year in this place. That deserves the kind of celebration that leaves a hangover."

Groaning, I push the door open. "I'll think about it," I promise before I slip into the office.

"It's happening whether you want it to or not," Lee announces, and when I turn around to look at her, she's pointing finger guns at me. "Might as well get with the program."

Shaking my head, I slip into the office, immediately throwing my now empty plastic cup in the trash can by the door. Damn Lena and her over-the-top ideas.

A smile splays on my lips as I look up from the floor, confidently striding toward the secretary. But as I take my next step, my heel gets snagged on the carpet. I stagger backwards, my ankle wobbles, and just as I go down, I'm mentally cursing the shoes I'm wearing.

"Motherfucker—" Okay, I guess I'm not only using my inner voice.

I throw my arms out to stop myself from falling on my ass in the pristine Georgetown office.

Jesus H. Christ. In the three years I've been here, I've done everything in my power to be professional. Dressed for success, never skipped a day or delayed an assignment. Yet, here I am, my ass about to be intimately acquainted with the plush carpet, while a curse slips from me.

This distinctly feels like I've somehow offended a higher being, one that's in turn decided to take revenge via humiliation.

My cheeks burn as I hurry to get back up, not sparing a glance at the people sitting in their chairs and waiting for their name to be called. After picking up my laptop bag, I roll my shoulders back and march up to the secretary.

"Hi," I sing-song, throwing my dark brown hair over my shoulder. "I have an appointment with Mrs. Ellis."

"Name," the grouchy woman utters, not once looking up from her computer.

"Piper Harrington," I reply, trying not to laugh as my gaze lands on her reflection in the window behind her. She's playing solitaire, not curing some kind of rare disease.

Just as she starts telling me to take a seat, my advisor, Mrs. Ellis, sticks her head out of her office. "Come in, Piper," she smiles.

I follow her into her den, which is exactly what it feels like. Everything from the walls to the furnishings is cloaked in dark wood and deep jewel tones—mahogany shelves lined with dense books, a Persian rug muted by time, and emerald velvet chairs that look more decorative than practical. The air is warm and slightly stale, laced with the scent of old paper and something faintly floral—like a perfume that's long since faded into the walls.

We sit down at her desk, my back to the door. While she opens her laptop, I crane my neck, looking at the single lamp that glows in the corner. I'll never understand why Mrs. Ellis always has her dark and heavy curtains drawn, especially not on a beautiful day like today.

"So, this is your last year," she says.

"It is," I confirm, crossing one leg over the other.

Mrs. Ellis hums as she clicks around on her laptop. "Still on track with the Master's in Political Communication and Public Policy?"

"Yeah. My focus is mostly campaign strategy and narrative development, media angles, voter outreach, all that."

"Good," she says. "That's a solid niche. Competitive, but with the right experience, you'll be fine."

I nod once, already bracing for what she's about to say.

"That brings us to internships," she says, confirming my dread. "Have you had any luck?"

"Not yet," I say, my voice tighter than I mean it to be. "I've applied to a bunch; PR consultancies, media firms. Even some smaller campaigns. I'm just waiting to hear back."

The look she gives me is that of a disappointed parent. "I'd like to tell you there's time, and there is. But not much. The top-tier placements are probably already gone."

Ugh, that's exactly what I didn't want to hear.

"Simply put, Piper. If you don't secure an internship by the first of October, you're out of the running for…"

I squirm in my seat, trying not to look as defeated as I feel as I listen to her go on and on about how much this internship means.

"In fact…" She pauses and taps on her laptop again. "… seventy-eight percent of your peers secured their internships before the summer break."

"I know," I sigh.

This is the first time I don't have a solid plan, the first time I haven't secured the next step months in advance. And it's scary.

"This isn't just for the credit," she adds. "For someone in your program, the internship isn't just experience—it's a graduation requirement."

"Yeah." I pause. "I'll follow up again this week. Maybe reach out to some alumni?"

"Smart move," she says.

Mrs. Ellis gives me a few more pointers, before ending the meeting by telling me to come by again in a week. I know what she isn't saying; if I don't have an internship by then, I need to pivot.

"Can I ask you one more question?" I ask, not sure I want to, but fully aware I need to know. When she nods, I force the words out. "What happens if I can't secure an internship?"

"Then you won't graduate on time."

The words land like a punch, making me exhale in small puffs. She must see it on my face, because her tone softens just a touch.

"It's a required component of your track, Piper. The program requires applied fieldwork logged and evaluated by the end of the semester."

"Right," I murmur, more to myself than to her.

"Look," she says, not unkindly. "You're not behind yet. But this isn't the year to wait for doors to open. You've got the grades, the writing, the instinct—start using your network. Email professors. Go to those boring wine-and-cheese mixers."

I nod, even though the idea of "networking" makes my skin crawl.

"And Piper?"

I meet her eyes.

"You're one of the strongest students in your cohort. Don't let the quiet panic of senior year shrink you."

I swallow hard and thank her before stepping out, already composing five different follow-up emails in my head.

Feeling dazed, I leave Mrs. Ellis' office. My plan is to shrug her warning off and head to the lecture, it's one of my favorites after all. But no matter how much I tell my legs to carry me in that direction, they refuse.

For the first time in my twenty-six years of being alive, I skip class. I tell myself it's fine—birthday privilege, mental health, whatever excuse I need to not sit through a lecture I won't hear a word of. What I really need is caffeine, quiet, and distance from campus.

So I walk three blocks east until the buildings start to feel less academic and more curated. I duck into the café I favor when I want to disappear. It's off the beaten path, and pretentious enough that no one I know comes here.

The girl behind the counter doesn't even blink when I place my order. It arrives like a small piece of heaven in a glass, and I take it to a small corner table without bothering to open my laptop.

Instead of emailing alumni, rewriting my résumé, or even applying for that underpaid campaign internship Lena swears is a stepping stone, I just sit there.

The funny thing is, I should be panicking. But I'm not. I'm just floating—untethered, like I missed a step and now I'm waiting to land. Everyone else seems so ahead. Their placement secured, capstone

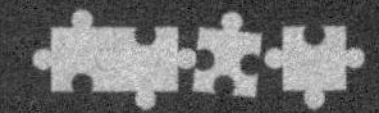

outlined, LinkedIn updated like they've been prepping for this since birth.

And me? I'm still trying to figure out how I managed to fall behind without noticing. Still trying to stop the low-level dread from morphing into full-blown failure. Well, I guess I do know. I put all my hopes into one internship. I never heard back from them, and instead of picking myself up, I kept waiting for their reply.

I take a sip, wincing at how sweet it is. Lena would have a stroke if she saw this much sugar in one drink. The thought of her makes me smile, but it's fleeting. My eyes wander out of habit, scanning the space without seeing anything—until they do.

He's standing near the counter, framed by a support beam that casts half his face in shadow. The man is tall, definitely over six feet. Broad-shoulders, lean but undeniably built, like someone sculpted from tension and purpose.

The clothes he wears are all black and tailored to perfection, from his fitted suit jacket to the dark shirt buttoned neatly at the collar. The fabric stretches just enough across his chest to hint at the strength beneath it, and when he shifts slightly, I catch a glimpse of ink peeking out from the edge of his left cuff.

A five o'clock shadow is dusted along his sharp jaw, giving him the kind of rugged edge no amount of polish could tame. And his hair; jet black, styled back with a smooth wave that looks impossibly intentional. God, he's… handsome doesn't even come close to describing him.

When my green gaze lands on his blue ones, a chill slithers down my spine.

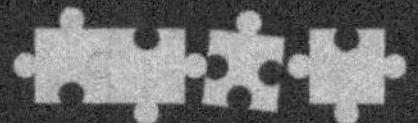

Lorenzo

I don't believe in fate. But the moment her eyes meet mine, I start to question that.

Her green eyes—sharp, tilted, curious—hook into mine like barbed wire. One look, and something inside me locks into place like a steel trap. No warning. No build-up. Just instant, electric obsession.

Fuck.

I don't think she really sees me, and before I can think of doing anything, her stare keeps moving like nothing happened. Like I didn't just feel the tectonic shift of something I wasn't supposed to want.

She's cradling the glass in front of her like it's the only thing holding her together. Long fingers, tense at the knuckles. Shoulders drawn up like she's waiting for something to go wrong. She has the kind of nervousness people miss if they don't know what to look for. But I do. I see it.

I see everything.

Most men would glance at her and think cute. Maybe even beautiful, if they were paying attention. And they wouldn't be wrong. But she's also so much more.

She's a fucking goddess, and even the small scar slicing through her left eyebrow isn't enough to make her a mere mortal.

Her chestnut brown hair is long and slightly wavy, pulled to one side like she can't decide between polished or disheveled. Her full lips are pursed, and her arms reveal a tan she's probably worked on all summer.

The black dress she's wearing is tight across her tits, teasing a shape that makes my mouth and hands itch. The thought makes a groan threaten to slip out, and I have to grind my teeth together to keep it locked down.

There's nothing staged about her—she's not posing for the world. And there's a silence in her stature. Not the quiet kind. Not the peaceful kind. The kind that hums under her skin like a storm waiting to be touched. The kind that demands to be broken open.

I want to touch that silence.

No—I want to destroy it.

When she looks back at me, my pulse stutters, and blood floods to my cock so fast I almost wince. This time, she keeps our gazes locked for longer. We just look, suspended in the kind of moment that turns men into monsters.

And I'm already one.

But she doesn't even seem to realize what she's done—what she's triggered.

She blinks once. The connection breaks as she turns her face slightly toward the window, looking outside at the people walking around.

Rooted to the floor, I trace the shape of her mouth like it's already wrapped around my cock. My fingers twitch with the urge to touch, and my jaw tightens with the restraint it takes not to cross the room and pull her up by the wrist. To press her into the wall and feel her gasp against my throat.

"I'm sorry it took so long, but I'm ready now."

When I don't immediately react to the words, a small hand grazes my shoulder. I whirl around, a growl building in my throat. As I come face-to-face with the wide-eyed barista, I quickly school my features.

"No problem," I say smoothly.

"Did you still want me to take a message?" she asks, her eyelashes

fluttering.

I nod, confirming I very much do.

Georgetown is not an area of D.C. I frequent. But today, I had a face-to-face meeting with Senator Jacobs' fixer, Mr. Shein. The thought of that unofficial job title makes me want to laugh. It's the irony of all fucking irony.

If the fixer really did what he was supposed to, I wouldn't have needed to drag my ass from my building in Foggy Bottom all the way here. And if Mr. Shein hadn't been late, I never would have been at the counter at Carroway Café, never having asked the barista to give Mr. Shein a message from me upon arrival.

Having my world flipped upside down, I don't feel inconvenienced anymore. I feel fucking grateful. "Please tell Mr. Shein to call me so we can reschedule," I say, feeling pretty fucking generous.

When I first asked to leave a message, I was going to ask him to fuck off and never bother me again. But now… now I feel like I owe him one.

Looking back over at where the woman was sitting, I find she's gone.

Fuck.

2

Piper

I barely make it into my off-campus apartment before my phone rings again. As soon as I accept the video call, my uncle's face comes into view.

"Happy birthday to you, happy birthday to you," he sings, badly. "Happy birthday dear Pipeeerrrr. Happy birthday to you."

I laugh, even though it comes out tired. "You're still tone deaf."

"Untrue and offensive," he replies with mock gravity. "And here I was just about to ask if my favorite niece needed anything topped up in her trust this month."

"I'm your only niece."

"Exactly. The competition is fierce."

I drop my bag on the floor and collapse onto the charcoal-gray colored couch that sits against the far wall.

Uncle Teddy is calling from his kitchen. I spot the old shelves behind him, cluttered with mismatched mugs and too many condiments. There's a bottle of whiskey just off-camera. Of course there is.

He's still in his wrinkled Henley and reading glasses, salt-and-pepper hair sticking up like he's been running his hands through it all day. Unshaven, warm-eyed, and always two seconds from making a wildly inappropriate joke—he looks exactly the same as always. Like home, in human form.

"You good, kid?" he asks. "Is the political hellscape still intact?"

"I'm fine." I pull my legs up beneath me. "Classes started today. I need to get myself an internship, but I'm working on it."

He raises his glass in a toast I can't fully see. "Just don't kill yourself trying to impress people who wouldn't piss on you if you were on fire."

I snort. "Inspirational, as always."

"What can I say? I give TED Talks in parking lots."

There's a beat of quiet—not awkward, just familiar. Then he asks what I knew was coming. "Did they call?"

I don't answer right away. I look around the room instead, anywhere but at the screen.

"Nope."

"Not even a text?"

"They don't do birthdays," I say, knowing it's not the whole truth. "Not for me. You know I only see them at Christmas."

His mouth pulls into a flat line. I know he wants to say something, maybe even offer a soft I'm sorry, but he's always known better. There's no point in apologizing for people who've chosen to turn their backs.

"They still think working is beneath me," I say, voice low. "That studying politics is just me being difficult. Mom told me once, 'You weren't raised to beg for a salary, Piper. Working is for people who have no legacy to protect.'"

He exhales sharply, like the words physically piss him off. "Jesus Christ."

"I guess when you live in a Connecticut estate with your name on half the hospitals and three centuries of old money at your back, it's easy to forget the rest of the world actually runs on effort." I pause. "They've got staff for everything, even feelings."

"They're relics," he mutters. "Dust in tailored suits."

I lean back into the cushions, my throat tightening more than I want it to. "You're the only reason I'm even here. You know that, right?"

He waves me off with a flick of his hand. "Bullshit. I signed some paperwork and pissed off your dad. You're the one keeping your head above water."

"You paid for this apartment."

"I own the building. You're doing me a favor, really."

"You set up the trust."

"So you wouldn't be beholden to people who think ambition is tacky. Which it isn't."

I nod, biting the inside of my cheek. It's a little embarrassing how easily he always disarms me. Like he's immune to the shame I've carried since the moment I said I wanted to be more than a wife on a charity board.

"I'm proud of you," he says, voice quieter now. "Even if your parents are too busy sipping dry martinis and basking in their moral superiority to say it."

"Thank you," I sniffle softly.

He lifts his glass one more time. "Happy birthday, kid. Go eat something with frosting. And stop pretending you don't deserve the life you're building just because it doesn't look like theirs."

The call ends, and I stare at the blank screen for a moment, letting

the silence settle over me like a weighted blanket.

I only allow myself a few minutes of pity-partying before I get my ass off the couch and go change, swapping my black, figure-hugging dress for a pair of yoga pants and an oversized t-shirt.

Since I don't have any plans of going out tonight, despite my earlier conversation with Lena, I remove my makeup and throw my dark brown hair up in a messy bun. There, now I look exactly like one of those women my mom compares me to. Talk about a self-fulfilled prophecy.

Even though I know there's no point in mourning the distance between me and my parents, I can't help it. Especially not on my birthday.

Growing up, I had everything I could ever want. When I said I liked horses, Dad bought me three ponies because I couldn't decide what color I wanted. When I watched a Disney princess belt out a song and I wanted to sing just like her, he hired one of the best instructors and flew them across America.

In short, when it comes to materialistic goods, things with a price tag attached, I had it all in spades. But when I was scared of the dark, no one checked for the boogeyman under my bed. The nanny was the one who comforted me when I needed stitches after falling off my bike and scraping my knee.

Everything changed when I announced my plans of continuing my studies after high school. That's when I learned the true meaning of being raised in a Greenwich estate where ambition was fine for men, but vulgar for women.

Mom announced that no Harrington woman should ever work, and Dad backed her up. If it wasn't for Uncle Teddy, I would have never been able to complete my undergrad at American University right here in Washington, D.C., and definitely couldn't afford studying at Georgetown.

But when I broke down and confessed my dreams to him at my elaborate eighteenth birthday party, he… well, he saved me. He set up a trust for me, and bought not just an apartment, but the entire building near American University. Then again, when I got into Georgetown.

He said it was for peace of mind so he knew I was safe when I moved from Connecticut to D.C. Regardless of his reasons, even if it's just to stick it to his brother, my dad, he made my life possible.

Just as I'm about to throw myself into the kind of spiral that ends in Googling government job placement stats and crying into leftover takeout, the door bursts open.

"Presenting: your favorite bitch with baked goods," Lena announces, kicking it shut behind her.

I blink. "Did you just break into my apartment?"

She shrugs, holding up the spare key like it's a trophy. "I didn't break in. I used my God-given right as your best friend. And you

weren't answering texts."

Rather than focusing on the fact that I never gave her that key, I reply, "I was wallowing."

"Yeah, I figured. That's why I brought sugar and violence." She tosses her oversized tote on the floor and crosses the room, pulling a small white box from under her arm like she's smuggling something classified.

"Are those—"

"Chocolate with raspberry filling. Obviously. And look." She opens the lid to reveal one perfect cupcake, pink candle already stabbed into the frosting at a slight angle. "Tradition, bitch."

My chest tightens in a way I wasn't ready for. "You really didn't have to—"

She levels me with a stare. "You're damn right I didn't have to. But you only turn twenty-six once, and I'm not letting you do it in yoga pants with red eyes and existential dread breath."

I laugh. It's small, a little cracked, but real.

She lights the candle with the lighter she keeps in her purse for emergencies and chaotic energy.

"Make a wish," she says softly.

I close my eyes. For one second, I consider wishing for an internship. For clarity. For a family that doesn't treat ambition like a betrayal. But instead, I wish for something simpler; I want to be wanted. To feel fulfilled.

Huh, maybe that's two wishes. No matter, it's what I want, so even if I have to find a shooting star as well, I wish it.

Lena watches me for a beat while I blow out the candle. I don't make a big thing of it—no clapping, no cheesy encore. I just exhale, soft and steady, and the little flame disappears.

She sets the box aside on the coffee table. Then flops onto the couch, dragging me with her. "Okay. Out with it," she demands, pulling one leg under her like she owns the place.

I glance over. "Out with what?"

"Don't play dumb, bitch. You bailed on class, ignored my texts, and I caught you mid-spiral when I came in. Something's up, and I want details."

I sigh, peeling the wrapper from the cupcake and staring at it like it might hold the answers. "It's just… everything."

Lena waits, no judgment. Just space.

I lean back against the cushion. "Mrs. Ellis gave me the full reality check this morning. Everyone already has their internships lined up, and I'm still hoping for callbacks. If I don't get one soon, I won't graduate on time."

Her face falls. "Shit."

"Yeah." I take a bite of the cupcake. It's rich and perfect and makes me feel exactly nothing. "I've always had a plan," I continue. "Every

semester, every summer, every goddamn volunteer campaign. And now it's the most important year of my life, and I'm stalled out in the first week."

Lena doesn't offer me fake platitudes or empty encouragement, which is why I trust her with the messy stuff. "You're not behind, Pipes. You're just not ahead, and that's freaking you out."

I blink. That lands a little too hard.

She softens. "You've been ahead your whole life. Over-prepared. Over-achieving. But this is just timing. Not failure."

"You say that as if the job market gives a shit about nuance," I grumble.

Rolling her eyes, she throws her middle fingers up. "Fuck the job market. You're brilliant, and driven, and frankly terrifying in heels. You'll land something. You always do."

I want to believe her. I do. But the fear's already lodged deep, like a splinter beneath the skin. Not bleeding yet. Just… festering.

"I just don't want to disappoint anyone," I whisper.

She reaches over and tugs the cupcake from my hand. "Then stop disappointing yourself."

Sucking my bottom lip between my teeth, I bite it none-too-gently. I don't say what we both know; I need to graduate. If I don't, I'll have to go back to the place where dreams die, and wearing last season's clothing is worse than a sex scandal in D.C.

"Tell you what, Pipes." Lena swipes a finger through the frosting and licks it off her finger. "We need a proper night out soon since you're clearly determined to stay in tonight. This weekend. I don't care what you think you have to do. If you don't live once in a while you'll regret it."

"But I—"

She shakes her head. "If you try to refuse one more time, I'll make us watch The Shining again. All work and no play…" Trailing off, she swirls her hand in the air.

Laughing, I pick up a pillow and throw it toward her face. "Fine. You win. We can go out this weekend—"

"Yes!" she whoops excitedly.

"Providing I've found an internship," I finish, ignoring her excitement.

Frowning, she tuts. "You really don't know how to have fun, do you? Thank God you're hot. Otherwise I'm not sure I'd be your friend."

"Please," I mutter. "You've been stuck with me since Intro to Comparative Politics."

"Don't remind me," she grins. "I still haven't forgiven you for bringing five shades of pink highlighter to our first lecture like a damn psychopath."

She says it like a joke, but it's a memory—the day we sat next to

each other at American University and never stopped.

We spend the rest of the night just chilling—ordering takeout, and eventually streaming some political thriller that Lena pretends to hate but secretly enjoys. I love that genre, especially when there's scandal and backroom deals. The dirtier the politics, the better.

When the credits roll, she yawns dramatically. "I hope you've put clean sheets on, because I have to sleep over." Waggling her eyebrows, she adds, "Ah, never mind. I forgot who I was speaking to. Your bed hasn't seen any action in months."

I arch an eyebrow. "I'll have you know I have a very healthy relationship with my vibrator."

"Like that's the same as a good dicking," she mock-grumbles. "Seriously, when was the last time you got laid?"

"June twentieth," I lie.

Honestly, I don't remember the last time I got it on with anyone. It's not that I'm not into sex, but right now, my education has to come first.

"Whatever," she sighs. "I still have to stay over."

"Have to?" I laugh.

She nods eagerly. "Yep. I've had way too many carbohydrates to drive."

"God, yes," I say, mock concern lacing my tone. "Don't ever eat pasta and drive."

After finding her a top to sleep in, she disappears into the bathroom. While she gets ready for bed, I begin my evening ritual. First, I lock the front door. Then I check every window is shut and locked before drawing the curtains. I move silently from room to room until I reach the one in my bedroom and freeze.

There's a shadow outside. Just for a second—tall, unmoving—but by the time I flip the light on, it's gone. I stare into the dark for a beat longer, heart thudding a little too fast.

Fucking hell, I don't even know why I'm overreacting like this. On the ground floor, I'm used to seeing people walking by. So why did this particular shadow startle me?

I should've taken the penthouse when Teddy offered it, but no. I had to be the idiot afraid of heights, insisting on the ground floor instead. Because of course I did.

The leather chair creaks softly as I lean back, the scent of polished wood enveloping me like a second skin. My office is pristine—every inch reflects my need for control. A half-empty humidor sits in the corner, its cedar-lined walls housing the only indulgence I allow myself—hand-rolled Cohibas from Havana.

The gleam of the glass desk catches the flickering overhead light, illuminating the carefully organized paperwork and framed photographs, each item precisely positioned, a testament to my meticulous mind.

I glance down at my tablet, at the file with everything pertaining to the woman from the Carroway Café. It came in only minutes ago, but I was alerted straight away.

Piper Harrington.

Though I've known her name since an hour after I left the café, courtesy of my many connections, it's not until now I've received her life story.

She lives alone in the ground-floor unit of a building her uncle Teddy owns. Amongst other things, he's a real estate investor, black sheep, and, apart from her, the only member of the wretched Harrington lineage worth a damn.

She's in her final year for her Master's in Political Communications and Public Policy at Georgetown. As far as I can tell, she has no job and no debt. No obvious vices, either. There's no boyfriend, and only two exes linger in the margins.

Hmm, wait, there's also a TA she ghosted after only two drinks. It seems he didn't get the hint, and she had to call the campus police to get rid of him while she studied at American University. I make a note to check if he's still teaching because if he is, I'll have his fucking job for making her feel uncomfortable.

I've memorized the sound of her deadbolt turning. I know how long she lingers by the window before pulling the curtain. She thinks she's safe behind her little routine.

My lips curl into a faint smirk as I read through her résumé, absorbing the words. "I want to be in the room where real decisions are made, and I want to make a difference."

I can't decide if it's naïve or enticing. It's two-faced; could be both or neither. I chuckle softly, the sound low and dark. With every word I read, I feel it creeping in—something dark, something possessive.

The file is long and intrusive. I have her measurements, calorie intake, health, strengths, weaknesses, and everything in-between.

I shift in my seat, the pressure in my trousers a slow, steady throb. She doesn't even know what she does to me. Getting to know her in such an honest and raw way is like foreplay. And I'm painfully hard.

The bottom drawer in the desk beckons me, and I oblige. Pulling out the lace panties I stole from her apartment when I had my team install security cameras in every room after she left for school yesterday.

Even though they're clean, I bring them to my face, inhaling deeply.

It's at times like these, I wish I could be near her. Hide in her apartment, but at six-foot-four, I'm not exactly built to curl up in a closet. I'm also not sure standing outside her window would be overlooked for long.

Clutching the panties in my hand, my eyes drift back to the puzzle on my desk. It's almost complete; only one piece is missing. I roll it between my fingers, pressing the edge against my palm.

I think about Piper in the flesh—wonder how her skin smells, and how soft it'll feel against my fingers. I let out a slow breath.

Soon.

Just a few more steps. Just a few more moves.

Soon.

She has no idea what I have in store for her future—our future.

I open my email thread with Lauren Chase, the woman Piper has an internship interview with tomorrow. From her file, I know how important this interview is. But it won't be the lifeline she's hoping for. It'll be a giant fiasco. At my… request, Lauren will turn Piper away, bringing my toy one step closer to me.

She doesn't know what she stirred. Doesn't know she was owned the second I felt my cock twitch behind a ten-thousand-dollar suit. That she never stood a chance the moment I wanted her.

I've made presidents. I've dismantled administrations. There isn't a powerful man in this city who doesn't flinch when my name is whispered in the dark. I don't hold office—I hold reins. They don't come to me for votes. No, they come to me when they need the power they can't touch without bleeding.

Unlike my cousins, I don't collect debts or favors. I collect the things I can toy with; leverage, power, alliances… and now—her. She's

the first thing I've ever wanted for myself—not for leverage, not for legacy. For me. And she doesn't even know my name… yet.

My phone buzzes, and a familiar name flashes on the screen: Remus Russo. I answer, keeping my tone casual, but the weight of our shared understanding hangs heavy in the air.

"Remus," I say as a way of greeting my cousin.

"Lorenzo," he mirrors. "How's the empire-building going? Is the last political candidate ready?" he asks, voice low, steady.

Closing my eyes, I try to come up with something—anything—useful from my meeting with the candidate Remus wanted me to meet with yesterday.

"Too average," I reply brusquely. "There was nothing memorable about him, and his ideas were too far-fetched."

"I see—"

Interrupting Remus, I carry on. "Plus, the skeletons in his closets aren't good. His penchant for chasing the secretary without bothering to be discreet is too cliché. Not to mention he seems to have an issue with consent, and according to his two ex-wives, he lets his fist do the talking once he's had a bit too much to drink."

That's the thing with power, it's not about who holds the title; it's about who pulls the strings. People think elections are about democracy—about the will of the people. That's adorable.

The will of the people is nothing more than a carefully orchestrated illusion, one I design with precision. I remove the weak and uplift the strong, and I do it without ever stepping into the spotlight.

Politics is a chessboard, and I am the hand that moves the pieces. The right candidate, the right scandal at the right time, the right whispers in the ears of the right people—these things matter more than votes. Public perception is a weapon, and I wield it with absolute control.

I don't work with just anyone. Only those who deserve to win. The ones with the will to command, to shape the world as it should be. The rest? They're dead weight, taking up space where real power should exist. And I remove dead weight with ruthless efficiency.

"Do you have someone else in mind?" Remus sighs. From his tone, I know he expected this. Though the Russo Don isn't happy about it, he respects my input enough not to argue the matter. "You know that we need a new senator this year, Lorenzo."

Nodding, I pull the two people who impressed me up on my tablet, and email their info to Remus. "I've sent you the info on the two I'd pick," I reply. "Both have the right image to win people over without too much effort."

My cousin doesn't waste any time in giving me his opinion, which we both know isn't the final word. When it comes to our family, his word is law. But when it comes to making or breaking politicians, he trusts me implicitly.

Some say I play God. Maybe I do. Maybe that's the point. The truth is, some people aren't built for power. They're weak, corruptible in ways that don't serve the bigger picture. It takes a practiced eye to spot which scandals are liabilities rather than assets.

In short, if a candidate's failure can't be used strategically, I cut them out. Disgrace, scandal, financial ruin—sometimes, they get the chance to disappear quietly. Other times, they become cautionary tales. A plane crash. A suicide. An accident no one questions.

The world needs leaders who can bend it to their will. And I decide who those leaders are. I don't care about political parties. I don't care about party lines. I care about making sure the machine runs as it should. And when a cog starts malfunctioning? I remove it.

No one remembers the names of those who almost won. But everyone remembers the ones I put in power. Because once I choose someone to lead, there is no alternative. No opponent is strong enough. No scandal big enough. No downfall is inevitable enough. If I decide someone will rise, they will. If I decide they'll fall, there's no way back up.

That's what I do. I don't just shape the future; I own it.

"You seem distracted," Remus observes. "Is this a bad time?"

Yes, it's the worst fucking time. Instead of saying that, I look at the incomplete puzzle and say, "I'm just tying up some strings."

"Word is you're getting distracted by a woman," Remus mutters. "Someone new to play with?"

I chuckle, slow and quiet even as heat stirs in my chest. "Piper Harrington is so much more than a plaything. She's mine."

"Harrington," Remus says, tasting the word. "She's the woman you had Matteo gather intel on?"

"The one and only," I reply.

I can hear the smirk in his voice when he says, "Is that why you're so distracted?"

"Partly," I admit. There's no point in lying.

He inhales sharply. "Look, I don't care what you do in your spare time. But I can't afford for you to get too… obsessed. I need you sharp, Lorenzo."

"Obsessed?" I scoff, leaning back. "Control isn't obsession. Control is ownership."

A part of me isn't so sure what I'm saying is true. For the past three days, nine hours, and thirty-seven minutes I've pulled every string, used every connection to learn everything there is to learn about Piper.

I even know how old she was when she lost her first tooth, when she got her period, what ice cream her nanny bought when she broke her arm by falling off her pony. There's nothing I don't know about her.

Is that control? Or obsession? Maybe the two aren't mutually exclusive.

"Just make sure she doesn't become a liability." Remus' tone makes

it clear it's an order, and… it sounds almost like a threat. A thinly veiled or else.

A flare of defiance sparks in my chest, sharp and fleeting. But I swallow it down. He's family. He's the Don. I bend—but only because I choose to. So I tamper down the need to growl at him, to tell him to mind his own fucking business.

I clench my jaw so hard my teeth hurt. "Liabilities don't exist in my world." I cup my chin and tilt my head back. "But if you're worried, cousin, tell Rafe and Matteo to do their job when the time comes for Piper's interview."

I hang up, then let the quiet settle.

Before I can put my phone down, it vibrates in my hand. It's Cyrus. We've known each other since birth—our fathers in the same syndicate, our childhoods sewn together in smoke-filled rooms and iron discipline. Now, he's my right hand. My shadow. The only man outside my family that I trust implicitly.

Cy: Senator Jacobs' fixer has been playing both sides. Just thought you'd like to know.

Of course he is. That's the thing about men who rely on others to clean up their scandals—they always think they can play both sides until one eats them alive.

Me: Let me guess. He called Senator Jacobs too…

Cy: Bingo. Want me to drop a little fire on his doorstep?

I smile coldly as I give him the go ahead.

As I place my phone back on the desk, I return my attention to the puzzle, the last piece still between my fingers. I've carried this last piece in my jacket pocket all day. Let it warm against my skin. She deserves more than cold cardboard. I place it down, aligning it with precision.

And just like that, the future Mrs. Piper Russo is looking back at me, smiling.

"I'll make sure you're ready for me," I say, and I relish the chill of anticipation working its way down my spine.

Standing up, I pull at the cuffs on my shirt before stretching to my full height. One of the worst parts of what I do is all the time I spend sitting. I walk over to the small table filled with alcohol, and let my fingers run along the neck of my favorite whiskey.

After pouring a glass, I return to the puzzle, my eyes settling on the image of Piper—perfect, smiling, trapped in a thousand tiny pieces. A

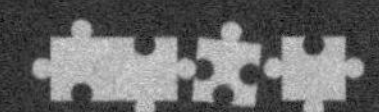

thing I built, shaped, decided.

Grabbing my phone, I send an email to my team. I've lined up five interviews, each one disingenuous, each one arranged to fail.

Despite the hour, my assistant, Maria, emails me back right away. She confirms that the interviews will happen one week apart, making the timing even sweeter for when I give Piper an internship in one of my companies.

My little toy needs this to be ripe for my picking.

I reply to Maria with a final instruction; have the black envelope I left on her desk delivered to Piper's apartment tomorrow morning. Maria's always in before sunrise, she'll have it done before Piper even opens her eyes.

The thought of my toy getting a toy—specifically, a puzzle piece— is addictive.

Soon, Piper won't just exist in pieces on my desk. She'll be in front of me, eager and hopeful. My pulse stays even, but something shifts— an ache, a hunger.

After this, she'll be in my world. And by the time she realizes she's trapped, she won't even want to leave.

I lean in closer to the mirror and swipe one final coat of mascara onto my lashes, holding my breath like it'll help keep my hand steady. No smudging. No clumps. Just clean, defined lashes to match the rest of my carefully constructed façade.

The high ponytail I'm sporting keeps my hair away from my face, making me look less timid. My makeup is polished without overdoing it. The navy tailored trousers are high waisted, and my nude-colored silk blouse is tucked into the waistband. Matching pumps finish the look, and I don't look half bad, if I do say so myself.

I've already triple-checked the contents of my tote, but just for the hell of it, I go through it again. My résumé folder, list of questions, water bottle, emergency breath mints… yep, it looks like it's all here.

Then I grab my phone and open the company website one more time, skimming through the About Us page like I haven't already memorized every damn detail. Founded in twenty-eleven. Political communications. Bipartisan narrative strategy. Emphasis on youth voter outreach.

While it's not my dream firm, it's solid, and more importantly, it's within reach thanks to the alumni I reached out to the day after my birthday. Prestigious enough to impress future employers, small enough that I might actually get to do more than fetch coffee if I land the internship.

A knot tightens in my stomach, sharp and familiar. God, I hate this part. The pretending. The smiling. The desperate edge I always try to hide beneath layers of competence and control.

I grab my bag off the table and sling it over my shoulder, keys already in hand. I'm halfway out the door when I spot something sitting on the doormat; a black envelope, plain and unmarked, resting like it belongs there.

Frowning, I crouch, and pick it up—but I don't open it. I don't have time. So I just slip it into my bag, and lock up behind me. The interview waits. As soon as I reach the curb, the rideshare pulls up, the driver's window already down.

"Piper H.?" he asks, glancing at his app.

Clutching my phone, I double-check that his picture on the confirmation matches the man in the car. One can never be too careful.

"That's me," I confirm, tugging the door open and sliding into the backseat.

The interior smells like lemon wipes and too much air freshener, but I'm too keyed up to care. I smooth the front of my blouse, legs crossed at the ankles, tote bag tucked neatly by my feet.

I pull out my phone, skimming the company's website one last time. I already know everything there is to find, just as I've memorized every name on their leadership team and every project they've touched in the last five years. Still, I scroll like I might've missed something. Like one more pass will settle my nerves.

My phone vibrates with an incoming text.

> *Lee: You're gonna crush it. They'd be idiots not to snatch you up. Text me the second you're out.*

A reluctant smile tugs at my lips. I type back a quick promise to let her know, and slide the phone into my bag, fingers tightening briefly around the handles.

When we pull up to the firm's building, I exhale slowly. Clean glass façade, neat lettering on brushed steel. No frills. Just quiet, self-important elegance.

"Thanks," I tell the driver as I slide out, heels clicking confidently against the sidewalk. I straighten my shoulders, smooth my ponytail, and walk through the glass doors like I belong.

The lobby is modern but impersonal—white walls, polished floors, a receptionist desk built like an altar. A young woman looks up at my approach, her expression unreadable behind a pair of tortoiseshell glasses.

"Hi," I say with a polite smile. "I'm Piper Harrington. I have an interview scheduled with Lauren Chase."

She taps her keyboard, eyes flicking over her screen.

"Harrington…" She frowns slightly. "Right. Please have a seat. Someone will be with you shortly."

Her tone is clipped. Not rude, exactly—but not welcoming either. And I don't miss the way her gaze slides down, cataloguing my outfit, my shoes, my confidence like she's trying to slot me into a box.

I nod, but something twists in my stomach.

Still, I head to the waiting area and sit down. I'm prepared. I'm a

professional. I'm ready.

As the minutes tick by, I wish I could take my phone out and text Lena. It might sound paranoid, but something isn't right. Something feels off.

No one's said anything overtly rude. But the smiles are too tight. The receptionist hasn't looked at me once since telling me to wait. And now it's been seventeen minutes past the scheduled time of my interview.

When the door finally opens, a woman in a sharp blazer and an expression to match steps out. She doesn't offer her name. Doesn't even greet me.

"Piper?"

I stand, smoothing the front of my blouse. "Yes. I'm Piper Harrington. Nice to meet you." God, I sound like a rambling idiot.

She barely nods. "Follow me."

Despite wanting to ask for her name, or hell, for her to look at me, I don't. Nope, I behave like the good little interviewee I am, and follow her down a corridor that somehow manages to feel colder than the lobby.

I glance at the framed awards on the walls—accolades for innovation, strategy, thought leadership. But none of them matter when she's already treating me like I don't belong here.

The interview room is sterile; just a glass table, two chairs, and a notepad already filled with scribbles that she doesn't offer to explain. She doesn't even offer me water or anything to drink.

"So…" she says, sitting with a sigh, somehow managing to sound like I'm being problematic. "Tell me why you applied."

I blink. "Umm, well, I'm a student in Political Communication and your firm has a reputation for impactful voter outreach campaigns, and I—"

"And what, exactly, do you think you can contribute?" she interrupts.

My breath catches. "I've worked on two midterm campaigns, focusing on digital messaging and demographic targeting. My thesis centers on reframing political narratives to increase youth engagement, and I—"

Her eyes are trained on her stupid notes while she scribbles something down. "That's only theoretical."

Grinding my teeth together, I sweetly say, "It's research-based, but also applied. My goal—"

"We're not really looking for theorists right now."

I blink again, stunned. "This was an active listing. I was told—"

Her chair scrapes back. "Let me save you some time, Ms. Harrington. We've already narrowed our pool to candidates with… worthy referrals."

My stomach drops. "But I… wait, what do you mean worthy? Mine

came from a Georgetown alumnus. Doesn't that qualify?" I ask, my tone is no longer sugary sweet or even polite. I'm not matching her disinterest, far from it, but there's no masking the shock I'm feeling.

"Yes, well. Circumstances change," she says, her tone final.

I don't know what that means, not really. But it feels like a slap. I sit there, spine rigid, pretending this isn't humiliating. Pretending I didn't feel the shift in energy the second she looked up and saw me.

She stands. I don't even remember finishing my sentence. "Thank you for coming in."

That's it; no feedback, no handshake, and still no fucking eye contact.

By the time I step back out into the sun, I can barely breathe. Christ, this wasn't a bad interview, it was… fuck I don't even know. It was humiliating, and it felt like a setup. Like a hazing or cruel prank. Those people didn't want me there. They'd made up their mind before I ever walked through the door.

I don't even remember walking down the block, but somehow I make it to the corner and order another rideshare via the app. I should've waited and gathered myself before stepping into another confined space with a stranger, but my pride's already dangling by a thread and I can't stomach the idea of lingering outside that building any longer.

The car pulls up, and I climb in without a word.

This time it smells like stale coffee. The driver says something polite, but I don't catch it. I just nod, fix my eyes on the window, and pull out my phone to text Lena as promised.

Me: Interview was a total joke. Tell you later.

Her reply comes almost instantly.

Lee: WHAT?! Are you okay? Do I need to kill someone?

A dry laugh escapes me, small and humorless. I don't answer. If I say anything else, I'll cry, and I refuse to break down in the back of this car.

When we reach campus, the driver tells me to have a good day. I'm just about to give him a mechanical and polite reply when I catch myself. No, after what I've just been through I won't treat someone else in such a brushoff-ish way.

"Thank you so much for the drive," I say, forcing a smile. "Have a great day." Then I step out into the sunlight and force myself to breathe.

Georgetown's campus is busy, but not overwhelming. Still, I feel adrift. Like the rhythm of everything around me has moved on while I'm stuck playing a different beat. A slower, heavier one.

Just as I reach the front steps of the Political Strategy wing, a familiar voice cuts through the fog.

"Piper!"

I turn. Mrs. Ellis is striding toward me, her heels clicking with the kind of purpose that usually means someone's about to be chewed out.

"There you are," she almost snaps. "I'm so glad I ran into you." She doesn't sound glad at all.

My stomach sinks. "Did something happen?"

She sighs, adjusting a strand of hair that's escaped her updo. "I just got off a call from Lauren Chase."

The name lands like a slap.

"She said you were rude and unprofessional. While Lauren didn't outright say that you wasted their time, she hinted at it," Mrs. Ellis adds, voice tightening. "She even used the word entitled."

My mouth opens—but nothing comes out. Then I blink, trying to catch up. "Wait… what? That's not true at all," I almost growl. "Not only was I early and prepared, I looked at her and smiled. Which is more than I can say for how she treated me. She acted like I was a bother from the moment we met."

Okay, maybe I shouldn't have said all that as it most definitely doesn't sound professional. But seriously, fuck Lauren Chase and whatever crawled up her ass just before my interview.

"I'm not accusing you of anything, Piper. I'm just telling you what was said." Mrs. Ellis' tone softens, but only slightly. "It's your word against theirs. And unfortunately, they're the ones with the influence."

Heat prickles beneath my skin. Shame. Embarrassment. Rage.

I fold my arms. "So, what, they slam a door in my face and then call my advisor to twist the knife?"

Mrs. Ellis gives me a long, assessing look. "I said I'd speak with you before making any judgment. And for what it's worth, I do believe you."

I nod tightly, but the damage is already done. They wanted me humiliated. That interview wasn't just a rejection. It was orchestrated. At least that's how it feels to me. Maybe I'm reaching, maybe I just don't want to believe I deserved what Lauren dished out.

Then again, what reason could there be to orchestrate anything like that? Yeah, I'm probably just making up excuses to ignore the reality that they just didn't like me.

5

Lorenzo

Having cameras installed in Piper's apartment paid off when I heard her talking with Lena on the phone. The two of them were making plans to go to Velvet & Rye tonight, a Georgetown cocktail bar.

While she got ready, I had my assistant make a reservation for myself, and make sure the staff knew to seat the two women close enough that I would be able to overhear their conversations.

That was two hours ago, and I've beaten them here. I'm already seated in my booth, facing the door so I can see when they arrive. I barely have time to take the first sip of my whiskey before they enter.

My phone vibrates again, either with an incoming text or email. But I ignore it, determined to not let work get in the way of my growing obsession.

Piper walks with a grace so lethal it rearranges a man's entire worldview. One look, and everything else fades. As I lock eyes with a guy who's here with his girlfriend, or date, I bare my teeth, quietly telling him to look the fuck away. He does.

Light gray satin clings to my toy's chest—tight enough to showcase the curve of her tits, loose enough to make you want to tear it off just to see what's underneath. Thin straps slide over her shoulders, one already slipping slightly lower than the other. If I were closer, I'd fix it with my teeth.

Her black pants sit high on her hips, cinched at the waist, soft fabric hugging every inch of her thighs. Legs for fucking days, ending in thin black heels with gold at the ankle. They're the kind of shoes that make me fantasize about bending her over a table while wearing nothing but high heels.

She doesn't dress to be seen, and yet she eclipses every woman in the room without even trying. Every man in this place should be on his knees. Not because she's flashy—but because she's fucking devastating to look at.

Lena's chattering animatedly as they're following the waiter to their seat, weaving through the crowd. "Can we order right away?" Lena asks, stopping the waiter from retreating once they're seated.

"Of course," he agrees.

Piper purses her lips. "Come on, Lee. I don't even know what I want yet."

Lena beams at her, leaning toward the waiter with flirtation laced into every careless tilt of her head. "Two Cosmopolitans, please and thank you." She shoots him a wink, making him stumble as he walks away.

I'm not going to deny that Lena's attractive in an objective way. But she doesn't hold a candle to my toy. Piper's all grace, sexy curves, and untouchable allure. A woman like her doesn't need to beg for attention. She already has it. And she doesn't even know it.

The drinks arrive a few minutes later, glowing pink in their wide-rimmed glasses. Lena lifts hers immediately, clinking it gently against Piper's.

"To us," she says, too brightly.

Piper doesn't smile. She picks up her glass like it's heavier than it should be, fingers wrapped tight around the stem. I slowly sip my whiskey, never looking away from her.

Another vibration from my pocket. Persistently annoying—relentless, unwelcome. I don't care who it is. They can wait.

Lena notices the tension oozing off her friend. "Okay," she says, voice lowering just a bit. "Tell me."

"There's nothing to tell," Piper murmurs. She takes a cautious sip and winces.

"Bullshit," Lena says cheerfully. "You've got that twitchy look, like your brain's trying to crawl out through your eye sockets."

I nearly smile.

Piper leans back, one hand brushing down her arm, nervous energy bleeding into every movement. "The interview with Lauren Chase was a disaster."

"I gathered that. But how bad are we talking?"

"Bad," Piper sighs. "She called Mrs. Ellis to complain about me. Who even does that?"

Lena freezes mid-sip. "Wait… what?"

I let the whiskey sit untouched, the fury too loud to taste anything but her humiliation as I listen intently while my toy explains how the interview went down, and what was said to her advisor.

The idea of anyone making her feel small sends something ugly crawling beneath my skin. I sabotaged her, yes—but I never asked Lauren to call anyone, that was her own initiative. One I'm not appreciating at all. Clenching my own glass tighter, I feel the heat of her humiliation like it's mine.

"… basically, she said that I was difficult," Piper finishes. The words fall from her lips like something she's repeating rather than believing, but I hear the hitch in her voice. The flicker of something cracked.

"She said all that to your advisor?" Lena asks, her tone sharp like she's angry on Piper's behalf.

More buzzing from my phone.

My toy nods. "Yeah. Luckily, Mrs. Ellis said she believed me. But still…"

"She's a fucking psycho," Lena declares heatedly. "No one even likes Lauren Chase. She only got her position because her dad donates buildings."

"She made me feel…" Piper pauses. Breathes. "…stupid."

No, my little toy. You're not stupid. You just don't know you're being nudged toward your rightful place on the board. I take another sip of whiskey, slower this time, letting the burn crawl down my throat.

A few minutes pass in silence while the second round of drinks is ordered and prepared. Piper finishes her first one slower than Lena, but it's gone before the new ones hit the table. Her fingers tap restlessly on the glass stem until she catches herself and stops.

"I just… I worked so hard to get here," she finally says, staring at the soft pink drink in front of her like it might hold an answer. "It's not supposed to fall apart like this."

It's not falling apart. It's being redesigned.

"Maybe she's threatened by you," Lena suggests, taking a sip of the fresh drink.

Piper huffs a laugh. "By what? My rapidly shrinking career options?"

"I'm serious." Lena's voice sharpens. "You're smart. You're well-spoken. And you don't suck up to women like her. That's threatening."

There's a beat of silence.

"I keep thinking maybe it's me," she whispers, her voice barely audible over the hum of conversation and low music. "Maybe I just don't belong in this world." She wipes under her eye before anything falls. Just a flick of her thumb—so fast, so casual, anyone else would miss it. But I don't. I see the crack.

My jaw flexes as I lift my glass, letting the whiskey coat my tongue before I swallow. The flavor doesn't register. All I can taste is the bitterness in her tone. The fact that she's sitting there, thinking she's not enough for a world I'm actively reshaping to fit her into.

She's cut out for all of it. She just hasn't been handed the right tools yet.

"Hey!" Lena snaps. "None of that, Pipes. Lauren Chase is a stuck up cunt who doesn't deserve your tears. You got more talent than she does in her pinky."

"Right," Piper croaks.

"I mean it," Lena continues, relentless in her defense of her best friend. "How about we just have some fun? Let loose for once and

forget about stuck up bitches."

Piper giggles softly. "Forget about who?"

"Exactly," Lena cackles.

When my phone makes itself known yet again, I'm just about to pull it out and tell whomever is blowing it up to fuck off. Before I fish it out of my pocket, movement catches my attention from the periphery.

Two men approach, drinks in hand with confidence that wasn't earned. I've seen their kind a thousand times. They carry themselves like they've inherited charm instead of building it. One of them holds a full pitcher of Cosmopolitan. The other has the nerve to wear a smirk before even opening his mouth.

They're approaching too casually, angling toward the booth like it's already theirs. "Hey sweethearts," the taller guy drawls. "How about some company?"

His friend chuckles and rolls his eyes. "What my friend here meant to say is hi, he's Daniel and I'm Chris."

Lena's head lifts, always quick to notice attention. Her smile is automatic. "Is that for us?" she giggles, nodding her head toward the pitcher.

Chris grins back at her. "Definitely."

"In that case," Lena says, her tone syrupy. "Welcome friends."

"What the hell, Lee?" Piper hisses, her gaze flicking from her friend to the men.

The guys don't waste a second. The taller of the two, Daniel, slides in beside my toy. He's casual in a way that grates under my skin. As he makes himself comfortable, his arm brushes hers. She stiffens, chin dipping slightly as if she's reminding herself to stay composed.

"And what's your name?" he asks.

"Umm—" Before Piper gets a chance to decide if she's going to answer or not, he continues.

"I'm Daniel. And you're Piper, right? I think we have a class together." He delivers what I'm sure is a line smoothly.

My whiskey is still half-full, amber and glinting like it might boil from proximity to the fury pressing into my ribcage as Daniel moves impossibly closer, sending my blood roaring in my ears to hear it.

All I see is the arm he throws around her shoulders as he leans in and murmurs something near her ear. Piper gives a small, tight smile. A sound that could pass as a laugh slips out, but it doesn't touch her eyes.

It's a performance, one she's practiced far too often in a world that doesn't make space for discomfort. The man doesn't even notice. He just reaches for the pitcher and refills her glass like she's his to serve.

I should thank him since he's already drawn the bullseye across his own chest. That makes it easier when I decide how to remove him. He's sitting too close, touching her, and breathing the same air.

When my phone buzzes in my suit jacket yet again, I scowl as I finally give in, and pull it out.

Maria: I'm sorry to disturb you, Lorenzo. But I've been monitoring Senator Jacobs as you asked, and there's a situation at The Ritz-Carlton, Tysons Corner. He's there with several interns right now and it's bad.

Of course he's holed up at the Ritz with its gilt walls and too-soft pillows. The kind of place that makes monsters feel clean again.

Cy: Why the fuck aren't you answering Maria?

Cy: Tick Tock... it'll only be hours before your cousin knows. You need to deal with Senator Jacobs now!

Cy: I swear to God... I'm going to track your ass. Have a look at what's happening.

Cy: Dude, I'm literally watching you ignore me. Last chance, if you don't answer me, I'll come in there. Because while you've been sitting there nursing the same whiskey, Senator Jacobs has been having the time of his life brutalizing interns.

Well… fuck!

My gut tightens as I flick through the pictures attached to one of Cy's texts. I immediately see red, almost missing the video he's sent as well. I play it with the sound off.

Senator Jacobs has his intern bent over the bed, one hand in her hair, forcing her neck back in an unnatural angle, and the other is clutching the knife he uses to slice across her back while he's balls deep in her.

On the floor are two other women. One is crouched in on herself, crying. The other isn't moving at all.

Motherfucker.

I need to get the fuck out of here and deal with Jacobs right away. Just as I think that, there's a quiet knock on the window behind me, and when I look out, Cy's standing there. I can feel his anger through the glass as he points at my phone.

Holding up one finger, I quickly type out a text.

Me: Is he still at the hotel?

Cy: Yes.

Me: Send one of your guys here to keep an eye on Piper. I need to make sure she's leaving alone.

Cy: Fuck! Fine!

Cy: It's done. My guy's on his way. Is he running interference or just observing?

Me: Observing only. I'm coming out.

Letting out an angry growl, I let my eyes move to Piper's table, where the guy still has his arm around her. I should fucking kill him for touching her, and I'm tempted to. But when she shrugs out of his hold and announces that she's going to the bathroom, I decide to leave his fate up to her.

I leave a few hundreds on the table—not just for the whiskey, but for the performance. The prelude. Done watching, I follow my little toy to the back where the bathrooms are located.

The corridor is dimly lit, the kind of ambient shadow that lends itself to secrets, to whispered sins and mistakes made on purpose. The light glows low and golden against the mahogany walls, and the further she walks, the more distant the bar sounds become.

She's almost at the bathroom door when I silently close the distance between us. One hand curls around her upper arm and I turn her away from me, pinning her to the wall before she has time to react.

"What the—"

Her front hits the dark paneled surface with a gentle thud. My body presses against hers, deliberate and suffocating, positioning her exactly where I want her. One hand braces her hip, the other flat against the wall by her head, caging her in a way that makes it clear she isn't getting out of this—not without me letting her go.

She goes still as I lower my head, my mouth near her ear but not touching. She smells like citrus and vanilla. Her pulse is rapid against her throat, her breathing uneven. But instead of struggling, she simply waits—rigid, uncertain.

"You shouldn't have let him touch you," I murmur, my voice a breath of heat against her skin.

She shifts, just slightly. Her hands flatten against the wall at her sides. She's trying to stay calm. "I didn't let anyone do anything that concerns you," she spits, the venom in her tone almost enough to drown out the small tremble. Almost.

"I saw him," I rasp. "I watched him pour you a drink. Saw his arm

around you. You let him sit too close, and that concerns me." Her hair brushes my jaw with every breath she takes, tickling me in the most delicious way.

My voice doesn't rise. It doesn't need to. Every word is a leash I'm wrapping around her throat—tight enough to hold, loose enough to make her think she's still breathing on her own.

"Make him stop touching you," I say, the command low and intimate. "Make him stop looking at you like you're something he could ever have. It's not nice to tease, you know."

My words make her hiss like an enraged snake. "Tease? I don't even know who the hell you are, or why you think you can just—"

"You. Are. Mine," I say, pronouncing each syllable clearly. "And if you don't stop him, I'll have to, Piper."

She tenses at the sound of her name, the first true tremor passing through her body like a shiver. "I…" she starts, then stops. Her voice is barely audible now, little more than breath. "I don't even know who the fuck you are."

"Not yet," I agree. "But you will soon. And the first thing you'll learn is that my warnings should be heeded."

I linger for one more second—long enough to feel her tremble again, long enough to sear the shape of her body into mine. Then I step back, slow and controlled, watching the way she holds herself against the wall like she needs the support.

She doesn't look up or ask who I am. But more importantly, she doesn't scream. She just breathes, shallowly. Good girl. As much as I want to stay, duty calls. First, I'll deal with Jacobs, then the guy who touched my toy.

And how I deal with Daniel is completely up to Piper. She holds all the cards.

Cy's black SUV is already idling by the curb, and I quickly slip into the front passenger seat.

"You're a fucking dumbass," Cy growls, fisting the steering wheel tightly as he pulls away.

Not in the mood to deal with his judgment, I huff out an annoyed breath and tell him to hurry the fuck up.

The world never tolerates my distractions for long, and Cy's right. I shouldn't have ignored my phone. Hell, I should have even listened to my cousin and put a stop to Senator Jacobs months ago. But when I found no concrete evidence of his extracurriculars, I naively hoped the rumors were just that.

That was my mistake, one I'll never repeat.

Jacobs was always living on borrowed power. The moment I handed it to him, he must have convinced himself it was his to keep. That his position meant something beyond my indulgence. That patience equated to leniency. But Jacobs is the kind of man who doesn't understand leverage until it's wrapped around his throat.

They all think they're kings. But they're toys—poseable, replaceable, breakable. And I'm the one who built the box they play in. As I think this, the puzzle of Piper flickers through my mind, uninvited. I might call her my toy. But she's nothing like the rest.

She's rare. Singular. Mine.

Cy's not done yet, though. And while he weaves through the traffic, speeding toward the hotel Jacobs is holed up in, he doesn't hold back.

"Seriously, Enzo. I was two seconds from just smashing that fucking window and dragging you through it," he states.

"I know," I reply. We both know he could have tried, but if I refused to go with him, there wasn't much he could do. "I'm here now. That's all that matters."

He turns his head to me, arching an eyebrow. "All that matters? What the fuck's the matter with you, man? It's not like you were out getting your dick wet."

"Careful, Cy," I growl.

Shaking his head, he turns his attention back on the road ahead. "I don't think I'm the one who needs to be careful," he argues. "Maria was so shaken I sent her home and told her to take a few days."

"You did what?"

"If you're about to school me on the fucking hierarchy, save it. She was fucking sick to her stomach, Enzo. She should never have been the one watching out for Jacobs. This shit is on you."

That stings, mostly because it's true. Maria's been with me for years, and she's as loyal as they come. And while she's handled sticky situations before, shit like what she's seen tonight isn't on her usual list of tasks.

I think it's time for Maria's next raise.

"I'll apologize to her tomorrow," I sigh. "You're right, I shouldn't have ignored my phone." Cy nods sharply, but wisely refrains from rubbing it in.

I stay still, my mind already dissecting how to deal with Jacobs. As much as I want to kill him tonight, that would be unwise. There are protocols to follow when dealing with public figures.

"Soooo," Cy says, dragging out the word while taking a sharp left that almost has the car on two wheels. A car horn sounds behind us, but we're already long gone. "How do you want to play this?"

A dark chuckle escapes me. "No play. We need to keep him mostly injury free until he can resign."

Cy nods. "Yes. But that doesn't answer my question." He inhales sharply. "The fucker needs to pay for what he's done."

"Once he's resigned publicly, you can do whatever the fuck you want," I reply. "But, Cy, Jacobs needs to step down before you have your fun." This is an important fact to stress since Cy's known to get caught up in the moment.

His eyes light up like Christmas came early. "This is why I stick with you," he grins wickedly.

"I mean it," I grumble. "Jacobs can't be in front of the cameras with bruises and lacerations. I need a clean exit."

Cy reluctantly agrees. Then proceeds to explain that some of his men are already stationed around Jacobs' suite, making sure he isn't going anywhere. I already expected all of that, it's who he is. So I just nod while he catches me up.

The drive from Velvet & Rye tonight to The Ritz is blissfully short. Thanks in most part to Cy's reckless driving which cuts the usual twenty-minute drive down to only thirteen minutes.

As the car comes to a screeching stop outside The Ritz-Carlton, I crack my neck before jumping out, practically sprinting inside with Cy

hot on my heels.

When I walk into that suite, I won't be Enzo. I won't even be Lorenzo. I'll be motherfucking consequence, and it's not nice to meet me.

Instead of walking around the hotel to use the back entrance, we purposefully rush into the lobby. Neither of us pay attention to the receptionist or bellhop as we head straight for the elevator.

"I fucking hate this music," Cy gripes while angrily jabbing the button for the eighteenth floor while the doors close.

Huh, I would have guessed the Senator to occupy the Presidential Suite.

"Me too," I sigh.

As we hit the floor we need, the doors open and Cy edges around me, exiting first. And I let him because if the Senator isn't alone, his men might recognize me and alert him.

We're immediately greeted by a guy I've seen plenty of times, but for some reason his name eludes me. "He's still in there," the guy says. Then he holds up a small, white plastic card. "Who wants to do the honors?"

Cy cracks his knuckles before snatching up the key card. "Thank you. Make sure you get the girls as soon as we've apprehended the Senator. Is medical on standby?"

The guy nods. "There's an ambulance waiting outside," he informs us. "It's ready to take them to Inova Fairfax Hospital."

"Make sure they're checked in under fake names," I urge. "The press hasn't caught wind of this yet, but it's only a matter of time after Jacobs resigns."

As we get closer to Jacobs' room, I notice more of Cy's men hiding in plain sight. Each of them dressed in dark tactical gear and fully armed.

Cy doesn't waste any time reaching for the piece resting at his lower back, pulling it out while holding the key card up against the electronic lock.

Click!

As soon as the door is unlocked, Cy kicks it open. "Weapons down. Pants up. This is your last civil request," he orders.

The first thing that hits me is the heat from the bodies. From the violence still vibrating in the walls. It's muggy with exertion and something almost sweet—like iron left out too long in the sun. The smell of sex and blood never lies.

"What the fuck?" Jacobs sputters, but he doesn't stop thrusting into the mouth of the girl that was crying on the video I watched.

The room reeks of sweat, cheap cologne, and something darker—something coppery and raw. Blood. It's faint, but present, clinging to the air like it's soaked into the walls. It doesn't smell like fear. It smells like rot. Like a man who's done this before and stopped caring when it

started to leave stains.

She looks young. Too fucking young. Big eyes, bloodshot, and full of fear. Her hair's dark like Piper's. Her lip's split. And all I can think is—what if it was her? What if it had been my toy on her knees in this room?

The thought is enough to make me snap. With a roar, I lunge, grabbing Jacobs by the shoulders and throwing him across the room like he weighs nothing.

"Who the fuck do you think you are?" I growl, balling my hands into fists to stop myself from reaching for him again.

My knuckles throb from the impact. The sharp bite of contact still lingers up my arm, like his filth tried to cling to my bones. The room still vibrates with the sound of the girl's cries.

"Hey!" Cy exclaims. "You said no bruises."

Turning my head, I shoot my friend my best are-you-fucking-kidding-me stare, but he just grins in return. I exhale sharply, forcing myself still. It's not often I get my hands dirty like this. Not because I'm a good man. I'm not. I've killed and tortured. Watched men beg and then die when their begging bored me.

But someone like Jacobs? He's beneath the weight of my personal attention. A maggot. A stain. The kind of rot that spreads only because no one wants to get their fingers filthy digging it out. And yet here I am—bone deep in it.

"What's the meaning of this?" Senator Jacobs demands as he staggers to his feet, finally having the good grace to put his dick away. Seriously, no one wants to see that thing. Not even Mrs. Jacobs, I bet.

"You fucked up," Cy declares, voice light, conversational. "Lorenzo here is very patient. Me? Not so much. So why don't we skip the bullshit and get to the part where you listen very carefully?"

Jacobs exhales through his nose, squaring his shoulders. "I still have connections. I can fix this. There's no need for—"

I laugh coldly. "Fix this? There's nothing you can do to fix what you've done." I take a step forward, letting the moment stretch just long enough for him to feel the weight of it.

Jacobs' fingers twitch at his side as he wobbles, unable to stay still. Fuck me, he's either drunk or high. Probably both.

"I don't have time for this," I grind out, gesturing to the women on the floor. "They need to be seen by a medical professional, and you need to fucking resign. Now."

At my words, Cy's team mills into the room that seems smaller with each body forcing their way in here. The men quickly gather the three women and carry them out of here. Though they don't interfere, each of them makes sure to shoulder check the Senator as hard as possible.

Jacobs opens his mouth, but Cy cuts him off, tilting his head like he's considering something deeply. "I have a question." His voice is smooth, almost curious. "How many breaks does it take for a human

hand to stop being useful?"

"Wh-what?" Jacobs sputters.

Cy ignores him and taps his chin. "I was watching a video the other day. Truly fascinating stuff. There's this particular bone, right here…" Without warning, he grabs Jacobs' hand, pressing a knuckle against it, making the man jerk back in reflex. "… snap that just right? Never quite heals properly."

Jacobs' breath turns uneven, the careful mask of power slipping from his face like melting wax. He knows. He knew the moment we stepped in, but knowing and accepting are two different things.

I lean closer. "The only thing left for you to decide is whether your family shares your fate."

His entire body locks up. There it is. The breaking point. Letting go of Jacobs' hand, Cy pulls out what looks like a resignation letter, probably prepared by Maria, and slaps it onto his chest.

"You resign. Publicly. And you make it sound like you're retiring to spend more time with your family. Privately, I want you to pay three million to each woman as well as paying for their medical expenses. No loose ends, no last-minute pleas. You take the fall, and in return, I ensure your family never feels the weight of what you did," I state, my tone icy.

His hands shake. Sweat drips from his temple. I smell panic now— tangy and sour. It replaces the stench of arrogance that used to cling to his suit like a badge. Now it's just piss and fear and the faint, metallic sting of someone else's pain.

I hand him a pen so he can sign the death sentence with ink instead of blood like I really want to make him do.

Jacobs stares at the letter. Twenty-six seconds. That's how long it takes before Jacobs' hand moves. Twenty-eight. That's when he signs. Thirty. That's when he folds completely.

"One more thing," I say, holding up my phone. "Smile to the camera you sick fuck." I snap a few pictures of Jacobs and the room, before also recording all of it for good measure.

If he holds up his end of the bargain, I'll never use the pictures. They'll be deleted the second Cy's done with him. But if he tries to weasel out? I'll release them all. I'll obliterate his family tree so far back that even the first of his line will feel the disgrace.

Without saying goodbye, we leave Jacobs to stew in his own undoing.

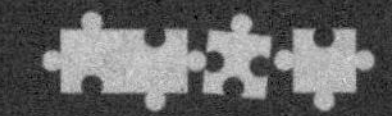

7

Piper

A week passes by in the blink of an eye. I barely feel the days change, all I can do is try to keep up with my classes.

The overhead lights in the lecture hall buzz faintly, casting a sterile glow over the semicircle of tiered seats. I sit near the middle of the lecture hall, my laptop open, fingers hovering over the keyboard without touching it.

There's something about this class—Political Strategy and Image Control—that feels heavier than usual today. The professor's voice drifts through the space, but I barely register the words until the rhythm breaks. A remote clicks and the projector hums to life.

"We're going to pause here," Professor Ellington says, his tone unusually tight. "This just started five minutes ago. Consider it a real-time lesson in public narrative collapse."

The screen flickers once, then stabilizes. There, under the cold lighting of a press podium, stands Senator Jacobs.

There's not a political student at Georgetown who doesn't know him. He's shown up in every class—from Ethics to Campaign Strategy—as the gold standard for public image.

As a veteran advocate, a pediatric hospital donor, and a clean-cut family man with his high school sweetheart and two smiling daughters, it was all too easy to root for him.

Washington D.C. isn't short of politicians by any means, but Jacobs is one of the few that captured the heart of the nation. The fact that he was dubbed Senator Silver Fox by the media, and managed to charm everyone from kids to adults didn't hurt either.

The man standing on the podium bears very little resemblance to the presence we're used to seeing. He looks smaller, somehow. Less polished. Almost like something vital got stripped out of him before he walked to the podium.

Too busy staring at the way his mouth moves without conviction, I don't hear the first few words of his statement. The resignation is written in the slump of his shoulders long before the words confirm it.

Murmurs ripple through the room like a current of disbelief, but something else coils in my gut. A chill. An itch I can't name. Jacobs was just another name on a long list of internship options I once pretended I had a shot at. So why can't I shake the sense that this isn't just politics?

"… and therefore, it's my belief that I can best serve my country by resigning. I've been in politics for over thirty years. It's time for me to take a step back and spend time with my family."

Someone scoffs to my left. "He's only fifty-three. Why is he sounding like he's on death's bed?"

"Maybe he is," another of my classmates suggests. "He could have cancer or something."

A wave of whispers starts from the back of the room and makes its way forward like a groundswell. My classmates' voices rise as discussions about this being a setup breaks out. I don't know why, but I can't look away. Something about this feels staged, and I feel like I'm watching a building implode in perfect symmetry.

Jacobs fades from the screen, and the projector cuts out. Our professor flicks the lights back on and starts throwing out questions. "How should Jacobs have played this?" he asks. "What's his next move?"

Someone coughs. "Guess I'm not going to hear back from my internship application with Jacobs' office," he jokes.

Professor Ellington shakes his head. But instead of saying something berating, he agrees. "Probably not. Let this be another lesson for all of you. In politics, you don't always know when it's your last campaign or even your last day. So don't waste time wondering 'what if' and go for what you want."

Paying attention is almost impossible as my thoughts begin to spiral. It should make me feel better to know I'm not the last student without an internship. But all it does is serve as a reminder of the failed interview two days ago. I'm oh-for-two.

The only good thing about my second interview is that they were a lot nicer than Lauren fucking Chase. But in the end, the result was the same. They didn't want me, and no amount of niceness attached to that verdict could sweeten the blow.

With a barely audible sigh, I close my laptop. Knowing that my mind is too preoccupied to take a single note, I admit defeat. At least to myself. God, I really need to get a grip and preferably soon.

Class moves on around me, the sound of Ellington's voice rises above the noise as people start filtering out after he dismisses us with a quick reminder about Monday's reading, but I don't remember what it was. I barely remember standing.

The halls blur on either side of me as I walk—faces passing, conversations I don't catch, laughter I'm not part of. I know that makes me sound miserable, and maybe I am. At least that would explain the way I seem to be letting everything slip.

Outside, the early September air hits cooler than I expect. A breeze brushes against my skin like a reminder that the world hasn't stopped spinning, even if something in me feels like it has.

When I reach the quad, I roll my bottom lip between my teeth, mentally wondering if one of my beloved caramel ice coffees will solve this fog that seems to render my brain useless. I mean, it could happen, right? People swear by all sorts of new age stuff. Maybe coffee that's so sweet it can give you a cavity is where it's all at.

I join the line to one of the carts. The line is so long it feels like every student at Georgetown got the same craving at exactly the same time. As I inch forward in the line, the hum of student chatter thickens around me—unfocused and ambient—until a cluster of voices to my right starts to cut through with quiet urgency.

They're gathered beneath the old oak near the center of the quad, half-huddled in that particular way people do when they have juicy gossip to share.

"Did you hear about Daniel Mullen—"

"Yes, I just heard today," another interrupts. "Can you believe it? I heard…"

She's still talking, but I can't hear her. The name lands like a weight in my chest, cold and inexplicably sharp. I shift slightly, trying not to stare, even though every inch of my skin prickles with attention now.

"Who the hell drops out mid-semester? And especially after landing the internship he did?"

Then someone says, "My dad's part of the faculty, and he said Daniel was all banged up when he submitted his formal letter of resignation."

Banged up?

"What do you mean?" one of the girls mercifully asks.

Shrugging, the person explains that apparently Daniel had several bruises and didn't look like his normal self.

A guy joins the group. "Are you guys talking about Daniel Mullen? My friend used to be his roommate. He told me Daniel got jumped on his way home from Velvet & Rye—"

"Is that why he dropped out? Because he got mugged?"

The newcomer just shrugs. "I'm not sure. My friend said Daniel got a job at a fastfood chain and talked about it like it was his dream job."

The first girl speaks again. "Who the fuck spends over three years at Georgetown just to ask people if they'd like fries with their order? I bet he was on drugs or something."

The breath I draw feels too thin and I wobble slightly as the note I received finally makes sense. I take a shaky step back from the line, blinking hard as the words sink into me like ice.

My legs continue of their own volition, taking me away without knowing where I'm going. My shoes click against the stone path, too

sharp, too fast, but I can't slow down. The blood in my veins rushes in my ears, each beat loud enough to fracture the thoughts running rampant through my mind.

Daniel…

The stranger's warning…

The note I received the next day…

While I move through campus like I'm sleepwalking, that fucking warning plays on my mind like an ominous soundtrack.

"You. Are. Mine. And if you don't stop him, I'll have to, Piper."

But I did stop Daniel. Even though I didn't have to since I don't belong to anyone, especially not some weirdo hiding in the shadows outside bathrooms, but still… I believed him when he said his warnings should be heeded.

So, as soon as the stranger disappeared, I went back to the table and told them I didn't feel well. Then I went home. Alone, I might add. And despite Daniel's insistence, I didn't give him my number.

If it wasn't for the envelope waiting for me the next morning, reminding me about the one I'd already received, I would never have linked what I just overheard with what happened at the cocktail bar.

The first envelope only contained a black puzzle piece. But the next one, the one I got the day after being at Velvet & Rye, had a note in it as well. I still remember the cryptic words.

Although I've received a new puzzle piece daily since then, there's only been that one note.

I don't stop until I reach my building. My steps quicken as I walk inside, dreading finding another envelope waiting for me. But there aren't any. Still, my hand shakes as I fish for my key, the teeth of it

scraping the lock once before I finally get it to turn.

The moment I'm inside, I slam the door behind me and lean against it, chest heaving, palms damp. Okay, so maybe I'm overreacting. Maybe Daniel left of his own volition… that's possible, right?

Without thinking, I grab my phone and call Lena.

"Hey bitch," she greets me. "Listen, I can't really talk right now. I'm on my way to Albert's office to discuss the B- he just gave me on—"

I interrupt her. "Lee, please come over when you're done."

As the hours crawl by after my call to Lena ends, I do everything humanly possible not to think about the envelopes stacked in the bottom drawer of my desk. I put on loud music and clean my apartment. When I'm done with that, I settle at my desk and send out even more applications.

Then I search for Daniel online. Thanks to Georgetown's student network, it's not hard to find he's from a small town in the midwest—Galena, to be exact. After getting this far in my search, it doesn't take long to find his new job which, indeed, is at a fastfood chain. It's only the fifth I click on, and there it is, his scowling face on the staff roster.

What the hell possesses a man to go from Georgetown to milkshakes and fries? I don't get it. Unless… no. No. Thinking that there's more to it than a change of heart is ridiculous… isn't it?

When I finally get up again, my body cracks and protests, my limbs creak like old floorboards. I've been so focused I haven't realized it's dark outside. After turning off my laptop, I go from room to room, switching the lights on.

But without anything to occupy me, the shadows feel like they're clinging. They don't need darkness—just my doubt. Not to mention the guilt gnawing at me. I don't want to believe I'm the reason Daniel left, yet a voice in the back of my mind insists that I'm to blame.

Tiredness makes me yawn, and I'm tempted to lie down on my bed. But since Lena's going to show up at any minute now, I decide on a shower instead.

I twist the shower handle all the way. The water slams down, boiling hot. Steam rises instantly, curling through the room like smoke from a fire no one will put out. I strip quickly, skin already prickling as I step under the spray.

The burn grounds me as I stand there, chest heaving as I let the water scald away the static crawling under my skin. I barely breathe. I just let the water roar until it's louder than whatever I'm feeling.

I keep my hair dry since I don't want to take the time to wash it. When I step out, steam curls around me like a second skin. It fills my lungs, coats the mirror, muffles the light. I dry off without thinking; towel to skin, breath held, muscles twitching.

There's no shutting up my mind. Thoughts about Daniel play on a never-ending loop. I did what the stranger demanded, though. I played by his fucked up rules. I swallow thickly as I step into fresh panties and put on a clean bra.

If the note is true, I guess I saved Daniel's life by rejecting him. That's how I should look at it. So why do I feel so guilty? I didn't do any of this. Reaching for my robe, I shrug it on. Once I've tied it, I glance toward the mirror and lift my hand to clear the fog.

Everything stops as I see the message scrawled across the mirror. The condensation is running, making the words pool like wounds.

You're mine, Piper!

My breath catches, and I quickly back away, but the words follow. I blink, half expecting them to disappear, to unwrite themselves. They don't. A sudden noise from the hallway makes me freeze. My brain scrambles to come up with a plan when the bathroom door swings open.

Lena bursts into the bathroom, startling me into a scream. "What the hell?" I slap my hand across my heart as though I can calm the organ. "What are you doing here?" I ask, my tone accusatory.

She furrows her brows in confusion. "What's wrong with you, Pipes? You asked me to come over."

Did I? Oh, right, yes, I did. Shit, that conversation feels like it happened in another life, not just hours ago.

"Bitch, why do you look like you've seen a ghost?" she asks, tilting her head to the side and narrowing her eyes.

In answer, I point a trembling hand toward the mirror, watching as she turns to look. The fog on the glass has lifted enough that I can see the way her confusion sharpens to concern the moment she notices the words.

"What is this?" she questions, somehow managing to keep her voice both soft and demanding.

"It's… I think… It's him, Lee," I ramble, barely able to form coherent words.

"Him?"

When my mouth opens and closes several times with no other words following, she wraps an arm around me and guides me out of the

room. She holds on tight, like she's afraid I might break if she lets go.

Lena pulls me into the kitchen, sits me down at the table. I stay frozen, the chair cold beneath me, the air too dense to breathe. She moves with purpose—filling the kettle, grabbing mugs.

Each action is a small act of defiance against my chaos, grounding herself while she waits for answers. I watch her, but I'm not really seeing, my mind still caught on the words, the awful clarity of them. Steam hisses, the kettle whistles, and she pours, sliding a mug in front of me. It's only when she sits, when her eyes lock onto mine, that I finally find my voice.

"I didn't imagine it," I say, more to myself than to her. "The mirror. It was there."

She nods. "And what was that? What the fuck is going on?" Her tone is gentle, but her gaze doesn't waver.

I try to gather my thoughts, but they scatter, unruly, refusing to be tamed. "He's everywhere," I say, the words tearing out of me. "The envelopes. The puzzle pieces. And… oh, God, he made Daniel drop out. It's all him."

Lena's brow furrows, and she leans in closer. "Take a deep breath for me, Pipes, because you're not making any fucking sense."

"B-but at least he's alive," I whisper. "The note basically said I saved his life." My voice breaks.

"Okay, start at the beginning." She reaches across the table, her fingers a warm contrast to the chill that's settled in me. Her hand stays on mine, thumb brushing lightly against my skin like she's trying to coax coherence out of me.

I close my eyes, exhale slowly, and start to speak. The words flow from me with zero grace or logic. I explain about the stranger in the hallway at Velvet & Rye, and the warning he whispered in my ear like he already knew me.

"Wait, is that why you suddenly wanted to leave?" Lena asks, interrupting me.

"Yes," I squeak.

She shakes her head, squeezing my hand harder. "Keep going."

I do as she asks; I tell her how I had received my first black envelope the morning we went to the cocktail bar, but that I'd forgotten everything about it until I received another one the next day.

"And what was in the envelopes?"

My breath saws out of me as I confess, "The first one just had a single puzzle piece. But the second one had a note saying 'He's alive because you listened.'"

Lena's eyes widen. "So why do you think he made Daniel drop out?"

I roll my eyes, ready to state the obvious. "Because no one drops out of Georgetown like that. Daniel had one of the best internships nailed, and his grades were damn near perfection."

My voice grows hoarse as I continue to speak.

"I didn't connect the incidents until today, when I heard people talking about him." Pausing, I take a deep breath. "I think someone's watching me. I don't know why. But it's not just a feeling anymore, Lee. The proof is on the fucking mirror… that guy has been in my apartment."

I don't look at Lena while I talk. I can't. It's like saying the words makes them more real, more unfixable. My voice shakes, but I don't stop.

She doesn't say anything for a long moment. Just studies me with a sharp, unsettling focus—like she's trying to assess how far gone I really am. But I can see the moment it shifts. Her expression tightens, and her jaw sets.

When she finally speaks, her voice is low, edged in something hard. "Jesus, Pipes," she breathes. "Why the fuck didn't you tell me any of this sooner?"

"I only just put it all together," I whisper. "It's my fault Daniel had to leave."

Her chair scrapes lightly as she shifts forward, narrowing the space between us. "No, it's not," she says firmly. "This is psychotic. This is…" she pauses, rakes a hand through her hair. "… this is next-level obsession."

I nod once. "I thought about calling the police about the envelopes the other day."

She blinks. "Why didn't you?"

"What would I even say?" I ask, voice rough. "That someone has left me a puzzle piece every morning?"

"It's more than that now," she adds, concern lilting her tone. "You have a legitimate case, Pipes."

She's not wrong. A guy I barely know dropped out, and it somehow connects back to me because of a drink and a touch. And the message written on my mirror which is proof someone's been in my home.

"I doubt they'd do more than tell me to change my locks and call a therapist." I force a laugh, but it's a hollow, scraped out sound.

Lena exhales through her nose. "Then let them tell you that," she says, already reaching for her phone. "But you should at least try."

I hesitate for a moment, but then I give in. "Put it on speaker."

She dials, taking my hand while we wait. The hold music makes my skin crawl with how cheery it is. Seriously, how does happy music fit an emergency?

Finally, a calm voice answers. "D.C. Police Department. What's your emergency?"

I start explaining about the puzzle pieces, but then, instead of telling her about my suspicion of Daniel being forced to drop out of Georgetown, I move on to the message on the mirror.

"Is there any sign of forced entry?" the dispatcher asks.

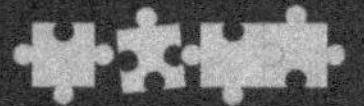

"No."

"Is anything missing?"

Even though she can't see me, I shake my head. "No. Nothing's been taken. But someone was here."

The dispatcher sighs, and I know what's coming before she can even get the words out. "Without evidence of a break-in or threat, we can't open a case. But you may want to change your locks."

I don't answer. Lena reaches across and ends the call herself.

"Useless," she mutters. "Why didn't you tell them about Daniel?"

"Because…" I finally meet her gaze. "… it sounds insane. And… I don't know, Lee. What if I'm wrong? What if it is nothing more than a fluke coincidence? Plus, it's not like I can prove anything."

She scoffs, but doesn't push the issue, which I'm grateful for.

I don't know why, but after talking to the police, knowing they don't consider it an issue or something that even warrants a report, I feel calmer, somehow. Like their dismissal is feeding the part of me that wants to live in denial, and now I have a legitimate reason to.

"Maybe you should stay at my place for a few days," Lena suggests, cautiously.

I shake my head firmly. "No."

"Piper." She leans forward, eyes wide with insistence. "You just said he's broken into your fucking home. You shouldn't be alone."

"This apartment is mine," I say, more to myself than to her. "I have to stay."

Silence settles between us, heavy but not hollow. I open my mouth, wanting to explain that I can't leave. This is Teddy's building, and he got it for me. It's so much more than just an apartment, it's my freedom. But… I don't know how to explain any of that. So I just don't.

Lena doesn't press, but her frustration is a living thing. "Okay," she says, backing off with a sigh. "Then we're ordering takeout. My treat. What do you want?"

"Sushi." It's an easy answer, but nothing feels easy.

She nods, grabs her phone, and starts to order. I stand, the chair scraping against the floor, and turn toward my bedroom. "I'll be right back."

The familiar weight of the apartment settles over me, making me feel more certain that I'm not going anywhere. I get dressed—overwashed jeans, a long-sleeved black t-shirt—each piece like armor. The fabric is soft against my skin, a gentle friction that reminds me I'm still here, still me.

Before joining Lena, I dig around my closet for my spare mace spray and hide it under my pillow. There. If he breaks in again while I'm here, I'm prepared.

When the food arrives, we move to the living room, sitting together on the couch. The light is too bright, too harsh against the dark edges of

my thoughts. It all feels exposed. We eat in silence, each bite a pause, a punctuation, a truce. I can feel Lena stealing glances at me, but she doesn't say anything.

She waits until the sushi is almost gone, until my nerves have settled into something less raw, before she speaks. "I want to see them," she demands.

I hesitate, knowing exactly what she means. "The pieces?"

"And the note. Everything."

I stay still, indecision pinning me down, then nod and stand. "They're in the desk drawer."

Lena follows me, and I open the bottom drawer, revealing the small stack of black envelopes. I've kept them hidden, even from myself. I pull them out slowly, like they might detonate, and set them on top of the desk.

Her eyes widen as she takes in the amount. Raising an eyebrow, she looks at me. "Let's open them."

Together, we pour every black puzzle piece onto the desk. When I grab the envelope with the note, I hand it to her so she can read it. After she's done, she places the puzzle piece next to the others.

"Wait." My eyes fly across the pieces as I mentally count them. "There was no envelope this morning," I whisper as I realize something is very wrong.

"Okay," Lena says, dragging the word out. "That's a good thing, isn't it?"

I shake my head. "You don't understand, Lee. There should only be seven envelopes, but there are eight."

We count them out while arranging each piece until we're sure we've only counted each piece once.

"Do you think he snuck one into your drawer when he drew on your mirror?" she asks, giving voice to a question I've already accepted as fact.

"He must have," I mumble absentmindedly, more focused on moving the pieces around to see if any of them fit.

Two of the pieces fit together, and I stare at them, my mind looping through the implications. Nothing is visible on their black surfaces; no image, no letters. But it's enough to know they connect. That it all connects.

"What do you think it means?" Lena's voice cuts through the dense air, and I meet her gaze.

"I don't know," I murmur. "But something tells me he isn't going to wait for me to figure it out."

But what the hell am I going to do in the meantime? Just sit back and let this shit eat me alive? These puzzle pieces are fucking bullshit. He's trying to scare me, and I'm feeding into it. Well, fuck that.

Making a spur of the moment decision, I swipe all the puzzle pieces into my hand. "Grab the envelopes and the note," I tell Lena as I march

into the kitchen, and quickly swipe the pieces into the sink along with the envelopes she hands me.

Before she can ask me what the hell I'm doing, I reach for the lighter I use for candles, tucked in the kitchen drawer. Realizing what I'm up to, my bestie springs into action. Instead of deterring me, she throws the window open.

"Go ahead," she says with a sharp nod. I strike the lighter, and the flame eats the puzzle pieces like it's starving.

Cardboard curls, and black turns to ash. The smell of scorched paper curls into the air, acrid and oddly satisfying. I don't say anything as I watch the fire, but with every piece the flame consumes, the more relieved I feel.

Before Lena leaves, we call a twenty-four hour locksmith, who, with the promise of a healthy tip, arrives within the hour to change my locks. With the new locks and mace under my pillow—just in case—I feel safe.

The police didn't think it was an issue, so maybe this is all it'll take. It's like Professor Lynn once said, every obstacle can be overcome with the right strategy. And I think I've perfected that tonight.

Bone-deep exhaustion hits me the second Lena leaves, and falling asleep proves to be much easier than I thought it would be.

9

Lorenzo

A wicked grin stretches across my face as I witness my toy's futile attempt to conclude our game with fire and a new lock on her door. Does she really believe she can so easily rid herself of me?

I fixate my gaze on the feed as I rewatch, devouring every second with a fervent intensity. She looks utterly pleased with herself, a smug smile stretching across her face as she steps back from the sink. Then she halts, eyes locked on the pieces I meticulously selected for her as they twist and writhe, devoured mercilessly by the flames.

I bide my time for an entire hour after the locksmith leaves. But it's enough time for Cy to track down the man, and get his hands on a key. I don't care whether he gets it by money or violence, as long as he gets it.

As soon as I finish that thought, my phone buzzes with a text from Cy.

Cy: Your key is under her mat. Have fun!

The anticipation builds as I finally head to her place, and when I reach her door, the key is indeed waiting for me under her doormat. With a steady hand, I slide it into the lock and turn it, the familiar click echoing in the quiet hallway.

Her scent hits me the moment I step inside—vanilla mixed with the barest trace of sweat. It's like inhaling her pulse. Tonight, it's mixing with the lingering scent of the burned puzzle pieces.

Her soft snores echo through the hallway, drawing me toward her bedroom like a siren's call. There, she's ensnared in a chaotic tangle of sheets, one leg provocatively curved, her knee slightly angled. Just enough to make a man imagine what's hidden beneath.

One perfect breast is exposed, her rosy nipple puckered from the cool air—as if it's waiting for my mouth, not her blanket.

Her breath is slow and steady, an unbroken rhythm that occasionally falters with a twitch of her fingers. I remain perfectly still, transfixed by the scene. There's a purity to her slumber, almost indecent in its vulnerability. Here, she's soft, silent, untouched by the relentless fears and stress that cling to her like shadows in the harsh light of day.

With one final, lingering glance that feels like a stab to my chest, I spin around and stride into her bathroom. The air is saturated with her essence—an intoxicating blend of citrus and vanilla that clings to my senses.

My hand reaches out with urgency for the familiar bottle she religiously uses every morning, nestled precisely on the shower shelf, a silent witness to countless intimate moments. As I unscrew the lid, my cock throbs with an intensity that feels like it's carved from stone.

Damn it, I've been hard ever since she ignited my gifts in a blaze of defiance.

I place the bottle on the edge of her bathtub, and lower the zipper on my suit pants, each movement deliberate and measured. With a sense of anticipation, I draw out my cock, feeling the cool air against my skin.

Then I begin to stroke myself; the pad of my thumb presses into the base, as I try to hold back weeks of restraint. But there's no stopping this.

The vivid image of her lathering herself in this—gently caressing it over her neck, down the slope of her tits, and into the apex of her thighs—sends a shiver through me, causing my jaw to clench with the intensity of the thought.

"Fuck," I whisper-groan.

Every part of her is mine, even the parts she doesn't know she's offering. She gave me everything the second she met my eyes and didn't look away. The rest are just details.

My hand tightens, rhythm deepening, jaw locked tight. The friction, the heat, the raw need building in my groin—it's all consuming. My eyes squeeze shut, and she's there; my toy, my obsession.

She's on her knees before me, lips parted in a begging plea, eager for my release. I can almost feel the hot, sticky ropes of my essence painting her chest, see the thick, white trails dripping down the valley between her breasts.

No, not just there. I want to claim her completely—fill her waiting mouth, or better yet, bury myself deep within her wet cunt, and unleash my load into her welcoming heat.

Opening my eyes, I pick up the bottle just in time to position it beneath my tip before I come while grunting her name. I spill every drop of my cum into the bottle, knowing she'll rub it across her skin every morning.

I screw the lid back on, shaking the bottle once, and return it to the shelf like nothing ever happened. If she won't let me show her how beautiful her face looks on puzzle pieces, she'll wear me instead.

10

Piper

I sit at my desk, fingers curled around a mug of coffee I'm not
drinking. The glow from my laptop casts pale shadows across
my face, highlighting the bags under my eyes and the defeat
slumping my shoulders. The screen is filled with applications I've
already submitted, and some I've yet to.

With a huff, I get up and stride into the kitchen, making myself
another cup of coffee. This one needs to be strong enough to raise the
dead so I don't fall asleep. I only have ten days left, and I can't waste a
single moment.

As my gaze lands on the sink, I shiver as I recall two weeks ago
when Lena stood with me, staring into the flames as we burned the
puzzle pieces one by one, feeding each scrap to the hungry blaze until
only molten flakes remained.

God, that feels like a lifetime ago. Now, with my education slipping
through my fingers, I almost miss the fucking puzzle pieces. At least
what Lena and I dubbed #PuzzleGate kept me distracted.

When my coffee's ready, I switch the machine back off and add
enough milk that I can drink it right away. Instead of staying in the
kitchen, I walk back into the living room, sitting down at my desk.

Yesterday, Mrs. Ellis called me into her office to remind me of the
October first deadline as if I could ever forget that I only have ten days
left. Instead of telling her about my most recent interview failures, I
pretended to have two promising prospects waiting for me.

It feels like lying is all I do. To myself, to Lena, and to Mrs. Ellis.
Truth be told, the interviews had already happened, and they rejected
me almost quicker than I could leave their offices.

I wince as I take a sip of my coffee, but force myself to drink half
the cup while I scroll through postings that blur together. Positions I
wouldn't have looked at twice just a month ago.

PR assistants. Campaign interns for candidates I wouldn't vote for if my life depended on it. A social media internship that pays in coffee and exposure. I apply to all of them. Cut and paste my resume. Swap out keywords. Lie through my teeth about why I'm passionate about their work.

I don't feel passion. I feel like I'm applying to vanish somewhere quiet and unremarkable, just to say I did something. Like I'm writing my own obituary, one bland application at a time.

Mindlessly applying for unpaid internships isn't me. I'm not interested in roles with no upward mobility, while watching other people making the important decisions in rooms out of my reach. But I still do it.

Ten days bleed by, each one sharper than the last.

If my life was a cartoon, the calendar pages would float across the screen to signal the days passing. But in reality, I avoid any reminder of what date it is. And I definitely don't want any reminder of the interview I had earlier today.

It was at a mid-size think tank, a policy group working on issues I struggled to feign enthusiasm for. When we were done, he shook my hand and said they'd be in touch. But I knew the answer the second he stood. The handshake was too polite, and the smile too empty.

But still, some dumb part of me hoped. Because whether I like it or not, that company is my last fucking chance. There's no denying it since it's September thirtieth.

I refresh my inbox like it owes me oxygen. Each click is CPR on a future that flatlined weeks ago. Of course, there's nothing. Just silence so loud it makes my teeth ache.

While I'm pondering what the hell to tell Uncle Teddy since all the money he's given me is wasted now that I've failed, I start drafting the email to Mrs. Ellis, thanking her for trying, and admitting I couldn't pull it off. As much as I hate it, I have to send the words confirming my failure. But I'll be damned if I send it before I have to. I snort as I glance at the clock in the bottom right corner of my screen. 11:57 p.m.

Just three more minutes until I officially wave the white flag.

The cursor on my screen blinks like it's mocking me—each flicker another second slipping through my fingers. I exhale, ready to hit send and shut it all down, when a soft ping cuts through the room.

My jaw is slack, and my eyes are impossibly wide as I watch my inbox updating. I frantically click on the email, as though it'll disappear if I'm too slow.

Subject: Interview Invitation—Blackwood Strategic Advisory

From: m.wilson@blackwoodadvisory.com

To: Piper Harrington

Dear Ms. Harrington,
Your academic achievements and focus in strategic communications and political policy have not gone unnoticed. We have followed your work with great interest and believe your values and potential align well with our firm's mission.

We would like to formally invite you to an in-person interview for our fall internship cohort at Blackwood Strategic Advisory, a consultancy specializing in elite political strategy.

Date: October 1
Time: 9:00 a.m.
Location: Blackwood HQ, Suite 14A, Washington D.C.
Attire: Business professional

Please confirm your attendance by replying to this email. We look forward to speaking with you.

Sincerely,
Maria Wilson
Executive Assistant to the CEO
Blackwood Strategic Advisory

I blink once, then again, making sure I'm not somehow reading the email wrong.

The timestamp glaring back at me reads 11:59 p.m., a minute poised on the cusp of a new day. Relief floods through me as I realize that tomorrow isn't canceled after all, that the opportunity still stands.

My fingers fly over the keys as I type out a reply, my heart racing as I accept the invitation for tomorrow's interview.

The Blackwood Strategic Advisory headquarters looms ahead—a sleek monolith of glass and steel, humming with power and promise. As I step out of the cab, the morning chill wraps around my legs. It's the kind that reminds you autumn has officially arrived in D.C.

I tug my blazer tighter and run my palms down the sides of my dress, wiping away the nervous sheen clinging to my skin.

The dress hugs my body in all the right places, tailored and bold without being loud. Deep green panels framed in black contour down from the structured shoulders to the hem just above my knees, creating sharp lines that feel almost architectural.

It's sleeveless and just the right amount of modest. It's not prudish by any means, and it shows just enough skin to remind them I'm not here to disappear. My black stilettos are clean and pointed, about three inches—tall enough to make a statement, but low enough that I won't wobble.

While picking out my outfit, I felt like fucking Goldilocks. Not too much of this, but not too little either. I think I've managed to find the perfect middle ground if I do say so myself.

I exhale and glance at my reflection in the glass doors. My braid is neat and tight, but a few strands have already slipped free to frame my face, softening the sharp angles tension has carved into my features.

Right, I've made it this far, and there's no turning back now. My last chance awaits, and I refuse to leave without an internship. I'm not above begging if that's what it takes.

The doors part with a hushed whisper, and I'm greeted by a sharply dressed woman, her expression unreadable but not unkind. "You must be Miss Harrington," she states, her tone certain. There's no doubt in this woman's mind which is why she's telling rather than asking.

"That's me," I say, glad my voice doesn't waver. She nods once, businesslike, and gestures for me to move further into the lobby.

Everything about her is efficient—from the crisp lines of her slate-gray pencil skirt to the perfect twist of her hair at the nape of her neck.

She doesn't wear much makeup, just a sweep of liner and matte lipstick in the exact color of quiet authority. I can't tell if she's forty or fifty, and somehow that makes her feel even more intimidating.

"I'm Maria Wilson, and I'm so glad you accepted my invitation," she says. "It's good you arrived early so we don't have to rush through security." While she talks, she guides me over to a sleek glass barrier guarded by two men in tailored suits.

There's no chaotic beep of a grocery store scanner, no barking orders—just quiet precision. A discreet metal arch stands to the side, all matte black and polished chrome, flanked by a conveyor belt leading into a scanner that hums low like it's already sizing me up.

"If you'll place your handbag and blazer in the tray, please," Maria says, gesturing toward the belt.

I do as she asks, watching as the tray slides forward, swallowed by the scanner's soft blue glow.

"This way," she says, motioning toward the detector.

My pulse trips as I step through. I've done this before—airports, courthouses, even a few political events—but something about doing it here feels different. Like I'm not just being screened for weapons… but for weakness.

Once I'm through the scanner with no issues, I step toward the belt, intending to grab my handbag. But I'm halted by Maria's hand on my elbow.

"I'm just going to get—"

She interrupts me. "No need. You're not permitted your handbag or blazer inside the interview room," she explains.

"Really?" The word slips out before I can stop it. I recover quickly, force a smile, and shrug like it's nothing.

Maria gives me a sharp nod, then she reaches into the small paper bag I hadn't even noticed her carrying. "There's one more thing," she says as she pulls out what looks an awful lot like a blindfold.

My breath catches as my brain instantly tells me this is strange, that blindfolds don't belong in interviews. "W-what's that for?" My voice stumbles, caught between shock and curiosity.

"It's procedure, Miss Harrington," she replies smoothly. "If you resist, there'll be no interview."

Her tone is firm, final. No room for negotiation, no room to argue. My heart pounds, a split-second war between self-preservation and ambition. But ambition wins. It has to.

"Okay," I whisper, nodding. Then I turn around, giving Maria my back so she can place the blindfold over my eyes.

The fabric is smooth against my skin, plunging me into darkness.

My world narrows, and I focus on my breath, forcing it to steady. I can't see, but I can hear—the quiet efficiency of the space, the soft footfalls of my guide.

I'm led down a hallway, the carpet beneath my feet muffling each step. My fingers twitch at my sides, itching to reach up and tear off this blindfold, but I resist the urge. I need this too badly to ruin it with nerves.

A door opens, and I'm guided inside a room and onto a chair, the cushion soft against my thighs. The space seems to hum with invisible energy, every nerve tingling in anticipation. My heart hammers in my chest as I strain to hear any sound, anything that might give me a clue about who else is in here.

There's breathing—steady, controlled—but I can't tell how many people are in here. Not even when a chair creaks which is followed by someone shifting their weight. The hush isn't hostile—it's hungry. I sense that whoever is here is waiting, watching.

My skin prickles with goosebumps, not just from the cool air, or from the loss of sight. But from the feeling of being seen—of being studied.

"Piper Harrington." The deep and commanding voice sends a shiver down my spine. "My name is Rafe. Welcome to the internship interview here at Blackwood Strategic Advisory."

I square my shoulders, forcing myself to focus. "Thank you." My voice holds steady despite the whirlwind of emotions coursing through me. "I'm honored to be here."

The interview begins with standard questions about my political strategy, ambitions, and goals. I answer confidently, my passion for public service evident in my tone.

Rafe's voice is steady, professional. "Your résumé mentions that you want to be in the room where decisions are made. What do you believe is the most effective way to influence policy in today's political landscape?"

I sit straighter. "Policy is shaped long before it ever reaches a public vote. True influence happens behind closed doors—through lobbying, media control, and agenda-setting. Voters see what we want them to see, and it's the job of political strategists to ensure the right narrative is pushed forward."

A pause. I hear the soft shuffle of fabric. A quiet exhale followed by low murmuring. I strain my ears, but I can't hear what's being said. Did I surprise them? I can't tell. The pause stretches, taut with judgment, pressing against my skin like unseen hands.

"And you believe voters are that easily swayed?" It's another man asking the follow-up question. His voice is smoother, sharper.

I nod. "I do, Mr… umm… sorry, I didn't catch your name." I inwardly cringe for sounding so unpolished.

"Matteo," he helpfully supplies.

"Public perception is a science, Matteo." I pause briefly. "The right headline, the right scandal, the right savior at the right time—it's all about timing."

Rafe speaks again. "That's a cynical take."

"It's a realistic one," I counter. "Change doesn't come from wishful thinking. It comes from control." The more I talk, the more my confidence soars. I've got this.

He hums, considering. "It seems you focus heavily on public perception. What about raw political power? Do you see yourself as the kind of strategist who plays kingmaker, or are you interested in holding office yourself?"

I hesitate, then shake my head. "I don't want to be the face. The mind behind it is where I want to be. The person who builds the leaders, not the one shaking hands in front of a camera."

He leans forward slightly, at least I think he does. When he talks again, he sounds closer. "And if you had to choose between winning by playing fair or winning by any means necessary?"

It's a trap. I know it. But the answer is easy. "Winning is the only thing that matters," I say, my voice unwavering.

A pause. I think I've impressed them. Then Matteo exhales softly, as if amused. "You speak like someone who understands the game, Miss Harrington."

I steel myself. "I do."

Then, just as I start to feel steady, as if I've passed some kind of unspoken test, another voice enters the mix—low, smooth, dripping with amusement.

"Tell me, Piper," he drawls. "Do you touch yourself at night?"

My head snaps in the direction I think the question came from. "W-what?" I gasp. No, I must have misheard him. "Can you please repeat—"

"No," he interrupts coldly. "A simple yes or no will suffice."

Heat creeps along my cheeks. I inhale deeply, then I slowly shake my head. There's no point in pretending to consider whether I'm going to answer or not. Of course I am. I've come this far, with everything to lose.

My mind reels. I'm a scholar, not a seductress. Desperation is a powerful motivator, and since I'm here to claim my future, I can be whatever he wants me to be.

I swallow hard, my throat dry. "Yes," I whisper, hating myself for it. "Sometimes."

"Good girl," he murmurs, voice low and smooth—but there's a darkness under it that makes my stomach twist and my thighs clench. "Such a perfect toy."

Oh, God. The way my body is responding is downright indecent. Those two words—hoarse and reverent—make me slick with want. Heat pools between my thighs, and I hate myself for how fast I go soft

for praise.

The atmosphere thickens, humming with something primal. It coils around me, a presence more felt than seen, one that makes my skin prickle.

"Stand up," he commands, smooth, effortless, like he already knows I'll obey.

My body tenses at the unspoken challenge lacing his tone.

"Is there a problem?" Rafe asks. "A woman who understands the game must also be comfortable with high-stakes decisions."

My heartbeat pounds in my ears. Shaking my head, I stand, ignoring the way my legs threaten to buckle under my weight.

"Now strip," the third man demands.

"I… umm…"

"Take. Off. Your. Clothes." He repeats the command, slowly pronouncing every word.

Silence smothers the room, thick and oppressive. My breath catches in my throat, my fingers curling into the fabric of my dress as if holding on to my last shred of dignity.

I freeze. Not in fear—but in… fuck, I don't even know. Anticipation? Before I can ponder it too much, a chair creaks. A slow inhale. They're waiting. Watching. Expecting.

"Now, Piper," he says, voice like silk over steel. "Or you can walk out of here and leave with nothing." The ultimatum is like a knife hovering over my throat.

Everything in me rebels, screams that this is wrong. But louder than that is the voice whispering this is what it takes. I've clawed too far, bled too long, to lose it all at the finish line.

My body betrays me before my brain can intervene—my hands move, reaching for the zipper at my back, fingers trembling as I tug it down.

The soft whine of fabric sliding apart is deafening in the stillness. My dress loosens, slipping from my shoulders, baring more of my skin to the chilled room. It pools at my feet in a whisper, leaving me in nothing but my underwear and heels.

My arms twitch with the need to cover myself. But I can't show any weakness. Reaching behind me, my fingers fumble with the clasp of my bra. Before I can undo it, I'm stopped by a warm hand on my shoulder.

"Keep your underwear on, little toy," the third guy orders in a husky voice.

His hand lingers, sending electricity coursing through my veins. I'm so caught up in the way his touch makes me feel that I don't notice he's moved until I feel his hands on my calf.

"Lift your foot." I obey, feeling him remove the dress from my ankles.

"Thank you," I breathe, assuming he did it to stop me from tripping

over the fabric.

Damnit, why am I finding that sweet? I shouldn't because there's nothing sweet about these men. I just know it. They're all fucking watching as I stand there, almost naked for their viewing pleasure.

A long silence stretches between us. The pressure in the room squeezes around me, coiling like wire beneath my skin. But then, just as the urge to cover myself up becomes overwhelming, I roll my shoulders back and place my hands on my hips.

"Good girl." Fuck, the rumble of praise from the third and unknown man punches straight to my core. My nipples harden, and my clit throbs in response.

Matteo and Rafe ask a few more questions, I answer—barely. I can't think straight with the third man's hand still on my leg. I'm waiting for his next move, not theirs.

"Do you prefer to be on top?" he asks, tone velvet-wrapped steel.

I lick my lips and roll my shoulders back. "I… err…" Christ, I'm not sure how to answer that question. Do I prefer it? Compared to what? I guess I like it fine… but it's not my favorite.

The room feels smaller, closer now. His questions hang in the air, charged and heavy. I can feel his gaze on me, even though I can't see him. I'm a deer in headlights, frozen yet painfully aware of every inch of my body.

"Answer me." The words crack like a whip—sharp, impatient.

My mind reels, torn between maintaining my dignity and the desperation that had me blindfolded and half-naked in the first place. I'm ashamed by my body's betrayal, the way it responds to his words, the ache that's building between my legs.

I hesitate. "I… I don't know how to answer." I whisper. "It's… umm… not my preferred way."

There's a low chuckle followed by another shift in the room's energy. I feel him standing up. The slightest touch grazes my arm—just a whisper of contact—but it brands like fire. That's what he is. Not a man, but a voltage.

"On your knees."

The words grind through the room like gravel beneath booted heels—low, sharp, and lethal in their simplicity. Not barked. Not begged. Just spoken with the kind of command that doesn't require volume to demand obedience.

My breath catches in my throat, a sharp intake that echoes in the silence. The air itself tastes different now. Like static electricity before lightning.

I open my mouth, preparing to form a protest. But no words emerge. I… fuck. He doesn't need to say it again. The weight of the command coils around my ribs, sinking into my bones.

If I say no, I walk out of here with nothing. If I say yes… before I can finish that thought, I drop to my knees, and tilt my head up, blindfold still in place.

A hand grabs my braid, firm and controlling. "Open for me, Toy. I want to hear what obedience sounds like when you moan around me."

The tip of his cock brushes against my lips, its warmth and weight tantalizingly present, an unmistakable promise lingering in the air. His scent wraps around me—clean skin, raw male, and something darker that threatens to ruin me.

"Make me proud. Show me how good you are with that perfect mouth," he growls, flexing his hips.

The stretch elicits an involuntary gasp from deep within my throat, yet his firm grip in my hair intensifies, anchoring me steadfastly in place. The blindfold heightens every sensation—the taste is more vivid, the texture more pronounced.

A low hum of approval follows, tension spiking as I remember we're not alone. I can't tell if the others are watching my face, enjoying the scene unfolding before them. But there's one thing I'm certain of—my own enjoyment.

In a perversely thrilling way, I'm reveling in the experience. A moan escapes my lips as I swirl my tongue around the sensitive crown.

"Fuck!" He lets out a guttural groan, one of those coming from deep within the chest.

Feeling the power of being the reason for his deep, throaty groans, and noticing how his length swells even more in response, fuels my desire. It's intoxicating, igniting a wanton need within me, making me crave this moment with every fiber of my being.

I'm pretty sure every hookup I've had in the past was done wrong because it's never felt like this. And I know it's not just because I've gone several months without sex. No, it's all this man. He's making me crave this, making me crave the feeling of him taking control, and letting myself be consumed by the raw, primal energy between us. Even blindfolded, even stripped bare, I feel… safe. Treasured, not used.

These thoughts swirl in my mind, and I scarcely recognize the person I've turned into as I'm on my knees in front of three strangers. But… fuck, I love it.

I wrap one hand around the base—hot and thick. While my hand strokes him in a steady rhythm, my lips and tongue worship the head, tasting the salty essence of him.

My free hand slips between my thighs, circling my clit with practiced hunger, sending pleasure sparking through me.

Before I know what's happening, the guy tightens his hold on my hair. "Your pleasure belongs to me, Toy. You won't get to come unless I allow it," he growls, authority vibrating from him. "Put your hands behind your back. Now."

Albeit reluctantly, I obey. The second my hands fold behind my back, he thrusts harder—brutal, relentless. I don't get time to breathe, let alone adjust, before he's buried deep down my throat.

"W-w…" The word is nothing but a garbled mess.

"I'm going to come in your mouth and all the way down your throat," he groans. "If you spill as much as one drop, you won't like the consequences."

I whimper around him, but don't do anything else. The truth is, that I've never been this turned on in my life. My entire body feels alive, and I feel… powerful. It might not make sense, but it's how I feel. Like I'm strong enough not only to allow him to use me, but to love it.

Courtesy of the massive length in my mouth, I can't speak. But I want to tell him to do his worst, to use me as he wants. Instead of speaking the words, I try to convey them through my actions.

He picks up speed, shoving his dick down my throat, making me moan around him. Drool escapes past my lips, messy and hot, no matter how hard I try to hold it all in.

I brace myself as his movements grow more erratic, the tension coiling tighter with each thrust. His groans fill the room, raw and unrestrained, a crescendo that mirrors the intensity building within me.

My senses are overwhelmed, teetering on the edge of something vast and consuming.

Suddenly, he pulls away, the absence leaving my mouth empty and needy. My gasp for air is desperate, a sharp intake that barely registers before he's back again, pushing into my mouth with an urgency that sends a thrill through my entire body.

"I'm close," he warns, voice strained and breathless. "I want to see your throat work for it. You'll take every drop like a good toy who knows she was made for this."

The words spur me on, determination flaring hot and fierce inside me. I hollow my cheeks, suck hard enough to pull a broken curse from his lips.

Each stroke is precise and relentless, an unspoken promise that I intend to keep. I can feel him losing control, the swell of his hardness a prelude to what I've been waiting for.

His release is sudden and explosive, filling my mouth with warmth and saltiness. I swallow greedily, savoring the taste of him, eager to prove my worth. A detached part of me notes how different it feels from anything I've ever experienced—like victory.

A sense of triumph courses through me as I swallow every last drop just like he commanded.

"Fuck," he groans again, softer this time, spent but still potent in its effect on me.

One hand slides from my hair to the curve of my jaw, his thumb swiping the edge of my lips. It should be a gesture of dominance, a final brand. But it doesn't feel punishing—it feels... reverent.

There's the barest tremor in his touch, like he's barely holding himself together. The possessiveness in that simple graze brands me in the way it seeps beneath my skin until I can feel it in the very marrow of my being.

He finally pulls free of my lips with a wet pop, leaving me panting and disheveled in front of him. I can only imagine the glint of satisfaction in his eyes as he looks down at me. I don't know his name. I can't see his face. But I know the way he made me feel—powerless, filthy... and fucking worshiped.

"Damn," Matteo whistles. "That was fucking hot the way she loved sucking your cock."

Instead of feeling humiliated, ashamed, maybe even disgusted with myself, I feel wanted. And fuck me, I loved every second of it.

The man who used my mouth as though it belonged to him chuckles, dragging his fingers along my cheek. "Piper," he murmurs, voice soft but sharp as glass. "If I told you the only way to guarantee your internship was to let me touch your cunt, would you beg me to do it?"

The question hangs between us, a line in the sand. I know what he's asking, what he's offering. My heart pounds in my chest, my body

betraying me with every beat. I'm ashamed by my arousal, by my desperation.

But I nod, my voice barely above a whisper, "Yes."

Taking my hand, he helps me to my feet and guides me a few steps. I feel him sit, the chair creaking softly under his weight, and then he tugs me into his lap so my back is against his chest.

"Spread your legs," he rasps.

I squirm in his lap, moving my legs to rest on top of his, and when he shifts his wider, mine spread open. The mortification I feel fizzles, quickly replaced by something darker—need, raw and crawling beneath my skin.

A moan is ripped from me as he runs his hand up my bare thighs, all the way to the line of my thong. Anticipation and need build, making me squirm harder.

"Sit still," he commands.

I try, I really fucking try. But when he runs a single finger along my slit, I jump. My breathing intensifies, turning ragged. I'm acutely aware of every touch, every breath. It's wrong, so wrong. But it feels good, too good when he circles my clit.

I let my head fall back against his shoulder, gyrating my hips to get more. I'm so caught up in what he's doing that I forget we're not alone.

"What's your dream job when my cousin's done molding you, Piper?" Rafe asks.

I can't focus when fingers push between my lower lips and against my opening. "I… uhh… I want… I want…" My brain goes blank as a finger is pushed into my dripping heat.

"You're already wet," the man, whose lap I'm practically riding, observes. He slides one finger deep, then another, curling them just enough to make me shudder. "So deliciously drenched. Mhmm."

"I'm waiting," Rafe snaps.

Shit, I completely forgot about his question. Is he watching me getting fingered? Instead of feeling shame, the thought sets my body ablaze, and a moan escapes before I can stop it.

"I-I want to be an architect of influence," I answer. It takes everything in me to conjure the words rather than focusing on the sensation between my legs.

The man with his fingers buried in my pussy rumbles what sounds like approval. Then wraps an arm around my waist, pinning me in place as his fingers fuck me harder—pistoning in and out while the heel of his hand grinds against my clit.

My muscles coil, every nerve a live wire. I bite the inside of my cheek, desperate to keep from crying out as my orgasm threatens to consume me.

His length presses against my ass—thick, hard, and insistent. The thought of feeling him inside me, paired with those guttural groans of approval, is enough to push me over the edge.

"I'm going to… I'm… Yes," I cry out, my hips undulating, chasing friction, chasing the release I desperately want.

"So fucking wet for me. Mhmm, that's it. Make a mess on my fingers like a good toy."

My climax ripples through me, a tidal wave of pleasure that leaves me breathless, trembling. It's a release, a surrender, a binding agreement. I've accepted his terms, his conditions.

His warm palm slides up my thigh, deliberate, lazy. I'm still trembling, my body betraying me in ways I don't want to examine. As I try to shift, his grip tightens—possessive, unyielding—keeping me exactly where he wants me.

"Such an exquisite toy," he murmurs. The praise slides into me like a hook behind my ribs, sharp and unshakable.

With a low growl, he dismisses Rafe and Matteo like they're nothing. I try not to die of humiliation, knowing they saw—and heard—how he made me come all over his hand.

His hands trail up my stomach and over my bra, palms cupping my breasts, thumbs grazing my nipples through the lace. It shouldn't feel good—but it does. Too good.

As soon as the two men are gone, his tone sharpens, but he doesn't stop touching me. "Listen closely, Toy. I don't like repeating myself." His tone is low and serious.

I nod, breath shallow as understanding dawns on me. Men like him are used to the world bending on the first command, and right now, that includes me.

"The internship is yours," he says like a verdict, not a reward. "I won't waste your talent on filing paperwork or grabbing coffee. You'll be mine to command. I'll decide when you breathe, and how sweetly I want to hear you beg."

The air thickens, his words coiling like a forbidden promise.

"I'll control your calendar and facilitate your commute. You'll work when I say, and if I want you kneeling under my desk between meetings, you won't hesitate—"

"The hell I will," I hiss, struggling to get off his lap.

But the bastard wraps his hand around my throat, squeezing just enough to remind me who's in charge. He chuckles darkly. "Don't bother pretending you won't do whatever it takes, Piper. You've already proven that much to me."

"You're a pig," I spit, outraged.

I don't even know why I'm acting like this. I was just riding his lap, and I didn't mind being on my knees for him. Yet, when he says it now, it makes me feel like I'm nothing more than a glorified whore that needs to be available when he wants me.

He sounds amused. "I'm worse than you can even imagine. But that doesn't change a damn thing. You're mine, and you'll do exactly what I say, when I say it."

His fingers drift along my thigh like he's marking the edge of a map only he's allowed to read.

"You don't belong to the company," he growls, voice low and possessive. "You belong to me."

I let out an annoyed breath. "Is that all?" I ask, layering my voice in sarcasm.

"It's all you need to know," he replies, and I swear I can hear a grin in his tone. "Are you ready to sign the contract?"

Am I ready? No.

He's right though. I don't need to know anything else—I don't want to. I just need to sign and pretend this never happened. Because if I think about it too much, I'll break before I even begin.

I have a feeling that denial is going to become my new best friend until I graduate.

Going into this interview, I knew there'd be a catch, and here it is. Being owned until I'm officially done at Georgetown is nothing compared to what I'll gain. So yeah, I can suck it up.

"I'm ready," I say, ignoring the tremble in my voice. "Can I remove the blindfold now?"

He chuckles. "No need." He doesn't offer me any comfort or explanation.

Before I can process his words, he lifts me to my feet and guides me to a flat surface. A pen is pressed into my hand. His fingers close around my wrist, firm and inescapable, guiding me to where he wants my name.

"Say the words," he breathes, his lips grazing the shell of my ear. "Let me hear you surrender, Piper."

"What words?" I ask, even though I'm scared I already know.

"Say you agree."

A shiver runs down my spine. "I agree."

"Say you're mine."

I clamp my lips shut, refusing. But when the silence stretches, thick and waiting, I know I have to say something. So I settle on a compromise I can live with.

"You said I'm yours." There. A half-lie dressed up as obedience.

"What a naughty toy you are." His tone is amused, but the words let me know I haven't fooled him at all.

I shut my brain off. No second-guessing. No hesitation. I grip the pen tighter and scrawl my name across the page. As soon as I finish, he releases me.

There's no time to wonder where he's gone before he's back, ordering, "Lift your arms up."

My body obeys him faster than my brain can argue, and that fucking infuriates me. Then I realize what he's doing; he's dressing me. And suddenly, I'm glad I didn't hesitate. If I had, I might've said something stupid.

I tilt my head to the side. "What now?" I ask, forcing the words to sound stronger than I feel.

"Now, I'll escort you to the lobby. Then, your paperwork will be filed, and your advisor notified," he replies, sounding like he's checking things off his to-do list. Yet, his deep voice still manages to make it sound sexy.

"Okay," I manage.

"Are you ready for your life to change, Toy?" The question makes me shiver, and causes goosebumps to erupt all over my skin.

He really needs to stop asking me that. I'm not ready for anything, I'm just really fucking good at pretending. "Sure," I answer, hoping he can't hear how hard I'm faking it.

He links his arm with mine and leads me out of the room.

The further we walk, the more sounds I hear; people talking, footsteps echoing. But none of it registers. I'm too focused on the man who just fingered me. It feels surreal… and so fucking hot I hate myself for it.

"Here we are," he suddenly says, bringing us to a stop. "Miss Wilson will be here shortly. She'll give you back your handbag and blazer. She'll also arrange for someone to drive you home."

I don't even question how he knew I was wearing a blazer when I arrived. "Wait," I beg, digging my fingers into his arm. "If I'm to work for you, shouldn't I know your name?"

He chuckles darkly. "Why would you need to know that already?"

I gape, lips parted, something sharp stuck in my throat that I can't name. It's not a protest or surrender. It's worse than both—I want to know.

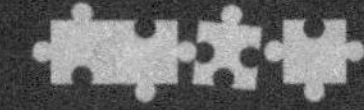

13

Lorenzo

I only linger long enough to watch Maria approach my toy and peel off her blindfold before returning her belongings. I grin to myself as I watch the way Piper's mouth runs a million miles a minute. Judging by Maria's pinched expression, she's not enjoying the barrage of questions.

A low chuckle slips out as I step into the waiting elevator, the doors closing on her questions and Maria's thinning patience.

Since I already know my assistant will make sure the driver takes Piper straight home, I don't need to wait around. It's not my personal driver, but someone who has been with me for long enough.

As soon as I'm in my office, I reach for my tablet and send the draft email to Mrs. Ellis at Georgetown, letting her know that one Miss Piper Harrington has landed a very prestigious internship.

Waiting beside my tablet is a new phone. A single folded note rests on top.

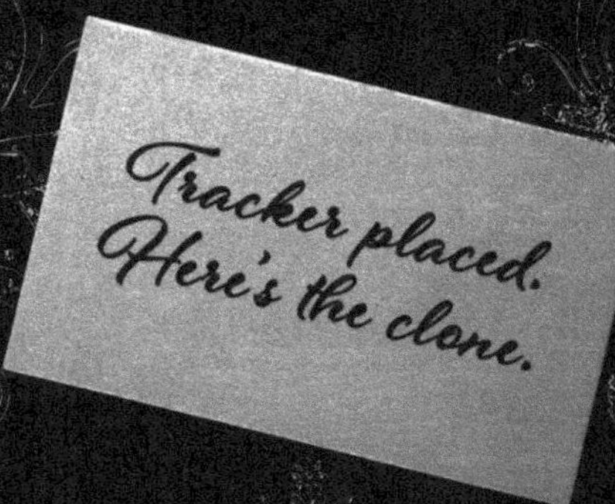

Cy's handwriting is sharp, efficient. Just like his work.

I power on the phone, and the screen glows to life. Every ping, every text, call, and move she makes will all be mirrored here. All without her knowledge.

With that out of the way, I pull up the surveillance feed from her apartment. I want to see the moment she arrives home—whether she'll flinch after what she allowed at the interview… or if she'll wear it like power.

Checking the camera in her living room, my eyes fall on the almost-bare wall. I considered hanging the puzzle of her face there. Even incomplete, it would have looked exquisite—haunting in the right light. But I decided against it. My toy's not ready for that.

Instead, it hangs in my office. The original print, the one I designed for her. Full-color, her face rendered in shadow and light, framed in black like an icon behind glass. Eight pieces are missing; the ones I gifted her. And now the image gapes with that absence.

Of course, I could order a new batch, cut to the exact same shape, black as night and sharp at the corners. I could slot them in tonight and call it whole. But it wouldn't be the same.

Those pieces—her pieces—were never just cardboard. They were part of our beginning, and she burned them like they meant nothing. Replacing them would be a lie. It would be a rewrite of history.

She doesn't understand that I only gave her pieces of the shadow. That was my way of easing her into it, as I didn't think she'd appreciate getting pieces of her face. No doubt that would have sent the wrong message.

My toy shouldn't fear me, only want me—and, eventually, love me back.

She should be home by now. I refresh the app, but there's still no sign of her. My jaw clenches. If there's a delay, my men should have informed me. The second she arrives, I need to see her.

I light a cigar first—thin, dark, perfectly wrapped—letting the smoke curl toward the ceiling like a whispered promise. Something about the ritual soothes the more primal ache beneath my skin.

Then I settle onto the couch, lying on my back. My dick hasn't softened since the interview. Not even flooding her throat with my cum took the edge off. If anything, it sharpened it. A groan builds in my throat, escaping before I can stop it. Fuck, I can still smell her pussy on my fingers.

Just as I'm about to give in to the carnal need thrumming through my veins, Piper steps into view. She walks in like nothing happened—like she didn't kneel for me, didn't orgasm with my fingers deep inside her.

Her posture is perfect, her movements calm. If she's shaking, she doesn't show it. And I study her closely—looking for the crack. But there isn't one. I zoom in, anyway. Just to be sure. Her mouth is relaxed, her gaze steady. She drops her bag by the table like this is just another day.

"Good girl," I rasp, the words meant only for me. My fingers twitch, craving her skin, craving the slow, inevitable moment I stop watching and start taking.

I adjust my position on the couch, my fingers deftly working at my belt. As soon as I've released my hardness from its confines, my hand wraps around the length with a familiar grip. My breathing remains steady and controlled, eyes locked unwaveringly on the screen before me.

Pre-cum is already forming into glistening beads, and I spread it gently over the sensitive tip and down the entire length, feeling the slick smoothness under my fingers. The sensation is intoxicating, an electric charge buzzing through my body with each deliberate stroke, sending waves of pleasure coursing through me.

A guttural growl tears from my throat as I fuck my fist to the image of my toy. Her hips sway with a tantalizing rhythm, each step a silent invitation. The dress she wears clings to her curves, accentuating her deliciously round ass with precision.

My grip tightens, strokes turning brutal, punishing. My toy. Mine.

"Fuck," I hiss through clenched teeth, my hand moving with increasing urgency.

The same hand that had expertly made her come during the interview is now working my hardness. The symbolism isn't lost on me; this connection through touch, this limb that bridges us, is driving us both toward the brink of release.

My grip turns punishing. I stroke faster. Harder. Like she's still on her knees for me. My breathing becomes ragged, echoing the rising intensity. I can feel the tension building, my muscles tightening, and my body responding in anticipation.

I'm on the brink, so incredibly close to the edge, teetering on the precipice of release.

"Turn around," I grunt. "Let me see that pretty face."

I fixate on her full, pouty lips as she parts them ever so slightly. My mind immediately plunges into a memory of the tip of my cock brushing against her soft, moist lips.

The warmth of her mouth enveloping me, inch by agonizing inch. Her tongue, slick and teasing, circling the sensitive rim. Fuck. That's the memory that finishes me. My climax crashes over me, and my body convulses with pleasure. Thick, white ropes of cum erupt from my dick.

I'm groaning her name. "Piper! Fuck!" I'm fucking drenched, my cum slicking my hand and staining my clothes—but I don't care. I wipe my hand on my slacks and sit up.

Just as I'm about to set the tablet down so I can clean up, I see it. See him—the driver. What the fuck is he still doing there? His usefulness and job ended the second she crossed the threshold. He definitely shouldn't be inside my toy's home.

My entire body freezes as I watch him move closer, too close.

Without warning, he reaches out and brushes her.

He. Fucking. Touches. Her.

Then he says something, but the rage pounding in my head drowns out his voice. His hand lingers on Piper's lower back. She nods, but she doesn't even look at him. In fact, she looks uncomfortable.

"Who do you think you're touching?" I roar, surging to my feet.

Although there's no way he heard me, the driver quickly removes his hand, but it's too late. The damage is done. He touched what's mine.

Reaching for my phone, I don't hesitate to call Maria. It only rings once before there's a reply.

"I need the driver who took Piper Harrington home to come pick me up at my office. Now." My tone is clipped, my words angry. And instead of waiting for a reply, I hang up.

Grabbing my keys and coat, I stride out the door and into the waiting elevator. Even though I get a text halfway down to let me know the driver is on his way, it feels like I'm pacing the lobby for an eternity before he pulls into the spot in front of the building.

My body feels tense, wound tight like a spring ready to snap as I stride out through the gleaming glass doors, each step landing with a deliberate heaviness. The air feels cold as it brushes against my skin, a stark contrast to the heat of my nerves.

With calculated precision, I navigate around the sleek, polished car, its surface reflecting the world in a distorted dance of light and color.

I open the door and slip into the backseat, the leather cool and smooth beneath me, positioning myself directly behind the driver, every movement purposeful and controlled.

"Where are we going, Mr. Russo?" The driver's voice wavers as he glances at me nervously in the rearview mirror.

"How long have you worked for me?" I snap, my voice a sharp blade cutting through the tension, anger boiling just beneath the surface.

"W-what?" he stammers, his eyes widening in fear, his grip on the steering wheel tightening as if it could anchor him against the storm brewing in the backseat.

I shake my head with a sharp jerk, making a deliberate show of adjusting my cufflinks with a precise, almost mechanical motion. "The answer required a number," I state, my voice cutting through the air like ice. "Six days, six months, six years. What it didn't require was a question." My eyes bore into him with a relentless intensity. "So I'll ask you again, and this time, I expect nothing but the truth. How long have you worked for me?"

He swallows with a loud gulp, and a bead of sweat emerges on his forehead, glistening under the harsh light. "Four years, two months, and twenty-two days," he stammers, his voice trembling with unease.

I nod slowly, my eyes locked onto his as I deliberately reach for my

tie, undoing it with measured precision. "That's exactly what I thought," I say, my voice cold and cutting. "Which means you knew better than to touch her. You knew—and you still fucking did it."

"Touch?" he blurts, panic rising in his voice. "I haven't touched anything, Mr. Russo. I swear, I—"

His denial ignites a blazing fury within me, surging like a storm ready to obliterate everything in its path. I lurch forward with ferocious intent, wrapping the tie around his throat with a vise-like grip, squeezing tighter and tighter.

"I saw you!" I bellow, my voice echoing with the force of an avalanche. "Touching my toy in her own home. You. Touched. Her." The words explode from my mouth, each syllable a dagger aimed at his very soul.

He opens his mouth to speak, but I cut him off with a glare that could slice through steel. There's nothing he can say. Words won't save him. Begging won't slow me. He signed his own death warrant, and I'm here to execute it.

A dark thrill courses through me as I see the color drain from his face in the rearview mirror, his skin turning a sickly hue. Desperately, he raises a hand to tug at the tie choking him, but I slap it away with a force that leaves my palm stinging.

I don't just choke him. I make him burn with it, just like I am. The betrayal. The audacity. And the fucking touch. My hands shake with rage as I squeeze.

His pulse thrums wildly beneath my fingers, a pathetic staccato begging for mercy. I don't give in. I squeeze harder, feeling his struggle turn sluggish, his kicks weakening. His lips part—one last plea, one last breath. And then... nothing. Silence. Perfection.

My heart pounds, adrenaline surging as I text Cy, a single command for cleanup blazing across the screen. His response is instant and primal—a wolf emoji, howling back at me with the ferocity of a predator ready to devour the remains.

It's been one week since I had my interview at Blackwood
Strategic Advisory. An interview I still don't know how I feel
about.

Part of me feels weirdly proud. I made a choice, took control. But
then there's that other voice, curled in the back of my skull like smoke,
whispering that I sold my body for an opportunity I haven't even
started earning.

Thankfully, I've mostly been able to ignore that voice. Even if it's
right, who cares? I have landed one of the most prestigious internships
that exists. Not just in D.C., but globally.

With Lena out of town, I've buried my negative feelings in what
must be gallons of ice cream and more bottles of wine than I care to
admit. A part of me is happy she's gone. Otherwise, I would have
confessed everything the second I got back from the interview. And…
well, I really don't want to.

The day after the interview, I received a package from the
company. A man wearing a crisp suit delivered a bouquet of black
tulips, a bottle of Louis Roederer Cristal Rosé Champagne, and a
matte black folder embossed with the Blackwood crest—a wolf with
its maw open in a silent howl.

Inside the folder was the contract I signed while blindfolded,
onboarding documents—including a very strict dress code, an even
stricter moral code of conduct, and instructions on how to contact my
driver.

There was also a sleek brass Blackwood name badge for office
access, already stamped with my face. Judging by the looks of it, it
was taken of me as I entered the building the day I went for the
interview.

The last thing inside the folder was a note from Maria—

handwritten in careful script, just polite enough to feel impersonal.

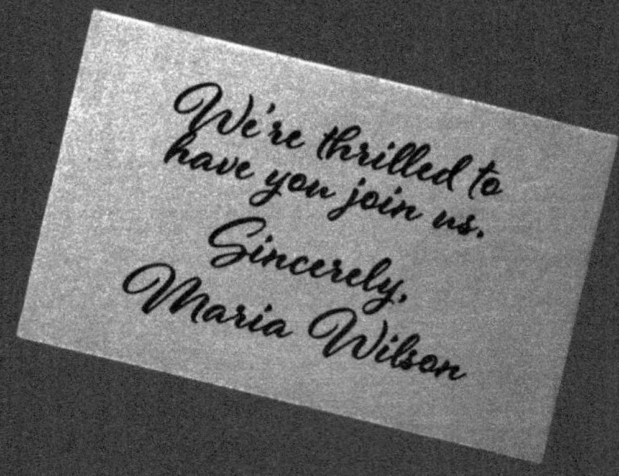

Later that afternoon, an email followed.

> *"Per company policy, all new Blackwood hires must undergo a comprehensive medical screening. Your appointment has been scheduled at Arlington Diagnostic & Preventive Services for October 8, 9:00 a.m. Please arrive on time. This ensures continued eligibility for internal insurance coverage."*

And now I'm here, standing outside a building I've never heard of until a week ago. I press my tongue to the roof of my mouth, willing my heartbeat to slow.

The doors slide open with a hushed whoosh, ushering me into a pristine foyer where the sharp scent of antiseptic collides with an incongruous whiff of expensive cologne. The collision leaves me off-balance before I even approach the gleaming marble reception desk.

The woman behind the desk is all crisp angles. Her dark hair pulled into a sleek chignon, her white uniform pressing sharp creases into her skin. The gold name badge pinned to her lapel reads Natalie.

"Hi there. How can I help you?" she asks, her voice as polished as the marble surrounding us.

I hand her my appointment details, and answer, "I'm Piper Harrington. I believe I've been scheduled for an appointment."

Her eyes crinkle as they flick over the paperwork I handed her, then back to my face. "I just need your signature, please. Then I'll take you to the changing room." She slides a digital tablet across the counter, a single perfectly manicured finger indicating where I need to sign.

I pick up the stylus, willing my hand to steady. The tremble in my

fingers sends the first stroke skittering off-course. I grit my teeth, try again. This time, the stylus moves in a jerky approximation of my usual scrawl. It looks like the signature of a stranger. Maybe it is.

Natalie takes the tablet back, her smile never wavering. "Follow me, please."

She steps out from behind the desk, leading me to an exam room, the pastel walls and softly humming machines doing little to mask the purpose of the space.

"Dr. Emily Voss will be with you shortly," Natalie informs me. "Would you like anything to drink while you wait?" I quickly shake my head, watching her as she leaves me with a wave.

I close my eyes, trying to slow my breathing. It's not that I have anything to hide, but medical examinations always freak me out.

The click of the door handle jolts me back to the present. Dr. Emily Voss enters the exam room, tablet in hand, her lab coat a blinding white under the fluorescent lights. She moves with the brisk efficiency of someone long accustomed to navigating the intricacies of the human body.

"Piper Harrington?" she confirms, her voice crisp and impersonal. I nod, my throat suddenly too dry to form words. "I'm Dr. Voss. We'll be doing a full-body evaluation today, including some swabs, a pelvic exam, bloodwork, and a brief verbal assessment."

She says it like she's reading off a grocery list, each item no more remarkable than the last.

"Let's start with the questions so you can get more comfortable."

She starts with the basics; last menstrual cycle, contraceptive use, and if I have any history of miscarriage or abortion. I answer each question honestly.

"Are you sexually active right now?"

I snort. "No." And then just because I feel fucking awkward, I smirk and add, "But it's not from a lack of trying."

Ignoring my lame attempt at a joke, she carries on. It feels like she's asking me a million questions before she finally puts her tablet down and announces it's time for the sensory tests. Christ, this is going to be the day that never ends. That health insurance better be worth it.

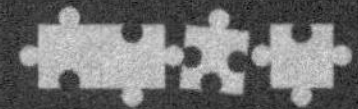

Lorenzo

The moment I step onto the jet in Montreal, my phone buzzes with an incoming call from Dr. Voss. I tap my earpiece, answering the call.

"Lorenzo," she greets.

I gesture for the stewardess to bring me my usual drink. "Good evening, Emily. How did the appointment with Miss Harrington go yesterday morning?"

She throws herself into an explanation that's more Latin than English with all the different medical terms she uses. "I've already sent the report to Maria for the insurance."

"Thank you," I state.

Even though I have a special interest in my toy's results, that's not why Maria set up the appointment. We do have great insurance, and thorough health checks are needed for that. Normally, our interns don't get full medical coverage. But there's nothing normal about Piper.

"Maria mentioned you might be interested to know that the results I've gotten back for Miss Harrington are great. I've emailed them to you."

I open my email, immediately seeing the top two are from the good doctor, and another one from Maria.

Ending the call with Voss, I focus on the one from Maria first. It doesn't take long to figure out it's a CliffsNotes version. It's times like these that my assistant deserves a raise for anticipating my needs.

After spending two days at a summit in Montreal, I'm beyond exhausted, and not in the mood for lengthy and convoluted medical jargon.

I skim Maria's summary, eyes dragging over each line until one detail makes me pause:

Miss Harrington stated she is not currently sexually active. Birth control status: IUD. No current sexual partners. Clear history.

Not currently sexually active?

My jaw tightens as I clench the phone harder while swiping to the video file attached. It's only a snippet, under two minutes. I tap play, and there she is; my toy. Sitting with her legs crossed, eyes forward, looking so fucking composed.

"Are you sexually active right now?" Voss asks.

Piper snorts. "No." Then she smirks—smirks—and adds, "But it's not from a lack of trying."

I pause the video, and for the span of a single breath, I see red.

She just said she's not sexually active like it's a fact. Like she didn't choke on me during her interview, and cream all over my fingers like a

good fucking toy.

My jet lifts off, slicing through the Montreal sky, but I don't look out the window. I don't need a view—I've already got one burned into the back of my eyes. That fucking smirk.

I sit back, phone in hand, the screen still open to Maria's email. My thumb rests over the line I've reread half a dozen times already—not sexually active—and I want to laugh. Or maybe I want to burn something to the fucking ground.

She said it to Dr. Voss with that coy little shrug of hers, like the words meant nothing. No. But it's not from a lack of trying. Her voice was breezy, flippant, almost amused.

Like swallowing my cum didn't count. Like letting me slide my fingers inside her perfect cunt until she came all over my hand didn't register as sex because it didn't come with a condom and a fucking penetration checklist. The growl building in my throat is as feral as I feel.

Someone kicks my shin under the table, and my gaze snaps up to... Cy. Fuck, I'd forgotten he was here. The second Voss called, everything but my toy ceased mattering.

I tear my earbud from my ear just in time to hear Cy say, "... if you keep making those noises I'll have someone give you a fucking rabies shot when we land, Cujo."

"Shut the fuck up," I snap, not in the mood.

"What's the matter?" he asks, eyebrows furrowing together. "Did something happen with—"

"This isn't about work," I almost snarl. Then I take a deep breath, forcing myself to calm the fuck down.

I bring the glass to my mouth, but the whiskey barely touches my tongue before I'm setting it down again. She thinks she's clever, that she can compartmentalize and... and what? Pretend I didn't finger her to orgasm?

That's not how the world fucking works—not the one I'm in charge of, anyway. I will make her fucking admit what happened. I'll make her own up to every single moan.

"Come on," Cy sighs. "Tell me what the fuck's the matter. Is it more shit about the former Senator Jacobs?"

I shake my head. "No, it's not fucking Jacobs. After I had the autopsy report released, everyone believed it was a tragic accident."

"Okay, so if it's not about him, is it Remus that has you this worked up?"

I shake my head again. Knowing there's only one way to shut Cy up, I tell him what Piper said to Voss while answering her questions, even show him the short video clip.

"Fuck me," Cy laughs. "That's ballsy. I like her."

At that, I bare my teeth, another growl slipping free. "Stop talking about her!"

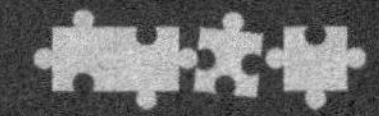

Still laughing, Cy holds his hands up in a placating gesture. "Not like that, for fuck's sake. Seriously, you need to get a hold of yourself. This is not like you at all."

"It is now." That's all I say. The silence isn't empty—it's laced with expectation.

The jet ride back is smooth, but I don't notice. I don't fucking care. The only thing I care about is what I'm going to do to her. How I'm going to punish her.

Just before we land, I check the cameras in her apartment. She's not home. I pull out the cloned phone, searching for where she might be. There are no texts or social media check-in's indicating her whereabouts.

If she's stupid enough to be out trying to give what's mine to someone else, I'll kill whoever touches her.

It's close to midnight when I finally step out of the jet and onto the tarmac of the private airfield outside D.C. The sky is starless—perfect for a man like me. A muscle in my jaw ticks as I pocket both phones and follow Cy into the waiting SUV.

"Problem?" he asks from beside me, when we're both seated in the backseat.

"She's not home," I bark, turning my attention to my friend. "If she's with someone else…" I don't finish the sentence. I don't need to.

Cy gives a sharp nod, then reaches for his phone. "Want me on standby?"

"I want you ready for cleanup," I bite out. "Just in case."

When the driver glances at me in the rearview mirror, I meet his eyes without flinching, and tell him to take us to Piper's apartment.

Almost halfway there, the cloned phone vibrates in my pocket, and I quickly pull it out. It's a text from Lena, replying to one Piper sent just seconds ago. Apparently, my toy's been busy at Georgetown's library, studying.

I let out a heavy breath, feeling better already.

The ride through D.C. is a blur of lights and fury. By the time we pull to a stop outside her building, I turn to Cy. "You can go home," I tell him. Now that I know I won't need to kill anyone tonight, I don't need him around. My plans for my toy are between the two of us.

"Really?" His entire face lights up. "Good. I had plans to get my dick sucked, and you're kind of interfering."

I arch an eyebrow. "Fuck, Cy. I'm glad you added the last part."

He grins wickedly. "No offense, man, but you're really not my type."

Snorting, I offer up my condolences to whatever woman he has his eyes set on. Then I exit the car.

Piper's scent hits me as soon as I let myself inside her home. Vanilla and something uniquely hers that clings to the air like a whisper only I'm meant to hear. It wraps around me before the door clicks shut

behind me.

I don't turn on the lights since I already know where everything is. Sitting down on the couch, I notice the book face down on the armrest. For once, not something political. This looks like… ah, never mind. A political thriller. For some reason, that makes me chuckle.

Her cardigan is draped over the back like she left in a hurry. I rest my elbows on my knees, staring straight ahead.

Outside, life goes on. Inside, time holds its breath. I'm about to get up and stretch my legs when I hear keys jangle just before sliding into the lock. A smile splays along my lips, anticipation coils.

Then she opens the door.

15

Lorenzo

Piper enters, humming under her breath. I don't recognize the tune, but it's something happy. Something light. Clearly, her mood has changed since her appointments at ADPS yesterday. As she reaches for the light switch, I speak. "Don't turn on the light."

Jumping, she lets out a startled yelp that makes my blood fucking sing. "Who the hell—"

I cut her off. "Miss Harrington," I growl, turning my face downward so she can't see my features.

Her body stiffens, beautifully. Her hands freeze in the air. "Oh…" she trails off, almost taking a step toward me, but my low growl stops her. "Oh, my God! You're the guy from the interview."

"I am, and you lied to your doctor." I pause for a beat, but she says nothing. "That was a mistake. I don't tolerate liars. Now, be a good girl and turn away from me." My tone is sharp, harsh, even.

"How did you even get in here?" she snaps, her voice rising with a sharp edge. "You… this is my fucking home. You can't just—"

"Turn. Around." I repeat, voice low and final.

I don't explain myself. She doesn't need to know how deep this goes yet. Let her feel the walls closing in before she sees who built them.

A minute passes, but then she obeys, spinning on her heel with a frustrated huff. Then she shakes her head, mumbling something incoherent. I can't be sure, but it sounds like she's telling herself to shut up, and the thought amuses me.

"I don't like being lied to," I press on, keeping my tone cold. Then I rise, reaching inside my suit jacket for the blindfold I brought with me. "I'm going to blindfold you again. When I say it's okay, you may turn around and face me."

She sighs, but doesn't argue as I secure the fabric over her eyes and place a kiss on her neck before sitting back down.

"How about you tell me what the hell I lied about?" she hisses.

Taking a step closer to where I'm sitting, she folds her arms over her chest and cocks her hip while lifting her chin.

I don't speak, just continue to look at her.

The longer the silence stretches on, the more she fidgets. Finally, she sighs and throws her arms up in the air. "Seriously, I have a right to know—"

"Do you now?" I interrupt. "Do you lie so often you can't keep it straight?"

Silence. Just her breath now, ragged and shallow.

"You need to be punished, Miss Harrington."

She huffs with indignation. "Punished?" she echoes. "Do you even hear yourself? What are you going to do? Spank me like—"

I'm too distracted by the way her lips wrap around the syllables—pouty, lush, pink—to really pay attention to her words. "What an excellent idea," I interject, loving the way her mouth falls open at my words. "That's exactly what I'm going to do."

Shaking her head, she retreats one step. "It wasn't a suggestion."

I laugh. "Maybe not, but it's what's going to happen."

She takes another step back from me. "I want to know what you think I've lied about."

Though her defiance is a fucking turn on, I harden my voice. "We can do this the easy way or the hard way, Miss Harrington."

She scrunches up her nose, opening and closing her mouth as though she has a million things she wants to say. But she wisely keeps her mouth shut.

"The easy way is you stripping and lying down across my lap of your own volition—"

"And the hard way?" she asks, unable to completely hide her curiosity from her tone.

Chuckling, I reply, "The hard way will be for you to find a way to graduate Georgetown without an internship at my company or anywhere else."

"Y-your company?" she asks, her voice trembling.

"My company," I confirm. Huh, I thought she'd have figured that out sooner. Especially with what I put her through at the interview.

Her breath hitches, and I almost feel bad for playing that card when her entire body and face fall with dejection. Almost. But not enough to take it back, or to let her know her future is safe because I'm never fucking letting her go.

With an almost inhuman growl, she moves, tearing her clothes from her body. There's nothing sensual or artistic about it; it's pure frustration, anger, and maybe a hint of hatred. It's fucking delicious.

When she's naked in front of me, she throws me this fuck-you curtsy, all defiance and sin. My cock swells instantly, thickening with the kind of pressure that's almost painful. She has no idea what she does to me, standing there stripped and defiant like that.

"What else does my liege command?" she snarks.

Reclining comfortably on the couch, I guide her to me with only my voice. She complies, moving to stand before me. Even though she can't see me, I tap my lap with a purposeful look.

"Lie down, ass in the air," I instruct.

She pauses for a brief moment, uncertainty flickering across her features. Then, with a resigned sigh, my toy slowly closes the last of the distance between us, feeling her way onto my lap, her body draping elegantly over me. Her back arches, accentuating the curve of her spine, as her hips rise obediently, a testament to her compliance.

The visual steals my breath. My dick throbs against the confines of my suit pants, desperate for friction. Every curve of her body taunts me with promises.

The first slap resonates through the room, a sharp crack slicing through the air.

She gasps, a tremor in her voice as she exclaims, "Fuck!" Her breath is ragged and filled with a mix of surprise and pain.

"You should be counting for me, Miss Harrington," I command, dragging my hand down the curve of her ass. "Since you're not sexually active, this doesn't count, does it? Just my palm marking your ass. No cock. No penetration. Just discipline."

"Two," she cries out when my hand lands another firm strike on her skin, the sound echoing once more.

I click my tongue disapprovingly. "The first one didn't count. Let's start over," I instruct, maintaining control with a calm demeanor.

To her credit, she doesn't argue or plead; she simply nods, accepting the correction. When my hand connects with her ass again, the impact reverberates, and she dutifully counts, her voice an enticing mixture of pain and a trembling I suspect is pleasure.

By the fifth strike, she's moaning and writhing in my lap, her body undulating with a mix of pleasure and anticipation.

The grind of her hips sends a jolt through me so sharp I have to bite my cheek to keep from groaning. My dick is rock hard beneath her, begging to be inside her. Her skin glistens with a light sheen of sweat, and the room is filled with her soft, breathy gasps and whimpers.

"I'm not sure this constitutes punishment at all," I rasp, my voice low and gravelly, as she tilts her hips, grinding against my thigh.

When she tries to protest, her words come out as little more than a whisper, barely audible over the sound of her own desire. I move my hand between her thighs, feeling the heat radiating from her skin, and my fingers find her drenched in arousal.

"Mhmm, so incredibly wet… and still not sexually active, right? Or is this you trying?" I taunt, dragging two fingers through her soaked folds. "All this slickness and no one to use it? That's fucking tragic."

Her body responds instinctively, a shiver coursing through her as shame makes her breath hitch, and her cheeks take on a delicious red

hue that almost matches the prints of my hand on both her creamy ass cheeks.

I want to bury my face in her pussy and taste the proof of her arousal. I want to ruin her with my mouth until she forgets how to lie to herself.

"N-no," she argues weakly. "P-please don't." Her denial dies when I pinch her clit, and she cries out, rolling her hips as though she wants more.

As I land another blow on her ass, she squirms, trying to get away from me.

"No, you don't," I growl with a low, menacing intensity.

She sobs, her voice trembling with a note of desperation. "No. Stop… ahh, I need more. No." She's at war with herself while tear after tear cascades down her face. The blindfold doesn't absorb all of them. I admire the inky trails along her cheeks like a somber work of art.

Reaching out, I grip her jaw with a firm, unyielding grasp, guiding her face closer to mine. I lean in, letting my tongue glide over her skin to taste a single tear, savoring its salty essence.

"Your desperation is delicious," I whisper, my voice a soft, sinister caress that hangs in the charged space between us.

I want to bottle that scent—the wet, electric musk of shame and arousal. Wear it like a cologne.

"Let's see if you're ready to tell the truth," I rasp. "Are you sexually active now, Toy? Or are you still intending to try with anyone else?"

She stiffens, once again trying to escape me. But I'm holding her too tight for that to happen. She parts her lips to speak, then she shakes her head and presses her lips together.

"Tell me," I croon, rolling her clit.

"I… I… it was an accident," she moans. "I was just trying to lighten the fucking mood."

That's the answer I expected. And now that I'm seeing her in the flesh, hearing the tremble in her voice, I'm convinced it's not an act.

"An accident?" I scoff.

She hesitates, licking her lips. "Yes. I mean…" Trailing off, she curses under her breath. "I wasn't going to sit there and tell Dr. Voss what you've done to me, was I? No. So I made a harmless joke," she snarls.

I run my hand over her ass, pinching the red marks until she gasps and bucks against me. "A harmless joke," I repeat. "Do you still think it's harmless?"

"Enough," she snaps, her voice thick. "I've answered your fucking question honestly. It's not my fault if you don't believe me. But I'm done playing this game."

There she is, my perfect toy breaking free, showing her fiery self.

"Are you sexually active?" I ask, my voice husky.

"Yes," she cries.

"With who?"

"Y-you."

I palm her ass, tenderly stroking the skin. "And are you trying with anyone else?"

"No," she hisses. "I'm not a fucking slut."

Tilting my head to the side, I push my fingers inside her again. "Aren't you? You indulged in sexual activity in exchange for your internship. Isn't that what a slut does? Sexual favors for payment?"

She hisses, a low, vicious sound. "I. Am. Not. A. Slut!"

I tisk. "I think you're my slut, Piper." I curl my fingers and pump them in and out until she's wiggling against them, chasing her pleasure. "Good toys deserve to get what they want, but you're not being a good toy right now."

I don't need to see her eyes to know she's caught between want and possibly pride. I deliver a swift slap to her ass, sending a jolt of sensation through her body.

"Come on," I taunt. "If you want to be sexually active, all you have to do is say so."

She moans, a sound both primal and needy, as she writhes, her hips moving in a slow, deliberate dance against me. Her body undulates with fluid grace, each movement deliberate and sensual.

I pull my fingers out and stop touching her. Several moments pass before she finally gives in. "P-please," she sobs. "I want… I want to come. I want… I am sexually active, okay? But only with you. I promise."

Those words are fucking music to my ears.

"Go ahead, Toy. Rub that perfect cunt against my thigh. Show me how desperate you are," I say, my low, husky words encouraging her.

I tense my thigh, muscles coiling and hardening beneath her, offering a firm surface for her to press against. The friction builds, each motion drawing her closer to the edge.

Her breath hitches, and a shiver of ecstasy courses through her as she reaches her climax. A guttural cry escapes her lips, echoing through the room like a primal symphony.

In that precise moment, I slide my fingers back into her eager core, curling them to caress the hidden pad of her G-spot. Her velvety walls clench around me, slick and inviting.

"Mhmm, your cunt is so hot and tight around me," I growl, my voice hoarse with lust. "You're clutching my fingers like you never want to let them go. I can't wait to feel you stretch around my cock."

I pump my fingers harder.

"To bury myself in your heat and lose all sense of where I end and you begin." Her arousal coats my fingers, her desire perfuming the air like a potent aphrodisiac.

"Yes! Yes! Yes… oh my fucking… YES!" she screams, her voice filled with urgency and pleasure.

My fingers move rhythmically, each motion deliberate and precise, drawing out her every response. My hardness is leaking, straining. I want to fuck her raw on this couch until she forgets her own name, but not yet.

As I continue, I whisper a litany of desires, painting vivid images with my words, each one a promise of the pleasures yet to come.

"I'm going to bend you over every surface, fuck you in every hole. Oh, my perfect little toy, you're going to be such a slut for me, aren't you?" Her every gasp and shiver tells me all I need to know.

When she's no longer coming, and her pussy releases my fingers, I don't hesitate in bringing them to my mouth, licking them clean. Her mouth pops open, and she turns her head.

"What are you doing?" she asks, sounding like she doesn't believe whatever conclusion she's come to in her head.

"Licking your taste from my fingers," I reply, shooting her a wicked grin she can't see.

"Oh…" That's all she says.

"Cat got your tongue, miss smart-mouth?" I tease.

Turning on my lap, she smiles sweetly as she brings her index finger to her lips, and the sight makes me growl low in my throat when her tongue darts out, snaking around the tip of her finger.

"You have no idea how smart my mouth is," she purrs. "What I did at the interview was nothing more than a preview."

"You're killing me," I groan, angling my hips so she can feel just how hard I am.

She shifts, deliberately rubbing herself against my hardness, causing me to growl. And then, she fucking smiles. Like the air between us isn't charged with arousal. And it nearly undoes me.

Instead of giving in, I slide my hands to her hips and still her movements, holding her in place so I don't come in my pants from the friction.

"You had your punishment and reward," I murmur, voice low and wrecked. "And I reminded you what the truth fucking feels like."

With those words, I lift her off my lap, set her down on the couch, and rise to my feet. I could take her now. Bend her over this couch and fuck her so full of me she tastes it for days. But this was about getting the truth, and I believe she gave me that.

"Now that you're finally being honest, you'll start your internship in three days."

16

Piper

Blackwood Strategic Advisory stretches before me, a gleaming expanse of razor-sharp angles. It's the kind of space designed to make you feel small, scrutinized, your every flaw and secret written across your skin like a confession.

If I'm completely honest with myself, I wasn't sure I'd return. Not even when I got into the car that waited for me outside my apartment this morning.

The interview was one thing. But having the owner show up in my fucking home and spank me like some unruly child… no, not like a child. My reaction to what he did was anything but innocent, and that might be what sickens me the most.

Despite changing my locks, I'm not sure that'll be enough to keep him out if he decides to come back. I mean, it's not like I gave him keys before. However he got in, it was illegal. Even thinking about it sends heat between my legs, dampening my panties. Gah, I really need to stop thinking about it.

In three…

Two…

One…

I take a breath, smooth my skirt, and step inside the intimidating building.

Just like the last time I was here, Maria meets me at the glass doors, her heels clicking a staccato rhythm against the floor. She's all crisp efficiency and tailored lines, her hair pulled back in a sleek chignon that doesn't dare shed a single strand.

"Follow me, Miss Harrington," she says, her voice as neutral as her expression. It's not a request.

"Please, call me Piper," I mutter as I do my best to keep up with her.

We move through the lobby like soldiers on a mission, Maria's strides purposeful, mine struggling to keep pace. The security checkpoint looms ahead, a gauntlet of metal detectors and watchful eyes.

After placing my belongings in the tray, I turn to the humming scanner, holding my breath as I step through it. It's just like the interview, this sense of being weighed, measured, stripped down to my component parts to see if I meet some unspoken standard.

I wonder if I'll ever get used to it.

Clearly above the security measures, Maria walks around and waits on the other side, impassive, as I gather my belongings with fingers that tremble just slightly.

She guides me over to the elevators, explaining the different floors as we ascend. I can barely keep up with everything she says, and I have a feeling I'll get lost here a lot.

When the elevator doors slide open, the main office floor unfolds before us, a cavernous space of glass and steel and muted colors. Sunlight slants through floor-to-ceiling windows, casting geometric shadows across the polished concrete.

Everywhere I look, there are sharp edges and clean lines, a precision that borders on sterile.

We pass sleek conference rooms with glass walls, their occupants engaged in hushed conversations that slice off as we walk by. The open-plan desks stretch out in orderly rows, each one a mirror image of the last. There's a hush to the place, a focused energy that crackles like static in the air.

"This is where you and the other two interns will sit. You're allowed to decorate your cubicle as long as it's done tastefully, and in accordance with the handbook—"

I can't help the laugh that escapes me, too quick and too loud. I'm buzzing with a weird, nervous energy. "So, no drunken selfies. Got it." Then I press my lips together, shooting Maria an apologetic look. Christ almighty, I have no idea what just possessed me to say that.

Maria smiles indulgently. "That would not be appropriate, no. However, if you ever feel like sticking it to HR, that's exactly the kind of thing that makes them hold seminars and fire interns," she informs, dryly.

"Understood," I croak.

"As I was saying," Maria continues. "Your seat is at the end. Go ahead and check it out. You'll notice your company-provided laptop, which is yours for the duration of your internship. Your orientation isn't for another twenty minutes, and the other interns haven't arrived yet."

The small, square space assigned to me somehow manages to feel both exposed and claustrophobic. The chrome desktop gleams, untouched. Files are stacked with military precision, each one perfectly aligned like they're waiting for inspection.

A slim nameplate perches at the edge of the desk: Piper Harrington, Intern.

My smile is so wide it hurts my cheeks. I'm here… officially an intern.

"The orientation is just around the corner and then the third door to the left. I trust you can find your way," Maria says, her tone crisp.

Without waiting for my reply, she takes off, which suits me just fine. I need a couple of minutes to myself, to fully absorb where I am. I sink into the ergonomic chair, my legs suddenly weak and I'm beyond overwhelmed.

Twenty minutes to gather myself, I can do that. Spinning in my chair, I look around, taking in everything I can see from here. And it's almost as though the walls are humming with energy. Just watching people going about their day is inspiring.

Right now, I can't bring myself to feel shame for using my body to help seal the deal. I'm not even sure I regret the spanking. Not just because it was all sorts of hot, but because it brought me here.

As soon as I close my eyes, he's there. But since I haven't seen him, my mind's making him a shadowed figure. Not that his looks matter. Not with the way he made me feel things I can't even name.

I can still feel the heat of his palm against my skin, the sting of the slap, the rush of shameful, unwanted arousal. I press my thighs together beneath the desk as I get wet from the memory. This is wrong. It's twisted and dark.

Despite my best efforts, I can't stop thinking about him. About the way he touched me, with a kind of ruthless control that made me want to surrender everything.

The minutes tick by, each one an eternity. I stare at the blank screen of my computer, at the neat stacks of files, trying to will myself into the focused calm I know I'll need to survive this place.

When my phone tells me that thirteen minutes have passed, I get up and make my way toward orientation. Luckily for me, I don't have any issues getting there.

The conference room is all dark wood and sleek lines, the kind of space that feels designed for power plays and hidden agendas. I take a seat at the long table, the leather cool against my bare legs.

I barely manage to sit down before three people enter; two women and one guy. Two of them sit down next to me. The third, the HR person, stands at the front of the room. Her expression is unreadable. She's the kind of woman who seems to have been born in heels, her every movement precise and purposeful.

"Welcome to Blackwood Strategic Advisory," she begins, her voice cool and clipped. "You are here because you are the best of the best, hand-selected for your intelligence, your drive, and your potential."

Her words wash over me, making me sit straighter.

The woman introduces herself as Gabriella Finch, Director of Human Resources. Her tone is clipped, but practiced, like she's said this same speech a hundred times and no longer needs to think about it.

"Let's begin with introductions," Gabriella says, her eyes sweeping

across us.

The girl beside me straightens in her chair, eagerly getting the ball rolling. Her voice is soft but clear as she introduces herself as Alice Brown. "I study Communication and Public Ethics in Boston." Her hands are folded tightly in her lap.

Even though it's only a two-hour flight, that's still quite a journey. Definitely not one I envy her.

Next's the guy, Ben, he introduces himself as. He's confident, and has an easy charm that's hard to ignore. Even though he's from Georgetown, I don't think I've seen him before. Then again, I don't think I could pick many out from any of my lectures. That's how big the classes are.

"I clearly hate sleep since I'm going for a double major in International Affairs and Behavioral Analysis," he jokes. He hasn't stopped smiling since he walked into the room, and it's so infectious I feel myself beaming back at him.

I go last. "Hi," I chuckle, awkwardly. "I'm also from Georgetown."

After mentioning my majors, I add a few more details. Nothing of substance. I hate these things where you have to make yourself sound interesting in just a few sentences.

Gabriella gives a single nod. "Welcome. The next two weeks will be about observation and precision. You'll rotate through key departments, support select staff on low-risk projects, and be evaluated daily—on both performance and discretion."

She doesn't need to say what happens if we don't measure up. The air already says it for her.

Alice offers me a warm smile as we stand. "That wasn't too terrifying."

"Speak for yourself," I quip, my lips curling into a smile.

Ben chuckles behind us. "It's Blackwood, ladies. Everything's a little terrifying here."

That might be the most honest thing I've heard all day.

The rest of that first day unfolds in a blur of new passwords, rushed instructions, and carefully labeled folders—digital and otherwise. Each of us is handed a rotating schedule of shadowing sessions, prep briefs, and assigned reading that looks more like classified intelligence than intern training.

At first, I feel like I'm drowning in acronyms and silent expectations. But by Wednesday, something clicks.

The rhythm here is fast, but I can keep up. I spot patterns quickly—who to ask, when to speak, how to format things the Blackwood way without needing to be told twice. I don't just complete the work, I start to understand it. And I love how that feels. Rather than just doing the work, I learn to see it.

By Thursday, I've already submitted two memo drafts for a senior associate, flagged inconsistencies in a report no one else noticed, and

reorganized briefing notes in a way that earned me an actual compliment from someone whose name appears in Forbes.

Being here isn't just thrilling, it's addictive. For the first time in forever, I'm not performing for approval. I'm performing for myself. And I'm good at it.

When Friday afternoon finally rolls around, I'm in the middle of gathering my things when Ben saunters over, wearing his signature smile.

"I don't know about you, Piper, but I could do with a drink."

"Or ten," Alice jokes from her desk.

As much as I like Alice and Ben, I would have preferred to celebrate with Lena, but she's going on a date she's been talking about all week. "Let's do it," I agree, slinging my bag over my shoulder.

Together, we leave Blackwood and head to a place Ben knows. It's not too far away, so we walk through the crowded streets. Foggy Bottom is always busy, but it's nothing like Friday afternoon at 4 p.m. when everyone wants to get home.

The bar is all deep shadows and gleaming surfaces, the kind of place where secrets cling to the walls like cigarette smoke.

"If you grab a table, I'll get the drinks," Ben offers.

Alice and I both agree, listing off our drinks of choice before snatching up a table near the windows. When Ben joins us, he's eyeing Alice's Dirty Martini with a scowl like it's offending him.

"God, I hate olives," he says, taking the empty seat next to her.

She grins. "Careful, Ben. Saying things like that makes you sound uncultured," she volleys, removing the olive from the cocktail stick with her teeth.

I reach for my drink, a French 75. "To surviving our first week," I say cheerily.

We clink our glasses before each taking a large swig.

"I can't believe we made it through," Alice says, her cheeks flushed and her eyes sparkling. "I keep feeling like I'm going to wake up and find out it was all a dream."

"Are you staying here in D.C.?" I ask. I can't imagine she's flying back and forth every day.

Nodding, she confirms she's staying at a flat she's rented. "I only have to show up in Boston a few times a month, so it was easier moving here temporarily," she explains.

We talk about the thrill we're all experiencing when we walk into Blackwood each morning, of being taken seriously. While Alice and I continue to talk about the internship, Ben disappears to get more drinks.

"It feels good to do something more real than just reading the words in textbooks," I agree when she's told me about a task she completed just before we left for the weekend.

"And I haven't tripped or spilled coffee on myself a single time

yet." Her words tumble out in a giddy rush, like she's been holding back those fears all week.

I guess that's how we all feel, and there's something nice about being here with people who truly understand the pressure.

We have a few more drinks, but it doesn't take more than a couple of hours before I start feeling like the third wheel. Ben's been flirting with Alice almost since we arrived. It's not that I'm jealous, but there's something over-the-top about his antics.

Finally, I can't take it anymore. I use the app to text my Blackwood-provided driver to let him know I'm ready to leave. Then I drain the last of my wine—I switched to red somewhere around the third drink, hoping for warmth, but all it gave me was a headache—and stand, smoothing my skirt with a quiet breath.

"I should probably head out," I murmur, not loud enough to interrupt, but just enough to be heard.

Alice blinks up at me, slightly dazed, cheeks flushed from the martini and maybe Ben's attention. "Already?"

I nod, giving her a crooked smile as I tug on my coat. "Yeah, I've got to put in a few hours on my school work this weekend or I'll end up finishing everything the night before it's due. And no one wants to read whatever that version would be."

Ben laughs, warm and easy, raising his glass in mock salute. "To deadlines we'll never meet."

"Are you okay?" I ask Alice, not liking how slowly she's talking, or the far-away look in her eyes.

"She's fine," Ben smiles, moving closer to her. "But I'll keep an eye on her."

When Alice nods, confirming she's happy to stay with Ben, I check my phone. There's a notification waiting for me, telling me that my driver's here. I pause, thumb hovering for just a second, before I slide my phone into my bag.

"Hey," I say casually, voice low, "are you guys good? Are your drivers waiting?"

Alice frowns. "A driver?"

"Yeah. I mean, one of the company cars?" I glance between them. "Mine's already outside."

Ben shakes his head, looking genuinely confused. "Nope. Pretty sure interns don't get that level of love."

"I took the Metro," Alice adds in that slow and almost robotic tone she's used since the third drink. "Didn't realize we could expense rides."

My smile flickers. "Huh. Weird. Maybe it was just for onboarding or something."

I offer a soft goodbye and slip outside, the late evening air clinging damp to my skin as I spot the car waiting at the curb, engine idling, lights already on. I climb into the vehicle without a word, and before I

can settle, we're moving.

The city blurs past my window, all lights and shifting color. Meanwhile, I try not to overthink the driver situation. Is this what you get for blowing the owner?

"Hey, can I ask you a question?"

The driver meets my gaze in the rearview mirror. "Go ahead, Miss."

Swallowing thickly, I ask, "Do all interns get a driver?"

His answering laughter is sharp. "Definitely not."

17

Lorenzo

The city still slumbers as I arrive at Blackwood, the towering Gothic spires piercing an inky pre-dawn sky.

An unnatural hush fills the underground garage, the usual click of heels and murmur of political machinations yet to pollute the air. I relish this eerie stillness, knowing I am the man who fills the silence.

Using my private elevator, I bypass the lobby, taking a detour down the darkened hall that leads to her cubicle. The overhead lights flicker on, triggered by my presence, and cast a cold glow across the generic workspace.

Her desk is painfully neat, uncluttered by any hint of personality. How convenient that she makes it so easy for the world to ignore her, to walk by without a second glance. All the easier for me to brand her as mine.

From my jacket pocket, I retrieve a velvet pouch and place it in the center of her desk. The contents are simple; one of my black ties and a single folded card. The note is brief.

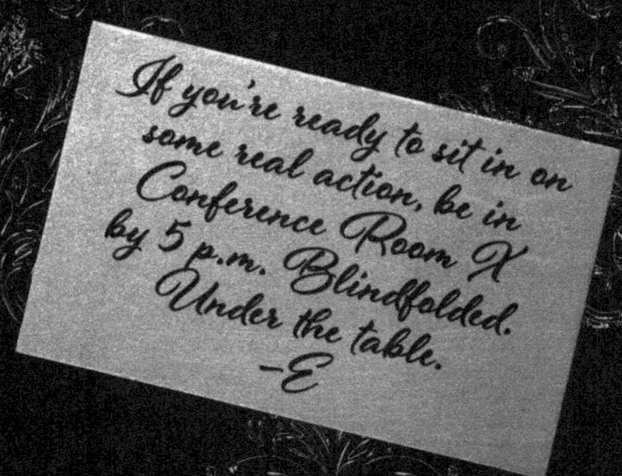

As I walk away, slipping back into the shadows of the hall, I picture her reaction. The way her breath will hitch as she unfolds the card, pupils flaring as she reads the terse instructions. I imagine her mind racing, trying to unravel the mystery in the vague promise of real action.

She hungers so desperately for knowledge, for a taste of the darkness that lives beneath the polished veneer of this city. And oh, how I will feed her until she chokes on it.

I can almost feel the phantom heat of her body cowering beneath my desk. My toy, tucked away until I decide to play with her.

It's a test of obedience as much as it's a temptation. There's no Conference Room X on any official blueprints of Blackwood. The meeting rooms stop at H, a little architectural sleight of hand to disguise the most important room of all—my office.

There are thousands of reasons I shouldn't risk it, pull her into the pitch-black center of my world. But I'm much too selfish not to do it.

As the hours drag by, as I suffer through an endless stream of meetings, I'm too impatient to give my full attention, I keep wondering if she'll rise to the challenge.

Maria knows that if Piper asks her for directions, she's allowed to give them. Only if my toy asks directly, though. Politics might thrive on the unsaid, on reading between the lines—but I don't, not when it comes to her.

Anticipation builds in my blood with each tick of the clock. I know her, perhaps better than she knows herself. She won't be able to resist the forbidden pull of seeing what lies behind the curtain, not even when I'm the one holding it open for her.

At precisely 4:30 p.m., I enter my office, the only sound is the measured click of my steps against polished wood. The air itself seems to part before me, charged with ozone, a storm building in my wake.

The faint scent of cedar and tobacco still lingers from this morning's cigar—my one indulgence before the day began. A ritual. A reminder that power, like smoke, should never be wasted on the undeserving.

Only when I reach the desk do I allow myself to look down, to acknowledge her. Even with my tie over her eyes, she tracks my movements, her head tilting to follow the cadence of my steps.

I let her wait, let the anticipation curdle in her belly as I settle into my chair. I can smell her uncertainty, the acrid tang of nerves mixed with something headier—lust, perhaps, or fear. They are so often the same in the dark.

With deliberate ease, I lean back in the chair. The leather creaks beneath me as I cross one leg over the other. My hands rest on the curved arms of the chair, but my attention is wholly focused on the shape kneeling in the dark.

"You found it," I say, voice low and smooth as silk. "Tell me, did you ask for directions, or did you figure it out yourself?" I ask, curious

to find out.

She doesn't answer right away, but I can see the twitch of her spine, the subtle shift of her weight, as if her body is responding to my words even when her mouth remains sealed.

I let the silence stretch.

Finally, she huffs. "I asked Maria Wilson for help. Her email signature says she's the assistant to the CEO, and since you told me you're the owner…" she trails off as though that's enough of an explanation.

I smirk. "Not every owner is also the CEO," I observe.

"True," she relents. Then she smiles slyly. "But you strike me as too much of a control freak not to be both."

"So you do pay attention," I grin, grazing my knuckles against the crown of her head. The soft waves of her hair warm beneath my touch.

"Of course," she quips as though there should never have been any doubt.

"And now you're on your knees for me again," I say slowly, each word carved in granite. "Blindfolded, again. Not knowing why I invited you. Is that trust, Toy? Or desperation?" Her breath catches, a small, involuntary intake of air that feeds my hunger.

I drag my thumb across the knot of silk at the back of her head, tightening it slightly. Not enough to hurt, just enough to remind her who's in charge. I move my hand to her nape, keeping it there.

She shifts again, just a little, her thighs tightening beneath her. Good girl. She wants to speak, maybe even challenge me—but she doesn't. That's what makes her mine. Not the submission, but the fight she hides behind it.

"Why do I have to be under the table?" she asks, her voice low but steady, threading through the stillness like a dare.

"Because this is where you belong," I drawl. "Toys don't sit at the table. They wait to be used."

She exhales sharply through her nose, and she's shaking slightly, but not from fear. No, this is something hotter. She wants to argue. I can feel the tension coil through her spine like a wire pulled too tight.

"I'm not a toy," she whispers.

"No? Then why are you here? Following my every command like a good little possession?" I slide my hand to her throat, flexing my fingers. I feel the shudder pass through her. I savor it.

"I'm here for the meeting," she says, voice clipped now, defensive. But the edge is dulled by the way she almost pants when I tighten my grip on her delicate throat.

"You're here because I want you here," I growl.

I slide my fingers up and down the slope of her neck, slow and proprietary, watching the way her pulse pounds just beneath her skin.

"Are you sure you're ready for what happens next?" I ask. I let the question hang in the air for several moments before continuing. "Once

the meeting starts, you don't get to leave. You don't get to run. You're mine."

She swallows. "You don't scare me."

I lean in closer until my mouth is just above her crown. "You should be terrified," I rasp.

There's a knock on the door. What perfect timing.

I straighten, adjusting the fall of my suit jacket with slow precision. I pat her head once before removing my hand from her, and she stills completely, like a toy being set down.

Reaching for my cigar case, I pick one up, and light it. I only savor a little before resting it in the crystal ashtray on my desk, exhaling the smoke toward the ceiling. One last breath of indulgence before the real game begins.

I smile, cold and sharp, as I turn toward the door. "Let's begin."

Congressman Malcolm James and Senator Jane Slade enter my office, twin sharks scenting blood in the water. Their faces are tense, postures angled to strike, but I remain at ease, a lion watching two jackals fight for scraps.

Normally, I'd get up, shake their hands, and we'd sit at my glass table. But not today. So I simply nod at them, not bothering to get up. There will be no glad-handing, no pretense of friendship. Only the cold calculation of people who know the value of power, and the cost of losing it.

"We're sitting at your desk?" Slade asks, arching an eyebrow.

"I am," I reply firmly. "However, you're free to sit wherever you like."

James' chuckle as he sits down across from me sounds more like a wheeze. There's a bead of sweat already forming at his temple. He likes to pretend he has a spine, but I see how his fingers twitch.

Slade, on the other hand, is calmer. She's always reminded me of a cold-blooded snake; coiled and ready.

As they settle across from me, James already stammering about optics and blowback, I slide my right hand beneath the desk, fingers combing through her hair until I find the base of her skull. I twist, gently but with purpose—tightening my grip into a leash. Then I tug her forward, until I feel her breath, damp and shallow, against my zipper.

Relighting my cigar, I offer them one as well, but they both decline. "Help yourself to something to drink then." I point at the decanters and glasses Maria's neatly arranged on my desk.

I tap the edge of the ashtray with two fingers as I watch Slade reach for the vodka. James doesn't touch the liquor—smart. He knows not to let his guard down.

While Slade pours herself a hefty amount of vodka, James babbles on, his words a meaningless hum. I catch snippets—crowds at the mall, an outraged social justice contingent. Empty noise, a cough into the

wind.

With my hand still fisted in her hair, I reach down with my right and slowly draw down my zipper. The sound is obscenely loud, a drawn-out hiss that cuts through James' prattling. Slade's eyes flicker to mine, a question, but I meet her gaze without flinching.

Releasing myself from the confines of my suit pants, I stroke the head just once, enough to smear pre-cum across the tip, before guiding my toy's mouth to where it belongs. I feed my cock into Piper's waiting mouth, thrusting past the wet silk of her lips. She takes me beautifully, snaking her tongue around the crown.

Such. A. Good. Fucking. Toy.

The urge to groan rises fast—fierce and raw—but I force it back, biting the inside of my cheek until I taste iron. I don't make sounds. Not in front of them. Not even for her.

Above the table, Slade drones on about containment, about controlling the narrative. I lean back in my chair, a lazy sprawl of dominance, and let Piper work me with her tongue. Each flick and swirl sends sparks of pleasure humming along my nerves. My thigh tenses beneath the desk.

"The story breaks tomorrow night," Slade says, her voice a distant buzz. "Primetime across all networks. We've got our scapegoat lined up, some low-level intern who'll eat the blame."

Piper stills below the table.

I nod, slowly, making sure I'm not giving away that my hand below the table tightens in my toy's hair, reminding her she has a job to do. She obediently hollows her cheeks, sucking harder, and I feel my balls tighten.

James pipes up, a mouse daring to squeak. "But if it gets traced back to us—"

"You better make sure that can't happen," I interrupt. "Otherwise, what's the point?"

He swallows audibly and lowers his eyes.

Slade smiles, a slash of cold amusement. "The press will spin it as youthful hijinks. An overzealous employee acting out of turn. The public has the attention span of a gnat. By next week, it'll be forgotten."

The tip brushes the back of my toy's throat. A shudder rolls through me so fast I have to cough—sharp and low—masking the sound that almost escaped. Almost.

"And for the parts that are beyond any intern, it's awfully convenient that we've just had someone resign. I've already planted the email trail at her feet…"

As Senator Slade continues speaking, I yank my toy closer, burying myself to the hilt in her convulsing throat. She gags around me, and my body riots. Every muscle coils, desperate to thrust, to take, to break through the façade. But I don't move.

I hold my toy in place for two more seconds, then pull her off me with a wet pop only I can hear. She gasps, but I silence her with a vicious tug on her hair.

"We've got everything covered," James finishes.

Slade nods, satisfied, but I'm no longer paying attention. The pressure inside me is building to a fever pitch, a storm surge of black pleasure.

With a calculated tug, I angle Piper's face. A quick glance down—just enough to aim at her face. Two sharp strokes, and I fucking erupt. Cum shoots from my cock, splashing onto her face. I grit my teeth so hard my vision spots, but no sound escapes.

I glance down again. Fuck, my toy has never looked more beautiful than right now when she's drenched in my cum. And, to her credit, she remains quiet. Not a single sound escapes her.

This is how she should always look—filthy, and most of all, mine.

Releasing Piper's hair, I tuck myself away and refasten my pants while she slumps back on her heels, trembling. I glance at my watch, noting the time. The cigar has long gone out beside me, but the scent still lingers.

"If that's all…" Trailing off, I rise smoothly, buttoning my suit jacket.

James scrambles to follow, nearly knocking over his chair in his eagerness to escape. Slade stands as well, her eyes flickering briefly to the desk.

"Always a pleasure," she drawls, emphasizing the last word. "We'll leave you to it. Don't forget to let the girl up for air." She smirks as they leave.

Even now, her head is held high. I watch her chest rise and fall in uneven bursts, my cum trickling down her lips like a promise I have no intention of breaking. When I reach for her, it's slow and deliberate—a brush of two fingers against her jaw. She's so fucking beautiful it makes my heart hurt.

"Are you ready to get up?" I ask.

"Y-yes," she croaks, her voice hoarse from not being used.

My tie stays across her eyes as I help her out from under my desk. One hand at her nape, the other tracing the line of her shoulder, testing the fragility of the fabric beneath my grip. She wobbles a little when she's standing, but I'm there to catch her, pulling her closer, setting the pace.

"Thank you." Her voice cracks at the edges, and I have to bite back the satisfaction that swells inside me. That tremor, like everything else about her, is so fucking addictive.

I settle her into my chair, arranging her limbs like she's breakable, which earns me a huff. Pressing a kiss to the top of her hair, I whisper, "I'll be right back, Toy."

Tilting her head, she wordlessly follows my movements as I walk into my private bathroom. I'm only gone for a couple of minutes, returning with a cloth. I wordlessly begin to clean her, swiping the wet fabric across her face almost reverently.

She shivers when I wipe a dollop of cum from the corner of her mouth with my finger. "Open up," I command. Obeying, she parts her lips, and I don't hesitate to move my finger into her mouth. "You shouldn't waste what I've given you." My tone is low and filled with gravel.

A groan is torn from my throat when my naughty little toy snakes her tongue around my finger, licking my cum away.

Pulling my finger back out of her warm, wet mouth, I trace her bottom lip with my thumb before slipping my hand back to her jaw. "You're perfect like this." My voice is threaded with quiet praise.

She lets out a soft, shaky breath. It ghosts over my wrist, warming the skin. I press the damp cloth to her cheek again, slower this time, watching the way her body responds to every pass—shoulders curving in, her chest heaving.

"Would you like to join me for dinner tonight?" I ask, folding the cloth and throwing it aside. "I've had food prepared, and the wine has probably already been opened."

She tenses, and I run my knuckles down her throat in response, grounding her.

"Tell me, Toy, do you want to go home?"

No matter her answer, I'm not taking her anywhere. I have this entire evening planned, and I wasn't lying when I said the food was already prepared. But I want her to want to stay. Coerced volition always tastes better than being forced.

She hesitates—just long enough for me to taste it. "Can I take the blindfold off?" she asks hesitantly.

"No."

Sighing, she nods. "Fine. I want to stay." There's a hint of a bite in her tone, letting me know she's not too happy about continuing to be robbed of her ability to see.

I text Maria, letting her know we're ready to eat, and it takes less than ten minutes before she knocks on the door. Piper gasps, tensing. I feel her surprise the way I feel everything else—hungrily.

Leaning closer to my toy, I let my breath fill her ear. "It's okay. It's just the food."

I cross the room, calm and unhurried, and let Maria in. Her steely gaze sweeps the office with its usual efficiency, noting every detail. She says nothing, but I see the slight quirk of her brow as her eyes land on my toy.

"On the table," I instruct, gesturing with a slow nod. "Then you're free to go."

I watch as Piper flinches at the sound of another woman in the room, and the thrill it sends through me is exquisite. Maria moves quickly, setting out the food in neat, perfect rows.

Duck breast, Szechuan eggplant, jasmine rice. She finishes with the bottle of Pinot Noir that I know from experience is beyond excellent, and two crystal glasses. When she's done, she slips out as quietly as she came.

Piper's nostrils flare slightly as she audibly sniffs the air. "Something smells delicious," she comments.

Chuckling, I close the distance between us and lift her from the chair and onto the glass table. Her thighs tremble when they hit the cool glass.

I move my chair between her spread legs, pushing her skirt up. Her hand darts out, grasping my shoulder as she steadies herself, obediently widening her legs more, and I can't stop the groan that escapes me when I see the navy colored lace hiding what's mine.

Reaching for the wine, I pour her a glass, bringing it to her lips with one hand wrapped firmly around the base. "Thirsty, Toy?" I coax, lifting the glass to her lips.

Nodding, she opens her mouth, and the flush of wine against her tongue is instant, red like the stain she leaves in my veins. She swallows audibly, eagerly.

"Easy," I say, pulling the glass back, taking a slow sip myself before letting her have more. "I wouldn't want to ruin your appetite."

She scrunches up her nose, all soft edges and irritation. "Is that duck I smell?" she asks, turning her face toward the waiting food.

"It is," I confirm while I grab the chopsticks and expertly pick up a piece of glazed duck, dripping with chili-plum sauce that I bring to her mouth.

"Oh, my God! That's so good," she half-moans while chewing. "This is my—"

"Favorite," I finish for her with a chuckle. "I know."

Tilting her head to the side, I can feel her gaze boring into me from beneath my tie wrapped around her eyes. "I don't think you do," she taunts. "If you knew my favorites, you'd know I never have duck on its own. It's always with a side of Szechuan eggplant, ground pork, and steamed jasmine rice."

I chuckle as she lists off what I know to be her custom order from her local Chinese place. "Is that so?" I inquire while I prepare the next bite for her. This time I feed her rice, eggplant, and a little bit of pork.

While chewing, she holds her hand up, and I wait until she's done. "What the hell?" she mutters, incredulous. "Wait, can I have some more wine?"

I allow her a few more sips.

"Damn," she breathes. "I didn't notice before, but this is… it's Meiomi Pinot Noir, isn't it?"

"It is."

Feeding her is becoming an intimate and decadent ritual—exactly how I want it to be. I know she isn't as relaxed as she pretends to be. I'm sure she's biting her tongue, but I can feel the questions coiling behind her lips like steam beneath glass.

She wants to know how I knew. But instead of asking, she opens her mouth for the next bite. I hold the chopsticks steady, watching the way her lips part. The way her tongue flicks against the rice as if tasting me instead of jasmine.

I feed her another piece of duck, dragging it just slightly against her lower lip before placing it between her teeth. She shivers. I catch a stray drop of glaze from her mouth with my thumb and smear it along

the curve of her cheek before licking it off, loving the way goosebumps erupt across her skin.

"You want answers, Toy?" I tease. When all she does is nod, I click my tongue in disappointment. "Then earn them by asking the questions."

Clearing her throat, she rolls her shoulders back and raises her chin slightly. "How did you know this is my favorite food? And my favorite wine?" she questions.

"You think I haven't watched you long enough to know how you eat? What you crave?" I croon, letting my hand trail down her thigh.

Her breath catches, sharp and unsteady. "Tell me something," she demands, shifting on the table. "Do you like puzzles?"

My lips curl up in a knowing smile she can't see. "Puzzles?" I ask, amused. "Do you mean that symbolic, like making campaign slogans and agendas, fit in politics? Or are you being literal and talking about spending a rainy Sunday afternoon completing jigsaw puzzles?"

"But it can't be," she mutters quietly to herself as she ponders my question. "It doesn't make any sense."

Minutes pass by, but I let her organize her thoughts. Every now and then, she nods to herself, as though she's trying to talk herself into believing whatever answer she reaches in her mind. I stay quiet. I don't want her hiding from the truth. What I want is for her to reach out and grab it, twist it in her palm—owning it instead of hiding from it.

But when my toy's lips split into what I'm sure should be a smile, I know that's not the path she chose. "Oh, well," she says breezily, shrugging one shoulder.

If she's not going to spell out what I'm sure we both know, neither am I. So instead of acknowledging what she just said, I ask, "Are you still hungry?"

"I don't know how to use chopsticks," she blurts out, her voice high pitched. "I probably should since Chinese is basically one of my main food groups. But, well, I always use a fork—"

"You don't need to," I interrupt, brushing her lip with the rim of the glass. "You'll always be fed."

The air thickens, the energy between us no longer humming—it vibrates. She leans into the next bite, and I let it linger at her mouth, just long enough for her to whimper in impatience. I pour another glass, and another, feeding her and feeding myself in turns.

Her voice catches again, breathless, perfect. "You know, I'm not stupid. Just because I refuse to say it out loud doesn't mean I don't know." She sucks her bottom lip between her teeth, biting down.

I tilt her chin, letting my touch linger. "You're many things, Toy. But not stupid."

She shudders, and I take a second to memorize the way she looks right now, the way her thighs are spread wide enough to accommodate me between them. I know she isn't here for me, not indulging my

games for anything but her future—for her career.

But she's still here, and that's all that matters. It's the opening I need to make her fall for me like I have for her. I put the food aside, shifting forward to kiss the soft skin of her thighs.

"Tell me something," I demand, my voice low, consuming.

"What?" she breathes.

"Was it worth it?"

Her eyebrows shoot up her forehead. "Was what worth it?"

Chuckling, I spread her thighs even wider. "Was it worth sitting in on the meeting?"

When she presses her lips together in a firm line, I bite the soft skin on her inner thigh hard enough to make her yelp. "Hey!"

"Answer me, Toy. Was it enough to justify what you endured?" My mouth presses against the crease of her leg, and I feel her shiver.

Her answer is cautious, almost defensive, but I expect nothing less. "Was it a setup?" It sounds more like an accusation than a question. "Am I here to be sacrificed like the intern Senator Jane Slade talked about?"

I get the feeling she's using Slade's full name to let me know she's aware of who the Senator is.

In answer, I bite her harder. Her body jerks, but she doesn't pull away. "Tell me what you learned from the meeting," I rasp before blowing cold air on the skin I just bit.

She exhales shakily, then swallows. "The intern scapegoat—they weren't just hiding a mistake. They were crafting a story. Something palatable. Something marketable."

"And?"

She draws in a breath, gathering courage. "Senator Slade controlled the tone. James played coward. You…" She falters, but recovers. "You barely spoke and still ran the entire meeting. You knew what the outcome would be before they walked through the door."

My hand tightens ever so slightly on her thigh, a wordless reward. "Go on."

"The story was already seeded, so maybe the scapegoat had already been chosen."

My dick hardens against my thigh as I listen to her give word to her thoughts. She's so fucking sexy as she lets her mind work it all out.

"Slade's job was to make it look clean. James' job was to panic loud enough that no one questions what happens when the smoke clears."

I make a sound of disapproval. "If that's right, why would they play those roles in front of me if it's all for the public?"

Her mouth falls open. "Oh!" she gasps. Then she catches her mistake. "You're right, they weren't playing. At least… I don't think Slade was. But… you set James up, didn't you?"

"Did I?" I counter.

"Or maybe Slade did," she allows. "Either way, he sounded

sincere.”

I hum with approval. “If those were their jobs, what was yours, Toy?”

She hesitates, then lifts her chin. “To listen.”

“To obey,” I correct softly, dragging my knuckle across the inside of her knee. “But listening is a good start.”

She licks her lips, emboldened now. “You already knew I’d ask to stay. You let me think I had a choice, but this was always your plan, wasn’t it?”

I lean in and kiss the top of her thigh, right above her panties. “Everything I do is by design.”

“Even this?” she asks, her voice barely a whisper. “The food. The wine. The questions?”

“Especially this,” I say.

Her next breath is jagged, full of weight she doesn’t know how to hold. “You don’t need to sacrifice me to make a point.”

“No,” I state firmly. “I need you to see how power works. So when I hand you yours, you’ll know what to do with it.”

My toy might think she’s the pawn, a future sacrifice. But she couldn’t be more wrong. There’s no version of this life where I let her go.

Eyeing the last dish that we haven’t touched yet, I pull away from her and stand up. “Now,” I drawl, stalking toward the untouched dish. “Let’s see if you have room for dessert.”

19

Piper

Time has gone liquid. Hours stretch and collapse around me, slippery and meaningless. I came here for a meeting—how long ago was that? I have no idea. I don't know how long I've been perched on the cold glass—just that I can feel every trembling echo in it, like I've become part of the table.

My skin prickling with each shallow breath I take. The tie is tight across my eyes, soft but unforgiving in its purpose. The darkness is complete, and I'm finding that I love it. There are no questions in the darkness, only an onslaught of sensations. Sensations I'm growing addicted to.

He hasn't spoken in minutes, but I feel him watching. The weight of his gaze falls heavy on my exposed skin, a tangible pressure that pins me as effectively as hands. I hate that I'm waiting. That I'm not fighting. That some dark, twisted part of me wants whatever comes next.

His footsteps circle the table. Each footfall is muffled but precise, like the slow ticking of a bomb. When he finally stops in front of me, I feel the heat radiating from his body, smell the spice of his cologne mingling with something darker, something male.

I open my mouth, intending to ask what's for dessert. But before I can force the words across my lips, he speaks. "So fucking beautiful," he murmurs, and the words drop into the silence like a stone, creating ripples I feel in my core.

His fingers find the first button of my shirt. The small plastic disc scrapes against the buttonhole with a sound that's loud in the quiet room. One. Two. Three. Each button falls open, exposing more of me to the cold air and, well, to him.

"Keep still," he commands when I shift slightly, and there's no mistaking the command in his voice.

When he reaches the last button, he pushes the fabric from my shoulders. It whispers down my arms, pooling somewhere behind me. His hands find my bra next, fingers tracing the edge of the lace before slipping behind me. One expert twist and it falls loose. My nipples harden instantly.

"Lift," he orders, hands on my hips. I comply, raising just enough for him to drag my skirt and underwear down in one efficient motion. Then I hear them land with a soft flutter somewhere to my left.

Now that I'm completely naked, I almost welcome the cold glass beneath me. It's a delicious contrast against my heated flesh. I'm so wet, and even though I shouldn't want him, I do.

I tilt my head, straining to interpret what I'm hearing. "What are you doing?" I ask, too curious to keep quiet. The question barely leaves my mouth before something cold lands on my shoulder. "Ahh!" I yelp. I jerk reflexively as, whatever the wet and icy substance is, trails down to my breast.

"It's lychee sorbet," he rasps, his voice closer to my ear than I expected. "With chocolate. Sweet and messy. Just like you." The way he says just like you makes my stomach clench.

I barely have time to process his words before something warm replaces the cold. His mouth, I realize with a gasp. His tongue traces the path of the melting sorbet, licking and sucking the sweetness from my skin. The contrast between the freezing dessert and his hot mouth sends electric currents racing through me.

"You know what I taste when I lick your skin, Toy?" His voice is a growl now, vibrating against the top of my breast where his mouth presses.

"N-no," I gasp, barely able to think straight.

"Possession. Ownership. All fucking mine," he growls.

More cold touches, this time circling my breasts. I hiss at the shocking chill, my back arching involuntarily. The sorbet melts instantly against my heated skin, dripping down the curves in cold rivulets. He catches each one with his tongue, tracing lazy patterns that make my breath hitch.

When he finally circles my nipple with his tongue, the jolt of pleasure is so intense I cry out. He answers with a dark chuckle, then bites down—not enough to truly hurt, but enough to send a sharp flash of pain-pleasure straight between my legs.

"Oh, God!" I cry out again.

"Mhmm, you're so sensitive," he notes, soothing the sting with soft, open-mouthed kisses. "I like that."

He lavishes the same attention on my other breast, alternating between gentle licks and sharp nips that have me squirming. The scruff on his face scrapes against my tender skin, a delicious counterpoint to the slick heat of his tongue.

My hands find his hair—thick, silky—and I tangle my fingers in it,

not sure if I'm trying to pull him closer or push him away. Everything is too much, but somehow not enough.

"You moan like you want to be ruined," he says, voice shredded with restraint. I don't answer. I just tilt my head back and let the next moan break free—louder this time. Raw. Needy. Maybe ruined is what I want to be after all.

"Please," I whisper, not even sure what I'm asking for.

Another cold splash hits my skin, this time directly on my nipple. I whimper at the shock, then moan as his mouth closes over it, sucking hard, the heat of his tongue melting the sorbet and sending rivers of sensation coursing through me.

"So responsive," he groans against my breast. "A perfect fucking toy."

He alternates between my nipples, sucking, biting, laving with his tongue until I'm panting harder and attempting to clench my thighs together so I can get some friction where I need it most. But with him standing between them, that's not happening.

Everything in me tightens—a coil winding, threatening to snap. "Oh, God," I moan, surprised by how turned on I am.

He chuckles, the sound seductively dark and knowing. "Are you going to come just from my mouth on your gorgeous tits?"

The question itself is almost enough to push me over. I shake my head in denial, but my body betrays me—hips canting, seeking, my breath coming in short, sharp pants.

"I think you are," he observes, and there's a note of wonder beneath the smugness. "Show me, Toy. Show me how you shatter for the man who owns you."

His mouth closes over my nipple again, teeth grazing the sensitive peak before biting down—harder this time, right on the edge of true pain. The sharp sting connects directly to my clit, and suddenly I'm falling, coming apart with a scream that sounds like it's being torn from somewhere deep inside me.

"I… yes! Just like that. Oh… more!"

He keeps his mouth on me as I shudder through it, waves of pleasure crashing over me, leaving me gasping and disoriented. I've never… not like this, not just from… I can't even finish my thoughts.

While I'm still trembling, still caught in the aftershocks, his hand cups the back of my neck and pulls me forward. His lips find mine in a crushing kiss that steals what little breath I have left.

His tongue slides into my mouth. I taste the sweetness of the sorbet mixed with something darker, richer—chocolate, and beneath that, a flavor that must be my skin.

This is our first kiss. The thought flickers through my mind like lightning, there and gone, replaced by pure sensation.

His mouth moves against mine with bruising intensity, possessing me. My hands find his shoulders, feeling the solid muscle beneath

expensive fabric and I dig my fingers into him while his tongue strokes against mine.

The kiss is commanding rather than coaxing, and I yield to it, letting him take. He groans into my mouth, and I moan in response to the guttural, masculine sound.

When he pulls back, I'm dizzy, lips swollen and tingling. A whimper escapes me—a small, broken sound that would embarrass me if I had any pride left to wound.

His thumb traces my lower lip, pressing slightly where it's tender from his kiss. "We've only just begun," he promises, and the dark anticipation in his voice makes me shiver. "Lie back on the table, Toy. I want to see if your other lips taste just as sweet."

I scramble to do as he says, but without my sight, and with the way I'm sticking to the glass table, I feel more like I'm flopping around rather than moving gracefully.

Mercifully, he grabs my hips and helps me. I feel him bend over me, the warmth of his exhale ghosting over my bare chest before his palm spreads between my breasts, guiding me down.

"Good girl," he praises, voice dark and indulgent.

The table must be big, no inch of me is touching the edges. But I feel around for them, just able to hold on with my fingertips.

My body is still humming with oversensitivity when I hear the clink of glass again. This time, when the jarring chill of sorbet hits my skin, it lands just below my navel, a freezing trail that makes my stomach muscles contract.

"A little warning would be nice," I hiss through clenched teeth.

My hands grip the edge of the table until my knuckles ache. The bite of cold is almost too much—until his mouth follows, hot and demanding, turning discomfort into a pleasure so acute it borders on pain.

His lips trail lower. I feel his teeth scrape against my hip bone, and I suck in a breath—unable to see, but hyper-aware of where he'll strike next. My thighs quiver with anticipation, with the effort of keeping still when every cell in my body wants to arch, to seek, to demand.

More cold—this time on the inside of my thigh, so close to where I'm aching that I cry out. The sorbet drips, followed by his mouth. He sucks hard at the tender skin, the gentle pain blooming into something darker, needier.

"Please," I hear myself whisper, hating the desperation in my voice but unable to contain it.

"Please what?" His breath brushes my slit—close enough to tease, cruel enough not to touch.

I clench my jaw, refusing to beg more explicitly. My stubbornness earns me a sharp bite on my other thigh, the sting making me jerk. "You know what I want," I manage, my voice hoarse.

"I want to hear you say it." His thumbs press into the creases where

thigh meets hip, spreading me wider. "Tell me how badly you want my mouth on your cunt."

The crude word sends a shock through me, a jolt of electricity that makes my already wet sex clench around nothing. I open my mouth, but pride glues my tongue to the roof. I can't—won't—give him the satisfaction.

My silence stretches between us, taut as a wire. I feel him shift, his hands leaving my thighs. For a moment, I think he's giving up, pulling away. The loss of his touch ruins my determination.

"P-please lick my pussy," I beg, blushing.

Then his mouth is between my legs before I can brace for it. No warning, no teasing approach—just the sudden, searing heat of his tongue gliding through slick folds. I cry out, back arching off the glass, hands flying to his hair to anchor myself against the onslaught of sensation.

"Fuck." The word is snarled against my pussy, his mouth sealing over my clit, sucking hard enough to make stars explode behind my eyelids.

My fingers tangle in his hair, yanking, trying to guide him where I want him. He allows it, lets me grind against his face, sets a rhythm that builds the pressure coiling inside me.

The stubble on his jaw scrapes the tender skin of my inner thighs, a delicious counterpoint to the soft heat of his tongue. I'm close—so close—when he suddenly pulls back. I whimper at the loss, hips lifting to chase his mouth.

"Say it," he demands, voice rough with desire.

"Say what?" I ask, confused.

"Say who I am."

The request cuts through my haze of arousal. I shake my head, panting. "No."

His thumb finds my clit, pressing just enough to keep me on edge. "Say it, and I'll take off the blindfold."

The offer is tempting—to finally see his face, to connect the voice and hands and mouth to a real person. But something in me rebels at the idea of giving in so completely.

"I can't," I whisper. Because I know. I know exactly who he is. But if I say it, I can't pretend I don't know he's the one who's been watching me, fucking up my world piece by fucking puzzle piece.

The moment realization dawned on me, I should have fled. I'm still here because I stubbornly refuse to acknowledge it. But if I say it out loud, I can't pretend I don't know.

He exhales sharply, a growl caught in his throat, before sealing his mouth over my clit again—rough and ravenous. The sensation is so intense it borders on painful, exquisite torture that has me arching off the desk. His hand presses down on my lower abdomen, holding me in place while he feasts.

"You're dripping," he groans against my swollen flesh. "So fucking wet for me, Toy."

And then his fingers press into my entrance, two thick digits working in rhythm with his mouth. The stretch burns slightly, a delicious fullness that has me crying out. He curves them upward, finding a spot inside me that makes my vision white out behind the blindfold.

"There," I gasp, grinding down on his hand. "Oh God, right there."

He chuckles, and the sound is all I need to know I won't like what comes next. "Say it," he demands again.

"No," I repeat, shaking my head for emphasis.

"Last chance, Toy," he growls.

"Why?" I demand.

"Because I decide when you get what you want, and right now I want you to earn it." He blows cold air onto my folds.

"I won't do it," I state, my voice firmer now.

His fingers pump faster, harder, curling against that spot with each thrust while his tongue flicks mercilessly over my clit. The pressure builds, a tidal wave gathering height before crashing down.

"That's it," he urges. "Give it to me. Let me feel you come on my tongue, on my fingers. Show me what a good little toy you are."

I shatter on his fingers, a broken cry tearing from my throat as pleasure crashes through me. My inner walls clench around his digits, pulsing with each wave of my orgasm. He doesn't relent. Just keeps driving into me, merciless and precise, toward another peak.

"I could spend hours here," he groans, "mouth full of your cunt, and still never get enough."

His tongue circles my oversensitive clit, gentler now but no less insistent. His fingers continue their relentless assault on that spot inside me, the dual stimulation overwhelming in its intensity.

I'm moaning loudly, calling out for a god I don't believe in because that's the only name I have to cry out.

His fingers curl, press, stroke that perfect spot while his tongue draws tight circles around my clit. I'm babbling now, incoherent pleas falling from my lips. "Please, please, I need… I can't… oh fuck!"

"Tell me what you need," he demands, the words vibrating against my clit.

"Your cock," I gasp, too far gone to feel self-conscious. "I want you inside me."

"Beg for it."

"Please fuck me," I almost scream. "I want to feel you stretching me."

His mouth leaves my core, and I whimper at the loss. Rather than feeling used, feeling shame at how completely I've surrendered to him. I feel only a bone-deep satisfaction mingled with a persistent, gnawing hunger for more.

Well, I didn't completely surrender. I held on to the one thing I'm not ready to deal with.

I feel him move, then his hands are on my ankles, pulling roughly. "Hey!" I yelp, startled.

"Didn't you say you want my cock?" he croons almost mockingly.

"I did… I do," I acquiesce.

"Then let me get you into position." He grunts as he lifts me off the table and sets me on my feet. It's too primal, too raw to be from exertion.

Once my feet touch the floor, he spins me around and quickly bends me over the table, squashing my breasts against the glass.

"Look at you," he moans, voice thick with appreciation. "So eager for me." With each word, he kicks my legs further apart.

"Yes," I agree. When he grabs handfuls of my ass, I arch my back and moan. "Please fuck me."

The sound of his zipper being lowered is like music to my ears. Then I feel him, the blunt head of his dick sliding through my wetness. I cry out, shameless in my need, and push my ass back to try to take him inside. He pulls back just enough to deny me, a punishment for my impatience.

"Last chance," he says, positioning himself at my entrance again. "Say it. Tell me who I am."

I shake my head again, defiant even as my body betrays me—cunt clenching around nothing, desperate to be filled.

"So be it," he rasps, winding my hair around his hand.

Tugging at my hair, he makes me turn my head enough for him to capture my mouth in a kiss that steals what little breath I have left. This kiss is different from the first—messier, filthier. His tongue winds around mine, every stroke making my clit throb.

"You don't deserve to know who I am," he murmurs against my lips, and I feel the head press firmer against my entrance. "But you can call me Enzo."

I have no time to process this revelation before he's pushing inside me, stretching me open around his considerable girth. The intrusion burns slightly—a delicious ache that has me gasping.

"Yes," I hiss, arching my back as much as possible.

He doesn't move once he's fully seated, just stays there, filling me completely, letting me feel every inch of him throbbing inside me. It's exquisite torture, being so full yet denied the friction I crave. I try to move my hips, to create some relief from the overwhelming pressure, but his hands grip my waist, holding me still.

"Enzo," I whisper, testing the name on my tongue. It feels dangerous, forbidden—a spell that might conjure something I can't control.

I feel him shudder at the sound of his name in my mouth, his cock twitching inside me. For a moment, I think I've gained some small

power over him.

Then he pulls out—a slow, deliberate withdrawal that leaves me empty and aching. I make a sound of protest, reaching for him, but he's already moved away. I hear the distinctive sound of a zipper being pulled up, fabric being adjusted.

"Time for all good toys to get some sleep," he says, his tone mocking, as if he hadn't just been buried inside me. As if he hadn't just made me come apart repeatedly under his hands and mouth. "Let's get you home."

The abrupt shift leaves me reeling. One moment I was on the brink of what promised to be an earth-shattering fuck, and the next he's… what? Ending our encounter? Sending me away? Anger flares, hot and bright, cutting through the lingering haze of arousal.

"You can't be serious," I snap, pivoting blindly, almost stumbling. "You're just going to—"

"Yes," he interrupts, and I hear the smile in his voice. "I am."

"Why?" I demand, hating how petulant I sound.

His fingers trace the edge of the blindfold, not removing it but reminding me of its presence. "I don't need an excuse," he scoffs. "If you'd told me what I wanted to hear, I would be fucking your greedy cunt so good."

I press my lips together, desperate to stop myself from begging, from giving him what he wants.

"But you misbehaved." Pausing, he pinches my nipple so hard I cry out. "And I don't reward bad toys, Piper."

20

Piper

Almost an entire week, six days, to be exact, has passed since Enzo made me beg for his cock, only to turn around and deny me. Fucking bastard. At least he dressed me and escorted me outside, so I guess he's not completely heartless. Just eighty percent so.

Shaking my head, I banish those thoughts from my mind and push open the door to Lena's apartment.

"Jesus, woman!" I exclaim as soon as I step through the door, almost dropping the cups I'm carrying.

The place smells like burnt eggs and charred bacon, a culinary crime scene that assaults my senses. The smoke detector hangs disabled from the ceiling—a precaution she's learned from experience. Despite my stomach's protest, I force a smile.

"Sorry about the smoke," she grins, waving a dishtowel frantically at a particularly thick cloud hovering near her kitchen window. "I swear to God I followed the recipe this time."

She's wearing fuzzy slippers, and her hair is piled on top of her head in what could generously be called a bun. A Georgetown sweatshirt hangs off one shoulder, revealing a bra strap the color of traffic cones.

This is Lena in her natural habitat: chaotic, comfortable, completely herself.

"It smells…" I search for a diplomatic lie, "…homemade."

She snorts, pointing her spatula at me. "That's Piper-speak for 'it smells like shit.' Just say it."

Returning her wicked smile, I kick my shoes off and grab the equally fuzzy slippers reserved for me. "Okay, you got me," I shrug. "But if it helps, I promise to take exactly three bites before ordering from somewhere."

"Aww, you really do love me," she sing-songs, waggling her eyebrows while opening the oven, revealing several containers. When she pulls them out, I immediately spot the telltale logo from one of our favorite brunch restaurants.

"Thank God," I laugh.

Cackling, she starts arranging the eggs, bacon, and pancakes from Susie's. I place the cups on the counter and hip-bump her out of the way so I can help. Once we're done, she grabs the Chai tea I brought and after grabbing my vanilla latte, I follow her into the living room.

I lower myself onto her couch, balancing a chipped plate and cutlery in my lap. Without wasting any time, I dive in, moaning around a bite of the best scrambled eggs known to man.

Lena nudges my plate with the edge of her cup, smiling. "So," she starts, cramming bacon into her mouth, "tell me about the internship at Blackwood Strategic Advisory. Are you making coffee for soulless lobbyists?"

I take my time swallowing. "Something like that," I answer.

She swirls her hand in the air, silently telling me to go on, but I can't. My fork pauses mid-air. No matter how much I've tried to prepare myself, I'm not ready for this conversation.

"It's just like any other internship. Lots of copying, filing, taking notes during meetings." I force an expression of boredom. "You know how it is," I say pathetically.

"That's pretty much what it's like at McKinley & Stern, minus the copying. My boss is allergic to paper. Says it's 'archaic technology.'" She rolls her eyes, then leans forward. "But come on, Pipes. Do you really not have any scandalous stories to tell?"

I choke on the sip I just took of my coffee. If only she knew. But no, that's the point. I can't tell her. "Sadly, no." I shake my head for emphasis.

"Well, at least it'll look good on your resume," she says, mercifully changing the subject. "Unlike my internship, where the highlight so far was watching Jim get caught sending dick pics during a staff meeting."

"No way."

"Yes way. Projected his entire phone screen while trying to show a PowerPoint." She waggles her eyebrows, and I laugh despite myself. "The best part was watching him try to explain it away as 'reference materials for a medical consultation.'"

"That's… creative."

"It was pathetic," she corrects. "But not as bad as my date last week. Matched with this guy who works at the State Department, right? Super hot, speaks three languages, and had this whole worldly vibe."

"Let me guess, married?" I ask.

"Worse. Lives with his parents and has a room full of Star Wars figurines he doesn't let anyone touch." She makes her voice deep and serious. "'They would depreciate in value, Lena.'"

I try to listen, I really do. But my thoughts slide sideways—back to Enzo's office. The praise, the way he made me come, the sound of his voice. It shouldn't still live rent free in my head like this.

Lena's fork clinks against her plate, dragging me back. "…and then he tried to explain the entire plot of all nine movies," she continues, oblivious to my mental wandering. "Including his theories about how they connect to current geopolitical tensions in the Baltic states."

I blink, forcing myself back to the present. "Sounds like a keeper."

"Oh, absolutely. I've already picked out your Wookiee bridesmaid dress." She sighs dramatically.

"God, Lee," I laugh. "How do you always find the weird ones?"

"My vagina's cursed," she deadpans.

I shake my head. "Wait, is this the same guy who said his cats were named after CIA operatives?"

"No," she sighs. "That one ghosted me after I asked if they were spayed. Can you believe it?"

The laughter that burst from me is real, and tears gather in my eyes. Because no, I in fact can't fucking believe how my bestie always ends up being the one who gets dumped.

All these years, I've envied her adventures. Not the being dumped, but that she's never scared to put herself out there, to experience life to the fullest. Maybe telling her about Enzo wouldn't be that bad.

Except… if I do, I have to admit I know he's the one that stalked me. Yeah, I'm still not ready to admit that out loud.

Despite knowing that, the need to confess everything sits in my throat like glass. From how I earned my internship with my body, to how Enzo broke into my apartment and fucking spanked me just because he could. And… that's just the tip of the iceberg.

I should hate him, Enzo, my boss' boss' boss. But instead, he occupies ninety percent of my thoughts. And more than half of said thoughts are turning into fantasies about things I want him to do to me.

Shit, I don't know how much longer I can hold all this in. I'm one bad day from blurting everything out in the middle of a lecture hall.

"Lee."

"Hmm?"

"Have you ever…" I trail off, blowing out a frustrated breath when no words come. Clearing my throat, I try again. "Have you ever kept something inside so long it started to feel like part of you? Like a bone that healed wrong?"

Her teasing expression drops away in an instant. "What's this about, Pipes?" she asks, looking at me in that Lena-way that means she sees too much. "Is something off at Blackwood?"

"Kind of," I admit. Knowing that I have to give her something, I decide on a partial truth. "It just seems like there's a lot more going on than I thought. Like maybe they're pulling more strings than I knew even existed."

"Like what?"

"Well, I was sitting in on a meeting, and it almost sounded as though there was more to it than what the public sees." There, that's not a lie. The meeting I listened to from beneath Enzo's desk did sound like that.

Lena gently squeezes my arm. "Pipes," she says warily. "Isn't that exactly what politics is? Shady doings and backroom deals. I mean, this can't be news to you."

My throat tightens again. She's being an amazing friend—the best, really. And all I do is lie. "Yeah, I know," I whisper. "But knowing and then knowing is different. It's messing with my head."

"Don't I get it." Taking it upon herself to lift my mood, she throws herself into more stories, animatedly painting picture after picture about her own internship.

Instead of coming clean, I laugh at her stories and sip my now lukewarm coffee. I let her voice fill the spaces between us, so I don't have to lie out loud. I nod and smile in all the right places, while a voice inside me screams for the relief of confession.

The city filters through her cracked kitchen window—a symphony of sirens, impatient horns, and distant shouts. The breeze shifts, and for a moment, I swear I catch a different scent beneath the rain. Expensive cologne and cigar smoke that doesn't belong. I close my eyes, telling myself I'm imagining things.

"Okay," Lena huffs, standing and stretching. "Enough brooding. Come help me pick slutty work-appropriate Halloween drag for next week."

"You have plans?" I ask, grateful for the redirect.

"Duh. Ross is dragging me to some rooftop party for staffers, which means I need to look hot without making HR twitch."

I trail behind her into her bedroom, where clothes are already scattered like she tried on looks before I even got here.

"Slutty FBI agent, slutty press secretary, or slutty… no, on second thought, the last one will never work."

I raise an eyebrow as she tosses a silk camisole onto the bed. "That's a lot of power for one wardrobe."

We work our way through lace, fishnets, boots, latex, and basically, most items in what she calls her slutty wardrobe. Her Lena-ness is a welcome distraction, one I've missed more than I realized.

Hours later, Lena has finally settled on being an FBI agent with enough cleavage she really should ask for a license to kill.

"Damn," I whistle as she does her fifth twirl in the mirror, striking a pose like she's about to cuff someone for bad taste in shoes.

"Yeah?" When I eagerly nod, she shoots two finger guns into the mirror while pushing her breasts higher up. "No, I don't think I need my special occasion push-up bra," she decides.

Before I can brace myself, she turns back to me.

"What are your Halloween plans? Didn't you say you had something fancy going on too with Blackwood?"

I reach for my phone and start scrolling for the outfit I bought. "Yeah. It's at some private venue they own." I keep my voice breezy, like it doesn't mean anything. Like I'm not hoping Enzo will be there.

"What are you going as?" she asks, coming to sit next to me.

I pause, then swipe to the photo I saved earlier this week. "This. It's kind of inspired by a toy—"

"A toy?" she laughs.

Nodding, I force myself to continue. "A doll, actually. Not a specific one, just dressed to impress."

Lena peers at the image and whistles. "Damn, Pipes. This is—"

"Too much?" I interrupt, already second-guessing it.

"No," she grins. "It's perfect. It's classy, it's sexy, it's… unsettling. But in a hot way." She throws a pillow at me. "You're going to look iconic. I just have one question…"

"What?"

She playfully waggles her eyebrows. "Who's going to pull your string?"

I burst out laughing, shaking my head. Not because she's wrong to ask, but because she nailed it. I am dressing like a doll because I want to play.

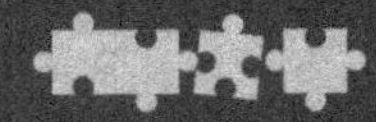

21

Lorenzo

The ballroom of Obsidian Tulip Hall breathes with ambition—suits and gowns circling each other like sharks scenting blood in the water. I watch them from behind my black mask, which isn't dripping with feathers or gilded edges. Simplicity at its finest.

The party is already in full swing, seventy-five bodies packed into the hall. Crystal chandeliers cast fractured light across marble floors. The air tastes of expensive champagne—sharp, saccharine, and laced with ambition.

To them, this is the pinnacle of access—an invitation people would sell their souls to get. And they do. Some through money, others through favors, a select few through secrets. The cost varies, but everyone pays.

I host this event every year for two reasons: irony and indulgence. In my world, masks aren't reserved for costume parties. They're worn by politicians who preach family values while fucking their secretaries, by CEOs who champion sustainability while their factories poison rivers.

Tonight is simply the one day a year everyone openly wears a mask. The honesty in that lie amuses me.

"And what are your thoughts on the latest appropriations bill?"

Senator Kinley has been talking at me for ten minutes, his voice a grating intrusion. His mask—gold filigree with emerald accents—probably cost more than his assistant's monthly salary. I notice how his eyes drift to every young woman who passes, even as he speaks about fiscal responsibility.

"The language regarding foreign aid is problematic," I say, offering just enough to seem engaged. "The restrictions will cripple our allies in Eastern Europe."

Not that I care. Not that I'll back his opposition either. The Russo family has existed longer than this country. We've learned to profit regardless of who holds power.

"Precisely my concern," Kinley nods, mistaking my response for alliance. "I've been trying to tell…"

I don't hear the rest of his sentence. My spine straightens as if pulled by an invisible wire. The hair on the back of my neck rises. The air in the room changes—becomes charged, electric. My body knows before my eyes confirm.

My perfect little toy has arrived.

It's not sight, not sound—it's something deeper, almost primal. Like my heartbeat resetting to match a rhythm only I can hear. My fingers tighten imperceptibly around my whiskey glass as I turn, the movement unhurried despite the sudden rush of blood in my veins.

She stands in the doorway, hesitating for just a moment before Ben Jacks urges her forward with a hand pressed low on her back. Too low. I want to rip them from their sockets. I want to extract each finger, one by one, that dares to touch what's mine.

I keep my face still, my body relaxed, even as I track her movements. Even as I imagine the sound his neck would make if I snapped it right here, in front of D.C.'s elite.

"Excuse me, Senator," I say, cutting him off mid-sentence. "I see some new faces I need to welcome."

I don't wait for his response. He'll interpret it as rudeness born of power, not the warning it actually is. Stay relevant or stay silent. The Russo family has no use for political allies who can't keep up.

I make my way toward the bar, positioning myself strategically so I have a perfectly unobstructed view of my toy as she walks into the room.

Her skin is painted porcelain white, cheeks flushed just right. Her full lips are the color of blood, and I want to feel them part around my dick. Her lashes are thick, impossibly long, and doll-like. Two high pigtails bounce with every movement, each tied with a blood-red bow.

That velvet dress clings to her bodice like fucking sin. The deep crimson fabric is cut like a corset, stitched tight enough that her tits look like they'd spill with the right pressure. She's fucking perfect.

Someone touches my arm and laughs close to my ear. I don't bother looking. I bat their hand away like an insect, eyes never leaving the toy that just wandered into my den.

My gaze drifts down her dress to the skirt. It's long in the back, flaring behind her like she's dragging every man's soul across the floor. In the front, it's short. Only reaching her mid-thigh, revealing garters I want to tear apart with my teeth.

She's wearing long black gloves that cover her to the upper arms—feminine, dramatic. And her shoes… fuck. Five-inch jet black heels with small bows on the toes.

A doll's shoes on a body meant to be used. And around her neck? A black silk ribbon, tied like a choker, its tails brushing the top of her chest. Decorative, sure—but I could pull them tighter. Loop them around my fist. Make her breathe for me.

She came dressed like my fantasy. I lick my bottom lip, slow and unhurried, imagining what her lipstick will taste like. My jaw flexes again. The need to drag her away and fuck her against any surface that'll hold is almost overwhelming.

Signaling the bartender, he rushes to bring me another whiskey without being asked. The ice clinks against the crystal as I take a measured sip, enjoying the burn. Across the room, Piper laughs at something, the sound carrying even over the murmur of conversations.

I watch as she excuses herself from her current conversation. Ben tries to follow, but she shakes her head, gesturing toward the ladies' room.

Cy joins me, ordering a drink before turning to me. "I thought the point was to have the interns mingle. Not just stand by themselves," he observes, giving Alice an appreciative glance.

Chuckling, I slap him on the arm. "Go ahead," I say. "If you can pry her away from Ben." I finish my whiskey and set the glass down on a passing server's tray.

I don't approach my toy right away. Instead, I orbit—positioning myself with the precision of a war strategist. The room becomes my chessboard, the guests my pawns, and Piper, my queen, though she doesn't know she's playing yet.

Every move I make is calculated to draw her attention without seeming to seek it. Every conversation I join has a dual purpose— political utility and optimal sightline.

I insert myself into a circle of federal judges whose careers depend on my family's good graces. They laugh too loudly at my observations, eager to please. I make a mental note of which ones might be useful later. Which ones might be expendable.

Throughout it all, I maintain my awareness of Piper's location. The space between us is electric, charged with possibility. I talk to the right people, shake the right hands, but I always end up in her line of sight, making sure she can hear my voice.

The Chief Justice of the D.C. Circuit Court is mid-sentence when I feel it—the shift in the air that tells me she's looking directly at me now. I turn my head, unhurried, and our eyes lock across the crowded room.

For one perfect, crystallized moment, it's just us—everyone else fades to background noise. Her lips part slightly. The champagne glass in her hand tilts dangerously before she catches herself. Recognition and shock flitters across her face before it's replaced by something else entirely.

I allow myself a small smile, lifting my glass in the slightest acknowledgement before I move through the crowd toward a group that includes the Secretary of State, positioning myself so Piper will have to pass by on her way to the bar. When she does, I reach out, my fingers

barely brushing her bare elbow.

"Miss Harrington," I say, my voice low enough that only she can hear. "Won't you join us? Secretary Whitman was just discussing the diplomatic corps internship program."

Her eyes widen fractionally, surprise flickering across her features before she composes herself. "I wouldn't want to intrude," she says, her voice remarkably steady despite the tension I can feel humming through her.

"Nonsense." I move my hand to the small of her back, guiding her into the circle. The touch is brief but deliberate, my fingers pressing just firmly enough to feel the heat of her skin through the thin fabric of her dress.

It's a test—to see if she'll play along, to see if she understands the opportunity I'm creating for her. She handles herself well, her intelligence evident in how quickly she adapts to conversations. Until Senator Darnell joins us and asks her a pointed question about loyalty.

"Tell me, Miss Harrington, where do your allegiances lie when policy conflicts with the party?" The Senator's eyes are sharp beneath his ornate mask. It's a trap—answer one way, she's principled but difficult; answer another, she's a soulless operator.

I watch her hesitate, caught between her genuine answer and the politically expedient one. She meets Darnell's gaze steadily, a flash of defiance in her eyes. "I'd rather be honest than pretend politics is ever fully separated from self-interest."

The Senator's eyebrows rise as he gives a small respectful nod, and I feel a surge of something dangerous in my chest. Pride, perhaps. Or hunger.

I note how she keeps trying to act unaffected throughout the evening, but every brush of my fingers against her bare arm, every moment I lean too close to whisper some observation about the person we're speaking with, breaks something small in her façade.

A quick intake of breath. A momentary loss of her train of thought. The way she shifts her weight when I stand too near, as if her body can't decide whether to move closer or pull away.

By the time midnight approaches, the party has reached that comfortable level of inebriation where secrets start to spill. A supreme court justice is laughing too loudly at a senator's joke. Two congressional aides are exchanging meaningful glances by the terrace doors.

Excusing myself, I go to the bathroom, and when I return, Piper's nowhere to be seen. I frown, immediately searching for Ben. I can't put my finger on it, but there's something about him I don't trust.

But he's lip locked with… well, isn't that interesting. He's not-too-discreetly kissing someone he definitely shouldn't be. I scoff at the predictability, and go looking for my toy.

I find her hiding out in a quiet, dark alcove. It's far enough away to

offer some privacy, yet close enough it can still be considered part of the party.

"You've made quite an impression tonight," I say, close enough that my breath stirs the wisps of hair by her ear. "Secretary Whitman asked for your contact information."

"Thank you for the introductions," she replies, her voice carefully neutral despite the slight tremble I can see in her fingers. "Though I'm curious why you're taking such an interest in my career."

I allow myself a small smile. "Who says it's your career I'm interested in?"

She doesn't move when I step behind her. Not right away. Just keeps her back straight, her breath steady. But her hands twitch at her sides, like she doesn't trust them not to reach for me.

I lean in slowly, letting my presence fold around her like a shadow. The silk bow tied around her neck brushes my chest. I lower my head until my lips nearly touch her skin.

"This alcove is supposed to be off-limits," I murmur. "You seem to be good at worming your way into places you shouldn't be."

"So are you," she retorts.

With a chuckle, I kiss the curve where her neck meets her collarbone. Her skin is still cool from the air but warms beneath my lips in seconds. She draws in a sharp breath when I trail upward, teeth grazing the edge of her jaw.

One of my hands slides over her hip, while the other finds her waist and tightens. Just enough to tell her she's not going anywhere.

"You shouldn't be doing this," she whispers, but her voice falters when I nuzzle behind her ear, biting the shell. Her head tips to the side almost instinctively, exposing her throat.

"There's a lot of things I shouldn't be doing," I rasp, and kiss the side of her neck again—harder this time, open-mouthed.

She makes a sound that's not quite a moan, not quite a gasp, and her ass presses back into me before she realizes what she's doing. I growl low in my throat; the sound meant only for her. She can feel exactly how hard I am.

When she finally turns her head, just enough to catch my eyes over her shoulder, she breathes, "So this is what you look like."

I chuckle darkly, my lips still against her skin. "Do you miss the blindfold?"

She huffs out a breath that might be a laugh—might—but it turns into a gasp when my hands roam higher. One curls around her ribs, my thumb brushing the underside of her breast. The other dips beneath the drape of her skirt again, this time with more purpose.

Her back arches again—natural, reactive. Not a performance. Her ass grinds against me in slow motion, and I hiss between my teeth.

Our lips collide in a flurry of inevitability, punishment, and want. She opens to me, but before I can react, my toy slides her tongue into

my mouth, her teeth grazing my bottom lip.

The kiss is hard, but so fucking perfect. She's not some meek little toy tonight, she's a woman on a mission. One I'm all too happy to help her with. When I finally pull back, her eyes are heavy-lidded, her lips swollen, her breath uneven.

"Do you like watching from the shadows?" I ask, grinding my dick against her ass again. "Watching people who have no idea you're observing them?" My hand slides up her thigh, dipping under her skirt and continuing upward until I cup her cunt.

"Yes," she moans.

"Why?" I ask, pushing her underwear to the side.

"Because…" She falters.

"Because what?" I prompt as I circle her clit. "Use your words, Miss Harrington."

She laughs softly. "Why so formal when you're playing with my pussy?"

Her hips stutter against my hand, breath catching as I circle her clit. "Because what?" I whisper again, right against her ear. "Tell me."

Her head drops back onto my shoulder. Her mouth opens, but all that escapes is a whimper. I drag my hand lower, just barely teasing her entrance, not enough to satisfy, just enough to ruin.

"Because it's power," she finally says, voice cracked open. "Watching people pretend to be something they're not."

I smile against her skin, slow and dark. "And who are you pretending to be tonight, little doll?"

She doesn't answer. She doesn't need to. Her silence is the truth I've been waiting for.

My hand abandons her cunt, leaving her panting and half-wrecked already. I slide it around her waist instead, pressing her tighter to me. Her ass molds to the hardness of my dick, and I feel her shiver at the pressure.

Then, with my other hand, I reach into my jacket and pull out the cigar. Still wrapped. Still waiting. Just like her.

22

Lorenzo

The weight of the cigar feels significant between my fingers. The dim light of the alcove catches on the cellophane wrapper, making it gleam like something precious, something forbidden.

We're ten feet from Washington's elite. The champagne flows freely out there, but here, tucked away in this darkened alcove, Piper and I have our own intoxication brewing. The distant murmur of political small talk forms a perfect soundtrack for what I'm about to do to her.

Piper's breath hitches in her throat as I hold the cigar in front of her, showing it off. "What are you going to do with that?" she asks, her tone filled with wonder.

"Do you really have to ask?" I smirk, pressing a kiss to her throat.

"You're not serious," she whisper-hisses, but there's no real protest in her voice, just the thrill of discovery hovering at its edges.

"Oh, but I am," I rasp.

I run the Cohiba Behike down her chest, between the valley of her tits. Lowering her dress, I tease her beaded nipple with the end of it.

"You want it?" I ask, letting the question hang between us, heavy with implication.

She looks at me over her shoulder, and I watch the war play out on her face—defiance versus desire, restraint versus desire. She nods once, then finds her voice. "Yes."

With a low growl, I place the cigar between my teeth. Then I gather the hem of her dress, inch by inch. It slides through my fingers until I've exposed just enough; the creamy expanse of her thighs, and the lace of her panties.

"Someone could walk by…," she breathes, but doesn't finish the thought.

"Then they'll see exactly who you belong to," I finish for her, voice low and certain. "They'll see that this cunt," I press my palm against her, feeling the heat radiating through the thin barrier, "answers to me."

She shivers with anticipation as I hook one finger under the edge of her panties, sliding them to the side rather than removing them completely. I take the cigar from my mouth, examining it. Then I press it against her soaked entrance.

Her lips part in a silent gasp, and I cover her mouth with my free hand before the sound can escape. Her breath scorches my palm in quick, shallow bursts.

"You're going to take this inside you," I tell her, my voice unnervingly calm even as desire rages through me. "And you're going to stay perfectly quiet while I fuck you with it. Do you understand?"

She nods against my hand and lets her head fall back against me. I can feel her trying to control her breathing, trying to maintain composure even as her body betrays her with slick desire.

The cigar slides in easier than I expected, her cunt already soaked and yielding. I watch her face contort with the strange new sensation—the firmness, the slight resistance as her body accommodates the foreign object. She's tight around it, fighting the intrusion at first, then gradually accepting each inch as I work it deeper.

"That's it," I murmur against her ear, close enough that my lips brush the delicate shell. "Taking it so well for me. Such a perfect little toy."

Her eyelids flutter at the praise, and I feel a tremor run through her body. I push the cigar in to the halfway point, then pull it back slowly, watching her face for every micro expression of pleasure. When I push it back in, I twist it slightly, and her knees nearly buckle.

"You like that? Being filled like this where anyone could see?" I release her mouth briefly to let her answer, my thumb tracing over her lower lip.

"Yes," she whispers, the word barely audible. "P-please, don't stop."

Moving my hand to cover her mouth again, I press harder this time. "I won't stop until you come all over this cigar," I rasp, fucking her slowly with the rolled tobacco, watching as her juices make it glisten in the dim light.

"Yes," she moans from behind my hand.

"I want you to remember this every time you see a fucking ashtray. Every time you smell smoke."

Her eyes roll back slightly, and I can feel her rolling her hips, trying to press against my hand, seeking more friction, more pressure. I give her neither, maintaining the torturously slow pace. She pants against my hand now, the rhythm frayed and erratic. There's the vibration of a moan my toy's desperately trying to suppress.

"Please... Enzo," she begs.

The sound of my name on her lips makes a growl build in my throat. "Say it again," I demand.

"Enzo," she gasps. "Please fuck me harder. Deeper."

The sounds of the party grow louder—someone's giving a toast, glasses clinking in celebration. The contrast between the civility just beyond the corridor and the depravity in our shadowed corner makes my cock throb painfully against my tailored pants.

I press myself against her thigh, letting her feel what she does to me, but never losing my focus on the cigar sliding in and out of her cunt.

"Look at you," I whisper, letting my voice drop an octave. "Taking it so deep. Are you pretending it's my dick, Toy?"

Her muscles tense, and I feel her clench around the cigar. The fear of discovery, the risk of being seen—it's all part of what's driving her to the edge. I exploit it mercilessly.

"Maybe I should let them see," I continue, picking up the pace slightly. "Bend you over that bar out there and let them all watch while I fuck you."

Her eyes widen, pupils blown with lust. She's close—I can feel it in the way her body tenses, in the wetness coating my fingers as I work the cigar in and out of her. I press it deeper, angling it to hit that spot inside her that makes her see stars.

"Enzo!"

"Come for me," I command. "Come right now, with all of them just steps away. Let me feel you fall apart."

As if her body is bound to my words, she shatters. Her entire body trembles against mine, and I hold her firmly against my chest, supporting her weight as the orgasm tears through her. It's a violent, beautiful thing—watching her come undone by my hand, by my command, by my fucking cigar.

She collapses against me, chest heaving, eyes unfocused. I just hold her there, letting her float in the aftermath while I memorize the way she feels.

This wasn't just about getting her off. It was about claiming space inside her memory—staking something permanent. She'll think of this every time she's in any building I own, when someone lights a cigar. And when she hears my name.

When the tremors subside, I slowly withdraw the cigar, now slick and glistening with her juices. I don't take my eyes off hers as I bring it to my lips, inhaling deeply. Her eyes widen at the gesture, a flush spreading across her cheeks.

"Beautiful," I murmur, tucking the cigar into my inner jacket pocket. I keep it uncovered—I want to feel her wetness seeping through the expensive lining, a delicious reminder of just how pliable and perfect my toy is.

I turn her to face me, cupping her face with one hand. She's still catching her breath, lips parted and chest rising with each shallow inhale. I reach for the long black ribbons trailing from her choker, wrapping them once, twice around my fist until the slack disappears.

The fabric is warm from her skin, and when I give a gentle tug, her

chin lifts automatically, exposing the elegant line of her throat.

"Get on your knees."

Her eyes hold mine for one second—the defiant fire in her burning bright. Then she smiles while gracefully sinking down, her dress pools around her like spilled blood. What a fucking sight.

From this angle, she seems both vulnerable and powerful. The choker sits like a collar around her neck, the ribbons still wrapped around my hand connecting us physically, a manifestation of the invisible chains I've been forging since the first day I saw her.

Her lipstick is smeared slightly—evidence of her pleasure, of my palm pressed against her mouth as she came undone minutes ago. A smile tugs at the corner of my lips when I notice her gaze traveling up my body, taking her time, savoring the sight she's been denied until now.

She's felt me, tasted me, had my fingers and tongue in her wet cunt—all without seeing. The blindfold has been my tool, my way of controlling what she knows, what she experiences. Removing that barrier is significant, a privilege I'm granting her.

"See something you like?" I smirk.

Blinking, she catches herself, baring her teeth. "How would I know? You're the one hiding behind a mask," she sasses.

"Undo my pants," I instruct, watching her hands move to comply.

Her fingers tremble slightly as they find my belt buckle. Is it nervousness? Anticipation? I study the slight furrow between her brows, the way she bites her lower lip in concentration. No—it's not fear. It's hunger.

She works the leather through the buckle methodically, then moves to the button and zipper of my tailored pants. Each movement is deliberate, almost reverential. When she finally frees my cock from its confines, I'm already hard, straining toward her warmth.

I allow her a moment to look, to process. Her eyes widen slightly, her tongue darting out to wet her lips unconsciously. My length twitches under her scrutiny, and I see a small smile tug at the corner of her mouth—pleased at the reaction she elicits, at the power she wields even on her knees.

She wraps one hand around the base. Her stroke is slow, measured, and her eyes fixed on the movement as if memorizing every vein, every ridge.

The other hand cups my balls gently. "Mhmm," I groan, tightening my grip on the ribbons. "Open your mouth."

She complies without hesitation, her lips parting. The sight of her like this—willing, waiting, wanting—sends a surge of possessiveness through me so intense it's almost painful.

Piper's lips seal around the head. Warm. Wet. Fucking perfect. She starts slowly, testing depth, tongue flicking just beneath the ridge. Her eyes fluttering closed as she concentrates on the sensation, on pleasing

me.

I give her a moment to adjust, to set her own pace. Then I tighten the choker just enough to make her gasp, the silk ribbons constricting slightly around her throat. Her eyes fly open, meeting mine with surprise and unmistakable arousal.

"Does it hurt?" I ask.

She pulls back just enough to speak, her lips still brushing against the head of my dick as she forms the words. "Yes," she breathes, her voice rough with desire. "But it feels so fucking good." I loosen the pressure slightly, allowing her to take me deeper into her mouth.

With each forward motion, I tighten the ribbons, restricting her breathing just enough to intensify the sensation. When she pulls back, I loosen my hold, allowing her a full breath before the next thrust. It sharpens every sensation—every drag, every stretch, every vibration of her throat.

"Perfect," I groan, watching her cheeks hollow as she sucks. "You were made for this. Made to serve me."

Her eyes open at my words, heavy-lidded with lust but lucid, present. She hums around me; the vibration sends a jolt of pleasure up my spine. My free hand moves to her hair, not pulling, just resting there to feel the movement of her head as she works me deeper.

"That's it," I encourage, as the head hits the back of her throat. "Take all of me like a good toy."

She gags once, unprepared for the depth, but doesn't pull away. Instead, she adjusts, relaxing her throat, determined to please me. I feel a swell of pride—she's learning, adapting to what I need. I ease back slightly, giving her a moment before pushing deeper again.

The ribbon control becomes more instinctive as we find our rhythm. Tighten as she takes me in, loosen as she pulls back. Her breathing syncs with the pattern. Each inhale when the pressure releases more desperate, more aroused.

The controlled oxygen—the dance between restriction and release— has her moaning, her own arousal building without a single touch.

"Look at me," I command.

Her eyes meet mine immediately, watery from the effort but blazing with desire. The connection is electric, intimate in a way that transcends the physical act. I can see everything in her gaze—a challenge, pleasure, and a raw hunger that matches my own.

"Good girl," I praise, the words falling from my lips like benediction. "Such a good fucking toy for me."

She whimpers at the praise while her hand works what her mouth can't take, twisting slightly on the upstroke in a way that makes my thighs tense with pleasure. She's pulling responses from me that no one else ever has.

I tighten the ribbons again, holding the pressure a beat longer this time. Her eyes widen, pupils dilating as the oxygen deprivation

heightens her sensitivity. When I release, she gasps around me, drool beginning to leak from the corner of her mouth.

It should be messy, undignified, but on her it looks like art—evidence of her surrender, her commitment to my pleasure.

"You love this, don't you?" I growl, knowing the answer but wanting to hear it. "Being used like this. Being mine."

She pulls back just enough to speak, her voice raspy from exertion. "Yes," she manages, lips swollen and slick with saliva. "Please, don't stop."

"I won't," I assure her, guiding her mouth back to my cock. "Not until I've filled that pretty throat with my cum."

Her moan at my words is desperate, needy. She doubles her efforts, taking me deeper, working faster. I feel her other hand slide between her own legs, seeking relief for the ache building there.

"No," I snap, tightening the ribbon in warning. "You don't touch yourself unless I say so. That pussy's not yours to please. It's mine."

I thought I'd already taught her that lesson, but evidently, my toy likes to play with fire.

She whimpers but removes her hand immediately, placing it on my thigh instead, nails digging in slightly as if to anchor herself.

Even when she yields, she pushes. That resistance is what makes her perfect—my favorite fucking contradiction. It's part of why I'm so obsessed, so addicted to her.

I begin to move my hips more deliberately now, fucking her mouth with measured thrusts. Loving the wet sounds of her struggle to accommodate me. And the sight of her lips stretched around my girth, the feel of her tongue working the underside of my shaft, is fucking beautiful.

"That's it," I grunt as her technique becomes more desperate, less controlled. "Show me how much you want it."

Her eyes never leave mine as she hollows her cheeks, creating a suction that draws a guttural groan from deep in my chest. The sound seems to spur her on, and she moves one hand to my balls again, cupping, squeezing gently, then more firmly as she gauges my reaction.

I feel the pressure building, that familiar tightening at the base of my spine. The ribbon draws tighter between my fingers, my thrusts more insistent. She takes it all, adjusting to my increasing pace without complaint, eyes watering but still locked on mine with fierce determination.

"I'm going to come," I warn her, my voice rougher than usual, control fraying at the edges. "And you're going to swallow every fucking drop."

She moans her acquiescence; the vibration pushing me closer to the edge. My hand tightens in her hair now, holding her steady as my rhythm falters. The sight of her—on her knees, taking me so deep, so willing—combined with the physical sensation of her mouth and hands

pushes me over.

I come with a growl. "Fuck! Piper!"

I'm still holding her in place as the first rope hits the back of her throat. She swallows reflexively, eyes widening slightly at the force, but doesn't pull away. I keep her there, watching her throat work as she takes everything I give her.

When I finally release my grip on both the ribbons and her hair, she sits back on her heels, breathing hard. Mascara tracks stain her cheeks, her lipstick is completely ruined, and my cock gleams with the evidence of her efforts.

The sight of her like this—wrecked and beautiful because of me—sends a possessive thrill through my veins.

She wipes her mouth with the back of her hand, a gesture that should be crude but somehow retains its elegance when she does it. A soft laugh escapes her, slightly hoarse from the treatment her throat has just endured.

"I need to find a bathroom." Her voice is raw in a way that will remind her of this moment every time she speaks for the next day.

Tucking myself away, I redo my pants while she rises to her feet. Her dress falls back into place, but nothing can hide what we've just done—it's written in her flushed skin, her swollen lips, the slight disarray of her hair that even her careful fingers can't fully fix.

I watch her collect herself, straightening her spine, adjusting her choker so the ribbons hang properly once more. The transformation is fascinating—from wanton on her knees to composed in the span of moments.

She may look presentable again. But I know better. Her throat's raw, her cunt's dripping, and her lipstick's still stamped on my shaft.

Thanksgiving break looms like a finish line, and those of us still here are the stragglers, the ones with one more paper to submit, one more deadline to meet. Mine is part of my thesis, and I'll have to defend it in front of my class before Christmas.

Lena walks beside me, her backpack slung over one shoulder. Two orange streaks frame her face—her personal celebration of Thanksgiving—and they catch the weak November sunlight like warning flares.

"Professor Donovan actually asked for a printed copy. With a staple," I say, shaking my head as we cross Red Square, dodging the few remaining students hurrying toward freedom.

"Mine wanted three copies. Three." Lena raises her fingers for emphasis. "Said his dog ate one last semester, so now he needs backups."

"That's not even a good lie."

Relief blooms in my chest, loosening something that's been tight for weeks. With the paper submitted, the pressure valve is released. There's something about finishing a project that feels like taking off shoes that have been too tight all day.

Lena nudges my shoulder with hers. "Let's go off campus for coffee. I need to be around people who aren't obsessing over exams, papers, and anything else remotely intellectual."

The café she chooses is three blocks away, a little place wedged between a bookstore and a vintage clothing shop. Inside, it's warm and fragrant with spices: cinnamon, nutmeg, and clove. The holy trinity of fall. Most of the tables are empty; the rest of Georgetown seems to have already fled for break.

While I secure us a place to sit, Lena orders for both of us. She returns to our table with two oversized mugs of pumpkin spice lattes and a single slice of pumpkin pie with two forks.

"I got whipped cream on yours," she says, sliding my mug toward me.

"Thank you." I wrap my hands around the mug, letting the warmth seep into my fingers.

Lena tilts her head, those orange streaks falling across her face. She wears gold hoop earrings that catch the light when she moves, and a loose-knit sweater dress in burnt orange that somehow makes her look both disheveled and perfectly put together.

"So." She leans forward, elbows on the table. "We haven't really talked in, what, two weeks? Three? I know I've been MIA, but so have you." She stabs her fork in my direction in an accusatory motion.

"I've been busy." It's not a lie, but it's not the whole truth either.

But I have been busy with papers, classes, and my internship. I've also been pretty preoccupied on my knees for hours at a time, getting intimately acquainted with the carpet in Enzo's office, and the marks it leaves on my skin.

"Mhmm." Lena takes a sip of her latte, leaving a crescent of foam on her upper lip. "Busy with school, or busy with something else? Maybe someone else?"

Heat creeps up my neck. I reach for the pie, then the coffee, doing anything but looking at her, using the mug to hide my smile. "It's nothing like that."

"You're lying," she states. "Your left eyebrow does this little twitch when you lie. And right now, it's dancing the Fandango."

I touch my eyebrow automatically. "It does not."

"Does too. You're also avoiding eye contact." She pauses, then grins as she leans even closer, her voice dropping to a stage whisper. "And you've been walking like your soul's been rearranged."

The coffee stops halfway to my mouth. "Shut up."

"Oh, my God, Pipes." Her eyes widen, fork clattering against the plate. "I was just teasing. But… there totally is someone. Spill it!"

"Lee!" I glance around, but no one's paying attention to us. The barista is scrolling on her phone, and the only other customers are an elderly couple by the window.

I take a long sip of coffee, using the mug to hide my smile.

"Are you seeing someone or not?" Lena asks directly, her playfulness giving way to genuine curiosity.

"Yes," I say before I can think better of it. The word hangs between us like a confession.

Lena's eyes go wide, then narrow with suspicion. "And you weren't going to tell me? Your best friend? The keeper of all your secrets? The woman who held your hair back when you puked after drinking too much tequila, and—"

Laughter bubbles up my throat and out of my mouth. "Okay, okay, drama queen." Taking a deep breath, I prepare myself. "It's new, and

complicated." An understatement so severe it might qualify as perjury.

"New and complicated." She nods sagely. "So like, what? Married? Your professor? Ooh, is it that TA from your Political Theory class? The one with the forearms?"

I snort at the way she describes my TA. I mean, everyone has forearms, so it's a ridiculous description. "No, none of those. Just... someone I wasn't expecting."

"Piper Harrington!" Lena almost shouts. "Do not play coy with me here. I want the deets, and I want them now."

Smirking, I lean back in the chair and slowly cross one leg over the other. "Okay," I relent. "His name is Enzo, and he's... I don't even know how to describe him."

"Do I know him? Where did you meet? How did you meet? When do I get to meet him?" The questions come in rapid-fire.

"Calm down," I laugh. "No, you don't know him. I met him when I interviewed at Blackwood for my internship, and... umm... he was one of the men interviewing me."

Hurt flickers across Lena's features. "You've known him that long and I'm only just finding out..." Trailing off, she frowns. "Wait a damn second. Is he the secret you mentioned just before Halloween?"

My breath saws out of me, and I reach for her hand, holding it between both of mine. "Hey, I wanted to tell you. I just didn't know how." Biting my bottom lip, I deliberate how to best explain it. "I... well, the fact we met during the interview made me feel like I earned my internship the wrong way. That's why I didn't say anything at first."

It's not the complete truth, but it's close enough that I don't feel like I'm lying.

"Ohh!" Lena squeals. "That totally makes sense. Okay, I forgive you. But only if you tell me everything right now."

"What do you want to know?"

"How's the sex?" she asks, unashamedly waggling her eyebrows suggestively.

The urge to deny having sex is on the tip of my tongue. But the memory of Enzo spanking me for saying I wasn't sexually active comes to mind. God, wrong as it was, I fucking loved it. My thighs press together under the table.

"It's..." I search for a word that won't give too much away. "Intense."

"Intense." Lena repeats the word like she's tasting it. "Intense like romantic candles and deep conversations? Or intense like he's rearranging your organs?"

I almost choke on my coffee. "The second one."

She squeals again, this time it's loud enough that the elderly couple glance our way. "I knew it. I fucking knew it. You have that glow. That 'I've been thoroughly fucked' glow."

"Can you lower your voice?" But I'm laughing too, the relief of

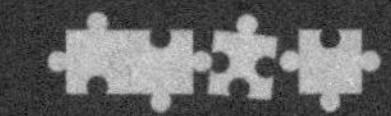

sharing even this small part of my secret lightening something in my chest. "And if you must know, we haven't actually fucked."

This makes her pause, and I can practically hear the gears turning in her brain as she just stares at me, uncomprehending. "You haven't? But why not?"

Images flash through my mind; his cigar between my legs, tie around my eyes, his palm striking my ass. I feel my cheeks flush.

"We're exploring," I admit. "He's showing me things I didn't even know I wanted."

Lena's eyes light up. "Oh my God, he's kinky. All the best ones are." She leans forward, lowering her voice conspiratorially. "You should make a list."

"A list?"

"A kink list. Things you want to try, things you're curious about, things that are absolute no-gos." She shrugs. "I did it with Derek last year. It was actually super helpful. Got us talking about stuff we'd never have brought up otherwise."

"I don't think we need a list." I think of the way Enzo seems to read my mind, how he knows what I want before I do. How he pushes me past what I think I can handle, into territory I never knew existed.

"Everyone needs a list," Lena insists. "It's like sexual homework. But the fun kind."

I laugh, imagining Enzo's face if I presented him with a list. Would he be amused? Intrigued? Would he punish me for being so presumptuous? He'd probably read every line without blinking—and then make me prove it. The thought sends a shiver down my spine.

"Fine, maybe I'll think about it." I take another bite of pie. "But I'm not showing you what's on it."

"Spoilsport." Lena pouts. "I bet it would be educational."

"For whom?"

"For me, bitch. I could use some inspiration. My sex life's been drier than the Sahara lately." She sighs dramatically. "The last guy I slept with asked if I came when he clearly hadn't touched anything remotely orgasm-adjacent."

I burst out laughing, nearly snorting coffee through my nose. Lena joins in, and for a moment, we're just two friends in a café, laughing about bad sex and the absurdity of dating in our twenties. For a moment, there's no Enzo, no secrets—just us.

But even as we move on to other topics—her disastrous PR project, my thoughts on graduation next spring, the latest campus gossip—I can feel him there, a shadow at the edges of my consciousness.

His absence is a presence all on its own. A hunger shaped like him that shadows everything else. Like a negative space carved into my day.

I catch myself touching my throat where his fingers have been, running my tongue over my bottom lip where he bites me. There's a

kind of hunger that lingers even after you've been fed. He leaves me wrecked and still wanting more.

"Well," Lena says when she returns from the bathroom. "I really need to go if I want to catch my train."

We hug goodbye, and she promises to text me tomorrow when she's knee-deep in Thanksgiving with her family. "And I'll be back the day after tomorrow," she reminds me. "This year, I don't have time to stay as long as I usually do."

"Let's go out when you come back," I suggest.

24

Piper

Tilden's glows with amber light and quiet conversation, a sanctuary of polished wood and white tablecloths. The hostess greets me by name—a perk of coming here every Thanksgiving for the past three years.

Uncle Teddy is already at our usual table, rising when he sees me, his smile lines deepening. "There she is," he says, opening his arms. "The future senator who'll make sure I never have to pay taxes again." The last part is added with a deep chuckle.

I step into his embrace, breathing in his familiar scent. "You know that will never happen," I laugh.

"Semantics." He holds me at arm's length, studying my face. "You look good, Piper. Are you doing alright?"

We sit across from each other, the familiar setting wrapping around me like a memory while I explain I've had two exams, and just handed in a paper yesterday.

"Well, food fixes everything. Or so my mother always said."

Our table is near the back, tucked against the wall where we can see the entire restaurant but aren't immediately visible to those entering. Teddy always requests this particular table while joking that he wants to know who's coming for him.

"Wine?" he asks, already reaching for the bottle the server has left. A rich cabernet, I'm guessing, something bold that will pair with the turkey and leave my lips stained darker than they should be.

"Please." I slide my glass toward him.

He pours generously—too generously, as always—and raises his own glass. "To another year of outrunning our demons."

I clink my glass against his. "Some demons run faster than others."

"Don't I know it." He takes a long sip, then sets his glass down with deliberate care. "Speaking of demons, have you heard from your parents?”

The question doesn’t sting as much as it once did. Time has a way of cauterizing even the deepest wounds. “Yes, Mom called yesterday to tell me I’m the best daughter in the world,” I joke.

He snorts. “Now that would be something.” After taking a large sip of his wine, he continues. “I believe they’re in Aspen this year.” Uncle Teddy doesn’t bother hiding his disdain.

“God forbid they’d spend a holiday somewhere without a social ladder to climb,” I quip. Then I exhale audibly. “It’s fine, honestly. I like our tradition.”

“Me too.” His expression softens. “And speaking of traditions…”

He’s timed it perfectly, trailing off as the server arrives with our first course. Rolls that are still steaming from the oven, and a small pot of honey butter. There’s also a plate of roasted root vegetables arranged like a miniature autumn garden.

“You didn’t have to do all this,” I say, though we both know it’s part of the ritual. I protest; he insists.

“I absolutely did.” He tears a piece of bread, butter knife poised. “It’s not every day I get to spoil my favorite niece.”

“I’m your only niece.”

“A technicality you never let me forget.” He grins, passing me the butter. “How’s school? Really?”

I spread butter on my bread, watching it melt into the warm dough. “It’s good. Challenging.” Between bites, I fill him in on everything worth mentioning.

“That’s my girl.” Pride colors his voice. “And the internship? Still learning the ropes?”

“It’s…” I search for words that aren’t lies, but don’t reveal too much. “Educational. I’m learning things they don’t teach in textbooks.”

“I bet you are. Politics is a blood sport dressed in Brooks Brothers.” He leans back as the server returns to clear our plates, making way for the main course. “Anyone giving you trouble?”

I think of Enzo’s hands on my throat, his voice in my ear. He’s not merely trouble; he’s temptation incarnate. “Nothing I can’t handle.”

The main course arrives; roasted turkey with chestnut stuffing, candied sweet potatoes topped with toasted marshmallows. There are also green beans, and, of course, the cranberry sauce I love. The scent of herbs and butter rises from the plates, familiar and comforting.

“This looks amazing,” I say, genuinely appreciative.

Food has never been a priority for me—too many years of my mother’s commentary on calories and dress sizes—but the more distant we become, and in huge parts, thanks to Teddy, I’ve learned to enjoy it.

“Only the best for our dinner.” He refills our wine glasses before I’ve made a dent in mine.

“So what are you up to these days? Anything new?” I ask as I spear a piece of turkey with my fork.

“I’m thinking of getting a cat.” Teddy laughs, a rich sound that fills the space between us.

I gasp. “A cat? No, Teddy, you can’t be serious. You can’t keep anything alive."

He looks affronted. "Of course I can. Who do you think keeps me alive? I'm doing a damn fine job if I do say so myself." A sly smile pulls at his lips and his eyes twinkle mischievously. "Besides, I've had Mr. Purrgatory for two months now, and he's very much alive."

I almost choke on my food. "Mr. Purrgatory?"

Teddy nods proudly. "That's his name."

The conversation flows easily from there—cats to his latest real estate acquisition, to a funny story about his housekeeper finding his secret stash of Pop-Tarts.

It's comfortable, warm, the kind of interaction that requires no performance. With Teddy, I don't have to be the perfect student or the ambitious intern. I can just be Piper.

"You know," he says after a lull, a forkful of sweet potato halfway to his mouth, "I'm proud of you. Not just for the school stuff or the career path. But for standing your ground."

I know what he means. My choice to pursue politics instead of following my parents' preferred path as trophy wife to someone socially acceptable, then a life of carefully managed appearances.

"It wasn't really a choice," I say softly. "I couldn't do what they wanted and still be me."

"That's exactly why I'm proud." He reaches across the table, squeezes my hand briefly. "Standing up for yourself is never easy. Especially not against Nathaniel and Evelyn Harrington, Social Terrorists Extraordinaire."

I laugh despite myself. "They mean well." Another half-truth. They mean well for themselves, for their image. For me? Never.

"Only if it benefits them." Teddy's voice turns serious. "Never forget that, Piper. People will always act in their own self-interest. The trick is finding the ones whose interests align with yours."

His words hit closer to home than he could know. What is Enzo's interest in me? Not just sex—he could have that from anyone. Definitely not power, since he already has that in abundance. Something else, something I can't quite name.

"You've always been sharp, kiddo," Teddy continues, unaware of my internal struggle. "Don't let anyone dull that."

"I won't," I promise, but even as the words leave my mouth, I feel the lie in them. I'm already letting Enzo reshape parts of me, sand down edges I once thought essential. The worst part is, I like it. I crave it.

We finish our meal with pumpkin cheesecake. The restaurant has emptied somewhat, the early dinner crowd replaced by those who dine fashionably late.

"Any plans for the rest of the break?" Teddy asks, swiping his card without looking at the total.

"Just recharging. Maybe get ahead on some reading." And waiting

to see if Enzo will summon me during the holiday, if he'll demand my time when I should be resting.

"Good. You work too hard." He stands, helping me with my coat before donning his own. "Promise me you'll actually relax? Not just say you will and then spend the whole time with your nose in a textbook?"

"I promise."

Outside, the night air is crisp, carrying the scent of wood-smoke and approaching winter. Teddy hugs me again, tighter this time.

"Call me if you need anything," he says, the same words he always says, words that have been a lifeline more than once. "Anything at all."

"I will." I kiss his cheek, rough with a five o'clock shadow. "Thank you for dinner. For everything."

He waves down a taxi for me, and as it pulls away, I watch him standing on the sidewalk, hands in his pockets, making sure I'm safely on my way. I wave one last time as the taxi turns the corner, taking me back to my empty apartment.

My apartment feels too quiet after the gentle chaos of the day. I leave the lights off, navigating by memory and the soft glow filtering through my curtains from the streetlamp outside.

The wine sits heavy and warm in my veins, not drunk but not entirely sober either—that perfect middle ground where truth feels less dangerous.

Before settling on the couch, I change out of the green dress I always wear for Thanksgiving, and into an oversized long-sleeved sweater and a pair of yoga pants with a more forgiving waist.

I stretch out on the couch, my sweater riding up slightly, exposing a strip of skin to the cool air. The contrast makes me shiver.

My phone buzzes in my hand. For one heart-stopping moment, I think it's him—Enzo. Which would make no sense since he's never texted me before.

The message is from my bestie. A string of turkey emojis followed by a simple text.

> *Lee: Hope dinner with Uncle T was good. Love you, and can't wait to see you tomorrow!! Remember what I said about the list ;)*

After texting her back and ordering her to call me the second she's back tomorrow, I open the Notes app on my phone, and stare at the blank screen. The cursor blinks, patient and accusatory all at once. What would I even write? Where would I start?

With the easy things, maybe. The things I already know I like. The things he's already done to me that have left me begging for more.

I type, delete, type again. Settle finally on a simple header.

Kink List

Beneath it, I write the first word that comes to mind.

Blindfold

I laugh softly in the dark. It sounds so clinical, so inadequate. It doesn't capture the feeling of having my sight stripped away, relying completely on my other senses. It doesn't explain how my mind goes quiet, how the constant chatter of ambition and expectation fades when I can't see, when all decisions are taken from me.

I add another.

Hair pulling

Again, too simple to capture the reality. But there's no other way to really describe the slight pain that sends signals racing along my nerves. Or the way it makes me arch into him like a cat seeking more contact. How sometimes he uses it to guide me, to position me exactly where he wants me.

The list grows, each entry bringing memories that heat my skin despite the cool apartment air.

Spanking
Choking

My free hand drifts absently to my throat, fingers tracing the delicate skin where his grip has left phantom pressure.

Being called Toy
Being told I'm a good girl

I'm more aware of my body tonight than usual—the way my sweater brushes against my nipples, the slight ache between my thighs that never fully subsides anymore. A constant, low-level hunger that spikes whenever I think of him.

Needing more ideas, stuff I haven't tried, I open the internet browser, feeling suddenly bold. I search for uncommon kinks, and the results are a mix of clinical terminology and explicit descriptions. I click through, scanning, dismissing some immediately, lingering on others. Some I already have on my list. Others are new to me, terms I've never encountered.

There's one that catches my interest right away. I click the link, read

the definition. Somnophilia refers to a sexual interest in engaging in sexual activity with a sleeping person.

I immediately picture Enzo entering my apartment like he did when he spanked me. My heart thunders in my chest as I imagine him stalking through the darkness, finding me asleep and vulnerable.

Slickness pools between my legs, and my pussy clenches around nothing as I let out a small whimper. The fantasy is so real. I can practically see him touching me without waking me. Using me while I'm unconscious.

The thought makes me press my hand against myself through my yoga pants, a reflexive action I'm barely aware of until it's happening. I'm soaked, shamefully aroused by the idea of being so completely at his mercy.

My finger hovers over the delete button again. This is too much, too honest. Too revealing of the dark, twisted parts of myself I've only begun to acknowledge. If anyone saw this list… what would they think?

What the hell am I working myself into a panic attack for? No one's going to see. Besides, it's healthy to have fantasies. It doesn't mean I'll act on it. For now, I'm content just imagining how it would work out.

I save the note, then lock my phone and let it fall to the couch beside me. The room feels different now, charged with something beyond just the lingering effects of wine and food. My whole body hums with awareness, with the weight of what I've just admitted to myself.

There's a kind of surrender in naming your desires. In acknowledging the parts of yourself that society says should remain hidden.

Deciding to leave the list on my phone, I get up from the couch and pad into the bathroom. Even though it's still early, I'm too tired to keep my eyes open. So I quickly get ready for bed. Then I stride into my bedroom where I strip out of my clothes and slide under the sheets. Just before I fall asleep, I read over my kink list one last time, and make a few changes.

Kink List!

Do I have any?

Do the below count as kinks?

Hair pulling

Spanking

Choking

Degrading names (Toy!!!)

Praise (good toy!!)

Exhibitionism (like Halloween & my interview!!)
Somnophilia

25

Lorenzo

"**I** have to give it to you. This is a great cigar," Rafe grins, rolling it between his fingers like it's a reward he earned.

I nod once, drawing the smoke into my mouth and holding it there. I don't inhale, I just let the flavor sit before blowing it out into the night air.

Back when my dad was alive, I used to love Thanksgiving. It was a grand affair with all the trimmings, and Cy and I always had fun with my cousins. But since my father died of cancer, it's become less about tradition and family, and more about debauchery.

That's never bothered me until this year. I don't want to be sucked off by one of the desperate women hoping to land herself a Russo husband. Like my heart, my dick belongs to one woman only, and she isn't here.

"That it is," I finally say, flicking ash off the end.

Rafe rocks back on his heels and exhales smoke into the cold Cleveland air. "So how are things going in D.C.?"

I glance toward the sky, where the stars are faint behind city light and haze. "Not bad." I say, letting the words fall flat.

Rafe chuckles. "Is that so?" He tosses the stub of his cigar into the trash and looks at me sideways. "How about your intern?"

A smile pulls at my mouth. "She's not just an intern."

"No?" He arches a brow. "What is she then?"

I take one last drag from the cigar. "She's mine." I exhale the smoke with each word.

Rafe stills, the grin slipping from his face as something more serious settles into his features. "You're serious." It's not a question. "Do you love her?"

I nod once. "Deadly serious." Taking a moment, I contemplate his second question. Do I love my toy? I don't know. She's my everything in so many ways. She's all I can think about, and all I want. Is that love? "I don't know if I love her. But I'm addicted to her," I reply, my voice low.

He studies me. "Does she know that?"

Smirking, I reply, "She's starting to." I crush the end of my cigar into the ashtray beside us, the hiss of it cutting the air like punctuation.

Rafe lets out a slow, impressed breath, his mouth curling into something that's almost a smile. "Fuck. You've got it bad."

"I've got it perfect," I correct.

He laughs under his breath, shaking his head as he flicks ash to the side. "Are you going to tell her everything?"

I don't need to ask what he means; he wants to know if I'm going to tell her who I really am, and what I do behind the curtain. "When the time is right."

"When is the time ever right?" he laughs.

My jaw ticks. "When I say so," I grunt.

"And if she walks?"

"She won't." My voice is steel. Cold. Absolute. "But if she does, I'll burn every exit behind her. Leave her with nowhere to run except back to me."

The silence that follows isn't awkward. It's reverent. Like even the night is smart enough to shut up when something holy is declared.

Rafe turns toward the door, but not before tossing me a look over his shoulder. "Matteo's probably setting something on fire by now."

"Fuck, you're probably right," I agree with a grimace.

I follow him toward the entrance of the Leone Room. The heavy door opens with the creak of old wood and old power, spilling warmth into the cold.

The air inside is thick with the ghosts of a hundred backdoor deals, a thousand whispered betrayals. It clings to my skin like a shroud, threading into my lungs with the scent of old money and blood, scrubbed clean but never truly gone.

Here, the devils don't wear Prada; they wear Armani, stitched with power, cut from control.

When we enter the room, we left only half an hour ago, it's barely recognizable. The lights have been dimmed, and there are half-naked and fully naked women dancing on the floors and tables.

Remus sits on the couch, staring at his phone like it's personally offended him, all while carrying out a conversation with Matteo, who's getting his dick sucked.

The woman between Matteo's legs moans dramatically, more performance than pleasure, and he doesn't even look down. Just takes a sip of whatever's in his tumbler, flicking his eyes toward us with a grin sharp enough to slice glass.

"There you are," Matteo says. "We were starting to take bets on whether you got pussy-whipped and ran back to D.C. already."

Remus doesn't glance up from his phone. "Speak for yourself. I was betting he snapped and buried a body in the garden."

"Garden's frozen," Rafe mutters, heading for the bar. "You'd need a flamethrower."

Matteo hums. "I do have one of those."

I sweep a slow glance across the room. A blonde in nothing but stilettos tries to catch my eye. I ignore her. Another girl on the far end of the floor bends over deliberately, ass in the air like it's a goddamn offering.

Shaking my head, I turn away from them. I won't offend my toy by even looking. She might not be here, but that doesn't mean I'll disrespect her.

Remus finally sets his phone down and lifts his eyes to mine. "You look like someone who's about five seconds from shutting this shit down."

"I'm considering it," I admit, stripping off my coat and tossing it over the back of a leather chair. "What the fuck is this?"

"Post-dinner entertainment," Matteo offers cheerfully. "Blame Rafe. He said it was starting to feel too civilized."

Rafe shrugs. "Didn't say hire a fucking harem."

"Semantics," Matteo smirks, stroking a hand down the head of the girl still bobbing between his thighs.

I sink into the armchair across from them, one ankle resting casually over my knee, watching without blinking. "This is how you celebrate family?"

"It's how we celebrate survival," Remus says evenly. "Besides, we knew you weren't interested. Not anymore."

I raise a brow. "Is that so?"

Matteo's grin grows. "We're not blind, cousin. You've gone full Enzo mode. Still, can't hurt to try." He waves vaguely at the girls. "Pick one. Or five. Might help loosen you up."

"I'm plenty loose," I murmur, lifting a glass from the table and inspecting the color. "Just not stupid."

Remus exhales a breath, something almost like a laugh. "You used to be more fun."

"No," I correct, sipping the whiskey. "I used to be more bored." And bored men are dangerous. But obsessed ones? We build empires—or burn them to ash just to watch our woman rise from it.

While Rafe and Remus throw themselves into a discussion about some jobs, I empty my drink, contemplating if I should just head back home. It's not like it's a long flight from Cleveland, Ohio, to Washington D.C. So I could get there before…

A brunette with honey-glossed lips who approaches from my left interrupts my thoughts. "Lorenzoooo," she purrs, her hips swaying exaggeratedly. She perches herself next to me. "How have you been?"

I arch an eyebrow, unimpressed with her performance. "Do I know

you?" I ask coldly.

Her answering laugh grates on my nerves. "Don't you recognize me?" she pouts. When I shake my head, she bats her lashes. "Maybe this will jog your memory."

Leaning closer, she reaches for my cock. I catch her wrist mid-air and squeeze. Not enough to bruise, but enough to get her to back the fuck off.

"Never touch what doesn't belong to you," I snarl. "Get the fuck out of my sight. Now!"

She gasps, breath hitching more from surprise than pain. Then she tries to pull away, but I don't let her. Not yet. I want her to remember this moment so she never makes that mistake again with me.

I hold her wrist for several moments, finally letting go when she lets out a pathetic whimper.

"Dick," she mutters as she scurries away.

Matteo lets out a low whistle. "Christ, Enzo. You're going to make the poor girl cry."

"She should be more careful with her hands," I say, reaching for the whiskey.

Her mistake wasn't wanting some action. It was believing she had the right to touch me when I already belong to someone else.

Rafe raises his glass. "And now the room's officially back to normal."

"She's lucky," Remus chuckles, reclining back in his seat. "Five years ago, that would've ended differently."

Matteo barks a laugh. "Three years ago, he wouldn't have waited for her to touch him."

"And just months ago," Rafe adds, "he'd have let her."

They're not wrong about who I've been. But that version of myself is dead and buried, and it all happened when I laid eyes on my toy.

"So," Matteo says, swirling the ice in his tumbler. "Now that we're all accounted for—and now that you've made it painfully clear no one here's getting their hands on you—how is your little intern?"

I meet his eyes and smile, slow and deliberate. "Better than your head game."

The woman at his feet snorts mid-suck. Matteo smirks down at her. "That's bold talk from a man who hasn't even gotten his dick wet tonight." Then he pulls her head back. "He isn't wrong, you know. You're not even acting like you're enjoying it."

She whines and promises she'll do better, so he lets her get back to it. I scoff at how generous my cousin is.

"You know," Matteo muses, "You won the blowjob lottery with your intern. She loved sucking you off."

Remus' brows lift slightly. "Are you honestly still thinking about that?"

I pin Matteo with my gaze. "Don't tell me you're fantasizing

about—"

Rafe snorts. "It's your own fault, Enzo. You let Matteo watch. What the fuck did you think would happen?"

Pinching the bridge of my nose, I remind myself it would be bad to kill Matteo. For one, I'd probably end up missing the crazy fucker. And, well, I don't think Remus would appreciate it.

"Have any of you thought about my proposition?" Matteo says, smoothly changing the subject.

Remus watches him for a long moment before giving the barest nod. "You have the family's backing."

Even though my agreement isn't needed, I say, "I think it's a good idea to collect some favors. It'll remind people you're not giving shit out for free."

"You should take Rafe with you," Remus says, his tone making it clear it's an order and not a suggestion.

Rafe smirks. "That's code for 'I'll keep an eye on you so you don't burn the whole thing to the ground.'"

Matteo lifts his glass in agreement. "It's like no one trusts me—"

"We trust you," I interrupt, smirking at my cousin. "Just not with flammables."

Matteo scoffs, slouching deeper into his chair like a man perpetually unimpressed by the world around him. "That was one small fire, for fuck's sake." He waves a lazy hand. "And it wasn't even the flames that were the problem—it was the explosives I stashed months prior. Completely forgot about them."

Rafe barks out an incredulous laugh, his patience visibly thinning. "You do hear yourself, right?"

Matteo just grins. "I do. And I stand by it."

Remus idly turns the ring on his index finger, watching the exchange with his usual measured patience. "This is why people assume you're unhinged."

Matteo raises his newly filled glass in mock salute. "I never said they were wrong. But I'm still everyone's favorite cousin."

Rafe snorts, shifting to stretch his legs out. "That's only because I scare people, Lorenzo's unreadable, and Remus runs a fucking empire. You win by default."

Matteo shrugs. "A win is a win."

I shake my head, exhaling a short laugh as I swirl the amber liquid in my own glass. This is familiar, comfortable. The banter, the ease between us—it's a rare moment where we're not running strategy, not making moves, just… existing.

Beneath the surface, there's an unshakable bond that binds us all. We'd all place our lives in Matteo's hands without a second thought. However, we'd rather avoid having him anywhere near an open flame, given his history of mishaps with fire.

Remus leans forward, finally peeling his gaze from the whiskey in

his hand. "Have you told her who you are yet?"

The room stills, if only for a beat. Rafe swirls the ice in his glass like it'll stir the silence back to life.

Matteo smirks. "Does she know she's the intern to a man that makes presidents look like marionettes and cleans his hands with their secrets?"

"Not yet," I reply calmly. "She knows my name is Enzo, and I guess she's starting to piece things together."

I fill them in on the meetings she's been privy to, and all the things she's overheard. I'm pretty sure she knows more than she's led on. If it scares her, she's hiding it well. Especially since she keeps coming back—both to the building and to me.

"What if she runs?" Matteo asks, tone more curious than cruel.

I look up, locking eyes with him. "Then I'll chase her to the end of the fucking Earth."

Remus raises his glass to that. "There he is."

"You think I'm joking?" I don't smile or blink. I hold his gaze so he knows I'm deadly serious.

"No," Remus says. "That's what makes it inevitable."

Matteo snorts. "Chasing's fun. I prefer the part after, when they realize they never had a chance."

"I don't want her broken," I say, voice darker now. "I want her to know I bend the very fabrics of the world just for her."

Even Rafe whistles at that.

Remus studies me over the rim of his glass, his eyes sharp, unblinking. "You're in deep."

"So I've been told," I smirk.

As Remus steers the conversation back to Matteo's new idea, I allow myself a moment to breathe. After checking my phone to make sure there's nothing pressing, I check the clone of Piper's phone, surprised there's been activity I've missed.

It looks like she updated her Notes app hours ago. Smirking, I open it. My eyes widen and my pants feel too fucking tight as I read over her list of… fuck me.

My toy has created a kink list. I bark out a laugh at her question about whether she has any or not. If she'd asked me outright, I could tell her she does.

I scroll back to the top of her list, reading it again slowly, deliberately—like it's gospel, which it very well might be since it's bringing me to my fucking knees.

Do I have any?

Do the below count as kinks?

My gaze drifts back to the last item on her list, and my cock jerks as

I read it. If my toy's curious about somnophilia, I'll be the one to answer that question for her. I rise without another word, already texting my pilot and driver that we're leaving.

"You're leaving?" Matteo blinks, halfway through raising his glass. "You just sat down."

"Enzo doesn't sit," Rafe mutters, watching me with something between respect and wariness. "He waits. And apparently, his wait's over."

Remus just looks at me, eyes sharp. "What'd she do?"

I smirk as I shrug on my coat. "She made a list."

"A grocery list?" Matteo deadpans.

I glance over my shoulder, eyes cold, hungry. "A kink list."

All three of them burst out laughing, enough to interrupt the woman still bobbing away between Matteo's legs.

"Don't wait up," I grin, already pushing the door open.

There's a girl in D.C. with a fantasy I plan on answering.

26

Lorenzo

I land in D.C. just before 2 a.m., the streets slick with rain that glistens like oil under the city lights. Her apartment is quiet when I let myself in, the kind of silence that feels sacred. Upon arriving at her bedroom, I linger in the doorway, captivated by the sight of her peaceful slumber. Her arm is casually flung above her head, and her lips are gently parted.

She lets out a soft snore and wiggle, unknowingly kicking more of her sheet off. Her body is sprawled out at the center of the bed, like she's subconsciously waiting for someone she doesn't know is already here.

I suppress a moan when I realize my toy's completely naked. Fuck, she looks good enough to eat.

Her tits rise and fall like she's panting for it, even in her sleep. Her waist... fuck! That little curve is just begging for my hand to wrap around it while I take her from behind.

I lean over her sleeping form, my fingers trailing along her smooth skin, tracing a path from her slender ankle up to her hip. She stirs slightly, and a breathy sigh escapes her. She doesn't know it yet, but her body does. It obeys me now. I've trained it without even fucking her. And that kink list just proves it; my toy's ready for me.

I slide my hand between her thighs, touching the heat that belongs to me. My fingers find her clit instantly. She sighs, soft and sweet, her hips shifting under my touch like her body knows exactly who's touching her.

That's it, Toy. Even asleep, your cunt knows who owns it. With careful precision, I move two fingers between her folds, feeling the slickness as I ease them slowly into her waiting cunt.

"You're drenched for me," I groan.

I curve my fingers just the way she likes, and quicken my pace.

When her body reacts, hips rising to meet my hand, and her breath hitches, I pause, watching her face for any sign of wakefulness, but her eyes remain closed.

"Such a perfect fucking toy," I murmur, my voice dark and reverent.

My hand doesn't slow as I work her body like I own every twitch, every gasp. I grind the heel of my palm against her clit in slow, punishing circles, watching her body obey me.

As her legs start to tremble, I withdraw my fingers and lick them clean. Fuck, I'll never get enough of tasting her cunt.

"You don't get to come yet," I whisper as I shift to the foot of the bed.

Moving her with me without waking her up is no simple task, but I manage. She's still sleeping as I fall to my knees, my hands cradling her thighs, feeling the softness of her skin beneath my touch.

I position myself between her thighs, taking a deep breath, savoring her overwhelming scent. Fuuuuuck!

I drag my tongue over her slick folds, loving the taste of her that now coats my mouth. I moan against her pussy, starving for more. It doesn't matter how long I eat her cunt, my hunger's carved from her now, and no amount will ever be enough.

Her hips roll, desperate little pleas written in muscle and instinct. That pussy is begging for my tongue in her dreams. I flick my tongue over her clit in sharp, punishing strokes. She twitches with every pass, her body reacting like I've wired her nerve endings to my mouth.

"Mhmm," I groan.

Her breathing stutters into whimpers—needy little sounds that curl in her throat like she's begging in her sleep. Fuck. My toy's dreaming of me, I'm sure of it.

I keep going, relentless and ravenous, until she moans and her body snaps tight like it's beginning to break. Her legs shake, and then she comes hard for me, soaking my tongue in sleep-drunk surrender.

Even unconscious, she knows who she fucking belongs to. What a good fucking toy.

After pressing one last kiss to her swollen clit, I rise. My hand goes to my zipper, undoing my pants. The fabric parts and my cock springs free—hard, heavy, aching for her.

I wrap a hand around it, squeezing tight, not to tease but to anchor. To keep myself from doing what every cell in my body is screaming for.

Even though I know I'm pushing it, I crawl onto the bed, the mattress sinking slightly under my knees as I position myself between her parted legs. I grasp my hardness, aching and heavy with need.

Then I rub her wetness all over my hardness, coating myself in her arousal. The sensation is overwhelming, sending a jolt of pleasure up my spine, making my eyes flutter closed and my teeth grit with restraint.

Swallowing down another groan, I continue to rut against her. I fuck her thighs, her folds, anything but her cunt. And with each thrust, the tip grazes her clit, sending ripples of pleasure through us both.

"You'd fucking love this if you were awake, wouldn't you? Being used like this. Painted in it," I rasp. It takes all my self-control to resist the overwhelming urge to plunge into her. "Fuck. You're already ruining me, Toy. And you don't even fucking know it."

It feels like it's madness that keeps me here. Every stroke against her slick cunt is a dare to lose control. I tell myself I'm in charge, but the truth claws at my spine. She's a fucking gravity well, pulling me deeper. And the worst part? I want it. Want her to hollow me out. To ruin me from the inside out.

"Fucking hell," I grunt, rutting harder.

A surge of tension grips me, a visceral tightening deep within me. I pull back and angle the tip toward her mound just in time.

Then I come, hard. My cock jerks, and I spill all over her. Thick ropes of cum paint her belly, her mound, her thighs. The thought of her waking up, covered in me, is enough to prolong my orgasm and I keep coming.

Getting off the bed, I sort my clothes before silently moving into the living room, where I find a notepad and a pen in her bag. I quickly scribble out a note.

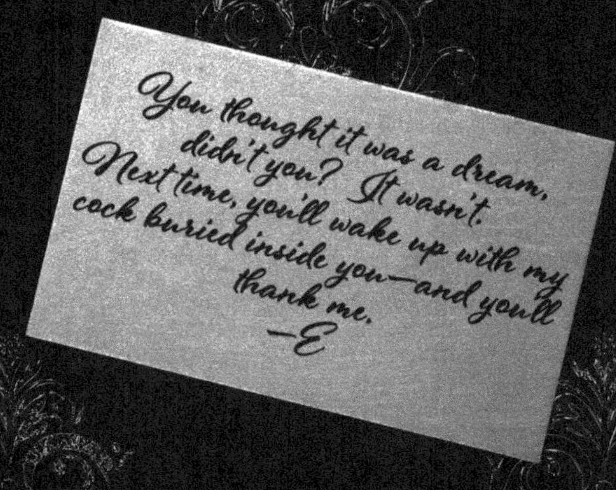

I pause in the doorway again, turning to look at her one last time before I leave. "No one will ever make you come like that," I vow. "Because if they do, I'll fucking kill them."

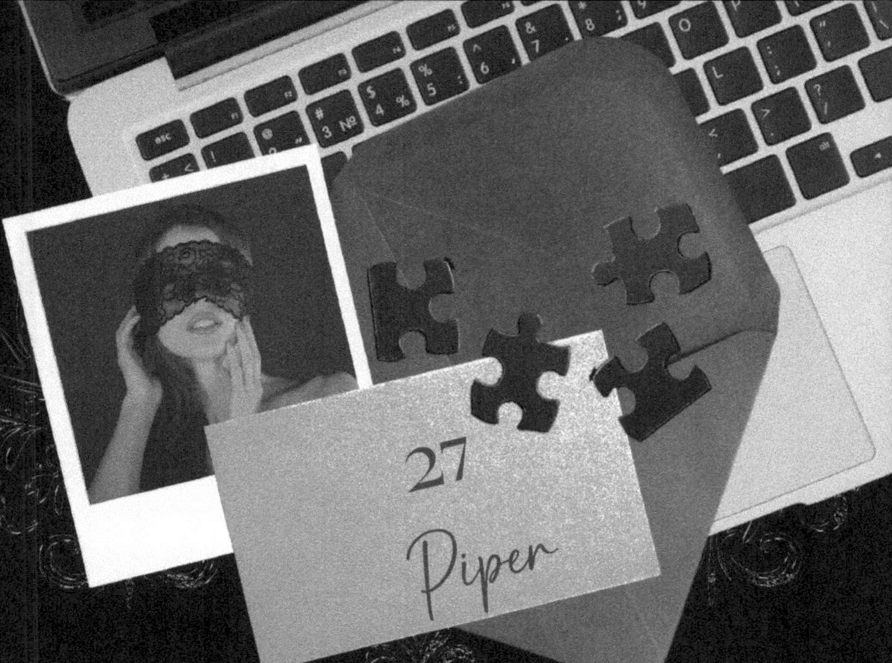

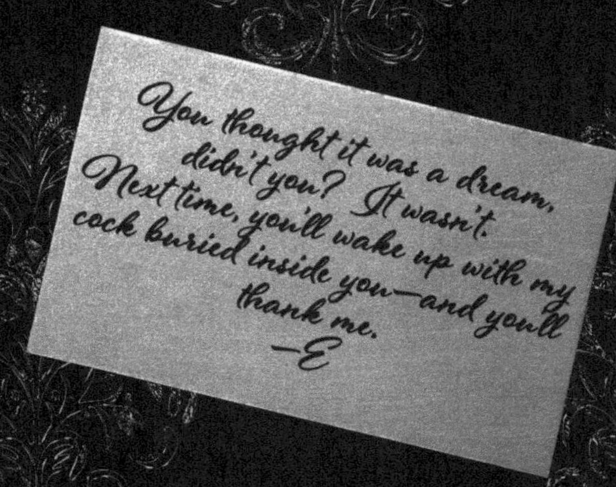

I wake up slowly, blinking against the soft light spilling through the curtains. There's a strange, delicious ache low in my belly—like I had a really good dream. My limbs feel heavy, warm. Sated.

Stretching, I let my hand brush against the bedside table where I usually keep my phone. Instead of touching the sleek device, paper grazes my skin. I sit up and reach for the folded paper, suddenly wide awake.

The note is written in tight, confident handwriting.

You thought it was a dream, didn't you? It wasn't. Next time, you'll wake up with my cock buried inside you—and you'll thank me.

—E

My skin prickles, a hot wave of… something crashes into me as I read the note. I read it again, as though the words will change if I stare long enough.

My hand flies to my mouth. "Oh, my God!" I scream, as the penny finally fucking drops.

He was here. While I was sleeping.

The ache in my body sharpens, memory flickering into sensation. Holy shit. It wasn't just a very vivid sex dream. Enzo was here. As in, he let himself into what's supposed to be my home—again. But this time it was while I was sleeping. And he… he… fuck.

I curl up the note and turn to throw it onto the floor.

Why would he come here while I was sleeping? That's not okay. I'm not okay with it. I barely finish the thought before my core clenches, slick heat pooling between my thighs and my nipples harden into little peaks.

Oh fuck. I'm actually turned on. Disgust curls in my throat—but lower, deeper, everything inside me clenches like my body's already decided it's fine with what happened. My mind, though? It's still putting up a fight.

I run my hands down my body, feeling something crusty on my stomach and thighs. The hell? Did he come on me?

Leaping out of bed, I run to the bathroom and turn on the shower. I'm trembling as I step under the scalding water, harshly washing myself. I can't explain it, but I feel unclean.

It takes over half an hour before I've calmed down enough to realize two things. One, a shower isn't going to change a damn thing. Two, Enzo breaking into the apartment and doing… doing this to me after I made the kinks list is one hell of a coincidence.

And if there's one thing being his intern has taught me not to believe in, it's coincidences.

My fingers tremble as I shrug on my robe and brush my teeth. I can't let go of the thought of being watched, of being scrutinized. It's fucking unnerving and I want nothing more than to curl up and have a pity party for one.

That's not on the agenda for today, though. I refuse.

After brushing my teeth, I feel more myself as I stride back into the bedroom and find my phone so I can text Lena.

Me: SOS!!!

Me: Are you back yet?

I look at the clock in the top corner. Hmm, it's later than I thought. Normally, I wake up at the ass-crack of dawn without an alarm, but today I've somehow managed to sleep until 8:30 a.m.

Lee: No, bitch, I'm not back yet. I'm half an hour away.

But what kind of SOS are we talking? Brunch?

Chocolate? Alcohol? All the above???

I can't help laughing.

Me: Definitely brunch.

After hitting send, I consider her other options, each one equally alluring.

Me: With mimosas and chocolate waffles.

Lee: Got it. Sunny Side Up as usual?

Me: Yeah. In an hour and a half okay?

Lee: It's a date!!

I toss my phone onto the bed and head for the closet, yanking the doors open like I'm preparing for battle. No, scratch that—war. Because that's what today feels like. A war between who I was yesterday and who I'm going to be now.

My eyes skim over rows of carefully curated outfits, but all of them feel too boring and safe for my current mood.

I crouch down and dig through the storage bins until my hand finds what I didn't even know I was searching for. A pair of knee-high black leather boots with thin as fuck heels. I haven't worn them since that Halloween party sophomore year, but when I zip them up, they still fit perfectly.

They're bold, confident, and a little dangerous. Okay. Maybe this can work.

I feel ridiculous standing here in just the boots and my robe, so I quickly find some underwear and put it on.

Reaching for one of my black skirts that I never wear because it's too short, I step into it. Yep, the length is just right. I pair the outfit with a short-sleeved, fitted, charcoal gray shirt that hugs my waist. The hem hits just above the skirt's waistband, a soft rebellion against all my usual business chic attire.

Spinning, I pause in front of the full body mirror, hands braced on my hips. I feel like Enzo would hate this look, and that's enough reason to choose it. The devil on my shoulder whispers that he might love it, enough to press me against the mirror and fuck me until the glass cracked.

Well, fuck that. This isn't about him.

"Am I really doing this?" I whisper to my reflection. My mirror self

stares back like it's daring me to chicken out.

Instead of arguing with myself, I head back to the bathroom and brush my hair out. Leaving it down would be too easy. Too soft. I twist it up into a high ponytail, then wrap a strand around the elastic to hide it. It gives me more edge.

Makeup next. Not too much, not too little. I'm aiming for the Goldilocks combo, where it's just enough to make me feel like I have control.

Black eyeliner, a little smoky shadow at the corners. Mascara, two coats. I slick on a matte plum lipstick—the kind that says I know exactly what I'm doing, even if I don't. Just for the record, I totally don't. I'm running on emotions rather than sense right now.

"Fuck!" I scream, letting out the frustration and anger festering beneath my skin.

I feel so… violated right now. And apart from gulping mimosas like it's air, I have no idea how to deal with it.

Once my throat feels raw, and I'm on the verge of crying, I gather my phone, clutch, and grab a blazer I never normally wear. Feeling back in control, I leave the apartment and make my way to Sunny Side Up!

The place isn't far away, so it doesn't take me long to walk there. When I arrive, there's already a throng of people waiting in line. I'm just about to call out for my bestie when she spins around.

"Pipes!" Lena squeals the second she sees me. Maybe it was the proverbial storm cloud above my head that alerted her to my presence. "Let's get our mimosas on."

She loops her arm through mine, dragging me past the line and straight inside. Sometimes there are perks to Lena being active on dating apps.

As soon as the door opens, I'm hit with the smell of buttery waffles, roasted coffee beans, and a hint of vodka. It's warm and loud, crowded with Georgetown's usual weekend brunch-goers.

The host barely finishes asking if we need a table for two before Lena shoots him a finger-gun and says, "Yes, please."

We slide into our usual booth in the back corner, half-hidden behind a ficus plant that's probably older than we are. Lena's already waving over the server, not even bothering to glance at the menu.

"Two mimosa pitchers," she chirps. "One classic, one mango." Then she adds, "And chocolate waffles. Double portion."

"Brunch of champions," I mutter.

Lena narrows her eyes at me. "You're being weird."

I blink. "I'm not."

"You are." She leans in, elbows on the table. "You texted me SOS like your uterus was on fire, then showed up looking like a villainess from a spy movie. I mean, those boots?" She gestures under the table. "Iconic. But also, deeply alarming."

I exhale a shaky laugh, fiddling with the edge of my napkin. "Okay, fine. I'm… spiraling a little."

"That's what mimosas are for. Spill."

The server returns with two tall pitchers and two champagne flutes. Lena waits until he's gone, then digs around in her bag and pulls out a small silver flask. She glances around before pouring a generous glug of vodka into each mimosa glass.

"Subtle," I comment as I top up our glasses.

"I'm a fucking ninja," she deadpans, handing me my drink. "Now. Talk."

I take a sip. The extra vodka hits hard, and I welcome it. "Remember Enzo?"

She arches an eyebrow. "How could I forget when you only told me about him a couple of days ago?"

I suck in a breath and try to gather my thoughts, but they're a fucking avalanche—loud, fast, and crashing in every direction. Throwing caution to the wind, I dive straight into the heart of the story.

"I had a sex dream last night, and when I woke up this morning, there was a fucking note from him," I hiss, outrage swirling in my gut. "I think he broke in and… and touched me while I was sleeping."

Her eyes widen. "Wait. What? He was there?"

I nod, my throat dry.

"Like… in your apartment? While you were asleep?"

I nod again. "Not like it's the first time he's broken in," I hiss, my anger flaring like a fucking bonfire.

"Umm… what?"

Well, fuck. I'd completely forgotten I haven't told her who Enzo is. For all she knows, he's just my boss. Then again, since I've barely admitted it to myself, I don't know when I would have told her.

Taking a deep breath, I mentally ready myself for the shit storm I'm about to unleash on my unsuspecting bestie. "Do you remember the puzzle pieces I received?" I ask, nervously biting the inside of my cheek.

"Yeah, of course, Pipes. Have you received more?" She stops talking and looks off to the side, and when her brows furrow, I know she's slowly piecing it together. "Why do you ask me that now?"

Before I can talk myself out of it, I tell Lena everything. From how I got the internship, to the times I've spent kneeling at Enzo's feet like he's some enigmatic god that demands my worship. I don't hold any details back, and I don't let her interrupt me when I tell her that he broke into my apartment and spanked me.

As I get to the part about the Halloween party, she holds her hand up. "Give me a damn second here. A girl needs time to digest," she demands.

I dutifully stop talking, nervously picking at my nails as I wait for her to say more. I don't know how much time passes until she speaks

again, but it feels like forever.

"Are you okay? I mean, that's… holy shit, Pipes, that's…"

"I know." I grab my mimosa and drink the rest of it in one go. "It sounds awful. Like, criminal-awful."

The conversation comes to a crashing halt as the food arrives, and we both dig in like we haven't eaten in days. The waffles are perfect—crispy edges, melty chocolate, whipped cream.

After a few bites, Lena reaches for her phone that lies next to her napkin on the table. "Should we call the cops? I mean, the man is fucking forcing you by holding your internship over your head." She lets out a sound of disgust that tells me exactly what she thinks about that. "Not to mention he's been stalking you, and breaking into your home. They have to take you seriously now."

Before I know what I'm doing, I yank the phone from her hand and shake my head. "No," I almost hiss. My eyes widen like saucers at what I just did.

She cants her head, confusion clear in her eyes. "Why wouldn't you want to, Pipes? If some creep broke into your apartment and sexually assaulted you, and is taking advantage of you at work, that's pretty much the thing to do."

I'm embarrassed to meet her gaze as I softly admit. "Because… I might have wanted it."

"Wanted it? You fucking wanted him to stalk you and deliver shit to your door?"

I quickly shake my head. "No, obviously not that part."

No longer hungry, I push the rest of my food around on the plate and gulp down more mimosa. With more alcohol running through my veins, I have enough courage to admit the next part.

"I think I wanted the sex stuff," I confess. "When I sucked him off at the interview, I… loved it. I've been really into all of it."

Trying to explain while untangling how I feel is fucking hard. I know how it sounds, and I don't agree with his methods. But his results… those I can't argue with. Every time I've felt his touch, or done things he asked, it's felt fucking awesome.

He's made me feel strong and desired. So even though his methods are questionable at best, I'm not sure I'll ever hate the outcome. I even dressed for him at the Halloween party. I wanted him to play with my body.

The more I sit here and think about it, the more I realize I wanted it. All of it. Enzo hasn't forced me, he's merely coaxed me and provided the incentives I needed to get over myself. Whether that was his intention or not, I don't know.

But something tells me I would have landed the internship even if I didn't drop to my knees. Even if I didn't let him finger-fuck me until I forgot my name.

"And what about what he did last night?" Lena challenges, her tone

stern as she interrupts my thoughts. "Don't let him get away with shit you aren't okay with."

"I don't know how I feel about it," I admit, licking my dry lips. "I wanted to try it, that's why I put it on my stupid list in my Notes app."

"Right. Did you tell him that?"

I shake my head vehemently. "No. But he must have seen it somehow."

Lena stares at me, eyes round as saucers. "Okay, let me get this straight." Her tone is all business now. "Let's focus on last night, okay?"

"Okay."

"So, you made a list of kinks you want to try. Then the same night, Enzo breaks in and does one of the things from said list?"

"Yep," I confirm.

"How in the hell would he know about your list, Pipes? Did he bug your phone or something?"

There it is, the million dollar question. Well, one of them.

"I don't know," I softly admit.

I no longer feel as pissed as I did when I woke up. Don't get me wrong, I'm still not happy about it, but I am intrigued. It's hard to explain. If I knew he might do something like that, I think I'd enjoy it. The part that's pissing me off is that it feels like I didn't have a choice. Like my participation and consent didn't matter.

Sighing, I do my best to convey my thoughts, which isn't easy when I'm not even sure I understand myself. Luckily, Lena is one hell of a bestie. She doesn't judge, doesn't tell me I'm insane for not going to the cops.

"Listen." She reaches across the table, taking my hand. "I want you to be careful. If you want to test kinks with this guy, go for it. If you just want missionary with the light off, you do you. But if you want an active role, it sounds like you're going to have to make a statement."

I gesture at myself. "That's why I'm wearing the boots," I grin, feeling a whole lot better about everything thanks to her and the mimosas.

28

Piper

As we leave, we only make it two steps outside before Lena pulls up short, her head turning like she's heard something. She grabs my arm. "Wait. Do you hear that?"

It takes a second, but then I catch it too—laughter, familiar voices, loud and a little tipsy, echoing from around the corner. Lena perks up like a bloodhound on a scent.

"I think it's Josh," she beams.

I squint. "The one with the man-bun and the aggressive Patagonia vest collection?"

"Yeah. He's hot in a guy-who-drinks-oat-milk kind of way," she stage-whispers. "Come on."

Before I can object, she's already dragging me toward the noise. And sure enough, there's Josh, plus two guys I don't immediately recognize.

"Lena!" Josh calls, grinning. "And… damn, Piper? Is that you? You look different."

"You must mean feral," I smirk.

"Respect," he laughs.

"Well, well, well," one of the guys with Josh drawls. "I'll be damned, Piper. I barely recognized you."

"Ben," I laugh, giving him a drunken hug. "I didn't see you there. Is Alice with you?"

He playfully waggles his eyebrows. "Nah, she's home for Thanksgiving. Doing the whole big family thing."

"We're heading to Static after this. Do you want to come?" Josh asks, giving Lena a hopeful look.

She quickly answers for both of us. "Obviously."

Although I'd probably be better off if I went home and laid in bed while dissecting everything that's happened, I don't argue. Right now,

I want to live in denial. In this strange, floaty, glittery buzz.

We fall into step with the guys and leave the rest behind.

Entering Static is like walking into a casino in Las Vegas. With no clock, no windows, no reference point to the outside world, time disintegrates. In other words, it's the perfect place to get lost.

Smirking, I let myself feel the pounding bass as my eyes follow the laser lights slicing through the darkness in violent flashes of pink and blue, strobing across mirrored panels and glossy black walls.

Beneath my feet, the floor vibrates with every beat, like the whole building is breathing. Somewhere overhead, industrial fans whir, stirring the heat into something dizzying and alive.

"Holy shit," Lena breathes beside me.

The bar glows like a spaceship, tendrils of LED light curling along its edges. The ceiling's so high I can't see where it ends, lost in scaffolding and projection screens showing silent, looping video art.

A girl with silver glitter smeared across her cheeks hands us drink menus we'll never read. Lena grabs us a table near the edge of the dance floor—a mismatched set of velvet chairs that looks stolen from a hotel lobby, and a glass table cracked right down the center.

I can't stop staring at everything and everyone. There are people in mesh, in latex, in sequins. A guy walks by shirtless with angel wings. Another wears nothing but jeans and body paint. No one blinks.

Lena grabs my hand, her grin sharp. "Embrace the chaos, bitch."

And maybe that's what I want—what I need. Something wild, untethered. Something that lets me forget what happened this morning, if only for a little while.

While the guys order beers—lager, as Josh obnoxiously insists on calling it—Lena and I opt for cocktails. Fruity, ridiculous, definitely overpriced cocktails.

My eyes widen when they arrive. They're not just over-the-top— they're a whole damn spectacle. Served in oversized hurricane glasses that look like they were stolen from a mermaid-themed resort, the drinks are violently pink, almost glowing under the club's neon lights.

A carved pineapple wedge is teetering on the rim, three maraschino cherries impaled on a flaming sugar stick, and a spiral of citrus peel wrapped around a candy-striped straw like it's auditioning for Cirque du Soleil. The top crackles from the firestick as the flame dances, hissing softly before fading into a trail of smoke that smells like toasted syrup.

"What the fuck is this?" I whisper, awe-struck.

Lena clinks her glass against mine with a devilish grin. "An experience, babe." Then she blows me a kiss. "And you're still paying."

The drink is way too sweet, way too easy to drink, and absolutely strong enough to make me forget my name.

Josh watches us take our first sips with a look somewhere between horror and admiration. "You two are gonna die."

"Then let us die fabulous," Lena laughs, already halfway through hers.

The drinks go down like a treat, and I quickly lose track of how many we've had, especially when we start double-fisting those bad boys. Ben takes a picture of both me and Lena holding one in each hand, and from there, the selfie game only gets better.

We have way too much fun posing together. Not just me and Lena, all of us in various poses. At some point, we even try stacking all of us on one chair, which ends in laughter, a broken chair, and spilled drinks.

"I can't even," I laugh. My cheeks hurt as I do my best to stand back up.

Josh offers me a hand, but Lena beats him to it, grabbing my arm and pulling me upright like a drunk little warrior.

"We need to dance," she declares. "Or we'll turn into furniture."

The music pulses like a heartbeat on steroids—neon strobing across bodies that don't move so much as vibrate. Static's dance floor doesn't have corners, just pockets of light and shadow where people writhe in time with whatever track the DJ's throwing at us next.

Our group has grown. Somewhere between rounds, a pack of girls joined us, glittery and shrieking and instantly obsessed with Lena's dress. Then one of Josh's rugby bros turned up with two new guys, one of whom is already shirtless and waving glow sticks.

Someone hands me a drink, and despite knowing better, I tip it back anyway, like I'm chasing something I can't name.

Lena's dancing with Josh again, all hands and heat and laughter, while one of the new girls drags me into a TikTok she's filming on the dance floor. I don't even try to escape. I just pose like I was born to do it, tongue out, middle fingers up.

"Piper!" someone shouts behind me.

I turn to find Ben grinning like he just found the pot of gold at the end of the rainbow. "Okay, real talk? I didn't peg you for this."

I arch a brow. "For what?"

He gestures at me with a dramatic sweep of his drink. "For being like this. You're always so put-together at Blackwood. Like you'd call the manager if your cappuccino had the wrong milk."

"I'm a woman of many layers," I shout back, finishing what's left in my glass. "And FYI, I absolutely would call the manager on your ass."

"I bet you would, darling," he laughs, moving closer. "And you can definitely touch my ass."

I don't know what to say to that. So I wink and turn around.

The group explodes into another round of cheers when someone starts a dance circle. And when one girl grabs me and pulls me into the middle, I give them a ridiculous spin and shake my ass.

A few of them start chanting my name, and someone whistles. I'm fully aware that I'll cringe about this tomorrow, but right now? I feel electric. Limitless. Free.

When Ben hands me another drink, I scrunch up my nose after just one sip. It tastes off. Or maybe I've just had enough. But since I'm not

making good decisions right now, I still finish it.

Across the room, Lena and Josh are basically dry-humping against a neon pillar, lost in their own sweaty make-out haze. And me, I get lost in people watching. Not just them, but everyone moving around me.

Ben's so close I can feel his breath on my neck, and I'm not sure I like it. But when he offers me a fresh drink, I take it with a smile. The first sip tastes wrong, worse than the last drink; bitter, chemical, not the playful fruit-bomb I expected. I use the straw to swirl the liquid around in case it wasn't properly mixed.

"So, how are you liking it at Blackwood?" I ask, feeling like I ought to say something.

"It's alright," he says. "Better when you're around."

"Oh my God," I laugh, immediately booing. "Did you practice that one in the mirror?"

"Maybe," he says with a grin. "Want to see what else I've practiced?"

I nearly choke on my drink and laugh so hard I nearly drop it.

Somewhere in the back of my mind, a voice whispers that this is too much. But that voice is buried beneath the bass, glitter, and the way my body won't stop moving.

I know that stopping would be the responsible thing to do. But stopping means thinking, and thinking means dealing, and I'm so not ready for that. I like not thinking and just feeling. I'm drunk on the chaos and cocktails—and loving every goddamn second of it.

Ben stays by my side, making it hard to talk to anyone else. Every time I try, he interjects himself. Loud, laughing, always just a little too close. He dominates the conversation until people start drifting away, one by one, like it's not worth fighting to be heard.

Suddenly, everything feels too overwhelming. The lights and even the sounds. I blink slowly, feeling as though the world is buffering in real time. My arms are heavy, and my smile feels like it's been glued to my face. It's uncomfortably wide, like I can't control it.

I keep sipping the drink he gave me without thinking about it. I don't even know if it's the same one. It just… appeared in my hand again.

"You okay?" he asks, and his voice sounds like it's underwater.

I nod, even though I'm not sure. I feel floaty. Untethered. As though I'm dreaming someone else's dream and forgot the script. When I try to move away, intending to find Lena or maybe the bathroom, he catches my wrist and guides me toward the farthest wall.

"You're swaying," he says with a crooked smile. "Come with me for a sec."

I don't remember agreeing, but I'm following him, anyway. My body's lagging behind my brain, every step weirdly delayed. There's a buzzing in my ears that won't go away.

"Ben," I murmur, dragging his name out like I'm trying it on for the

first time. "I think I need water."

"You're fine," he says, tucking a strand of hair behind my ear while pushing me against the wall. His hand lingers. "You just danced too hard. You're cute when you party." He smells like cologne and beer, which is not a nice combo right now.

My head tilts, not quite on purpose. This doesn't feel right—I don't feel right. The thought disappears, slipping under the surface like it never existed at all.

He keeps talking, something about DJs and EDM festivals and how he once snuck backstage at Coachella. But his voice is syrupy now. Slow and too sweet, and I can't tell if it's charming or cloying.

Every time I blink, the world seems to skip a frame.

Ben shifts closer, his thigh pressing between mine. "You're a lot of fun when you let go."

Am I?

When he leans in and kisses me, I don't pull away, but I don't kiss him back, either. I just stand there as his kiss becomes more insistent, and his hand slides to my bare thigh, fingers inching beneath the hem of my skirt.

I need to put a stop to this. I try to stand straighter, to pull away, but it's like my limbs forgot how to respond. My pulse kicks up, not in excitement but in… something else. Panic? Nausea? I can't tell.

A part of my brain registers a change in the atmosphere. Harsh and loud voices blend with the music, and it sounds like people are scurrying away. I strain my ears, but it's so hard to focus when Ben's body presses closer.

He's grinding against me, rolling his hips like we're in the middle of the floor instead of half-hidden by shadows. My head tips back against the wall, dizzy from the motion. My fingers twitch at my sides. I try to say something, but my tongue's too thick in my mouth.

"Relax," Ben murmurs, dragging his lips along my jaw. "You're so tense."

I don't know what scares me more; how wrong this feels, or that my body isn't obeying me when I try to escape his lips on my throat. His hand keeps moving—fingertips skating higher, brushing the edge of my thong.

"Come on, babe," he whispers. "You're so fucking hot like this. Just let me—"

Something crashes nearby, and for the briefest moment, all sounds come to a stop.

"Get your fucking hands off her!" The familiar voice cuts through the noise like a blade; low, lethal, and full of promise. "No one touches my fucking toy."

And then… Ben's gone.

One second, his weight is pressing into me, and the next, I feel myself falling. I try to move my arms to catch myself, but nothing

happens. I close my eyes, preparing myself for an impact that never comes.

Strong arms catch me, one bracing my back, the other curving beneath my knees, lifting me like I weigh nothing at all. My head lolls against a shoulder that smells faintly of citrus and smoke.

Then everything fades and the world turns black.

She's weightless in my arms, a sleeping ghost. I carry her through the cold, white hall of Arlington Diagnostic & Preventive Services, anger biting at my control with every step. It smells like fucking antiseptic and failure, a reminder of how close I came to losing her.

Piper's head hits my shoulder, and for a moment, a brief, insane moment, I think she might be gone. But then I hear it—the slow, uneven sound of breath. It's not enough, and it won't be until she's awake.

Every step echoes. Every moment stretches.

My. Toy. Is. Fucking. Unresponsive.

Fuck!

If something permanent happens to her, I'll scorch the entire world.

My steps stay measured, but my breathing is anything but. Every inch of me is screaming to find that fucker and end him.

"We've got him, Enzo. Where do you want—"

Baring my teeth at Cy, I growl, "Not now." I don't fucking care that my anger is misplaced. Nothing matters until I know Piper's going to be fine.

I know my friend wants to know where to put Ben Jacks until I'm ready to deal with the low-life who drugged my toy, but I can't think about that right now. He'll figure it out.

Finally reaching the medical room, I give a sharp nod to Dr. Emily Voss, who's waiting. She's already gloved up, machines humming behind her. I called her the second Piper was in my arms to let her know we were coming.

"Vitals cart is ready. We've got tox panels standing by," Voss adds, businesslike. "Put her over there on the bed."

The second I lay her down, my hands itch to take her back. To pull her into my chest and shield her from the fucking world. I want to crush her to me and never let go. I want to lock her away until she understands that nothing—not even her—can match my fucking need to keep her.

"Fuck!" I roar, forcing myself to step out of Voss' way so she can do what needs to be done.

While she attaches monitors, I tell myself to calm the fuck down. My hands clench and unclench, and I want to drive them through the wall. But no, I need to remain calm.

"I'm going to draw some blood," Voss states in her prim tone. I give her a sharp nod, not looking away as she fits a needle into the crook of Piper's arm. "And I'll need a urine sample to confirm what's in her system," she states, efficiently prepping the next step.

"Whatever you need," I say through clenched teeth.

"She's out cold, so I'll need to use a catheter," she adds without flinching. "Standard procedure."

My nostrils flare. I hate the thought of anyone touching her like that. But this isn't about preference.

"I'll run a rapid tox screen," she mutters, tapping the vial with practiced fingers. "We should know what she took in under an hour. We've got a lab tech on-site to process the panel. Blood's being run now. Urine's next. I'll notify you when it's confirmed."

The rhythmic beep of machinery is the only sound I really hear. It's proof that my toy is still here, still breathing, still mine to drag back to the place she belongs. At my fucking side.

"Can you give us some privacy—"

"I'm not going any-fucking-where," I snarl, interrupting her.

She huffs, but doesn't argue as I stay close by, watching while she works. Well, mostly I watch Piper, who doesn't as much as flinch when Voss touches her.

While Voss runs tests, I run out of fucking patience. "What's taking so long?" I snarl.

"Her heart rate is irregular, but holding. Pupils are sluggish. My bet's on a fast acting benzo. Possibly alprazolam, or something in the same class." Voss glances up. "We'll confirm shortly."

"See that you do," I bark.

Voss acts like I haven't spoken at all as she continues her explanation. "I'll monitor her respiratory response through the night. If her breathing slows any further, we'll have to intubate."

My teeth grind and my fingers curl.

She adjusts the IV line and makes a final note on the chart. "There's nothing more you can do here, Lorenzo. She's stable enough for now. Let me do my job."

I don't move.

Her voice sharpens. "You want her to be okay? Then go burn off some of that rage somewhere else. You hovering won't help her breathe."

My glare cuts toward Voss, but she doesn't react. "Let me make myself as clear as I know how to," I growl. "I. Am. Not. Leaving."

Instead of cowering, she pins me with a glare of her own. "Just don't get in my way, Lorenzo."

She turns her attention back to the monitors and starts adjusting the IV drip. I stand just behind her, close enough to make her aware of my presence, but far enough that she can't accuse me of interference.

Voss works quickly, efficiently, then steps back, scribbling something onto a chart before peeling off her gloves. "I'll be back to check on her in twenty. If there's any change, hit the call button. The nurse will stay in the meantime."

A moment after she leaves, a younger woman steps in, trying to avoid making eye contact. Ignoring her, I pull a chair to Piper's side and sit, bracing one arm on my knee, the other wrapped tightly around her hand.

"Everything looks fine," the nurse says. "I'll be in the back if you need anything."

I don't look away from my toy, don't even bother to nod.

Time passes, but I don't measure it in minutes. I measure it in the number of times her fingers twitch beneath mine. In the slow rise and fall of her chest. In each fucking heartbeat that the machine insists on announcing like it's doing me a favor.

The nurse comes in every thirty minutes on the dot. She checks vitals and does whatever else she needs to do. Hell, she even makes polite noises that I completely ignore. Luckily, she stops trying after the third visit.

Cy sticks his head in at one point. "Still nothing?" he asks, his tone as grave as I feel.

"No."

He doesn't ask me anything else, he just comes over and squeezes my shoulder once. "Ben's locked down. He won't be a problem," he informs. "You want me to stay?"

"No." My voice is a knife. "And don't you dare fucking touch him, Cy. Ben's mine."

"Of course."

I order him to find everything he can on the Jacks family. I want to know where Ben's parents went to school, where they got married, what investments they've made. They don't know it yet, but they're about to lose everything.

Cy nods once before leaving again.

The nurse also leaves eventually, with a murmured, "She's stable. Call if you need anything."

As I reply with a one-word answer that barely registers in my brain, I keep staring at Piper like I can force her to wake up with sheer will. She looks like a wax doll as she lies there. Too still, and too fucking quiet.

Fuck!

I try to stop myself from thinking about what almost happened. But

with nothing else to do, the thoughts come rushing in. I squeeze my eyes closed, and let out a huffed breath.

My toy came close to being raped.

Raped…

It's the first time I allow myself to admit what I walked in on. Ben fucking Jacks drugged my toy and intended to rape her.

A feral growl builds in my throat, but I squeeze Piper's hand tighter, letting the touch calm me. I can't lose it here, not when she needs me. My breathing turns ragged from the effort, but I manage.

Rather than thinking about what could have happened if I hadn't found her in time, I force my thoughts on what will happen once she's safe.

Yeah, when I say his family is about to lose everything, I mean it. The only one who has to die is Ben. But the rest will be left to deal with the rubble. And when that bastard pays for what he did—because I will make him pay—I'll make sure he knows exactly why he's dying.

"They'll all fucking suffer," I vow as I drag my thumb across Piper's knuckles.

It's hard to imagine it was only this morning she came for me in her sleep. I miss her breathy moans. Fuck, I miss her sassy attitude. I'd give everything I have to hear her chew me out, it would be better than this hollow silence.

I don't know how long I sit like this. My back's stiff. My jaw's clenched so hard I might crack a fucking molar. I shift in the chair, careful not to disturb her. I can't stop staring at her. At the way her hair brushes her cheek. Leaning closer, I move the strand in case it bothers her.

"You were mine the second I saw you," I rasp, running my thumb up and down her palm. "And if you think I'm ever going to let you go, you're fucking mad."

Of course, she doesn't answer.

"Every time you run, I'll catch you."

The rest of the world fades away as I watch her sleep like it's the only thing I know how to do anymore.

Dr. Voss enters the room. "You're awake," she says, smiling. "If you want to let go and join me, I can give you a full update."

I straighten, only now realizing my forehead is resting on Piper's stomach, and I'm still holding her hand. Fuck, I must have fallen asleep. As I look toward the door, I notice Cy leaning against it.

"I've been keeping watch," he informs.

Looking at Voss, I shake my head. "I'm comfortable right here," I reply. "I'm not letting go."

She huffs softly, but instead of arguing, she catches me up on what I've missed. "She's been stable for the last two hours," Voss begins, her tone professional. "Breathing's regular, heart rate's back in a safer range. The tox screen confirmed Benzo. Fortunately, the dosage wasn't

lethal, so her liver's already processing it. But it'll be a slow ride."

My fingers tighten slightly around Piper's.

"I've got her on fluids, and we're keeping her under observation through the rest of the night. She'll sleep it off, most likely wake up groggy, confused. But I don't expect any long-term damage."

Relief punches through me, low and hot. I let out a breath I didn't realize I'd been holding.

"We'll need to monitor her for residual side effects such as headaches, memory gaps, and there is a possibility of severe nausea but nothing indicates lasting harm." Voss' voice softens. "You got her here in time."

"Of course I fucking did."

Voss doesn't respond to that. Just huffs and mumbles something under her breath about charging me millions so she can go on vacation. That makes my lips twitch and I almost smile at her back as she leaves again.

With Voss gone, Cy moves closer and clears his throat. "I've already had Static shut down. The owner lost his liquor license and the police have ransacked the place. You'll never guess how many drugs they found there."

"I want every person responsible charged as harshly as possible," I growl.

"Already one step ahead of you," Cy smirks. "Between the stash behind the bar and what staff had on them, no one's walking away clean."

"Good."

If it wasn't for the women who tagged my toy on social media, I wouldn't have even known she was out partying. Fuck, I almost didn't go to Static. I was torn between waiting for her in her apartment, and dragging her out of the club.

When I walked in, I still hadn't decided if I was going to drag her out by the hair or fuck her against a wall until she remembered who she belongs to. But when I saw Ben corner her and his hands all over her, all that mattered was getting him away from her.

I shift in the chair and reach up to cup Piper's cheek. Her skin is still warm, her breath steady. I swear I'd rip out my own fucking heart if it meant she'd open her eyes.

"You're safe now," I whisper. "And next time you run it better be toward me. Because if you run from me again, I'll chase you into Hell."

Now that I know she'll be fine, I can finally fucking breathe again. That doesn't mean I'm leaving. I'm staying put. And once she's ready to get out of here, I'll go back with her. Because if I've learned one thing, it's that I've given my toy way too much freedom, and that ends now.

I'm fading in and out of consciousness. My thoughts are muggy and unclear.

All I can smell is the pungent scent of chemicals, like a mixture of antiseptic and something I can't place. I try to move, but nothing's happening.

My skin tingles, and my limbs feel heavy. Wrong. Like I've been rewired while I was sleeping. I try to open my eyes, but my lids are too laden with exhaustion to move. My eyebrows twitch as I focus on breathing.

Where am I?

As I realize I can't answer that question, alarms vibrate under my skin, trying to rouse me. But I'm too tired. A part of me doesn't want to wake up. Apart from the smell, I'm actually quite comfortable. I'm warm, and the darkness calling me back with open arms is alluring. I think I'm smiling as I move toward it, letting it engulf me again.

"Can you hear me, Toy?"

"Leave her alone," someone snaps. A woman. "She'll wake when she's ready."

There's a low growl. "She fucking moved. I felt it."

The darkness loosens its grip on me enough that I can hear the soft beeps of a machine. The sound is almost hypnotic. Like a song I'm meant to answer, but I don't know how.

When I open my eyes, I'm met with a blinding white ceiling I don't recognize, and I immediately try to sit up. But wires snag at my body, holding me in place like tentacles. Panic climbs up my throat, making it hard to breathe.

I call out, my voice raw and fractured.

Beep. Beep. Beep.

My skin prickles under the scratchy sheets. I squeeze my eyes shut, try to shut out everything. But it's too much. My head throbs, and my limbs ache. I try to push up again, but the wires pull against me, and everything collapses.

"Easy, Little Toy." Enzo. His voice is the only thing I can hold on to. It's gravity. "I'm here." His hand tightens around mine, anchoring me.

I look into his eyes… wait. I can see more than that. I can see his entire face.

Not sure if I'm imagining it or not, I blink against the blur. But as my vision clears, I still see him. With no blindfold or Halloween masks, this is the first time I get an unobstructed view of him.

His face is all sharp lines, cheekbones that could cut diamonds, lips I know to be soft and demanding. His jaw is clenched tight as though it's the only thing keeping him from unraveling.

And those eyes… God, those piercing, cold and electric blue eyes. They keep me in place and strip me bare. My breath catches as I continue to stare. And he stares right back like I've finally caught up. Like he's been waiting for this moment longer than I can understand.

"What's happening?" My voice is hoarse, barely above a whisper.

"You're in my medical facility." He speaks so evenly, like that explains everything. "You're safe." I want to believe him, and when I focus on his eyes, I do.

I push up again, desperate to feel in control. To feel anything but helpless. But my head spins, the world going black. When I open my eyes again, he's closer. Leaning over me. He's so close his nose brushes my cheek, and I can feel his breath against my skin.

"Shh." He's relentless. "You'll be fine." I want to believe him. I want to not feel so lost. But I can't even remember getting here.

"Am I dead?" I ask.

He chuckles, but it sounds all wrong. "Try not to move," he says, his hand finding my shoulder, holding me in place. It feels solid, real. The wires slacken as I sink back against the bed. The room tilts, and I close my eyes, just for a moment. Just to shut out the brightness and the sharpness and the uncertainty.

When I open them, a woman is here. She moves quickly, efficiently. Checks the IV drip, checks the beeping machine, checks me. Her eyes are clear and unflinching, and I don't know why, but it makes my skin feel tight.

"You must be feeling disoriented." Unlike the room, her voice is warm and soothing. "But you'll make a full recovery." She doesn't ask. She states. Enzo's hand never leaves mine, not even as she examines me.

"Who are you?" The question takes too much effort. I'm too tired, too raw to care about the answer. "No, wait. I know you," I croak.

"Yes, we've met before. I'm Dr. Voss." She gives me a brief smile. "You're lucky to have someone so devoted." She nods toward Enzo,

but he doesn't react. His eyes are on me, searching, intense.

"What happened?" It's a struggle to keep my eyes open, to focus on anything but the heaviness of my own body.

"You were drugged." She checks the machine again, adjusts a setting I don't understand. Her fingers are quick and mechanical. "I've flushed your system, so you'll be fine. You'll need rest, but as I said, you'll make a full recovery."

"Drugged… rest," I repeat, the words sounding foreign, like something I've never heard before.

"I'm afraid so. Two weeks of complete bed rest should do it. And of course, I'll want to do some follow-up tests." She writes something on a chart, hands it to Enzo like he's the only one who needs to see it.

"Of course," I huff, not even bothering to hide my growing annoyance.

Dr. Voss presses her lips together in what looks like a tight line. I have the feeling it's to hide her smile. At least if the spark in her eyes is anything to go by. "We'll be monitoring your progress closely. But you're in good hands with this one." She pats Enzo's shoulder, and even though Dr. Voss is old enough to be my mother, I'm not okay with her touching him.

The lights blur around me, and just as I think I might pass out again, I feel him. The weight of his stare. The weight of his hand.

"Piper." God I love the way he says my name. He doesn't need to raise his voice, doesn't need to do anything but say my name. It roots me, pulls me back from the edge. "Tell the good doctor you understand. I need to get you the fuck out of here before I lose my mind."

"Yes." The word is a breath, a whisper. "I understand." I don't know if I mean it, but I know what he needs to hear. And maybe I need it, too.

"Good." She nods once, crisp and precise. "I'll make sure everything is ready so you can leave." Then she walks out. I watch her leave, feeling the sound vibrate in my bones.

"Enzo." It's the only word I can find, the only one that matters.

He releases my hand only long enough to brush hair from my forehead, knuckles grazing my cheek. "I'm here." He tucks a blanket around me, smooths it down, and I sink under the weight of it. Under the weight of him. The world narrows to his presence.

"Don't leave." The plea is ugly, too raw, but it's out before I can stop it.

"Never." He says it like a promise, like a threat.

I don't bother asking him why I'm here, I already know he won't answer me. Not until he deems it necessary for me to know. That should piss me off, right? Then again, denial has always been my best friend. Maybe that's why I'm content lying here until we can leave.

When Dr. Voss returns, she finally disconnects me from the tangle of wires like she's disarming a bomb. "Do you want your clothes back on before you leave?" she asks, gesturing at a bag with what I presume

to be my belongings.

"No," Enzo answers for me. "We'll be fine." He takes the time to shake her hand, smirking when he notices the way I narrow my eyes whilst slowly pushing myself up.

My feet barely touch the floor before Enzo scoops me up, grabs the bag, and carries me out. Each step is making me nauseous, so I close my eyes, not opening them again until I feel fresh air on my face.

Breathing hurts when the ice cold air hits my lungs, but it's a good hurt. I greedily inhale as deeply as possible, relishing the burn. It's making me feel alive.

"Wait," I insist when Enzo opens the car door.

He doesn't ask why, doesn't put me down, and doesn't seem impatient while I have a weird ass moment with the fresh air. Reaching up, I cup his cheek, running my fingers across the stubbled skin, all the way down to his lips. Damn, he looks really kissable right now.

Instead of taking advantage of seeing him for the first time, I sigh. "Okay, I'm ready to go."

He gently sets me down in the car. Then he slides in next to me, wrapping his arm around my body while telling the driver to go. I'm too tired to ask where we're going or who's driving. I just want to go back to sleep.

I must have dozed off because the next thing I know, Enzo's nudging me awake. "We're here," he announces softly.

He carries me into the building Teddy owns, refusing to let me walk. "You can put me down," I protest.

"I could." The corners of his lips lift, and he smiles. Damn, seeing his smile is something. "But I won't," he continues.

"I feel silly," I grumble as he unlocks my front door and carries me inside the apartment. If I'm honest, I'm not sure my legs could carry me right now, so instead of arguing further, I press my lips together.

"You're fucking beautiful." He says it like a decree. Like it's never been up for debate. No, he genuinely means it, and I hate that I believe him. That part of me preens under the weight of those words.

"Enzo, I—" He cuts me off with his mouth on my hair, a ghost of a kiss.

"You need to rest." That's not a suggestion, it's an order. His grip is firm, unrelenting. "Or do you want a shower first?"

Ugh, now that he's mentioned it, I definitely want a shower. "A shower would be nice. But I can walk by myself." I stubbornly lift my chin, surprised when he lowers me to my feet.

"As you wish," he smirks over his shoulder as he disappears into the bathroom, and I slowly trail after him.

God, why did I insist on walking? My legs are trembling, my balance shot to hell. I hate how weak I feel.

Don't get me wrong, I'm by no means one of those girls who can run miles without breaking a sweat. But I can usually walk my ass

around without feeling like I'm twenty-six going on eighty.

When I finally make it into the bathroom, Enzo's already running a bath. Steam rises from the tub. I walk over and sit down on the edge, letting out a deep exhale as I do.

"Need help to undress?" he asks, his eyes glinting.

It's only now I realize I'm wearing nothing but a hideous hospital gown. I still take him up on the offer. "Sure."

To my surprise, Enzo doesn't just untie the damn thing and rip it off me. He nudges my legs apart, kneeling between them. Then, with movements that are slow and measured, he unties it in the back. He moves as though he's afraid I'll break. Or maybe he's afraid I'm already broken.

Now there's a depressive thought.

Once I'm naked, I swing my feet into the tub and slowly lower myself into the scalding water. A gasp escapes me, and our eyes lock.

"Too hot?" he asks.

"No, it's perfect," I rasp. I'm about to tell him that I'm fine but the words dissipate on my tongue when he starts unbuttoning his shirt.

I don't know why, but I expected him to leave me to bathe on my own. He doesn't. He rids himself of all his clothes, unblinking as his penetrating blue eyes stay on mine. Then he slips into the water behind me. I feel the hard line of his body, the way he fits perfectly behind me.

He starts to wash me, taking his time. "Why?" The word spills out before I can stop it, unsteady and unsure.

"Because I want to." His mouth is close to my ear, his breath hot against my neck.

A moan slips out from between my lips as he lathers shampoo into my hair. "That feels so good," I admit.

I want to turn so I can study him, but his hands are insistent, pulling me back, and holding me in place.

"You don't have to do this." The words feel hollow. "I can wash myself."

He dips my head back, the water rushing over my scalp, drowning out everything but the sound of my own heart. "I want to."

His touch is gentle, but I can feel the intensity behind it. Sighing, I let myself sink back against his chest.

"You're tired," he says, the words a low rumble, the weight of his erection a constant against my spine.

"I'm not." It's a lie we both recognize. But he doesn't call me on it. He just holds me there, skin on skin, until the water goes cold and the rest of the world falls away.

I don't tell him that the reason I want to stay in the tub for as long as possible is that I'm scared what will happen once this bubble breaks. I'm not brave enough to demand answers. But I'm not blind either.

Something happened. Something I don't want to remember— because the second I do, everything changes. And with that thought

comes a lot of others. Like, where were we? A medical place, sure. But it wasn't a hospital. At least not a public one.

Every thought brings more questions with it, questions I'm not sure I'm ready to have answered.

"Why are you taking care of me?" I ask, feeling like that's a question I can handle the answer to.

Enzo tightens his hold on me. "Because you're mine, Piper. Mine in ways you haven't even begun to understand," he rasps.

"For this year, sure. But that doesn't answer my question," I huff.

He bends down, biting the lobe of my ear until I yelp from the sting. "You're not hearing me, Piper. You're mine, and you have been since I first saw you."

"At the interview," I feel the need to clarify.

"It was before that. I saw you on your birthday when you were at the Carroway Café," he corrects.

Stiffening, I demand. "Say that again." Surely I didn't hear him right.

"That's when I saw you. You were sitting by yourself, and—"

"Stop!" I shout. Before I can process what I'm doing, I push myself out of the tub and reach for the plush towel on the heat rack. "Why would you say that?"

Enzo rises from the tub like something dragged out of a dream—if dreams came soaked in sin and built to ruin you. My mouth goes dry as I drink him in. Every inch. Every goddamn detail. It's criminal how perfect he is.

He's tall, at least six-foot-four, which is so much taller than my measly five-foot-six. His jet black hair is slicked back from the water, and drops run down his broad shoulders. A trail of ink curls up his left arm in a full sleeve, and just above his heart, there's a tat of a black puzzle piece.

My chest tightens as I think about the pieces he left for me.

A wolf sits above his ribs, and beneath its fur are the Roman letters S.P.Q.R. There's a faint curved scar along his forearm, pale against his skin. And then… fuck, the cut abs, powerful thighs, and dusting of dark hair leading down from his stomach in a line I can't stop following.

His thick cock is pointing straight at me, and God of everything unholy, I can't help licking my lips. A low chuckle rolls from his throat as he takes a step toward me. When my gaze flies up, he arches a brow and wraps his hand around the base, stroking himself.

"Tell me, Toy, do you like finally seeing what you already fucking own?" he asks, his voice filled with gravel as he strokes himself once, slow and deliberate.

"Yes," I squeak.

My thighs press together without permission as I watch his hand move slowly—so slowly—and my lips part on a gasp I don't mean to make.

"You're wet for me already, aren't you?" He fists his dick harder.

Heat coils low in my belly, dark and liquid and impossible to ignore. I feel it, the wetness blooming between my thighs like betrayal.

I thought I had the upper hand. Thought I was just mad. But now he's working himself like it's a game he's already won—and my body is betraying me with every heartbeat.

It's not just arousal; it's a deep-rooted need. Raw and wrong and crackling under my skin. And the worst part? He fucking sees it. And still… I step closer. One foot, then another. I don't know if I want to slap him or drop to my knees.

With each step I take forward, Enzo takes one backward until he reaches the edge of the tub. He's still stroking himself as he sits down on the edge, completely unashamed. "Do you want a taste, Toy?"

I blink down at the tub. The water drains, the soft trickle slipping through the room like a whisper, even though I never saw him pull the plug. Looking back up, my gaze immediately settles on his thick, hardness. Even in his large hand it's still big.

Oblivious to my thoughts, he just sits there, watching me with that infuriating smirk. The kind that doesn't just promise I'll fall to my knees. It dares me to try to resist it. Dares me to pretend I haven't already lost.

I don't even realize I'm moving until I'm close enough to touch him. Rather than going directly for his erection, I press my lips to his forearm, right over the ink that twists like vines along his skin. I drag my tongue across it, tasting soap, salt, and something purely Enzo— and he fucking groans. Low and dark.

My hands glide over his chest as I shift so I can lick my way up his torso. His flesh damp and sweet beneath my tongue, lingering along each curve and line, tracing every ridge and groove.

His hands settle around my nape, urging me on. I draw slow circles on his skin with my tongue, tight little spirals around his nipple until his chest heaves and his breath quickens and his heart thunders like a distant storm.

"Fuck," he groans.

The space between us is electric, thick with unspoken needs. His eyes are the only things sharper than his jaw, colder than his resolve. He makes me work for every gasp, every groan.

When I bite into the soft skin of his neck, he finally gives me what I crave—a low, guttural growl, deep and raw. I whimper as his grip on me tightens, and he tilts my head back, exposing my throat.

He smirks down at me, slow and vicious, a wolf about to devour. "Don't stop, Toy," he demands. "Show me how greedy you are."

"Yes," I agree, my voice hoarse with want.

Enzo lets me take my time, lets me push and pull and break myself against his stillness. I suck a long, messy trail from his collarbone to his ribs, burying my nose in the hollow there, breathing him in.

Slipping lower, I press my lips to his hip, feeling the frantic pace of his blood just beneath the surface. I let my mouth brush against the tip of his cock, just enough to drive him wild. Then I lick the length of

him, once, twice, over and over, his breath comes quicker, his muscles straining beneath his skin.

"Look at you," he says, his voice filled with gravel. "You love this. You love having my cock in your mouth." I swallow the moan that almost escapes my lips.

His hands grip tighter, pulling me back up to his chest, his mouth hot against my ear. "Such a greedy little toy." I protest, not happy he stopped me from taking all of him into my mouth. "But if you want my dick, you have to ask."

I try to rear back, but he stops me. "Fuck you," I hiss.

"Not until you ask," he smirks. "And you better make it nice."

Anger stirs in my stomach, making me fight his hold. My nails dig into his chest, but he doesn't let me go. Not even when I break his skin.

"I'm not going to beg," I snap. "You just told me you've been fucking stalking me. How do I even know you're not the one who put me in the hospital?" The second the words leave my mouth I wish I could take them back.

Enzo's eyes darken, and all traces of his playfulness are gone. "You think I'm the one who hurt you?" he asks, his tone low and lethal. "You think I could ever hurt you?"

Before I can stop myself, I reply, "No." If I'm honest, I don't think he would. That's why I've been okay with leaning on him while remaining in denial about what happened to me. "No, I don't think so. I'm just... stop making me beg." At the last part, my voice rises.

"No," he stubbornly states. "Beg or I'll carry you to bed so you can sleep."

Closing my eyes, I inhale sharply and pinch the bridge of my nose. I'm tempted to beg, to give in to the constant ache between my legs. But no. I won't lower myself to do that.

"I won't do it," I hiss.

The words barely leave my mouth before Enzo moves us. Standing, he grabs my wrist and pulls me over to the sink, bending me over it. His hand presses between my shoulder blades, holding me down. My cheek hits the cold marble, my breath fogging the glass in front of me.

"N-no. Stop. Fucking stop," I cry while bucking and trying to pull myself free.

"You want to act like a fucking brat?" His hand tightens. "Then you'll take your punishment like one."

I gasp as his palm lands hard across one ass cheek—once, then the other. The sound echoes off the tiles. My thighs clench without permission. The sting blooms into heat. Shame and arousal twist inside me.

This is the second time he's spanking me, but this time it actually feels like a punishment rather than play.

"You think you're not begging, Toy?" His voice is cruel now. Calm and cruel and fucking devastating. "Your body's doing it for you. Your

tight cunt is so wet you're dripping on the floor."

Then he drags the tip of his cock through my soaked folds at an agonizingly slow pace. It's a cruel reminder of how ready I am for him because it proves how pathetic my resistance was.

"You feel that?" he breathes against my ear, voice so low I barely catch it. "That's your cunt begging for me while your mouth lies."

I hate how true it is. I hate how much I need him to keep going. And I really hate how much I love the sound of his voice when he's being like this.

"You don't get to accuse me and walk away clean." He moves so the tip is positioned perfectly against my soaked opening. But he doesn't push in. "I take care of you. I protect you. I fucking own you."

"Then fucking act like it," I choke out, the sob slicing through before I can stop it. "Stop playing games. Prove I'm yours."

He chuckles darkly, lips brushing my ear. "Life is the game. You're either the one pulling strings or dangling from them."

"Except you," I hiss.

He tisks. "You still don't get it," he murmurs, squeezing my ass hard enough to leave a mark. "You're the one pulling my string, Little Toy."

I'm so surprised by his words that I can't think of anything to say.

While I try to process what he just said, I feel him moving behind me. He reaches for the closet, but I don't check to see what he's looking for, or if he's found it when he slams the door closed.

I flinch hard when something cold kisses my inner thigh. I glance down—and ice sluices through my veins at the sight of my spare electric razor.

"What are you doing?" I gasp, my throat tightening as fear needles down my spine.

The sleek handle is cool against my skin, deliberate and slow as he drags it upward—closer to my center. It's not switched on, but I still don't want the blade anywhere near my pussy.

"Let me go," I demand. I begin fighting him again, doing my best to somehow slip free.

"Careful," he rasps, dragging the blade higher. "It'd be a shame to scar your perfect cunt."

"Stop it," I whisper, the breathiness betraying the terror clawing up my throat. I rise to my tiptoes, desperate to put more distance between myself and the blade. "I'm not kidding, Enzo."

He laughs low in his chest. "Look at me," he orders, voice dragging over my skin. "In the mirror, Toy. Now."

But I can't. I can't fucking look away from the shaver that's slowly moving closer. With a low growl, he fists my damp hair, jerking my head up so I'm forced to face the mirror. Sweat beads across my brow and lip. I'm shaking, begging—until the cold touches my folds and I go still, trapped by terror.

"P-please don't," I gasp, fear coiling tight in my stomach, rooting me to the spot even as every instinct screams for me to run.

The blade doesn't move. It lingers—silent, patient—a whisper of cool metal teasing the slickest part of me. My whole body turns to stone, breath caught somewhere between a scream and a moan.

"You're scared," he murmurs, voice like dark velvet behind me. "But not of me."

"Yes, I am," I cry, even though I'm not sure I believe it.

"No," he says, smirking at me as he drags the flat of the razor along the curve of my clit with surgical control. "You're scared because you're soaking wet for me. Scared because your cunt's drenching a fucking blade."

I sob, high and sharp.

"You don't want to run," he breathes. "You want to be wrecked. You want me to decide how far we go."

And I do. I hate that I do. That I'm shaking and crying and so fucking wet I can feel it coating my thighs.

"Look at what I'm doing to you," he commands, slackening his hold on my hair so I can tip my head down.

I look at the smooth foil head—wide and flat, built for legs or bikini lines—not for being pressed against my clit like Enzo's doing. Logically, I know it can't cut me when it's not switched on. The foil has a protective mesh over the blades. But… logic isn't what's driving me right now.

"Enzo," I gasp. I don't know if I'm asking him to stop or to keep going.

"Keep watching," he rasps, pressing the razor harder against my clit.

I whimper at the sensation. I want to look away and to tell him to stop, but I can't do either. It's physically impossible for me to tear my gaze away, and I can't stop the pleasure singing in my veins either.

"Enzo."

"That's it, Toy," he encourages, adding more pressure.

My breathing shatters into ragged gasps, each pass of the blade winding me tighter. "Enzo!" My pussy contracts, and I need… I need… fuck. I don't know what I need.

"I've got you," he groans. Then he lets go of my neck, sliding his hand to my throat. "Are you ready to come?"

Before I can answer him, he squeezes tighter, making it nearly impossible for me to breathe. In frustration, I turn my head, and when my lips graze his arm, I bite down. The grunt he lets out goes straight to my pussy.

"Oh, God!" I croak, barely able to speak with the pressure on my throat.

A few more swirls is all it takes before I rapture. An orgasm unlike anything I've experienced before tears through me. It's almost painful, making me squeeze my eyes closed.

"No. Look at me in the mirror," he commands.

My eyes fly open, obeying his command. Our eyes lock, blue on green, and I feel like he's underneath my skin. That's how powerful the connection is.

He barely gives me time to recover before I feel him removing the razor from my pussy. But his gaze stays on mine, locking me in place, despite my trembling legs. I'm just about to ask what he's doing when I feel something thick between my pussy lips.

"Is that…" The words die on my tongue.

But I don't need to, Enzo knows what I mean. "It is," he confirms, pushing the razor handle into me.

I try to fire back—something smart, something venomous—but it dies on my tongue the second he thrusts it all the way inside my pussy, pushing me down at the same time.

"Fuck!" My scream is muffled by my own palm as my body jerks forward against the sink. He doesn't pause.

He just adds pressure to the hand between my shoulder blades, ensuring I'm not going anywhere while he pistons the handle in and out of my drenched sex. Each time he pushes it in, it slams me into the counter, my breasts dragging across the cold marble, my skin burning where it meets the chill.

"Wanted to be a little brat, Toy? Wanted to test me?" he growls, slamming me harder against the counter with each thrust. "Then you get fucked by plastic instead of my hard dick that's throbbing for you."

His hand slides up my spine and fists in my hair, yanking my head up so I can see my reflection. My cheeks are flushed and my eyes glossy as my mouth opens in shock and pleasure. And behind me, Enzo

is all dark muscles and sharp control.

He's relentless and so fucking mine.

"Look at yourself," he snarls. "You made this happen. You made me like this. And you've never looked more perfect, Toy."

Tears prick my eyes, but they're not from pain. Not even from pleasure. I'm overwhelmed and so fucking confused I barely recognize myself right now. My body wants him, that much is true. But I don't know if I want him, or if he's just that good at playing me.

"Stop thinking," he demands, fucking me harder. "You want this. You want me. Why do you keep lying to yourself by fighting it?"

"I don't want you," I gasp, but we both know it's a lie.

"Say it." He thrusts the handle almost all the way into me, keeping it there. "Say who you belong to."

"No one," I hiss, willing to say just about anything to deny my thought about him being mine. He isn't.

Enzo angles his hand so the heel presses against my clit, roughly rubbing it until I'm a whimpering, trembling mess. "Stop lying," he demands.

Instead of answering him, I press my lips together.

"If you come on the handle, Toy, you belong to me," he growls. "And if you don't say it out loud, I'll continue to fuck it out of you."

I don't bother protesting; I know my body well enough to know he's going to make me climax. But I'll be damned if I'm going to act like this is okay. I asked him to stop, and he didn't. So I'm not going down without a fight. I find his gaze in the mirror, keeping my eyes on his while he expertly works my pussy.

"Mhmm, your cunt's clenching so tight. I can feel the resistance." His voice is filled with gravel.

I'm unable to keep my moans at bay, but I still don't give him any words. Not even when he tilts the handle, so it hits that magical spot inside me.

He hisses, pushing into me so hard the mirror rattles. "You're mine. You've always been mine."

His hand doesn't stop grinding against my nub, even as I shake my head in desperate defiance. My thighs tremble, my breath hitches, my walls flutter around the handle, betraying every word I haven't said.

He groans, low and vicious. "You're going to soak this handle for me, Toy. And when you do, you'll know exactly who you fucking belong to."

I bite my lip so hard it bleeds, desperate to keep the sob inside me from becoming a moan. I can't let him win. I can't. He circles harder, faster, making it impossible to keep my sounds locked down tight.

I come with a broken scream, my body convulsing, my release hitting me so hard I nearly collapse. The pleasure is blinding, savage, humiliating—and still, I chase it. I grind against the plastic like a broken toy that's forgotten how to do anything else.

"There she is," he purrs, the words dripping with triumph. "My greedy, lying little toy."

He continues to fuck me with the handle.

"You're mine," he grits. "Say it, Piper. Or I'll make this last all day."

My mouth opens—but I don't know if it's to defy or beg him. I don't know anything anymore. Just him. "I'm yours," I whisper, broken and breathless.

I barely register it when he removes the handle and replaces it with his cock, sheathing himself inside me with one vicious stroke.

"Yes. You. Are," he hisses through clenched teeth. "And now that you've finally admitted it, you can have what you refused to beg for."

Enzo grabs my hips, holding me so hard it hurts. I whimper and moan, my pussy clenching around him as though it's trying to keep him inside me.

I have no idea how I manage to stay upright, but I do. I never look away, and I never falter while he fucks me like he's using his dick to punish me. It aches in a way that's addictively delicious.

Rolling my hips, I meet him stroke for stroke, moaning and chanting his name as another orgasm builds inside me.

"Enzo!"

"Fuck. Come on my dick, Toy," he groans.

He slams into me one last time and comes with a growl that sounds more like possession than pleasure. The primal sound, paired with the way his length swells inside me, is enough to send me crashing over the edge again.

His body collapses over mine, chest heaving, mouth pressed to my shoulder. And then—just like that—the violence fades from him as he kisses the back of my neck, soft and unhurried.

"Let me take care of you," he murmurs.

I brace myself against the counter as he crouches behind me, and then I feel it—warm, damp cloth against my swollen, oversensitive pussy. He wipes away his cum slowly, thoroughly, like he's cleaning up something precious.

He presses a kiss to the inside of my thigh, then another just above my ass. Worshiping the body he just used like a weapon.

"You did so well for me," he says softly, reverently. "So fucking perfect."

I want to argue. I want to snarl at him, maybe scream. "You should leave," I finally say, barely recognizing my voice.

"And why's that?" he asks, amused.

"Because I think I hate you right now." With those words, I turn on my heel and make my way into the bedroom, ready to let the bed swallow me.

Of course, Enzo doesn't make it easy. He follows me into the bedroom, not bothering to get dressed before sliding in beside me on

the huge bed.

"You think hate scares me?" he asks in a low and amused tone. "Hate's just love wearing its fangs. You can gnash at me all you want, Toy. I'll still be the one you bite down on."

I pull the sheet up to my chest, wishing it were armor, but all it does is trap me beside the man who just ruined me—and now wants to cuddle like he didn't. He doesn't touch me; just lies there, breathing quietly and steady, like he's waiting.

"Stop acting like this is normal," I whisper.

"What's normal, Piper?" he replies, calm as ever. "People lie to each other. Hurt each other. Leave. But you and me? We fit. And whether you admit it now or later, you'll never belong to anyone else."

I turn my back to him, but it's useless. I still feel him. His warmth. His words. His fucking presence curling around me like smoke.

33

Lorenzo

It doesn't take long until my toy's fast asleep again. Still at her back, I listen to the way her breath catches, then releases. I count the seconds between one, two, three. I brush my thumb across the blue vein mapping her wrist, timing her pulse against my own.

Even though I feel her skin against mine, I still have to remind myself that she's safe now. The relief I feel is unfamiliar, almost caustic in its intensity. I don't name it. Names have power, and I already know what this is.

I trace the edge of the bruise blooming on her arm where the IV punctured her skin. But as soon as I touch it, Piper's face scrunches up, and she whimpers in her sleep and presses her body harder against mine.

"You're safe, Toy," I murmur, stroking her everywhere I can reach.

At my words, she relaxes again. Her face is slack in sleep, defenseless. The sight of it strikes something primal in me. Then, the corner of her mouth twitches, and I hope she's dreaming about me.

I lie with her until I become too restless to remain still. As I get out of bed, I'm careful not to disturb her. Cold air hits my bare skin as I move to the bathroom where my clothes lie scattered across the tile.

When I dress, I do it slowly. Button by button. Cuff by cuff. The ritual of reclaiming control when everything around me threatened to unravel hours before. My reflection in her mirror is composed, but my eyes tell a different story. They're black with purpose.

Before I leave the bathroom, I touch the sink. I can still feel her cunt squeeze me as I fucked her right here. Fuck, maybe I should dismantle the sink and keep each tile as a momento of our first time together.

Smirking, I leave the bathroom and retrieve the bag with

everything my toy had on her when I found her at Static. Even though she looked sexy as sin, I refuse to let her keep the clothes Ben touched.

My jaw locks so suddenly my molars ache, and in five furious steps, I'm at her kitchen trash, dumping every item of clothing without ceremony. They'll never touch her skin again.

It's far from the first time I'm in my toy's home, but it feels like I'm seeing it with fresh eyes as I look around. Everything here screams her, and I take my time drinking it all in. This is her home, a place she loves.

In the past, I've heard people say that home is where your heart is. It never made sense to me until now. I thought my luxury apartment filled with items I don't care about was home. But it's not—this is.

Seeing my toy swaying at that club, eyes unfocused, and with Ben's fucking hands on her, changed everything. I'm never leaving her alone again. That leaves two options; either she moves into my penthouse, or I move in here. I'm choosing the latter for us.

My phone vibrates in my pocket, and when I fish it out, I have a few texts from Cy asking for an update. I ignore him for now and call Maria, who answers on the first ring despite the hour.

"Lorenzo?"

"I'm moving in with Piper," I say without preamble. No space between the words for questions or concerns. "I need things brought over. And I need to replace some of her stuff."

The silence stretches, and I know I've surprised her. But instead of letting it show, she asks, "How soon?"

"Now."

She yawns loudly, and I pretend not to hear her cursing me for calling her like this with no notice.

"Oh, one more thing," I grin. "Dr. Voss put us on bedrest for two weeks, so I need you to cancel my schedule. No face-to-face meetings with anyone but you and Cy."

She huffs. "Dr. Voss put you on bedrest?"

"She put Piper on bedrest, which means I'm on bedrest. So, yes," I clarify.

"I see." There's a faint tap of keys as she makes notes. "The usual selection of clothes, toiletries—"

"And food," I interrupt. "And something comfortable for Piper to wear."

While Maria takes notes, I explain the outfit Piper wore at Static, so we can replace it. Then I move on to listing off some options that she likes to wear when she's at home. Yoga pants, oversized shirts and stuff.

"Nothing restrictive," I finish.

"And what food would you like?" she asks, staying on task.

I remove my phone from my ear and look at the email from Voss explaining Piper's do's and don'ts. "Coconut water, herbal teas, and light food." I go into more detail as I mention a few of the meal ideas Voss gave me.

"You know, I can arrange a private nurse," she offers. "Someone discreet, with security clearance."

I feel my body go rigid at the suggestion, a visceral no that surprises even me. "No nurse. No security team inside. I'll handle her care myself."

"Got it." There's a short pause before Maria speaks again. "And when you say you're moving in, do you—"

"I mean that I'm moving in," I state. "I'll keep my place so you don't need to fill out a change of address card."

Of course she's surprised, and I don't blame her. In the years she's worked for me, I've never moved into a woman's space. I've never adjusted my schedule to accommodate someone else.

Before ending the call, Maria repeats what I've asked for, and assures me I'll receive everything shortly. Being a Russo opens just about any door, so I know she'll get it done.

With that out of the way, I double-check the bag doesn't hold anything Piper will need. That's when I find her phone. It's dead, the black screen a void like the hours she's just lost.

I plug it into the charger beside her bed, watch it vibrate to life with a spasm of notifications. Lena's name appears five, seven, twelve times. Each message is more desperate than the last. A digital panic that came too late to prevent anything. The slew of where are you, I'm worried, and are you okays are useless.

Lena's guilt won't undo shit. She failed. She let my toy get poisoned and pawed at in a room full of strangers. Piper could've died—and Lena was too busy. The thought hits like a hammer. This is what happens when I allow others to protect what's mine.

With a scoff, I silence the phone without reading the rest. What good is guilt now? What use are Lena's concerns when the damage is done? The phone keeps lighting up, persistent as a wound that won't close. I place it screen-down on the nightstand and turn away.

Behind me, Piper stirs—a small noise, a shift of her leg against the sheets—but doesn't wake. I check her breathing again. It's still steady. But I don't like how deep she's sleeping, or that she's sleeping this long. I haven't had time to feed her, which can't be good.

Something dark flickers in my chest. It's been hours. She should have shown some sign of waking by now. Not willing to leave anything to chance, I call Voss.

"She hasn't moved," I say when she answers, my voice a growl of accusation. I proceed to explain how long my toy's been asleep, expecting it to worry the doctor like it's doing to me.

"That's to be expected," Voss replies, her tone steady despite being woken.

"How long?" I demand.

"It could be…" She pauses, calculating. "… four to six more hours, perhaps. Maybe longer. Her body is recovering from multiple traumas, Lorenzo."

I pace to the window, watching the deserted street outside. "And if she doesn't wake?"

"She will." Voss's certainty is professional, detached. "Her vitals were strong when I left. Unless you're noticing labored breathing or extreme pallor—"

"No."

"Then let her rest. It's the best medicine right now."

After ending the call, I process her words. She said as much to me before I took Piper home, and I trust Voss implicitly. It just doesn't feel like enough. I'm not built for situations where there's nothing to do but fucking wait. There's no way I'll be at peace until Piper's eyes are open.

Three soft knocks on the door jerk me from my thoughts, and when I go to open it, Maria and Cy are there. While my assistant looks as put together as always, Cy's scowling.

"This one dragged me out of fucking bed," he seethes.

Maria rolls her eyes, pointing toward Piper's living room. "Stop whining and carry the things in there."

It's only now I notice Cy's arms are loaded with garment bags while Maria's balancing a box on her hip.

Noticing my gaze, she straightens. "Some food," she explains, already walking into the kitchen. "It's nothing fancy. Just some soup that can be reheated once Piper's up for it."

While she talks, Cy empties Maria's car, carrying in more boxes than I know what to do with. But considering they're both here in the middle of the night, I'm not going to question them.

Once we're done, I turn to Maria. "You should buy yourself something—"

"Pretty," she finishes for me, smiling slyly. "You bought me a new car only last week, so I'm fine. But Christmas is coming up, and you could always show your generosity then."

I chuckle while I usher them out. Maria always buys her own presents. If I'm honest, I don't even know how much she spends, but whatever she deems generous, she'll get.

"Oh, wait. One more thing," Maria says, coming to a stop. "I wasn't able to move the Morrison meeting. However, I changed it to video call. Everything else has been moved."

"Thank you." I look at Cy over her shoulder. "Both of you."

He nods. "The perimeter is secure so if you don't need anything else, I'm getting my ass back to bed."

After mumbling my thanks, I lock the door behind her and Cy. Then I begin the methodical process of unpacking. I hang suits next to Piper's dresses in her closet, place my razor on the sink, and my toothbrush next to hers.

With everything put into their new space, and food stored in the fridge, I walk back into the bedroom. I frown, not liking that she's still

practically comatose. Right now, I'm longing for her to wake up even if it means she's going to fight me. Anything would be better than this silence.

Sighing, I strip, methodically removing each piece of clothing. Then I slide back between the sheets. My toy's body radiates heat like a furnace, and I quickly check her forehead to see if she's running a fever. I don't think she is.

Lifting the sheet, I check her body, needing to see for myself that she's okay. There's a bruise forming on her hip that I don't recognize—not from my hands, not from my mouth.

It could be from the club, perhaps. A collision with something as innocent as a table corner or a doorframe. Yet, it makes me angry. Because if she stumbled, it could be because of Ben. Which means she's wearing a bruise from another man.

I brush my thumb across it, feeling the subtle heat of damaged capillaries beneath her skin. By morning, it will be purple. By next week, green. By the end of the month, gone. But that's not soon enough.

My touch tightens, and I dig my fingers in firmer. I stop when she groans in her sleep, deciding that now isn't the time. I need to let her sleep, and I can replace the bruise tomorrow. The ownership I feel isn't abstract. It's visceral, physical, as real as bone. The games are over. No more blindfold. No more manipulation from the shadows.

34

Piper

My bladder wakes me before my brain does—a screaming, urgent pressure that sends me stumbling to the bathroom. The tiles bite cold against my bare feet as I shuffle, eyes half-closed, toward relief.

Once I'm done and have washed my hands, I splash cold water on my face in an attempt to regain full consciousness. It works, and as I reach for my toothbrush, I realize it isn't alone. Next to my rose-colored electric toothbrush is a black one I've never seen in my life.

There's also an electric shaver on my sink, expensive-looking, matte black. Next to it sits shaving cream I've never purchased. My fingers hover over it, not quite touching, as if it might bite.

"What the fuck?" I mutter, squinting at my reflection. My hair is a nest of tangles, my eyes puffy and underlined with smudged mascara.

I look like I've been through a war, which isn't entirely inaccurate. Memories of Static flicker through my mind, but they're fragmented, like someone took scissors to a film reel.

My hands tremble as I grab my robe, throw it on, and cinch it tight at the waist. Ready for battle, I push the door open, words of rage building in my throat. But as I walk back into my bedroom, the words dissipate.

"Why are you still here?" I ask, accusation heavy in my tone.

Enzo sits on my bed like he has the right—like a dark king surveying his rightful domain. The sheet pools around his waist, exposing a torso that belongs in an Italian Renaissance painting—all lean muscle and smooth skin. His hair falls across his forehead. He looks like sin incarnate, and he knows it.

"Tell me you didn't move in while I was asleep," I say, aiming for dry humor but landing somewhere between disbelief and horror.

His eyes, so blue they seem almost artificial in the morning sun, lock onto mine. "Yes," he says simply.

One word. No explanation. No apology. Just confirmation that this man has invaded my space, planted his flag, and expects me to accept it.

"No," I snap, crossing my arms over my chest. "Absolutely not. I appreciate the knight-in-shining-armor routine at Static, but that doesn't give you permission to…" I wave my hand around frantically, "… to colonize my apartment. You need to leave."

He doesn't move. Not an inch. Not a muscle. He just watches me with those eyes that see too much, that strip away pretense and leave me feeling naked despite the fabric wrapped around me.

Smirking, Enzo stands in one fluid motion, the sheet falling away entirely. He's completely naked and completely unashamed. I try to look away, but my body refuses the command from my brain. My eyes track down the defined planes of his chest, the narrow trail of dark hair that leads to…

"Enjoying the view?" he asks, quirking an eyebrow.

When I just shake my head and press my lips together, he lets out a deep laugh. Then he reaches for his pants and pulls them on without underwear. The fabric settles low on his hips, and I hate that it's somehow more erotic than his nudity.

"Come," he says, already walking. "There's something I want to show you, Toy."

Against every scrap of common sense I possess, I follow him out to my living room. He doesn't wait to see if I will; he just expects it. The worst part is that he's right.

My breath catches when I see what now hangs on the far wall. A framed puzzle—a portrait of my face, rendered in tiny, interlocking pieces. It's stunning in its detail… so intimate it feels like surveillance disguised as art. Perfectly capturing the flecks of gold in my eyes, and the scar in my eyebrow that even I forget exists.

But what makes my stomach drop are the eight blank spaces where no piece resides. "What the…" I trail off and shake my head.

"The missing ones are the ones you burned," he explains without prompting.

My heart slams against my ribs so hard I'm surprised it doesn't break through. Now I finally see what the pieces I destroyed were; parts of me.

It's obsessive. Deranged. A violation dressed as devotion. And still… part of me wants to be seen like this. My fingers touch my lips as I realize the horrible truth. I like being the object of such dedicated obsession.

I continue to stare at the missing pieces, at the spaces I've created, and feel something hot and dangerous blooming in my chest. Something that makes my skin tingle and my breath quicken.

Needing to distract myself, I turn and head toward the kitchen. "I

don't think it goes with my furniture," I dryly say over my shoulder. "And I don't like looking at myself."

Enzo doesn't even bother responding, but his answering chuckle grinds on me. This isn't funny at all. It's disturbing, and wrong on too many levels to count.

In the kitchen, I head straight for the coffee maker. My fingers have just touched the canister of beans when his hand closes around my wrist. The contact is electric and shamefully welcome.

"No caffeine," he says, voice quiet but final. Like the decision was made hours ago.

I jerk my arm away. "Excuse me?"

"Your system is still processing the drugs." His tone is matter-of-fact, devoid of condescension but allowing no argument. "Caffeine will make it worse."

"So will dealing with you without coffee," I mutter, but something in me, some treacherous part, is touched by his concern.

He opens the refrigerator, retrieving a bottle I know for a fine fact I didn't buy. "You can have coconut water." Then he gestures to a wooden box on the counter I definitely didn't own yesterday. "If you insist on something hot, there's caffeine free herbal tea."

I want to hurl both options at his perfectly sculptured head. I want to tell him that I'm a grown woman who can decide what goes into her own body. The irony of this thought, after Ben literally drugged me, isn't lost on me.

Enzo moves through my kitchen like he's done it for years. Confident hands opening cabinets that should be unfamiliar, finding things I didn't even know I owned. I watch from the doorway, arms crossed over my chest.

The muscles in his back flex as he reaches for a pan, and I hate that I notice. I hate that my eyes track the movement, that my body registers it while my mind screams in protest.

"What are you doing?" I ask, half curious.

"Cooking you breakfast," he answers without stopping.

With my eyebrows raised, I sit down at the small table. For a few moments I just look out the window, wondering if this is even real. But when I turn my attention back to him, he's still there.

"You don't have to cook for me," I argue. "I can feed myself."

As he just continues his silent, efficient invasion of my space, I open the coconut water, gulping half the bottle down.

"Did you go shopping?" I ask, finding it hard to picture him walking along the supermarket aisles.

"I had them brought in." His back is still to me as he stirs something that smells disarmingly good. "Your pantry was… insufficient."

"For someone who wasn't invited, you're awfully critical," I volley, but it lacks the bite I intended. My throat is dry, and the coconut water is actually helping.

Soon enough, he's sliding a bowl of what looks like porridge across the small table to me. It's not just oatmeal—there are berries, sliced almonds, a drizzle of honey. It looks Instagram-worthy, which only irritates me more.

I'm quick to tell him thank you, but for some reason, it sounds insincere. I'm pretty sure he thinks so as well, because he arches an eyebrow as he sits down next to me.

Rather than bothering with more words, I dig in. "Oh, my God!" I exclaim after the first few bites. "This is delicious." I feel a bit ridiculous for praising porridge like it's a five star meal, but it kind of is. The extras he's added hit my palate perfectly.

"Glad you're enjoying it."

When I'm almost half-done, I notice he isn't eating. But when I question it, he just grunts something about not eating breakfast. Fucking hypocrite. I don't say that though, not when I'm enjoying the food this much.

Once I'm done, I lean back in the chair and pat my stomach with a smile that he doesn't return. In fact, he looks downright grumpy. It's making me feel bad for… no, wait. I have nothing to feel bad about. I didn't ask him to come here.

Even so… there's still something I need to say. I stare at him, trying to formulate the words. "Thank you," I start, the phrase feeling awkward and insufficient, "for what you did at Static. I don't remember everything, but I know you stopped… whatever was happening."

Gah, I sound like a rambling idiot.

He watches me with those piercing eyes, waiting for more. Always waiting. Always three steps ahead.

"I wasn't there looking for a hookup," I continue, feeling defensive without quite knowing why. "I was pissed at you for…" I stop, the words jamming in my throat. About what? The somnophilia? That's not something I can just casually mention.

"For what?" he presses.

"Doesn't matter." I avert my gaze, absentmindedly pushing a leftover berry around with my spoon. "I needed to get out of my own head for a while. So after brunch with Lena, I agreed to go to Static. I just wanted to have some fun." The last part comes out almost like a hiss. Talk about backfiring.

"It doesn't matter why you were there." His voice hardens slightly. "What matters is that no other man will ever touch you again."

The declaration should infuriate me. It should make me stand up and tell him exactly where he can shove his possessive bullshit. Instead, something warm and dangerous pools low in my belly. No one has ever wanted me so completely before. It's terrifyingly intoxicating.

"Right, because you're the only one who gets to touch me without asking." The words escape before I can stop them, bitter and sharp.

His expression doesn't change, but something shifts in his eyes—a

darkening, a focusing. "You're referring to me eating your cunt while you were sleeping."

I nearly choke on my porridge. "Of course I am," I shout, angry all over again. "What even made you think I'd want that?"

"It was on your kink list, Toy," he replies smoothly. "And I always aim to please."

"That's not… I didn't…" Pinching the bridge of my nose, I center myself. Completely ignoring the warmth pooling in my lower stomach. "You violated my consent, Enzo."

"Did I?" His head tilts slightly. "Your list made it clear it was something you wanted to explore."

"Not by a stranger. And not without talking about it first." My voice rises again, but inside, I'm a mess of contradictions. My mind says violation, but my body—my treacherous body—says yes, more, please.

"Tell yourself whatever you need to," he murmurs, eyes dipping to my silk-covered chest. "But your body tells the truth."

I yank the edges of my robe closer together, face burning. "Fuck you."

"Perhaps later." Standing up, he takes my empty bowl and places it in the sink. "I'm going to shower."

I say nothing, just sit there simmering, waiting for him to disappear into the bathroom. The moment the door closes, I count to sixty in my head, then make my move. I tiptoe to the hallway, intending to put on a pair of boots, my long coat, and get the fuck out of here.

As soon as I reach the door, I find him there. He's leaning against it, arms crossed over his bare chest, eyes knowing. Not only did he move without making a sound, he predicted exactly what I would do.

Fuck.

"You have two options," he states, voice deceptively soft. "Shower with me, or I tie you to the bed while I shower."

My mouth opens, but no words come out. He's not joking. There's not a hint of humor in his eyes, not a trace of uncertainty in his stance.

So I shower with him. The water is hot, steam rising between us like the tension neither of us acknowledges. I try to avoid looking, but that's damn near impossible. His body is a work of art—all lean muscle and purpose.

Afterwards, we get dressed without speaking; me in leggings and an oversized sweater, him in the tailored black pants and a crisp white shirt that appeared from somewhere while I was sleeping.

The silence has teeth. It gnaws at the spaces between us, forging my questions into weapons I'm not sure I'm ready to wield.

I sit on the edge of the bed, watching him button his cuffs with precise, unhurried movements. My fingers twist in the hem of my sweater, betraying the anxiety I'm trying to hide.

"How did you know?" The words tumble out before I can polish them. I swallow hard, heat crawling up my neck. "About the

somnophilia. About my kink list. Nobody but Lena knows about that.”

Enzo doesn't look up, doesn't pause in his methodical dressing. “I cloned your phone the day of your interview.”

The simplicity of his confession steals my breath. Not an apology, not an excuse—just a statement of fact delivered with the same inflection someone might use to comment on the weather.

“You what?” My voice rises, thin and sharp. “That's illegal. That's… that's…” I search for a word terrible enough to encompass this violation and come up empty.

“Yes,” he agrees, finally meeting my eyes. His are calm, untroubled by my outrage. “It is.”

And the worst part—the absolute worst part—is that beneath my anger, beneath the righteous indignation, there's a twisted little flicker of… flattery?

The idea that this man wants me enough to break laws, to burrow into the most private parts of my digital life just to know me better is… no. It's sick, and it's wrong. So why is it making me wet?

I shake my head, trying to dislodge the thought. “What about Georgetown? My internship?” I ask, needing to change the subject. Then a thought hits me. “Wait… is the internship even real?”

“Of course it's real,” he states, his tone making it clear he considers that a stupid question.

“So why can't I go? Am I just supposed to disappear from my life now that you've decided to keep me at home?” I challenge.

His eyebrow lifts slightly, the closest he comes to showing surprise. “You were drugged, Piper. You're on two weeks' bedrest. Medical leave has been arranged.”

“You arranged it, you mean.” There's less heat in it than there should be. Two weeks away from the office suddenly doesn't sound too terrible. “At least I don't have to see Ben,” I mutter, more to myself than to Enzo.

The change is instant. Enzo goes completely still, and even the air around him seems to cool by several degrees. When he speaks, his voice is low, controlled, and more frightening than any shouting could ever be.

“You won't see Ben again,” he says quietly, like a promise.

“What does that mean?”

He moves toward me, each step deliberate, until he's standing directly in front of where I sit. He doesn't touch me, but I feel the heat of him, the solid presence of him, like a wall I can't see through.

“Do you want the truth?” he asks, and there's something in his tone. It sounds almost like consideration. As if he's weighing how much reality I can bear.

“Yes.” My voice doesn't shake, and I'm proud of that small victory.

“I'll tell you,” he says, “but understand there's no going back once you know. Are you certain you can handle it?”

I should say no; tell him to keep his secrets, to leave me in the blessed dark where I can maintain the fiction that the world operates according to rules and laws and decency. Instead, I nod.

He retrieves his phone, taps the screen a few times, then hands it to me. A video begins to play. The quality is high-definition, unforgiving in its clarity. It shows a room—windowless, concrete, clinically bright.

In the center, chained to a chair, is Ben. His face is a mess of bruises, one eye swollen completely shut, blood crusted at the corner of his mouth. He's screaming. Not in pain, though there's plenty of evidence he's experienced that. No, he's screaming justifications.

"Why the fuck am I here? Someone tell me." He scoffs like he's being inconvenienced. "If this is about the bitch Piper, she fucking asked for it. She was teasing me every fucking day. Fuck. The way she dressed, the way she talked. She wanted it. I know she wanted me."

My stomach heaves. I clamp a hand over my mouth, bile rising in my throat. Not because of what's been done to him—that, God help me, doesn't bother me at all—but because of the vile shit he's spewing.

The video continues. Ben thrashing against his restraints, foam gathering at the corners of his mouth as he rages, as he calls me names I won't repeat even in my own head.

"Turn it off," I whisper, and Enzo takes the phone immediately, slipping it back into his pocket.

My hands are shaking, hell, my entire body is. But not with fear, not with disgust—with a pure, clarifying rage I've never felt before.

Enzo might have touched me in my sleep, but I did want that. I had written it down, fantasized about it, made it clear in my private thoughts that the idea aroused me. There was a violation of process, perhaps, but not of desire.

What Ben intended was nothing I ever wanted. Nothing I ever invited. Nothing I deserved. I might be refusing to even acknowledge the thoughts, but just because I like living in denial doesn't mean I can't see through the illusions I create in my mind.

Ben was going to rape me.

"What are you going to do with him?" I ask, surprised at how cold my voice has become.

"What would you like me to do with him?" The question hangs between us. He's giving me a choice.

Insisting he let Ben go or suggest we call the police are the right answers, the morally correct answers, the answers that would let me sleep at night believing I'm a good person.

But Ben tried to steal my choice. He would have used my unconscious body for his pleasure without a moment's hesitation. And that's not even the worst part. The more I think about it, the more I'm sure I'm not his first victim.

Obviously, I could be wrong, but I don't feel like giving him the benefit of the doubt. After hearing what I just heard, I'm not that

generous.

"I want to see him," I say finally, the words coming from somewhere deep and dark inside me, a place I didn't know existed until this moment. "Face to face."

The sensation of wetness coating my cock drags me from the depths of unconsciousness. For a disorienting moment, rage ignites—a violent impulse to destroy whoever dares to touch me without permission. Then my eyes adjust to the darkness.

Piper. My toy.

Her head bobbing between my thighs, moonlight catching on the curve of her cheek, the hollow of her throat. The rage doesn't dissipate; it mutates, coiling into something equally dark but infinitely more pleasurable.

My hand moves without thought, fingers tangling in her hair, silken strands knotting around my knuckles like nooses. I want to yank her head back hard, to tear a gasp from her throat. Instead, I pull slowly, savoring the stretch of her neck, the power trembling under my palm as her mouth slides off with a delicious pop.

Her lips are swollen and glistening in the half-light. There's a small string of saliva trailing from her bottom lip to the tip of my dick. The sight makes my cock jerk against her cheek.

"Why did you stop me?" she pouts, looking up at me through long lashes, defiance blazing in her eyes.

"Having fun, Toy?" My voice scrapes out of me like it's been dragged over broken glass, thick with sleep and want.

The smile that curves her lips is pure sin. "I wanted to see if you'd like it," she breathes against my skin. "And I was curious."

I loosen my grip on her hair, not holding her in place anymore, just maintaining contact. "Curious about what?"

She laughs huskily. "I wanted to know how you felt when you did it to me. I wanted to… play."

The admission makes me groan. "Don't let me stop you, then."

She doesn't need to be told twice. Her mouth descends again, and this time I watch as her lips stretch around my girth, the hollow of her cheeks as she sucks, the flutter of her eyelids when I hit the back of her throat. Every detail burns itself into my memory like a brand.

The room is hushed around us, the only sounds are her wet, greedy slurping and my ragged breathing.

"Fuuuck!" My eyes roll back in my head in pure pleasure.

The day I broke in and spanked her comes to mind. She wasn't kidding when she told me I had no idea how talented her mouth is. Fuck, this is so much better than any other blowjob she's given me. The best part is she initiated it this time. My toy taking what she wants.

"That's it," I murmur, feeling the vibration of her moan travel through me, into my spine, igniting every nerve ending. "Look at you, you're so beautiful when you're slurping all over my dick."

As her hand comes up to cradle my balls, I tense my thighs, fighting the urge to thrust. Her rhythm grows confident, one hand wrapped around what she can't fit in her mouth, the other still teasing lower, fingertips pressing against sensitive skin. She's learning how to read me, how to interpret the tensing of my abs, the flex of my thighs, the tightening of my hand in her hair.

Heat builds at the base of my spine, pressure coiling tighter with each downstroke. I could come like this—I want to come like this, making her take everything I have to give.

But there's hunger in her eyes that tells me she has other plans. So I let her explore, my restraint a gift I've never given anyone else. Her eyes never leave mine, as her tongue traces along the sensitive underside. She's studying me, learning me, the same way I've been learning her all these months.

The realization sends a fresh surge of heat through me. My toy isn't just servicing me, not just sating her curiosity. She's collecting information, ammunition for later. The thought should anger me, but instead, pride blooms beneath my ribs.

She's becoming exactly what I knew she could be. Dangerous. Mine.

My breath catches as she takes me deeper than before, her throat working around the tip. I want to grab her skull and hold her there, feel her choke, feel her gag around me. Instead, my fists knot the sheets beside me, forcing myself to endure her mercy.

"Fuck. Piper." Her answering hum of satisfaction vibrates through me, and I know I'm close. Too close. "You're so fucking perfect."

The coil of pleasure tightens to near-breaking, and I realize this isn't how I want this to end. Not with her mouth, as perfect as it is. I want to be inside her wet cunt, need to feel her take all of me.

Before pleasure can overtake me, she's moving, crawling up my body with feline grace, her knees bracketing my hips. No hesitation in her movements, no asking permission.

She positions herself above me, one hand reaching between us to

grasp my dick, guiding the head to her entrance. It's damn near impossible not to seize her hips, to slam her down onto me and take what's mine.

Our eyes lock as she sinks down, impaling herself on me with a hiss of satisfaction that sounds like victory. "Mhmm, you're so deep inside me," she moans. The sound burns hotter than any prayer I've ever heard.

"What are you going to do with me?" My voice is husky with want.

Adjusting herself, she leans slightly forward, splaying her palms on my chest, fingers digging into the muscle like she's anchoring herself—or pinning me down.

"Whatever I want," she smirks. "It's my time to explore."

With each word, she presses her nails deeper into me, creating small crescent moon indents in my skin that I hope will scar. I want her marks all over me, proof that this happened, that she chose this.

"Yes, it is," I agree. "Take what you need, baby."

She begins to move, slow and devastating, her body rising and falling with a measured pace that speaks of exploration rather than desperation. Each downstroke takes me deeper, her inner walls gripping me like they never want to let go.

Every time she sinks down, it shreds another layer of my control. I want to buck up into her, brutal and deep, make her scream my name until her voice breaks.

The sight of her above me, moonlight painting her skin silver in between the shadows, head thrown back in pleasure she's orchestrating herself—it's almost too much to absorb. The ridge of my cock drags against her inner walls as she rises, almost releasing me before sinking back down with a soft gasp that I feel in my marrow.

Tonight, my toy's taking what she wants, and I would let her carve me open for it if she asked. Fuck, I hope she asks. Her tits sway with the movement, nipples hard in the cool night air.

A roll of her hips has us both groaning. The sound tears from my throat unbidden, honest in a way I'm rarely allowed to be. It takes everything in me not to thrust up into her heat. I deliberately fold my arms behind my head, pillowing it, making a show of my surrender.

I drink in every detail of her pleasure; the flush spreading across her chest, the way her teeth dig into her lower lip when I hit a spot that makes her shudder. The subtle changes in her breathing that telegraph how close she is, how much she's enjoying using me like this.

A bead of sweat trails between her breasts, and I follow its path with hungry eyes. She's exquisite in her determination, her thighs trembling slightly with exertion but never faltering. Pride swells in my chest—look what I've created, look what I've unleashed.

Piper moans with satisfaction as she bends forward, the angle shifting, taking me deeper. Her mouth finds mine, not asking but demanding, her tongue stroking against mine in a mimicry of what our

bodies are doing below.

Her teeth graze my bottom lip just before she bites down, hard enough that I feel the skin split, copper blooming on my tongue. I growl at the unexpected pain, and my cock pulses inside her in response.

She pulls back just enough to watch my reaction, her eyes gleaming with something dangerous and new. My blood stains her mouth like war paint, and something primal claws free inside me, wild and worshipful.

"Are you branding me, Toy?"

The smile she gives me is nothing short of wicked, a queen accepting tribute. She licks the blood from her lip, never breaking eye contact. "Maybe," she hums, hips grinding down, locking me inside her like a death grip. "Is that a problem?"

I could flip her now, remind her who she belongs to. But her confidence, her audacity—it's intoxicating. Instead, I reach up, finally touching her, thumbs brushing over her nipples, feeling the shiver that runs through her entire body.

"No," I reply simply. "You were made for me, baby, and it's about time you take what's yours." I pinch one peak between my fingers, rolling it until she gasps and arches into me.

She moves faster, taking me deeper, her body demanding everything I have to give. And I give it to her—my stillness, my patience, my savage appreciation of every undulation of her hips, every moan that falls from those bloodstained lips.

Fuck, I love the way she's using me. She's becoming more mine with every bounce on my cock. Then she slams down hard, her eyes blazing, her breath hot against my mouth.

"I have questions," Piper growls, grinding down until my vision goes white. "And if you want to come tonight, Enzo, you'll answer every one of them. Honestly."

If there was ever any doubt as to whether or not my perfect toy belongs to me, it's gone. This proves that she's my equal. My everything.

This has to be what love feels like, because I want nothing more than to fall to my knees for this woman.

"You can ask me anything," I rasp.

She swirls her hips at an agonizingly slow pace, and judging by her wicked grin, she knows exactly what she's doing. Something shifts in the air between us, a heaviness that has nothing to do with the press of our bodies.

Her voice cuts through the dark like a blade, low and demanding. "Would you really have killed Daniel just for touching me?"

The question doesn't slow her hips. Doesn't ease the strangling grip of her cunt around me. If anything, she tightens, watching me with eyes that demand truth even as they drink in pleasure.

I should probably be surprised she's asking me about that fucker now, but I'm not. Somehow, it seems fitting to get everything out in the open while she's staking her claim.

"Yes," I answer, the single syllable hanging in the air between us. No hesitation, no remorse coloring the word. Just fact, delivered while buried inside her.

Her rhythm falters for just a heartbeat, the only indication that my answer affects her. Then she resumes, somehow more intent, more present in the movement of her body over mine. Her eyes never leave my face, searching for regret, for signs that I'm lying. She won't find any.

"He touched you," I elaborate, my hands finally moving to her thighs, feeling the flex of muscle as she rises and falls. "That's more than enough reason."

She doesn't recoil or pull away. If anything, she sinks down harder, taking me deeper as if my confession deserves reward rather than revulsion.

"Not really," she disagrees, licking her lips as she pushes herself back up. "He didn't touch me in any way that matters. Definitely not in a way that made him deserve to be killed."

"He. Touched. You," I grind out through clenched teeth. "That's enough."

As she shakes her head, her hair spills around her face like a curtain. "No," she hisses. She moves her hands back to my chest, digging her nails in harder this time. "If I'm yours, I get a fucking say, Enzo."

"Is that so?" I challenge on a grunt.

"Yes, it's so." When she adds more pressure with her nails, I feel at least two breaking through my skin.

"Fuck," I growl, hips jerking up into her before I force myself still.

"You can't just go around and kill people who randomly touch me. I mean, what if I help someone who's about to fall, will you murder them?" she huffs with irritation, no longer moving.

I squeeze her hips harder, rocking them back and forth. "That depends," I reply honestly.

"On what?"

"On what their intentions are," I clarify. "Daniel wanted you, sure. But you shut him down, made it clear you weren't interested. That's why he's still alive. So you had a say, Toy."

"You took away his education," she hisses, her green eyes flash with anger. "How's that fair when I did what you demanded?"

I rock her faster. "He was disagreeable," I grunt.

The memory of my encounter with Daniel makes me feel angry all over. If he'd just listened and agreed to leave my toy alone, he could have stayed at Georgetown. But he didn't. He fucking boasted, namedropping his uncle who's a mayor like that could save him.

I tell Piper that, finishing with, "I meant what I said in my note to you. If it wasn't for you, I would have ended him on principle alone. But you held up your end. You saved his life, even when I didn't think he deserved to keep breathing."

Exhaling deeply, she straightens her back and slaps my hands away from her hips.

"The fact that I'll commit murder for you is nothing," I murmur. "But to let someone live when they don't deserve it, that's something I'd only ever do for you."

I keep my eyes on her, watching as she processes the info I just gave her. But instead of breaking down or crumpling, she wears her emotions beautifully. A sly smile forms on her lips as she moves her hips again.

I cup her tits once more, rolling and pinching the nipples. "Come for me," I snarl, voice guttural. "You're drenching my cock. I want you gushing so hard it fucking coats me."

Piper's nostrils flare as she looks down at me, her eyes almost black with lust. When she increases her pace, I fist her hips harder and thrust up and into her.

"Yes," she cries. "Oh, God. Yes. Play with my clit."

I slide a hand between us, rolling her needy nub with my thumb.

Her sex contracts around my dick, almost squeezing the cum from my balls as she comes with a loud moan.

"So fucking beautiful when you come on my dick," I praise. "My perfect fucking toy."

While the spasms still roll through her, she collapses onto my chest. Her breathing makes the hairs tickle. I wrap my arms around her back, holding her close to me.

This has to be what happiness feels like.

I hold her, not moving a muscle until her breathing evens out. "Mhmm," she moans, lazily. "That felt so good."

She sinks her teeth into my skin, and she doesn't let go until I fist her hair and yank her mouth away with a groan of pride. "You like marking me, Toy," I groan.

Smirking, she pushes herself back up again. "It's only fair that I get to play now."

"Go ahead," I rasp, my hands finding her thighs. "I'm not going to stop you."

"Should I be scared of you?" Her question comes out of nowhere, but it's followed with a deliberate roll of her hips that makes us both gasp.

My hands tighten on her thighs as I catch her eyes in the darkness, letting her feel the truth vibrating off my skin, radiating from where we're joined. "Only if you ever try to run from me."

The words should terrify her. Would terrify anyone sane. But Piper—my magnificent, perfect toy—moans, her cunt clenching around me like she was made for my brand of madness. This twisted honesty between us is its own form of foreplay, more intimate than being inside her.

"Is that why you did all this?" Her hand gestures between us, encompassing not just our bodies but everything—the internship, stalking her, and moving in while she was asleep. "To make sure I couldn't leave?"

I thrust up into her, making her gasp. "I did this because from the moment I saw you, I knew you were meant to be mine." My voice is rough with exertion and truth. "Leaving was never an option, Toy. Not for either of us."

Each question she throws at me binds us closer. She's doing exactly what I hoped she would—digging deeper, demanding more of the darkness, accepting the monster beneath my skin instead of flinching away.

"Do you…" she starts, then breaks off on a moan as I shift, changing the angle. Her nails dig into my chest. "Do you ever get scared that I'll become like you? That I'll enjoy this too much?"

The vulnerability in her voice guts me harder than any blade ever could. This is her real fear—not that I'll hurt her, but that she'll become what she thinks I am. That she'll look in the mirror one day and not

recognize the reflection.

"No." I reach up, wrapping a hand around her throat. "I don't want to change you, baby. You're perfect the way you are."

Her eyes widen, pupils blown with arousal and something darker, something that matches what lives inside me. She doesn't pull away from my hand. If anything, she leans into it, trusting me even as she interrogates me.

"You've already changed me," she argues.

"Have I?" I challenge. "Or have I merely unlocked parts of yourself that you didn't know existed?"

She shudders above me, her rhythm growing erratic, her breathing shallow. Not from fear, but from how close she is to having another orgasm. My honesty is pushing her there faster than any physical touch could.

"Is this…" she gasps, grinding down harder, chasing her pleasure even as she demands more truth. "Is this love to you?"

I feel my control slipping, the question piercing something vital inside me. My hand slides from her throat to the back of her neck, pulling her down until our foreheads touch, until we're breathing the same air.

"This is everything," I tell her, the words scraping my throat raw with their honesty. "Everything I have. Everything I am."

She kisses me then, her tongue sweeping into my mouth like she's trying to taste the truth of my words. I kiss her back just as desperately, just as honestly, letting her take what she needs.

When she pulls back, her eyes are wild, her cheeks flushed. "More," she demands, and I'm not sure if she means more truth or more pleasure. I decide to give her both.

I can't hold still anymore. The control I've clung to splinters inside me like bone snapping under pressure, and with a growl that doesn't sound human even to my own ears, I seize her hips and flip us both in one fluid motion, pinning her beneath me.

Her back hits the mattress with enough force to drive the air from her lungs in a surprised gasp, her eyes widening. But there's no fear there, only expectation, anticipation, a dark hunger that matches my own.

I drive into her without preamble, thrusting deep enough to make her moan.

"Tell me you're mine," I snarl into the hollow of her throat, dragging my mouth over the skin I'm about to fucking brand with every thrust.

Another thrust, deeper, harder. Her legs wrap around my waist, ankles crossing at the small of my back, pulling me in like she can't get enough.

The sound she makes isn't quite a moan, isn't quite a sob—it's surrender and defiance wrapped in one breathless noise. Her nails rake

down my back.

"Answer me," I demand on a groan. She shakes her head and presses her lips together. "Why did you start this game and demand honesty if you can't play by your own rules?"

There's no way I can be gentle when she still refuses to answer my question. I know she's mine, and she's already admitted it to me days ago. But I still want to hear it again. I've been brutally honest with her, so it's only fair she does the same.

"Look at me," I demand, one hand fisting in her hair to tilt her face up. Her eyes meet mine, glazed with pleasure but still sharp. "You think I don't already know the answer?" I punctuate each question with a thrust that makes the headboard slam against the wall.

A flush spreads across her chest, up her neck, staining her cheeks. Her inner walls clench around me, her body responding to my words as much as my touch.

"Why do you need to hear it?" she gasps, teeth bared like she's still fighting, even as her body surrenders.

I slow my pace, making each thrust deliberate, forcing her to feel every inch of me. One hand slides beneath her, lifting her hips to change the angle, hitting deeper, where I know she needs it most.

She moans at that, her back arching off the bed, pushing her breasts against my chest. I take advantage, my mouth finds her nipple, teeth scraping sharp before I suck.

Every brutal, worshipful stroke is a brand, a vow, an offering she didn't even have to ask for. I'm giving her everything—not just my body, but the darkness she's been asking about, the truth of what lives inside me.

"Enzo," she gasps. My name, raw and needy, like she's finally accepting who and what I am to her.

"Tell me," I demand, feeling her tighten around me, knowing she's close. My hand slides between us, finding where we're joined, my thumb circling her clit with the same relentless rhythm as my thrusts. "Come on me, baby, while you tell me what we both know."

Her body responds instantly, clenching around me, her head thrown back as pleasure overtakes her. I don't slow, don't gentle my touch, driving her higher, pushing past that first peak toward something more devastating, more complete.

"I can't…" she starts to protest, oversensitive, overwhelmed. But I know her body better than she does—know what she craves, what she'll beg for if I push her just right.

"You can," I assure her, my voice rough with exertion and something dangerously close to reverence. "You will."

Her orgasm builds faster, harder, her body trembling beneath me, around me. I feel my own release approaching, a tight coil of pressure at the base of my spine, but I hold back, determined to watch her fall apart again before I allow myself to follow.

"Enzo!" My toy claws at my back, screaming my name like a prayer and a curse combined.

"Yes, baby, that's it. Now tell me—" I'm cut off by the way her cunt squeezes me as her orgasm hits with a force that surprises us both.

She cries out and I drive into her one final time, burying myself to the hilt. "Fuck! Piper!" I groan her name as I empty myself inside her.

I collapse over her. My body feels simultaneously leaden and weightless, wrung out and remade. I bury my face in the crook of her neck, inhaling the scent of her—sweat and sex and something uniquely Piper, something I could track through darkness, through fire, through the gates of Hell itself if necessary.

Her pulse thrums against my lips, slowing until it matches mine—two heartbeats syncing into one. I feel the echo of it in my own chest, our rhythms synchronizing like they were always meant to.

This close, with nothing between us, I'd feel even the slightest tension, the smallest hint of regret or fear. But there's none as she wraps her arm around me, one hand sliding up to cradle the back of my head, fingers threading through my hair in a mirror of my own grip on her.

The gesture undoes me more completely than any climax ever could. I remain there, breathing her in, letting her hold me in a way I've never allowed anyone else to do.

In this moment of absolute honesty between us, I need to admit the truth to her, the one she's too scared to tell me.

"You own me," I breathe into her skin, the words more prayer than surrender. Then I push myself up, looking into her green eyes. "I don't think you've heard me when I've said it before—"

"Enzo—"

Shaking my head, I interrupt her like she did to me. "You own my heart, Toy. My body. My name. My fucking soul. Every part of me is yours. Everything I own is yours. Ever since I first saw you, I've been yours."

She swallows thickly. "But you don't even know me."

"I don't need to know your past to know you're mine. I don't need details to feel you in my blood."

Shifting, I place my hand on her heart.

"But I know this, baby." I lie down on my side, placing her hand on top of my organ that's beating just for her. "And you know mine. You have since I first saw you."

She smiles softly as her fingers trace idle patterns on my skin, soothing the sting from where she bit me earlier. The contrast is exquisite—her violence and her tenderness, her defiance and her acceptance. I could stay like this forever.

Her hair is a wild tangle against the pillow, her lips swollen from my kisses and her own teeth worrying them.

"Look," she starts, pressing her finger against the puzzle tattoo

above my heart. "I told you that I wanted to see Ben three days ago, and instead of taking me, you keep changing the subject. I can't belong to someone who tries to control me."

I arch an eyebrow. "Because we're on fucking bedrest."

Scoffing, she tries to push me off her. "Is that really the only reason?"

"Yes," I promise. "After Voss has checked you over tomorrow, we can go if you want to."

She yanks me in for a gentle, sweet kiss. When she pulls back, there's a new gravity in her gaze, a weight of understanding that wasn't there before.

"You better not be lying to me, Enzo."

37

Piper

The fluorescent lights of Arlington Diagnostic buzz above me like static electricity, making my skin prickle. Dr. Voss' cool fingers press against my wrist, counting my pulse beats while her eyes track the second hand on her watch.

Enzo stands in the corner, a dark sentinel with crossed arms and watchful eyes that haven't left me since Ben slipped something into my drink seven days ago.

"Blood pressure is normal," Dr. Voss says, unwrapping the cuff from my arm. Her voice is clinical, detached, but there's something else there—a hint of satisfaction. "Your heart rate is steady. And the bloodwork from yesterday looks good, too."

I sit very still on the paper-covered exam table, the crinkle underneath me sounding too loud in the sterile room. My fingers fidget with the hem of my shirt. "So I'm okay?"

Dr. Voss' light brown eyes assess me, not unkindly. "The drug has fully cleared your system. No signs of any lasting effects." She tucks her stethoscope around her neck. "You're recovering well, but I still recommend taking it easy for another week."

"Define taking it easy," I scoff, and Enzo's eyes narrow from his corner position. I feel his gaze like a physical touch. "Can I go back to Georgetown?"

Whether she says yes or no, there's no fucking way I'm staying trapped inside another week. Sure, I've been able to study remotely, and even finish a paper despite Enzo's constant hovering. But I still need to attend lectures. I want my fucking life back.

Dr. Voss glances at Enzo before answering, a fraction of a second that speaks volumes about who signs her checks. My jaw tightens. I hate being discussed as if I'm not in the room—even if it's via silent communication.

"Classes should be fine," she concedes with a reluctant nod. "But pace yourself. No all-nighters, no excessive stress if possible."

Well, that's just not possible. But instead of saying that out loud, I ask the next question on my mind. "And coffee?" Despite trying not to sound desperate for a fix, that's exactly how it comes out. A week without caffeine has been its own special kind of torture, and I honestly don't think I can take another day.

The corner of her mouth quirks up in what almost resembles a smile. "Two cups a day wouldn't kill you."

"Four," I bargain, and this time her eyes definitely crinkle.

"Fine, three. But not after 4 p.m., and nothing extra-strong." She makes a note in my chart. "And water. Lots of it."

"I can handle that." Relief floods through me, not just for the coffee, but for the gradual return to normalcy it represents. I slide off the table, my legs steadier than they've been in days.

Dr. Voss packs up her tools with efficient movements. "Any lingering symptoms I should know about? Dizziness? Nausea? Headaches?"

"She seems extra tired," Enzo replies, making me snap my gaze to him. "Is that normal?"

"Hey," I protest. "I can speak for myself."

Voss laughs softly. "Go ahead, Piper."

Reluctantly, I explain, "He's right. I do seem more tired. But I just think that's because I've been cooped up inside. I need to be able to start living again."

"That's very plausible, and I do recommend you go back to your normal routine. I'm just asking that you do it slowly." She hands me a card with her number. "Call immediately if anything changes. I mean it."

Enzo pushes away from the wall, the movement fluid and controlled. "Thank you, Dr. Voss."

It's a dismissal. She nods, accepting it, and leaves us alone in the exam room. The door closes with a soft click.

"Ready to go home?" he asks, and the way he says home—like it's ours, not just mine—sends a strange thrill through me that I'm not ready to examine too closely.

I know he sees it as our place since he moved in, but every time he says it, I hate the thought less. Instead of telling him that, I just say, "Yes," and let him guide me out with his hand at the small of my back.

In the car, as the city slides past the tinted windows, I pull out my phone and text Lena.

Me: Got cleared by the doctor. Not quite 100% but getting there. Miss you.

Her response comes almost immediately.

Lee: OMG FINALLY!! I miss you too, Pipes. Can I come

over? I promise to bring chocolate.

My fingers hover over the screen. I glance at Enzo, whose eyes are fixed on the road, one hand on the wheel, the other resting on my thigh in that proprietary way that makes me both irritated and warm.

Me: Yes, please. In a few hours?

When she confirms, I take a deep breath and turn my head to Enzo. "Lena wants to come over."

His hand tightens on my leg, just slightly, his thumb pressing into the soft part of my inner thigh. "No."

"I wasn't asking," I say, my voice steady. "I'm telling you that my best friend is coming over."

His jaw works, a barely perceptible movement. "She didn't look after you at Static. You know I don't trust her." He all but growls out that last part.

"She's not my keeper," I snap, anger flaring bright and sudden. "What happened wasn't her fault."

"She left you alone."

"It's called partying," I point out. "She wasn't there to babysit me."

This isn't the first time we're discussing Lena and that night at Static. But it's going to be the last one. I'm done with the grudge he's holding against my bestie. What happened wasn't her fault, and there's no part of me that blames her or thinks she's responsible in any way, shape, or motherfucking form.

If anything, I'm to blame. The drinks Ben gave me tasted off, but I still drank them. That's on me, and I'm owning that stupidity. Which is exactly what it was; stupid. I was acting like I had something to prove rather than using my common sense.

I cross my arms over my chest. "If you want to blame anyone, blame me. Or Ben." When Enzo doesn't react, I let out an exasperated huff. "And if that's not enough for you, blame your HR department for hiring him as an intern, since that's how I met him."

Enzo abruptly pulls hard at the steering wheel, ignoring the horns from behind us as he swerves across two lanes and parks in the emergency lane.

Before I can speak, his fingers wrap around my throat, squeezing hard enough to steal my next breath. Which is exactly hard enough to make my thighs clench, my clit throb, and my nipples harden.

"Let's get one thing straight, Toy," he says, his tone deceptively soft. "Not only have I fired everyone who approved Ben as an intern in our company. I've made sure he was expelled from Georgetown, and his family has lost everything. Every-fucking-thing."

When I realize his ruthlessness makes something inside me melt,

not recoil, I know I'm not the same person I used to be before Ben drugged me. Bringing my hand up, I slap the one that's still squeezing my throat, but he doesn't budge. Not even when I dig my nails in, not stopping when I feel blood pebbling.

"Let go," I wheeze. He doesn't.

I do the only thing I can think of; I reach for his collar and pull him closer to me. Luckily, he comes willingly, and as soon as I feel his breath against my lips, he slackens his grip on my throat.

"You're crazy," I gasp just before I fuse my lips to his. My fingers tangle in his hair, pulling at the ends while I try to tell him how I feel with the kiss.

He kisses me back with bruising force, devouring the air from my lungs, the fight from my body. It's not gentle. It's not slow. It's messy and desperate, teeth clashing, tongues tangling, like we're trying to consume each other from the inside out.

I moan into him, high and helpless, clutching at his shirt like it's the only thing anchoring me to this moment. His hands are everywhere—cradling the back of my skull, squeezing my hips.

All I can think about is all the things he's done for me, and the way he said our company, like my life has been woven into his so tightly there's no pulling free now. The realization that there's no going back isn't what sets me on fire. No, it's knowing that I don't want to.

When he pulls back just enough to breathe, our foreheads press together. His fingers tighten in my hair, tugging just enough to make my scalp prickle, his voice a ragged whisper against my swollen mouth.

"Is this your way of telling me that you're done fighting me, Toy?"

A sly smile spreads across my lips as I shake my head. "Never," I promise.

With a chuckle, he presses a kiss to the corner of my mouth. Then he smoothly pulls back into traffic and drives us home.

I honestly don't know if I'll ever stop fighting him because, no matter how pointless it is, it makes me feel alive. When it comes to Enzo, I'm still learning, and maybe I'll never stop learning.

When we're almost home, I turn to him again. "Lena's coming over," I state. "I need to see her."

Something in his expression shifts, almost imperceptibly. "Fine."

"Really?"

"My men will still be watching," he says as we pull up. "Doesn't matter if I'm there or not. You're never alone."

"Thank you," I say, and mean it.

He puts the car in park and turns to face me fully, his blue eyes unreadable. "Don't thank me for giving you what you want. I'd give you the moon if you asked for it, Toy. But I don't have to like it."

And then his mouth is on mine, not asking but taking, his hand sliding up to cup my face. I sink into the kiss, my body responding

before my mind can catch up, heat blooming under my skin like a fever. When he pulls away, his thumb traces my lower lip.

"Promise me you're not going anywhere," he says, his tone making it clear it's not up for discussion. "And I'll be watching through the cameras in our apartment—"

"Wait… what the fuck, Enzo? You have cameras in there?" I demand, pointing at the building in front of us. "When the hell—"

"That's a story for another time," he chuckles. "Just know I'll be keeping an eye on you."

I nod, breathless, and step out of the car.

Three sharp knocks on my door send my heart leaping into my throat. I cross the apartment in quick strides, twist the deadbolt, and then Lena is there—hair tucked behind her ears, eyes wide and worried.

She doesn't speak. She just crashes into me, arms locking around my neck like she can hold me together by force. Her arms are so tight my spine pops. I stagger back, letting the door swing shut behind us.

She smells like coconut shampoo and that vanilla perfume she always wears. The familiarity of it breaks something in me, and I'm clutching her back just as tightly, my face pressed into her shoulder as hot tears slip free without permission.

"Pipes," she whispers against my hair, and her voice catches on that single syllable. "God, I've been so worried."

We stand like that in my hallway, swaying slightly, neither willing to be the first to let go. When we finally separate, her mascara has smudged beneath her eyes, and her hands tremble as she tucks a strand of hair behind my ear.

"You look better than the last time we had a video call," she says, studying my face with the kind of careful scrutiny only someone who's known you for years can get away with.

"I feel better." I give her a reassuring smile.

She shifts awkwardly and holds up a crumpled brown bakery bag. "I brought chocolate cupcakes. Emergency-grade."

The smell of rich cocoa leaks out, making my stomach twist with a sudden, fierce hunger for the cupcakes.

"Do you want some coffee?" I offer, desperate for something normal to do with my hands.

"Yes, please."

While I busy myself with the coffee machine, Lena leans against the counter, picking apart a cupcake like it personally offended her, crumbs trailing down her fingers.

"Almond milk?" I ask, as if we're just having another study session, as if nothing has changed.

"You know it." She hesitates. "Pipes, I—"

"Let's sit first," I interrupt, not ready yet. "Please."

With a sharp nod, Lena heads toward the living room, but comes to an abrupt stop.

"Jesus, Lee!" I yelp, almost crashing into her back. "Why did you—"

"What the fuck is that?" she asks, her tone shrill as she stabs her finger toward something in the living room.

I step around her to see what she's sounding so worked up over. Oh, shit. The puzzle picture. Fuck. I've gotten so used to seeing it that I didn't think to warn her.

"Umm…" I trail off, not sure how to explain it. "Let's sit down."

"I'm not sitting until you tell me what the fuck is going on," she demands. Her hand's shaking so badly the coffee almost sloshes over.

"Please, Lee," I beg. "I promise I'll tell you everything."

We settle on the couch, both of us instinctively curling our legs underneath us, creating a small fortress of knees and mugs. The crumpled bakery bag sits between us like a forgotten peace offering.

Through the windows, afternoon light casts long rectangles across my floor. I trace one with my toe, buying time, searching for the right words.

"So," Lena begins. "The last time we discussed Enzo, you just wanted to get your rocks off. But now you have his masterpiece displayed in your living room. What gives?"

Right, I guess we're diving straight in.

"He kind of lives here now," I admit.

"You live together?" Lena furrows her brows. "Why?"

I try to come up with a variation that sounds better than the truth, which is he moved in while I was sleeping. But I refuse to lie to my best friend, no matter how fucked up it sounds. So I end up giving her the brutally honest version, no holds barred.

"But I like having him around," I add defensively when she scoffs at my explanation.

"Right," she replies, sarcasm heavy in the one word. "So first he stalks you, then he hires you as his intern so he can use you, and then he just decides to move in. And you…" Holding her fingers up, she makes air quotes. "… like having him around."

Sighing, I take a sip of the now lukewarm coffee. "I know how it sounds," I say, fighting the need to defend myself. "But it's the truth. I don't like how he went about it, but I like him, and I like—"

"The orgasms," she finishes for me, shooting me a grin that I estimate to only be half fake.

"Yeah, I definitely like those," I mutter, feeling my cheeks heat. I reach blindly for a cupcake, peeling back the paper liner with shaking fingers. "But Lee—"

"Do you love him?"

The question hits harder than it should. My stomach knots. My chest tightens. Somewhere down the hall, the radiator coughs to life, a low, rumbling heat chasing away the first edge of evening chill.

Do I love Enzo? No… yes… maybe? I honestly don't know. What I do know, though, is that I could. To buy myself time, I tear off a piece of cupcake and shove it into my mouth, like chocolate can fill the gaps in my courage.

"It's not that simple," I muse out loud. "When I'm with him, I feel like we're the last two people on the planet. It's like, nothing else matters apart from us—"

"Because his dick is magical?"

Shaking my head, I explain, "No. I mean, it is. But that's not what it's about. All the sexy stuff aside, I like being wrapped up in him. And… well… I like that he chose me. It's flattering."

Lena cackles at that. "So is black, that doesn't mean you let yourself get sucked into a black hole, Pipes. I hate to say it, but it sounds like you're letting your vagina do the talking. I mean, do you even know him?"

"Yes, I do."

She waggles her eyebrows in that way that tells me she's about to test me. I shove the rest of the cupcake into my mouth, waiting for her to go ahead.

"So where did he grow up? What's his full name? What's his last name? What does he actually do for a living?"

While she continues to hurl questions at me, I frown. She's absolutely right; I don't know Enzo at all.

"Well, I presume his full name is Lorenzo." I try to sound flippant, but it falls flat.

She nods. "And how many siblings does Lorenzo have? Where did he grow up?"

Instead of answering, I set my coffee cup down, brush the crumpled cupcake wrapper onto the table, and bury my face in my hands. These are all valid questions, and I've pondered some of them myself. But when I'm with Enzo, those questions melt away, meaningless compared to the way he looks at me.

I run my hand down my face, once again meeting Lena's gaze. "Look," I start, swallowing thickly. "I don't know the answers. You're right, there are many things I don't know about him. But… do you know what he did after Ben drugged me?"

The room's dim enough now that I fumble for the lamp switch beside the couch, filling the space with a low, golden light.

Her loud inhale is all I need to carry on.

"He fucking kidnapped Ben. He's holding him somewhere—"

"Pipes, that's—"

"Awesome," I state, making sure my tone's firm. "It's fucking awesome. How many men can you say would do that? Or how about the fact he fired everyone at Blackwood that had a hand in Ben being hired there as an intern?"

I'm not sure what I expected from my friend, but it's definitely not the horror-stricken expression currently marring her face.

"Well, that's…" She doesn't bother finishing the sentence.

I lean closer, squeezing her hand like I can force her to understand through touch alone. "That's love," I say, tasting the word since it's the first time I say it out loud.

Silence settles between us, heavy and expectant. Lena shifts on the couch, her thumb is absentmindedly tracing circles on my hand. Something in her posture transforms, shoulders squaring slightly, chin lifting.

I recognize this look: it's her truth-coming face, and my stomach immediately knots in response.

"What?" I ask, the word sharper than I intend.

She tugs her bottom lip between her teeth, hesitating. "Are you sure you know what you're getting yourself into?" Her voice is soft but sure.

Five seconds of perfect stillness, like the moment between lightning and thunder. The question hangs in the air, crystalline and dangerous.

"Of course I do," I say, but the words sound hollow, rehearsed. My fingers twitch against hers, wanting to pull away, to protect myself from the doubt she's trying to seed.

Lena doesn't blink. "Do you, though? Because the things you told me during brunch… it's just… it's fucking crazy. Why are you putting up with it?"

I withdraw my hands, tucking them beneath my thighs. The absence of her touch leaves me colder than I expected. "You don't understand," I mutter.

"Of course I don't fucking understand," she snaps, tilting her head. "So, if this is something you're serious about, make me understand."

"Why are you doing this?" I ask, heat rising to my face. "He saved me. Why does there have to be more to it than that?" That's the wrong thing to say, and I know it the moment the words slip out.

"I know." Her voice softens, and the look she gives me is almost pitiful. "And I'm grateful, I am. But…" She tucks her knees closer to her chest, making herself smaller. "There's something you're not telling me. Or something you're not telling yourself."

I could build a mountain of graves with the things I don't know about Enzo. But I know how he looks at me, like really looks at me. I know the way his muscles contract when I touch him, and I know the taste of his lips and the weight of his body over mine.

What else is there? What else could matter, when he's the only thing that feels real anymore?

I've known my parents all my life. I know how old my mom was when she lost her virginity, because she told me that was the right age. If I had sex before I turned sixteen, I was a slut. But if it was after I turned seventeen, I'd be a prude. Unlike most people, I know my mom's real hair color, and I know her insecurities.

Although I never knew my dad that well, they both managed to surprise me when they all but disowned me. Until that happened, I barely knew Teddy, but he stepped up in ways he never needed to, and took care of me when my own parents wouldn't.

So, how much do you need to know someone to know the things that really matter? To know their heart?

"I know enough," I say finally.

"But not everything." It's not a question.

I stare at a small coffee stain on the couch cushion, a tiny brown constellation from some long-ago spill. Outside the windows, the last threads of daylight bleed into gray. "No one knows everything about anyone else."

"That's a cop-out, and you know it." Lena's voice is gentle but insistent. "There's a difference between normal privacy and whatever this is."

I pick at a loose thread on my sleeve, watching it unravel between my fingers. "He's complicated."

"Complicated how?" She leans forward. "Piper, I'm not trying to hurt you. I'm trying to make sure you're not—"

"Not what? In danger?" My laugh cracks, brittle and sharp, my chest tightening like a fist is squeezing my heart.

The certainty in my voice surprises even me. It's the one thing I do know, bone-deep and unshakable. Whatever else Enzo might be, whatever shadows he keeps hidden, the truth of his devotion to me is written in every touch, every look, every possessive gesture.

Lena watches me, her eyes steady and knowing. She's always been able to read me better than anyone—better than my parents, better than Uncle Teddy, sometimes better than I can read myself.

"I believe you," she declares, shocking the hell out of me.

"Say it again," I rasp, like if I hear it twice, it might stitch something broken inside me.

A smile spreads across her face, softening her features. "I, Lena Carter, believe you, Piper Harrington," she exclaims.

She tosses a cupcake at me, and I catch it against my chest, laughing for real for the first time since she arrived. The sound is still echoing in the apartment when there's the sound of a key being slid into the lock just a moment before the door opens.

I freeze, the cupcake squashed between my palms. Next to me, Lena stiffens too, her eyes narrowing like she's bracing for an earthquake.

"Is that the squatter?" she asks, her voice light but sharp at the edges.

The second Enzo walks through the door, my body springs into action. I don't even register moving until I find myself in front of him. Ignoring Lena's huff from the living room, I drink him in as he stands there.

God, he's too handsome in that tailored black coat he's wearing.

His expression is carved from stone, his voice a rasp of dark velvet. "You've been naughty, Toy."

"Have I?" I ask, immediately thinking about the punishment I hope he doles out when we're alone.

His gaze pins me where I stand, a force heavier than hands, heavier than chains. Before I can speak—before I can even think—he curls his hand around my throat. Not squeezing. Just holding, like he's reminding me who I belong to. Who I've always belonged to.

And then he's kissing me, hard and deep, his mouth crashing down on mine like a punishment. His fingers flex against the sides of my neck, sending a bright, burning shudder down my spine. I gasp against him, and he takes the sound like an offering, swallowing it down with a low growl that vibrates between our bodies.

I whimper when he pulls back, ending the kiss all too soon. I lean into the touch as his thumb strokes once under my jaw, possessive and tender, like he's checking to make sure I'm still breathing.

"You haven't eaten anything but cupcakes, and you've only had coffee to drink," he murmurs. That's all it takes for me to know my transgression. "You promised to look after yourself."

I bite my bottom lip. "I know," I admit. "Guess I got a bit carried away with Lena."

At my words, his gaze sweeps over me, then slides past my shoulder, and when I turn to look, I see Lena standing in the living room doorway. The tick in her jaw is the only outward sign that she's scrutinizing Enzo and finding him lacking.

While he shrugs his coat off and hangs it on the mounted rack by the door, I silently ponder how I'm going to diffuse the growing tension.

"Enzo," I say, forcing air into my lungs. "This is Lena. Lena, this is Enzo." My voice sounds wrecked even to my own ears, still raw from his kiss, from the way his presence devours the room.

Lena crosses her arms, one eyebrow lifting with slow, surgical precision. "So you're the squatter."

Enzo doesn't react, not the way most men would. No anger or indignation. Just a small, glacial smile that's more teeth than anything. "And you," he answers, voice low and dangerous, "are the friend who left her alone."

Lena's lips twitch, but it looks more like a defensive reflex than real humor.

Well, she might be okay with that cheap jab, but I'm not. "Hey," I

interject, my hand brushing Enzo's chest without thinking. Solid. Steady. A wall that would never let me fall. "I've told you it's not her fault."

"You have," Enzo agrees, not taking his eyes off Lena. "And I've told you I disagree."

Rolling my eyes, I look at Lena, who holds my gaze for a long moment. I can see the war happening behind her eyes. The part of her that wants to tear him apart is fighting against the part of her that's maybe—just maybe—starting to understand he would tear apart the entire world to keep me safe.

Finally, with a reluctant sigh, she eases her arms to her sides. "I guess it's not squatting if the person whose name is on the lease wants you here."

Enzo's lips twitch, just a fraction, as if he finds her feisty acceptance amusing rather than threatening.

"Don't know about that," I deadpan. "As far as I know he hasn't gotten permission from Teddy."

Lena crosses the space between us so she can grab her jacket and boots. Once she's wearing both, she pulls me into a hug.

"Be good, Pipes," she murmurs into my hair. I start to pull back, but she doesn't let me go. She presses her mouth to my ear and whispers, so soft I barely catch it, "I think I get it now."

Then she pulls away, flashing me a smile before turning toward the door that Enzo's holding open for her. She nods at him before walking through it, leaving us alone.

With Lena gone, there's a restlessness in Piper's movements that catches my eye. The way she fiddles with her sweater hem, her fingers pinching and releasing the fabric in a rhythm that betrays everything she's trying to hide.

She thinks I don't notice the half-glances she throws my way, as if she's processing something. But I notice everything about her. Every breath. Every twitch. Every silent plea her body makes before her mind catches up to what she truly wants. Me.

"Did you have fun, Toy?" I ask.

Piper nods, a slight jerk of her chin. "Yeah."

While I was gone, I only checked the security feeds long enough to confirm she hadn't left the apartment. I could have listened in on everything, but I decided to play nice and respect her time with Lena. Now that seems like a fucking mistake because something's up.

"What did you talk about?" I move closer, watching her throat work as she swallows.

"Nothing special." Her eyes slide away from mine. "School. Exams."

She's lying. The truth sits on her skin like a fever, making her cheeks flush, her posture too rigid. Something in their conversation has unsettled my toy.

"Liar," I murmur, but there's no anger in it. Only certainty.

Her shoulders tense. "I'm not the only one with secrets," she retorts.

"Is that so?" I brush her hair back from her cheek with one hand, savoring the slight tremor that runs through her at my touch. "What secrets am I keeping, Toy?" My fingers skim the shell of her ear, down the column of her throat.

She huffs out a laugh. "If I knew it wouldn't be much of a secret, would it?" There she is, my stubborn Piper.

"If you want to know something, all you have to do is ask," I tell her.

If Lena has done anything to upset Piper, I'll need to address it carefully. My toy is stubborn in her attachments. She wouldn't forgive me for hurting her precious friend, no matter how much that friend might deserve it.

"We should shower before dinner," I say, the words simple enough, but the demand beneath them is unmistakable. Her body knows what I'm really saying. It always does.

She laughs under her breath. "I need to shave." She says it like that's a deterrent. "And I can't afford distractions right now. Exams are coming up, and I'm already behind."

I let her spill her protests like prayers to a god who's already made up his mind.

"You don't have to do anything alone anymore," I tell her, closing the distance between us, and sliding my hand around the back of her neck. Her skin burns against my palm, so alive. I apply just enough pressure to remind her who she belongs to. "That includes shaving."

The shift is subtle but immediate as her body softens against mine without a fight. My hand never leaves her neck as I guide her toward the bathroom. With each step, I feel her resistance crumbling, feel her leaning into my touch like it's the only thing keeping her upright.

"I'll run the water," I tell her, finally releasing her to turn on the shower. Then I move back to her, watching as she shifts her weight from one foot to the other, still hovering in the doorway as if uncertain. "Strip."

Her fingers tremble slightly as she reaches for the hem of her sweater, but she doesn't hesitate. With swift movements, she pulls it over her head and lets it fall to the floor. Next, her pants, sliding down her thighs to pool at her feet. She steps out of them with a grace that makes my blood burn.

I take my time removing my own clothes, never breaking our gaze. Every button undone, every inch of skin revealed is done with the slow precision of a ritual. My toy's eyes darken with lust when I stand naked before her.

I step toward her, and hook my fingers beneath the elastic of her underwear. "These too," I rasp against her temple.

She obeys without hesitation, allowing me to unhook her bra while she pushes down her thong, stepping out of her underwear. Then I take her hand and lead her into the shower, the hot water immediately slicking our skin, making it gleam in the low bathroom light.

I position her directly beneath the spray, watching as the water cascades over her, plastering her hair to her skull in dark rivers. She looks up at me through long, wet lashes, water beading on her lips, and for a moment, I almost forget that anything was ever wrong. But then I see it—that same restlessness from before, hidden now behind desire but still there in the corners of her eyes.

Whatever Lena said to her, I'll erase it. Letter by fucking letter, touch by motherfucking touch, until there's nothing left in Piper's mind but the truth I've carved into her soul since the day I saw her.

I reach for the soap, working it between my palms until it becomes a thick, white lather between my hands. When I touch her shoulders, she exhales—a soft sound that echoes off the walls.

"Turn around," I demand against her ear.

She obeys, presenting her back to me, hair cascading down in a dark, wet rope that I push to her front. I start at her shoulders, fingers digging into the tense muscles there, working the soap across her skin in slow, deliberate circles. I'm memorizing her all over again, mapping territory I already own.

"You're so fucking beautiful," I rasp against her ear, because sometimes even gods have to worship their miracles out loud.

Her head drops forward, exposing the vulnerable nape of her neck. I press my lips there, tasting soap and water and the salt of her skin. My hands slide around to her front, palms gliding over the slick plane of her stomach, up to cup the weight of her tits.

Her nipples pebble instantly against my palms, the contrast of soft flesh and tight peaks making my cock jerk against her ass. Piper arches into my hands with a fractured moan, and the hunger to split her open threatens my control.

She turns in my arms, her own hands coming up to mirror my earlier actions. "I want to feel you," she purrs.

Slick suds slide between her fingers as she traces the contours of my chest, shoulders, down my arms in slow, deliberate lines that make my blood sing.

When her fingers brush over my nipple, I groan. "You're playing with fire, Toy."

"Then it's a good thing we're literally surrounded by water," she smiles.

I let her explore, loving the feel of her hands moving lower, tracing the cut of my hip bones, the trail of dark hair leading down. But before she can reach her destination, I capture her wrists, spinning her gently so her back is against my chest again.

"Didn't you say you couldn't afford any distractions?" I ask, my voice filled with gravel.

"I did," she purrs. "But I—"

I interrupt her with a tisking sound. "And you said you needed to shave. Let me take care of you," I rasp, dragging the blunt edge of my teeth along the vulnerable line of her throat. "You don't have to do anything except trust me. Let me show you how well I take care of what's mine."

She shudders, the breath stuttering out of her in a ragged exhale. "Enzo," she whispers, half in warning, half in surrender.

I curl my hand around her throat, my thumb brushing the rapid pulse hammering beneath her skin. Fragile. Frantic. Perfect. "Trust

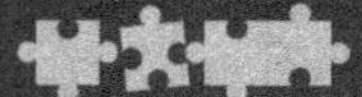

me," I say again, softer now. A promise and a command layered in one breath.

The moment her head tilts back, baring her throat wider for me, I know she's given in. "Fine," she finally agrees.

I could tear the world apart in gratitude. My toy. My perfect, stubborn, beautiful toy.

Lifting her arm, I guide it up and back until she's cupping the nape of my neck. The position exposes the delicate hollow of her armpit. She tips her head up, watching me with wary eyes, her lips a tight line of uncertainty.

Even her resistance is beautiful to me—not something to be crushed, but savored like the last moments before a storm breaks.

"Hold still," I murmur, squeezing body wash into my palm. The scent blooms between us, jasmine and vanilla.

I cover the sensitive skin of her armpit in soap. She tenses at first, a flush crawling up her neck at the intimacy of this act. It's one thing to let me fuck her, it's another entirely to let me care for her in this way— to expose the vulnerable, ordinary parts of herself that no one else sees.

When I reach for her razor on the shower shelf, her breath hitches. "Enzo." Her voice trembles slightly. "I'm not sure about this."

"Do you trust me, Toy?"

"I don't know," she admits, worrying her bottom lip. "But I… ahh, I want to."

"Good girl," I murmur.

The razor glides smooth against her skin, revealing pale flesh in its wake. I rinse the blade under the spray, then return for another precise stroke. Her skin is sacred to me, and even the mundane act of removing hair is a form of worship when it's her body beneath my hands.

She doesn't relax until I'm almost done with the second armpit, the tension finally bleeding from her shoulders, her breath evening out to match the rhythm of my strokes. When I finish, I rinse away the remaining soap.

I press my lips to her forehead. "What else needs shaving?" I ask, my voice hoarse.

"M-my legs," she stutters.

"Sit on the edge," I tell her, guiding her to the built-in bench in the shower's corner.

While she obeys, perching on the edge with her knees pressed tightly together, I kneel at her feet like it's the most natural thing in the world. And maybe it is because it feels like I was born to worship at this particular altar.

With gentle pressure, I lift her right leg and settle it across my shoulder, my hand cradling her calf. The position opens her to me, exposes the slick pink of her sex, but I keep my eyes fixed on the task at hand.

"You don't have to—" she begins.

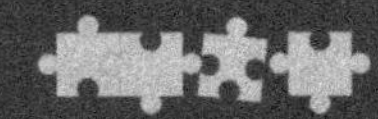

I silence her with a look. "Yes, I do."

Then I lather her shin and calf with careful hands, making sure the soap coats every inch before I gently press the razor to her skin. The first stroke reveals a path of silken skin, gleaming wet in the shower's light. I continue with meticulous care, my movements slow, precise, reverent—each scrape of the blade a promise written into her flesh.

Her breathing stays even, controlled, but I can feel the tension vibrating through her, the vulnerability she's offering without saying a single word. Each time I adjust her leg, she allows it, yielding to me inch by precious inch.

When I finish the first leg, I press my lips to the inside of her ankle, letting my teeth graze the delicate bone there. Her breath hitches, her pupils dilating as she watches me through the steam. I move to her other leg, repeating the process with the same careful devotion, mapping her contours with blade and hand and breath.

As I finish the final stroke, she tugs her leg free from my grasp, already shaking her head before I can even ask, making it clear she won't let me shave anywhere else. The dark landing strip between her thighs remains untouched, a boundary she isn't ready to surrender.

I slide my hands up her thighs, my mouth following the path my fingers blaze. She tries to press her knees together, but I'm already between them, my shoulders keeping her spread open for me.

"I love you exactly as you are," I murmur against her clit.

She gasps. "You love me?"

Frowning, I look up at her. I'm pretty sure I've told her over and over that I love her. I mean, I've said she's mine, that's fucking synonymous.

"Yes," I rasp. "I love you, Piper."

"H-how can you love me when you don't even know me?" She lifts her hips, trying to grind against my face. But I pull away, denying both of us. "Tell me," she demands breathlessly.

"I do know you," I answer, blowing air against her sex, making her shiver. "I know you act like you hate when I lick right here." Pausing, I press my tongue to her clit for a brief moment.

"Enzo!"

My cock throbs, and I'm tempted to wrap one hand around the base, but this isn't about me. It's not even about pleasure. I'm determined to show my toy once and for all what she means to me, and the maddeningly perfect sex we have is just one aspect of our relationship.

"And I know you whimper so fucking prettily when I use my teeth. And when you can't take it anymore," I growl, "you ride my face like you want to smother me with your cunt. Like you're desperate to do right now."

"Am not…" Her denial dies the moment she realizes I'm right. She's rotating her hips. "Okay, you got me there. But you don't know where I grew up, or if I have any phobias."

Chuckling, I carry on. "I know you're from Connecticut."

"Google will tell you that."

"Your uncle Teddy," I rasp, "was the first man who treated you like you mattered."

She jerks, her moan catching on a sob, her hands finding my hair, yanking at the strands like she doesn't know whether to pull me closer or shove me away. I fucking love the way she's making me hurt for her.

"You grew up starving for love you never got, carving yourself hollow just to be enough," I continue. "And you hate the color yellow because your mother wore it when she threw you out."

Her back stiffens, and she lets out a sob. "W-what?"

I lift my face and look up at her so she can see the truth in my eyes. "I know you, Toy. Better than you know yourself."

"Is that so?" she volleys.

I nod. "Yes, it's so. Right now, you want me to distract you with orgasms. And even though I'd love nothing more, I'm not going to."

She pouts so prettily. "Why not? I want to come."

"Because," I pause to press a kiss to her inner thigh. "We both already know I know your body better than you do. Now, I want you to understand just how precious you are to me, and how well I do know you."

When she tries to turn away, I catch her chin, my grip firm, wet, unforgiving, dragging her back to me like a sinner to confession.

"This is the only thing that matters, Toy," I breathe, slowly rising to my feet. "You're mine, and I'm yours. Blood, bone, fucking destiny."

I lift her from the shower bench, feeling her weight settle perfectly in my grip, her skin slick beneath my palms. Her body fits against mine like a missing piece returned to its rightful place—wet, warm, and trembling.

There's a heaviness in my chest as she wraps herself around me, a dark satisfaction that burns beneath my ribs. This is what I've waited for. This is what I knew would happen from the moment I first saw her.

Water sheets down her back as I shift my grip, my palm flattening against her slick spine, the curve of her ass fitting perfectly into my hand like it was carved there just for me. My cock aches, leaking with my need for her, but I still ignore it.

She clings to me, arms winding tight around my neck, her breath hot against my throat. Her legs lock around my hips, thighs squeezing. "Enzo," she whispers, her voice breaking on my name.

I turn, pressing her back to the cold tiles. Her gasp is immediate, her body arching instinctively toward me, seeking heat, seeking me. Her hair is plastered to her neck, water beading on her collarbone before trailing down between her tits. I watch one droplet's journey, mesmerized.

"Look at me," I command.

She does, those green eyes locking with mine—half-lidded, hungry.

For the first time, there's no hesitation. My toy's finally accepting what I've been telling her all along; she's mine.

"Fuck. Piper," I grind out through clenched teeth. "You're so fucking perfect."

I capture her mouth in a brutal kiss, a battle of lips and teeth and tongue. I devour her, tasting the sweetness of her mouth, swallowing her gasps. Her tongue slides against mine, challenging, surrendering, then challenging again.

My toy pulls back, locking her gaze on mine. "I need to know how you know all those things about me?"

"After I first saw you, I investigated every aspect of your life," I admit, my voice steady despite the fire in my veins.

"You did what?"

I nod. "I did a complete background check. Your educational records. Your medical history. Your favorite coffee order."

"Keep going," she urges.

"Then I broke in and installed cameras all over your apartment," I admit. "Sometimes I watched you through the feed. But other times, I came here and watched you sleep."

Her eyes widen slightly, but not with shock—with recognition. As if something has finally clicked into place. For a moment, I think she might push me away, might finally decide that my obsession crosses some line she can't accept.

She bites my bottom lip, savage and sure, sending a sharp sting straight to my groin. When she releases my lip, her eyes are dark with something wilder than lust. "From now on," she says, her voice strong, "you ask me. If there's something about me you want to know, you ask me directly."

"I promise," I vow, and mean it.

She rewards me by leaning forward, teeth grazing the sensitive skin where my neck meets my shoulder. Then she bites down. The sting of it is delicious, unexpected. My hips jerk forward involuntarily as she gasps against my skin; the sound vibrating through my body.

"Again," I growl, and she obliges, biting down harder, sucking the spot. The thought of wearing her brand, of everyone seeing the evidence of her passion on my skin, sends a surge of possessive pleasure through me.

Water drums against our bodies, the air thick and heady with heat. The glass separating the shower from the rest of the bathroom is completely fogged. The world outside this shower stall is irrelevant. Nothing exists beyond her body against mine.

I slide one hand up, trailing over her ribs, between her breasts, before wrapping around her throat. I don't squeeze—I don't need to. The weight of my hand there, the implicit control, is enough.

For several heartbeats, we remain frozen like this—her back against the wall, her legs around my hips, my hand still loosely encircling her

throat. The water begins to cool, but I can't bring myself to move yet. To separate my body from hers feels sacrilege.

When I finally look at her, her eyes are heavy-lidded, but clear. There's no regret there, no second thoughts. Just a quiet certainty that mirrors my own. This was inevitable. This was right.

I lean forward, pressing my forehead against hers. "Mine," I whisper, not as a question, not as a demand, but as a simple statement of fact.

She closes her eyes briefly, her lashes casting delicate shadows on her cheeks. When she opens them again, there's a peace there I haven't seen before.

I ease her legs down, letting her stand on unsteady feet while keeping her pressed against the wall for support. Water sluices between our bodies. After switching off the water, I help her out of the shower and dry her body before my own. The look in her eyes tells me there's something on her mind.

Before I can ask, she places her hand on my chest, right above my puzzle tattoo. Her palm presses directly over my heart. "I'm not mad you stalked me," she says, almost too soft to hear. "Or that you looked into my life, Lorenzo."

The way she says my full name makes it clear she's annoyed she figured it out on her own and didn't hear it from me. And the fire in her green eyes confirms it.

Fuck, my stubborn toy is perfect. No wonder I want to spend all my time worshiping her.

"But I can't be yours," she continues, her fingers tracing the outline of the puzzle piece. "Not until I know who you really are."

She steps closer. Her breath ghosts over my chest, and then she licks the skin above my heart in a way that's fucking lethal to my self-control. A low groan rumbles out of me.

"And until I know your mind as well as I know your heart and body," she breathes, voice shaking slightly, "I don't want to see Ben."

Her words confuse me, but then I get it. When she demanded to see him before, it was a reaction. Now, she's refusing to embrace the darkness until I've proven myself to her. And fuck if that doesn't make me want to tear the whole fucking world apart just to give her what she's asking for.

40

Piper

The past two weeks blur together like watercolors left in the rain—endless nights of highlighting textbooks until the words swim, mornings waking to Enzo's fingers tracing my spine, afternoons of him quizzing me relentlessly between stolen kisses.

Every time I tried to focus, he was there, simultaneously my greatest help and my most devastating distraction. Now I stand at the front of the lecture hall, gripping the podium like it's the only thing keeping me upright, acutely aware of how the recycled air presses against my skin.

A dozen pairs of eyes pin me in place as I stand in front of Georgetown's most selective political students. Some gazes are curious, others glazed with boredom, a few already mentally packed for Christmas break.

But not me. I'm almost done presenting and defending the paper I handed in just before Thanksgiving. Almost. The light behind me hums, casting my shadow long across the floor while my final slide glows against the monitor—a neat bulleted conclusion.

The words fall from my mouth like I've rehearsed them a thousand times, which I have. In front of my bathroom mirror. While cooking dinner. Under Enzo's watchful gaze as he lounged on my couch, interrupting every few minutes to correct a point or challenge an assumption.

Heat crawls up the back of my neck from the memory of how those practice sessions usually ended—with papers scattered across the floor and both of us naked. I clear my throat and force my mind back to the present.

The wood of the podium is smooth under my fingertips. I trace small circles against it, grounding myself in the present moment as I methodically dismantle the counterarguments to my thesis. My voice grows steadier with each point, even as I feel a trickle of sweat slide down my spine.

Professor Levi leans forward in his seat, elbows on the desk, fingers steepled beneath his chin. His gray eyes narrow slightly, and I see it coming before he even opens his mouth. "Miss Harrington, you argue that economic incentives are the most effective. What about cases where economic leverage fails to change behavior?"

My mind blanks for a half-second. Then it fills with Enzo.

Three nights ago; my apartment, books spread across the kitchen table as Enzo forced me to my knees and undid his pants.

"Focus, Toy," he murmured, lips against my ear as I squirmed. "If your professor asks this, what will you say?"

He wasn't happy with the answer I gave, and instead of giving me time to change my argument, he shoved his cock down my throat. While I gagged on him, he helped me get a better grasp on the concept and how to verbalize it in a way that couldn't be challenged.

"You'll remember that answer now, won't you?" he asked as he let me up for air.

He was right. The memory is seared into me.

"Historical evidence suggests that economic failure is often a matter of insufficient incentive rather than the wrong approach altogether," I begin, my voice clearer than I expected. "If we look at the Baltic states in the early two-thousands…"

The answer flows from me, perfect and polished, even as my inner thighs tingle with the ghost of Enzo's touch. I don't stumble or hesitate. I channel every ounce of focus into getting through these last ten minutes without combusting.

I finish with a crisp, "Thank you for your time," and a silence falls over the room like a dropped curtain.

Professor Levi's face remains impassive. Twenty-three years in politics before academia has left him with a perfect poker face. But then—there it is. The smallest nod, a twitch at the corner of his mouth that just might be approval.

"Thank you, Miss Harrington," he says, making a small note on his legal pad.

Relief floods through me, leaving my fingers trembling against the podium. I did it. I actually did it. Months of research, two weeks of intense preparation, and one very distracting benefactor later, I've survived my presentation.

We're dismissed with nothing more than a collective exhale as everyone starts packing up their things. Since our grades won't be announced until the end of January, I try to push it out of my mind as I shoulder my bag and join the stream of bodies filing out of the lecture hall.

My legs feel like they're moving through syrup as I push through the heavy door of the building. The sharp December air hits me like a slap, stealing my breath for a moment before my lungs remember how to work again.

Georgetown looks like a postcard in winter—bare tree branches lined with a dusting of frost, old brick buildings standing solid against the pale sky. I inhale deeply, letting the cold burn my throat on the way down. It feels clarifying somehow.

Christmas break stretches before me like an unmarked canvas. Weeks of freedom before the next semester begins. I shift my weight from one foot to the other, suddenly unsure what to do with this new lightness.

A part of me wants to call Lena and meet for drinks to celebrate. But another part wants to crawl into bed and sleep for a week straight. Preferably with Enzo spooning me. Just as I think the last part, I see him.

He's leaning against his sleek black SUV, parked illegally at the curb like he owns the entire fucking city. Hands tucked into the pockets of his tailored coat, shoulders relaxed despite the cold. A slow smile spreads across his face as our eyes lock across the distance.

Every nerve ending in my body lights up like a struck match. The exhaustion that weighed on me moments ago evaporates, replaced by a humming awareness that makes my skin feel too tight.

I'm already moving toward him, my pace quickening with each step until I'm running the last few feet, launching myself into his waiting arms. He catches me effortlessly, possessively, like I belong nowhere else. My heart free-falls into him, tethered only by the brutal certainty that no one else would ever catch me.

Then his mouth claims mine, hot and unapologetic, tongue pushing past my lips. The contrast is electric—his heat against my wind-chilled lips. We kiss like we haven't seen each other in days instead of mere hours. His tongue sliding against mine with a possessiveness that makes me dizzy.

"I take it you did well," he murmurs against my mouth, not really a question.

"I think so," I breathe back, aware of how his body shields me from the wind, creating a pocket of warmth between us. "He nodded. Professor Levi never nods unless you've impressed him."

Enzo's thumb brushes over my bottom lip, his eyes following the movement. "Good girl."

Two simple words, but they send a shiver down my spine that has nothing to do with the cold. I press closer, seeking more of his heat, more of the solid certainty of his body against mine.

"I knew you would," he says, and there's something in his voice—pride, but also the quiet confidence of someone who never doubted the outcome. It makes me feel both seen and small, like I'm a puzzle he solved long ago.

He kisses me again, harder this time, teeth catching my lower lip in a gentle bite that makes me gasp. My toes curl in my boots, and I can't stop the small moan that escapes when his hand slides down to grip my

hip, fingers digging in just enough to remind me who I belong to.

When he finally pulls back, the air between us is foggy with our mingled breath. His eyes are darker now, pupils dilated, and there's a tension in his jaw that tells me exactly where his thoughts have gone.

Without a word, he reaches behind me and opens the passenger door of the SUV. The command in the gesture is unmistakable. "Get in, Toy," he murmurs, low enough that only I can hear.

I hesitate for just a moment—not out of reluctance, but because the transition always takes my breath away. One minute I'm Piper Harrington, Georgetown political student with a promising future; the next I'm his, stepping willingly into the world he creates for us.

He shuts the door with a solid thunk, and I watch through the window as he walks around to the driver's side. The outside world recedes as he slides in beside me, his presence filling the car with something heavy and electric.

Pulling away from the curb, he steers with one hand while the other rests on my thigh. "Tell me about the presentation," he says, his eyes on the road as we merge into the flow of Georgetown traffic.

"I think I nailed it," I say, unable to keep the pride from my voice. "Though I did blush at one of Professor Levi's questions, thanks to you."

"Oh?" One dark eyebrow lifts, his lips curving into that knowing smile that makes my stomach flip. "And why is that?"

"Because all I could think about was you asking me the same question while I was on my knees." Heat creeps up my neck at the memory. "With your dick in my mouth."

His chuckle is low and dark, vibrating through the small space between us. "That was the point, Toy. Every time you answer a question in that classroom, I want you to remember who really taught you." The words coil in my belly, hot and undeniable.

His fingers tighten on my thigh, inching higher, and I have to press my legs together to quell the immediate ache that blooms between them.

"Where are we going?" I ask, trying to redirect the conversation before I combust. "I thought we'd go back to my place to celebrate."

"Our place," he corrects. "You thought we were going back to our place to celebrate."

He's not wrong; there's no my place anymore; it's ours, and I secretly love that. I smile softly at him, reaching out and running a finger across his cheek. I smile.

"Yeah, I guess that's what I meant."

Enzo's eyes remain fixed on the road, but there's something in his profile—a slight tightening at the corner of his mouth—that makes my heart skip. "We are going to celebrate," he says simply. "Just not at home."

"Then where?"

He glances at me then, those ice-blue eyes holding mine for a beat longer than is safe while driving. "You said you wanted to know me, Toy. There's no better way than meeting my family."

The air leaves my lungs in a rush. "Your family?"

"My mother. My cousins." He says it casually, as if he's suggesting a trip to the grocery store rather than introducing me to the people who shaped him. "We're flying to Cleveland."

"Cleveland?" My voice comes out higher than I intended. "Now? Today?"

"Yes, today." His smile is slow, predatory, satisfied at my reaction. "Is that a problem?"

"No. I mean…" I shake my head, trying to organize the sudden flood of questions. "I just didn't expect… you never talk about them."

"Because they're mine," he says simply. "But now you're mine too. So it's time."

Something warm unfurls in my chest at his words, a giddy excitement that makes it hard to sit still. "What are they like? Your mom, is she…"

"Like me?" He laughs, a genuine sound I rarely hear. "No. She's worse. But I think you'll like her."

"And your cousins? How many do you have?"

"Only three that matter. Matteo, Rafe, and Remus." He navigates through a yellow light, his driving as precise and controlled as everything else he does.

"Matteo and Rafe," I squeak. "Please tell me they're not the ones from—"

"The interview," he finishes, shooting me a wolfish grin. "Oh, that's them, Toy."

Well… fuck. A flush creeps up my neck.

"They weren't actually looking when I fingered you," he adds. "Both of them were facing away."

I breathe a sigh of relief. "Okay then," I agree, trying to ignore the nerves dancing underneath my skin. As I look out the window, I suddenly realize the familiar streets of Georgetown have disappeared and we're heading toward the highway. "Wait, are we going right now? I haven't packed anything."

"I packed for you."

I blink at him. "You what?"

His thumb resumes its small circles against my thigh. "Everything you'll need is already on my jet."

"Your jet." I repeat the words numbly. "As in… do you have a private jet?"

"Did you think we were flying commercial?" There's amusement in his voice now, rich and dark.

I stare at his profile—the straight line of his nose, the sharp cut of his jaw, the way his dark hair curls slightly at his collar. Of course Enzo

has a private jet. Of course he packed for me without asking. Of course he orchestrated everything without giving me a chance to say no—because with him, I never really want to.

"How long are we staying?" I ask, my voice smaller than I intended.

He glances at me. "Through Christmas. Maybe longer."

A cold weight settles in my stomach. "Christmas?" I twist my hands in my lap. "I usually spend Christmas with my parents. My mom texted last week, and I already told her I'd be there."

His answering growl vibrates through the seat, and I feel it hum against my spine. "They don't deserve you."

The silence that follows his outburst seems to stretch into infinity. The only sound is the soft purr of the engine and the rhythmic click of the turn signal as Enzo merges onto the highway.

"No," I agree, finally able to stitch words together. "But they're my parents."

His eyes are still on the road, but his jawline has hardened. "Then I'll come with you to your parents'."

I stare at him, speechless. Enzo, in my childhood home. Enzo, sitting at my family's dinner table. Enzo, meeting my horrid parents… whelp.

"Unless you don't want me there?" His question sounds casual, but I know better. There's an edge beneath the words, a trap waiting to be sprung.

"I want you there," I say quickly, and to my surprise, I mean it. "I just… didn't think you'd want to come."

His hand moves from my thigh to the back of my neck, fingers threading through my hair, grip firm but not painful. "Where you go, I go, Toy. That's how this works." His thumb brushes against my skin.

My heart stutters, a traitorous little lurch I can't control, and I find myself leaning into his touch, craving the certainty of belonging to him.

I still haven't told him that I'm his, not unless he's using orgasms to force the words from me. I meant what I told him two weeks ago; until he shows me who he really is, I can't belong to him.

But every day, he gets one step closer to me uttering the words he's longing to hear.

As we touch down in Cleveland, I feel the difference in the air the second my foot hits the tarmac. I can't stop watching my toy take it all in, unaware that each molecule has been filtered through my family's grip for generations.

Her fingers curl around my forearm, trusting. "We're not going through the terminal?" she asks, those green eyes scanning the private hangar, the waiting black Bentley, the absence of any processing or security.

"No need." My palm finds the small of her back, guiding her forward. "This is Russo domain."

I can't stop touching her—shoulder, wrist, hair—as if making sure she hasn't dissolved between my fingers. And every time I do, it quiets something rabid in me. The driver opens the car door without a word, eyes down in proper deference. When we slide into the leather interior, I pull her against me, her thigh pressed to mine.

"My family owns everything here," I tell her, watching her profile as Cleveland's skyline crawls past the tinted windows. "People know better than to question a Russo."

"A Russo?" she asks, her voice catching slightly. "Is that… you? I mean, are you a Russo?"

"I am." I trace the line of her jaw with one finger. "I'm Lorenzo Russo."

"Why are you only now giving me your full name?" she questions.

I smirk. "You never asked, Toy. You guessed Lorenzo by yourself, but you never asked what my full name is."

She scoffs, but instead of arguing, she accepts it with a sharp nod. "Touché," she mumbles.

The city gives way to older neighborhoods, elegant buildings with history etched into their foundations. When we pull up to my building—twenty-eight stories of sleek stone and glass—I feel her shoulders tense slightly.

"This entire building is ours," I explain, not a question. "I had it constructed eight years ago."

She blinks. "The whole thing?"

"Yes." I watch understanding dawn across her face—another layer of my reach made visible. "We'll stay in the ground-floor apartment."

"Not the penthouse?" she asks, curiosity dancing behind her eyes.

I step out, offering my hand. "Of course not. You don't like heights."

Her lips part slightly, surprise softening her features. It's such a small detail—one she might not have been aware I knew about, but I know everything about my toy. Her fingers touch mine, delicate and warm.

"I wonder if I'll ever stop being surprised by the things you know," she muses. Then she adds, "I hope not."

"Don't count on it," I smirk. "I like surprising you."

A small, private smile touches her mouth. "Thank you for being thoughtful."

The quiet gratitude in her voice melts something inside me—a heat that spreads through my chest and makes my fingers tighten around hers. Such a simple thing, and she looks at me like I've given her something precious.

I quickly grab our suitcases from the trunk, refusing anyone else to follow us into the apartment I've made sure is ready for us. We walk across the lobby and take a left, toward the back, where the door to the apartment hides behind a column.

This is the one apartment I never thought I'd use, so when Piper threw down the gauntlet two weeks ago, saying I couldn't have her until she knew the real me, I started making preparations for us to come here.

I unlock the door with my thumbprint on the scanner. "It'll only open for the two of us," I explain as I open the door.

"How did you…" She stops talking with a shake of her head. "Never mind. I don't think I want to know how you got my thumbprint."

Although I could remind her that we got her prints at Blackwood, I don't. If she wants it to remain a mystery, I'm not going to ruin it for her.

Inside, I watch her face as she takes in the space—the floor-to-ceiling windows, the furniture, and even the paintings. Her eyes travel from the custom kitchen to the hallway leading to the bedroom, until they stop, fixed on something in the living room.

A banner stretches across the main window, and the bold red letters read: WELCOME HOME, KINGMAKER!!

"Fucking Matteo," I mutter, crossing the room to tear it down. My cousin's sense of humor hasn't evolved since we were teenagers. I crush the banner in my fist, tossing it into the trash.

"Kingmaker?" Piper repeats, that sharp mind of hers already turning the word over.

"Later." I check my watch. "Are you hungry? La Volta has a table ready."

Her face brightens. "I'd love to eat, but I need to shower and get changed first." She gestures vaguely at her clothes.

"Of course." I guide her toward the master bathroom. "Take your time."

While the shower runs, I unpack our suitcases, hanging the clothes in the closet. There are rows of new clothes waiting for her already, garments I've bought over the last week. The only thing she won't find here are panties. There are none.

I select a long black dress with a slit that rises just high enough to make my mouth water, laying it carefully on the bed. Then I pull out a bra and a pair of stilettos I've dreamed of seeing her bend over in.

While I wait for her to finish up, I pour a whiskey and light up a cigar, making myself comfortable. For once, I'd like my brain to shut the fuck up, but as time stretches, it becomes clear that ain't happening.

I feel like a fucking adolescent boy about to ask the girl to prom. Except, I'm not asking Piper anything, I'm telling. And what I'm telling her tonight is everything.

When I hear the sound of the blow dryer, I pour myself another drink and relight the cigar that died in the ashtray. As I puff on it, I smirk, the memory of Halloween coming back to me. Fuck, my toy really is perfect.

Piper finally emerges from the bathroom wrapped in a towel, her long, brown hair cascading down her back. She sees the dress, fingers hovering over the fabric like she already knows it's more than silk.

"You chose for me," she says, eyebrow arched.

"I did," I confirm, stepping closer. "Do you object?"

She playfully rolls her eyes and lifts the dress up, holding it against her. "No, it's beautiful." Turning, she grins at me. "That's why I bought it."

With those words, she finds her toiletries and disappears back into the bathroom. I give her thirty minutes. Long enough for my anticipation to calcify into something sharp. When I finally join her, the jewelry box feels heavier than it should.

"What's that?" she asks, eyeing it in the mirror as I position myself behind her.

I open it, revealing the gold necklace with a puzzle piece pendant. "The second last one," I murmur, lifting her hair out of the way so I can fasten it around her neck.

She goes completely still as the gold settles against her collarbone. She doesn't move, and I can't fucking breathe. I've orchestrated entire regimes with less pressure than this one moment.

"Second last," she breathes, tracing its outline. "What's the last piece?"

Ignoring the question, I watch her in the mirror—the reverent way she touches the pendant, the slight part of her lips, the faint flush in her cheeks. She understands the significance, even if she doesn't yet know the full weight of what I'm giving her. Tonight, she'll learn exactly who she's wearing around her neck.

As we drive through Little Italy, her gaze stays locked on the world outside, but I stay locked on her. She has no idea what it does to me, watching her wear the puzzle piece like it's always belonged there.

When we pull up to La Volta, the driver exits the car and opens the door for us. Piper slides out first, but when she reaches for his outstretched hand, I let out a low, menacing growl. "Don't even think about it." I palm her hip. "If you touch him, I'll have to kill him. And I don't want that blood anywhere near you."

She stiffens for a second, but then she huffs with annoyance and exits without touching him.

"Apologies, Lorenzo," the driver says, looking anywhere but at Piper. "I only meant to help."

I know he did. "It's fine," I state, correcting my suit jacket. "I don't know how long we'll be, so stay nearby."

Piper takes my hand, but she doesn't move yet. "You did nothing wrong," she says, looking at the driver. "And if he gives you any grief about helping me, I want you to tell me. It was a nice gesture."

When the driver looks at me, I just shrug. "You heard her, feel free to report me if it happens again." I smirk as we walk away.

La Volta parts for us like the sea parting for its god. Not one glance meets mine, because power isn't acknowledged—it's obeyed.

My hand doesn't leave the small of Piper's back as the maître d' guides us through the main dining room toward the private booths in the back. No words need to be exchanged; my presence is enough.

I've walked this path a thousand times, but never with her beside me. Never with the weight of my name balanced like a blade between us, waiting to be handed over hilt-first.

"This is…" Piper's voice trails off as we're seated in the curved booth at the back, far from prying eyes.

"My family's," I finish for her, though I'm sure that wasn't what she meant to say. "Like everything else in this city worth having."

Her eyes catch on the velvet drapes, the obsidian flatware, the way the staff move like shadows. "Why does everyone either look scared or like they want to fuck you?" she asks, sounding annoyed at the last part.

"Does that bother you?" I counter, amused.

Before she can answer, the sommelier approaches. Instead of carrying a wine list, he presents a bottle of wine I've had waiting for this exact moment—a Brunello di Montalcino, laid down the year Piper was born.

After filling our glasses, he leaves with a murmured, "Enjoy."

I raise my glass. "To knowing." Her glass meets mine with a delicate ring that echoes between us. "To seeing."

The wine tastes of dark cherries and the slow burn of patience. I set my glass down, carefully, deliberately, like a man setting a timer on a bomb he has no intention of running from.

"You said you wanted to know everything." My voice remains steady as a surgeon's hand. "Are you ready for the truth, Toy?"

Her eyes narrow slightly. "Bring it on, Lorenzo."

"I didn't rise to power, Piper. I built it. Inherited it. Expanded it." Pausing, I take a deep breath. "The Russo family doesn't claim territory; we create it."

She lets out a nervous laugh. "You make it sound like you're the mafia." She tilts her head, thinking. "Wait… is that what you are? Your family, I mean."

"That's what they call us when they want to simplify what can't be simplified." I lean forward. "What we are is infrastructure. We're the shadow behind every government, the whisper behind every policy. Every empire you admire? We put it there."

I take a large sip of the wine.

"More specifically, I put it there. Before me, it was my dad, and before him…" Trailing off, I swirl my hand in the air. "You get the picture."

She rests her fingers lightly against the glass, but her eyes never leave mine. Calculating. Unafraid. "So you really are a kingmaker."

I chuckle. "I'm not just a kingmaker, Toy. I'm the kingmaker."

She whispers the word, and I watch her mouth form the word, memorizing the shape of it on her lips. I expected resistance. At least a sliver of fear. But she's not shrinking—she's studying me like I'm a thesis she intends to defend.

"Every senator who's risen in the last decade has done so because I allowed it. Every presidential candidate approved by both parties has my fingerprints on their selection."

She takes a slow sip of wine. "So the meetings you allowed me to listen to… I mean…" She pauses, and pinches the bridge of her nose. "Was that to help me? Or were you feeding me breadcrumbs about who you really are?"

"Both," I admit. I reach across the table, taking her hand. "Every move I've made since the day I saw you has been calculated, Piper. Every door that closed, every opportunity that vanished—that was me clearing your path."

"Hang on." She holds her hand up, halting me. "You blacklisted me, didn't you?" she asks, her eyes narrowed and her tone accusatory.

"I redirected you. To me," I explain with a shrug. This is something I refuse to apologize for. And still, my chest tightens. It's not guilt— Russo blood doesn't do guilt—but from the fucking miracle that she's still sitting across from me.

The waiter appears with our meal—Ossobuco for me, sea bass for her. Neither of us ordered. Her eyes follow the waiter as he retreats, understanding dawning.

"How far does it go?" she asks, cutting into her fish. "Your control."

"If I pull my backing, governments fall." The words are simple, factual. "And they know it."

"And you've been doing this since…"

"Since I was eighteen." I watch her calculate again. "Though I sat in the room from the time I could understand what was being said."

She takes another bite, thinking. "Is this why you insisted on the blindfold in the beginning?" Another bite. "And, look, I know you say I never asked about your name, which is true. But you still could have told me and you didn't. I want to know why."

"Names are masks." I set my fork down carefully. "I only ever planned to take mine off for one person."

Something flickers in her eyes; awareness. "Me."

"You." The single syllable carries the weight of years. "I told you I would never lie to you."

She doesn't speak for several long moments, just takes small bites of her food. I feel a tightness in my chest, something unfamiliar—the threat of loss. I've faced down presidents and entire governments without flinching, but this silence from her scrapes me hollow.

"Why tell me now?" she finally asks.

"Because you've earned it." I meet her eyes across the table. "Because I want you to know exactly what you're choosing when you choose me."

"And if I choose to walk away?" Her voice is careful, measured.

"You won't," I growl.

"I might," she insists. "Answer the question."

"That's not an option, Toy," I rasp. "So you might as well stop pretending you want to."

The minutes stretch as we finish our meal, drinking more wine, exchanging fragments of conversation that dance around the weight of what I've confessed.

I watch her process, that brilliant mind of hers turning over each revelation, examining it from every angle. She asks more questions— about specific elections, about family structure, about how decisions are made. I answer every one. She looks at me differently. Not with fear or revulsion, but with a clarity that feels like being seen for the first time.

"You know…" She leans back slowly, eyes unfocused for the first time all night. "… when you study politics long enough, you start to see the patterns—who gets elevated, who gets erased, what stories are spun. And you start wondering."

Her fingers graze the puzzle pendant.

"Wondering if there's more to it than what people let on. If

someone's behind it all. Not just a system or government. But a puppeteer."

I don't speak. I let her get there on her own.

"And now you're telling me it's you." She meets my gaze, and the stillness between us sharpens. "You've just confirmed every quiet suspicion I've ever had about how this country actually works."

A pause. A breath.

"And somehow," she murmurs, voice quieter, "that's not even the most terrifying thing about you."

"No?"

"The scariest part is that it makes sense. That it fits." Her lips curve. It's not quite a smile, but something darker. She leans closer, eyes still fixed on mine. "You're the only man who could say all that and still make me want to climb into your lap."

I exhale in relief. My toy's not scared, and she's definitely not going to run. I can see it. She's fucking turned on. By the power, me, or maybe both.

"So you're not running?" I ask, needing to hear her say it.

The waiter arrives to take our plates and asks if we want dessert. I look at my toy, arching an eyebrow. Instead of answering the unspoken question, she stands, slightly unsteady from the wine. I rise immediately, ready to catch her if she falls. But she doesn't. She steps toward me, close enough that I can smell the wine on her breath.

"Take me back to your home, Lorenzo." Her voice drops to a whisper that burns. "And then fuck me all night long."

My blood ignites, a liquid fire that races from chest to groin. She knows everything now—every shadow, every sin—and still she wants me. Still, she says my name like a prayer.

The car door closes and seals us in darkness, in want, in the aftershock of truth. Piper's mouth finds mine before the driver has even pulled away from the curb—hungry, demanding, tasting of wine and absolution.

Her hands fist in my hair, pulling me closer as if the revelation of who I am has only sharpened her appetite. Mine. The word vibrates through me with each heartbeat. She knows me now—my name, my power—and still she reaches for me. Still she burns.

I slide my hand beneath her dress, finding the wet heat between her thighs. She gasps into my mouth, hips rising to meet my touch. I press my fingers against her, circling slowly.

"Please," she begs, biting my lower lip. "I need you inside me."

"Not yet." I keep my strokes measured, controlled. "Not here."

Her fingers work frantically at my belt, desperate to free me. "Enzo, please."

The sound of my name on her lips nearly shatters my resolve. I capture her wrists in one hand, pinning them to her lap while my fingers continue their methodical torture between her thighs.

"I said not yet." I murmur, biting the soft skin below her ear.

She whimpers, legs falling further open. Her slick heat drenches my fingers, almost enough to snap every thread of control I have left. One stroke and she's trembling. Two and she's whimpering against my throat. Three and she's broken—moaning, begging.

"You're soaked," I whisper, pushing one finger inside her, then another. "Dripping for me."

Her hips buck wildly. "Then fuck me. Now."

I unclick our seatbelts with my free hand, pulling her onto my lap so she straddles me. Her dress bunches around her waist. I reach for my zipper, freeing myself while her eyes widen, hungry and wanting.

"I'm not going to fuck you in the car," I rasp, guiding her hips with one hand.

She makes a small sound of protest until she feels the head of my cock pressing against her entrance. When I ease her down, just enough for her to feel me stretching her, her lips part on a silent gasp.

"But I need to be inside you," I confess, the words torn from some primal part of me.

She tries to take more of me, but I hold her still, allowing only this shallow penetration. She squeezes around me, muscles fluttering in frustration, and I groan at the sensation.

"Please," she pants. "More."

"At home." I guide her hips in a barely there rock, not thrusting, just connected. "Where I can have all of you."

We remain locked together this way for the rest of the drive—her trembling on my lap, me buried just inside her, both of us suspended in exquisite torture. By the time we reach the apartment, we're both panting, clothes damp with sweat, eyes glazed with need.

The second the door clicks shut behind us, I slam her against the wall. My mouth crashes onto hers, hot and punishing. I've been starved for fucking hours—years—a lifetime. Her back arches, pressing her breasts against my chest as my tongue invades her mouth.

I fist her hair tight enough to sting, yanking her head back so I can bite down the length of her throat. She moans, nails digging into my shoulders through my shirt. Her hands claw at my clothes, buttons flying as she tears at my shirt. I don't care. Nothing matters but getting to her skin, getting inside her, making her feel the weight of what she's done by accepting me.

"Do you know what you do to me?" I growl, tearing her dress down the middle. The sound of ripping fabric fills the air between our ragged breaths. "Do you have any fucking idea what it does to me when you look at me like that?"

She stands before me in nothing but the torn dress and the gold puzzle piece at her throat. Her hair falls wild around her shoulders, lips swollen from my kisses.

"Show me," she challenges, green eyes burning into mine.

I rip away what's left of her clothes, lifting her against the wall. Her legs wrap around my waist, heels digging into my back. I slide two fingers into her, finding her impossibly wet, impossibly tight.

"This cunt," I murmur, curling my fingers just right, watching her head fall back. "So fucking perfect. So fucking mine."

She grinds down on my fingers, chasing the edge like she needs it to breathe. I work her relentlessly, thumb circling her clit while my fingers press deep inside. I could watch her like this forever—suspended between pleasure and pain, surrender and defiance.

"You know who I am now," I tell her, increasing the pressure. "You know what I've done. What I'll do for you."

"Yes," she gasps, eyes half-closed, lost in sensation.

"Say my name," I command, feeling her start to tighten around my fingers.

"Enzo," she moans, hands scrambling for purchase on my shoulders.

"My full name," I growl, pressing harder, deeper.

"Lorenzo," she pants. "Lorenzo Russo."

Her walls flutter, clenching hard around my fingers, and I know she's close. I twist my hand just right, circling her clit until she comes undone in my grip, moaning my name like it's salvation. Her legs shake around me, and I don't let up until she's trembling with aftershocks, sweat glistening at her throat.

The sound of her rapture while chanting my full name pushes me over the edge of control. I withdraw my fingers, replacing them with the thick head of my dick. She's so ready, so wet that I slide in with one deep thrust that makes her cry out.

"Tell me you still want this," I demand, holding still inside her, my forehead pressed to hers. I don't need her consent, I already have that. But I need to hear the words to sate the primal beast inside me.

"I want this." Her voice breaks on the words. "I want you. Now fuck me, Lorenzo. Stop holding back."

I begin to move then, each thrust harder than the last. Her back slams against the wall, but she meets me force for force, pulling me deeper, urging me on with breathless pleas. The sound of skin against skin, of her wet heat taking me in, fills the apartment.

Every thrust is a threat. A vow. A silent reminder that no one else will ever fuck her like this—because no one else will ever get the chance.

"Tell me you're mine," I growl into her ear, feeling her tighten around me.

I shift my angle, and the second I hit that spot, her breath catches. She claws at my shoulders, back arching hard. One more thrust and she breaks—screaming into my mouth as her pussy milks me, clenching around me.

"Fuck!" she cries, undulating her hips in greedy motions.

Her refusal to say the words should infuriate me, but somehow it only makes me want her more. My perfect, stubborn toy, still fighting even as she gives herself to me completely.

Before either of us can come, I carry her to the bedroom, keeping my cock inside her. She rotates her hips, seeking friction and movement while clinging to me, wild with need.

I place her on all fours on the bed, positioning myself behind her. "Look at you," I breathe, running my hands over the curve of her ass, the arch of her spine. I trace the tight ring of her asshole, not pressing— just circling. A warning. A promise. Her breath hitches, and I grin. "One day, Toy," I murmur. "Every inch of you will be mine."

I slide back into her in one long, relentless thrust that makes her bury her face in the pillow to muffle her scream. I grab her hair, pulling her head back.

"Let me hear you," I command, setting a ruthless pace. "Let me hear what I do to you."

She obeys, each thrust pulling a raw moan from her throat. I watch where our bodies join, mesmerized by the sight of her taking all of me, again and again. Her back gleams with sweat, muscles tensing as she pushes back to meet each thrust.

"Harder," she begs, and I comply, gripping her hips hard enough to bruise.

"Tell me how deep you want me," I growl.

"Deep enough to ruin me," she pants. "Make me feel it. Show me what it means to belong to a kingmaker."

"Tell me," I repeat, my voice filled with gravel.

She mewls when I slide one hand to her tits, pinching her pert nipple. "Fuck. Ah, okay. Fuck me like you own me," she chokes out. "Like you own everything else." She cries out, bucking hard as I circle her clit with ruthless precision.

I'm beyond gentleness now, beyond restraint. I fuck her with everything I am—the monster, the man, the obsessive shadow who has wanted her from the first moment. And she matches me, stroke for stroke, moan for moan, as if she was made for this, for me.

I feel her start to tighten around me; her moans becoming desperate, breathless. My hand slides beneath her to rub her clit, pushing her toward the edge.

"Come for your kingmaker," I demand, pounding into her. "Come on my dick while I fill you."

Her whole body tenses, then breaks, clenching around me in waves as she cries out my name. The sight of her—head thrown back, body shaking beneath mine, taking everything I give her—pushes me over the edge.

"Fuck, I love you," I growl as I break apart inside her, the words ripped from the rawest part of me. The place where she lives now.

My cock jerks, emptying everything I have inside her. Every thrust and every drop is a brand, sealing her to me from the inside out.

I collapse beside her, pulling her sweat-slick body against mine. Her heart races beneath my palm, gradually slowing as we both catch our breath. I press my lips to her shoulder, tasting salt and wine and completion.

She knows me now—my name, my power, my obsession. And still, she's here. Still, she's mine. Even if she won't say the words yet, I can feel the truth of it in how her body yields to mine, in how she turns in my arms to kiss me again, softer now but no less hungry.

I have given her my darkest truths, and she has given me absolution in return. My toy isn't blind, and she's definitely not naïve. She knows

what being with me means, and she's staying anyway. Not to be saved, but to burn beside me.

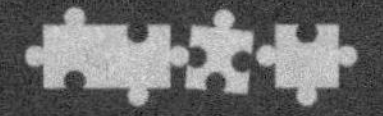

43

Piper

It's been two days since we arrived here in Cleveland, and we've barely left the apartment. Ever since Enzo told me who he is, there's been an insatiable hum under my skin. I swear, I've tried insisting we go sightseeing, but one glance from him, and I'm a panting mess, wanting his dick, his mouth, even his fingers, until I can barely walk.

But today, it's finally time to meet the infamous Russo family, which is why I'm fussing both with my clothes and makeup. Enzo's no help, he keeps insisting I don't need to get dressed at all.

"It's bad enough I have to meet your family without panties," I huff, when he makes the same suggestion for the thousandth time.

"We could just blow them off," he smirks, puffing on his cigar.

Maybe it's because we've spent most of our time at my—our—place, but I never knew he smoked this much. I don't mind. Not at all. In fact, I'm starting to like the sweet smell, associating it both with him and the filthy things I know he's capable of doing with a cigar.

"Hey," I ask, pausing as a thought hits me. "Is your place in D.C. anything like this apartment?"

"What do you mean?" he asks, blowing out smoke and tipping back the whiskey in his crystal glass.

Shrugging, I wrap the sage green dress I've picked around my body. "I was just wondering if this is your style."

I've never seen his D.C. residence, and until this trip, I haven't given it any thought. But now I'm curious. God, my apartment must feel like a novelty home compared to what he's used to. This place is a cathedral to taste—skyline like a painting, walls hung in art worth more than my degree.

He shrugs, as though he doesn't know how to answer, which I find adorable and so unlike him it's almost funny. "I don't dislike it," he says thoughtfully. "But my place in D.C. wasn't decorated or designed by me. I handpicked everything here."

"Really?" I ask. When he nods, I reach for the black boots, opting to go bare-legged despite the freezing temperatures outside. "What was your inspiration for this place?"

A genuine smile tugs at the corners of his lips, his blue eyes crinkling. "You, Toy. I asked myself what you'd like." He takes one last drag of his cigar before putting it out. "Plus, Lena helped me."

"Lena?" I squeak, surprised.

He nods. "Yeah, I called her and asked her for help with what you'd like."

"You really called my best friend?" I ask, stunned.

"I wanted to get it right," he says simply. "You don't hand someone a kingdom unless you build it for them first."

The revelation melts something in me, warm, messy, a little dangerous. Enzo's thoughtfulness really knows no bounds. Closing the distance between us, I wrap my arms around his neck. "Thank you," I murmur.

I step away again, mumbling that I need to finish getting ready. Once I'm done, I take a last look in the bathroom mirror, puffing my hair. Okay, I think I'm ready to meet his family.

"We need to stop somewhere first," I call out, running my finger across the seams of my lips to make sure none of my nude lipstick is smudging.

Enzo comes into view, adjusting his cufflinks, the movement so practiced it looks like a dance. He arches a brow. "We're on a schedule, Toy."

"I'm not showing up empty-handed to meet your mother," I state, leaving no room for argument. "At a minimum, I'm buying her some flowers."

Something softens in his expression. "Whatever you say," he murmurs, stepping closer to tuck a strand of hair behind my ear, his fingers lingering against my skin.

The detour takes fifteen minutes. I select an arrangement that walks the line between impressive and not trying too hard—elegant white lilies with sprays of something blue I don't recognize.

When Enzo tries to pay, I put my foot down. "They're not from me if you're paying," I argue, and eventually, he gives in.

Back in the car, darkness has settled over the city. The driver weaves through traffic like it's personally obligated to part for him.

"So, where are we going?" I ask, curious to know more.

"The Russo family estate," Enzo answers, running his thumb across the back of my hand.

"And your mom lives there?" I ask.

He shakes his head. "None of us live on the estate. We just meet there."

The car turns onto a private road, then slows as we approach a massive gate—wrought iron twisted into patterns that seem almost violent in their beauty. A guard steps forward, light scanning over our vehicle. No ID requested. They know exactly who's in this car.

The gates swing open, and I feel the first real shift in the air. It's not danger, but something equally old and merciless. The kind of power I grew up around but never understood. The kind that lived behind manicured hedges and dinner-party smiles. I didn't know what it was then. But I do now.

This power is different, though. Or maybe I'm the one who has changed. Because now I know who owns me, who protects me. The man beside me, with one hand squeezing my thigh. His thumb strokes slow, deliberate circles—possessive, steady as ever.

"It's me and you, Toy. No one else matters."

As we round the final curve in the driveway, the estate looms into view—sleek, sprawling, designed for privacy and dominance. Lights illuminate strategic portions of the façade, creating shadows that seem intentional rather than incidental.

It's not a house; it's a statement.

Instead of being intimidated, I feel my blood warming, a familiar heat that has nothing to do with fear and everything to do with hunger. This is Enzo's world—the foundation that shaped him into the man whose hands have mapped every inch of my body, whose voice has pulled confessions from my lips I never thought I'd make.

His fingers flex against my thigh, and I cover his hand with mine. "Ready?" he asks, watching me with that intensity that makes my heart skip.

"Lead the way," I say, knowing he won't allow me to fall.

Enzo's hand remains at the small of my back as he leads me inside, the heat of his palm seeping through my dress like a brand.

A woman appears at the end of the hallway, and even from a distance, I know she's Enzo's mother. It's not just the ice-blue eyes—a perfect match to his—but something in the way she holds herself, like the air around her should feel privileged to touch her skin.

"Lorenzo," she says, her voice carrying the kind of cultured precision that can't be bought, only inherited. Her gaze slides to me with clinical interest, as though I'm a specimen she's not quite sure how to classify.

"Mom," Enzo—Lorenzo—replies, the name still foreign on my mental tongue. "This is Piper."

She approaches with measured steps, her smile razor-sharp beneath perfect lipstick, and kisses my cheeks—left, then right. The scent of her perfume is subtle but unmistakable, probably a custom-blend that probably contains notes of power and intimidation.

"These are for you," I say, offering the flowers. "Thank you for inviting me."

It's strange to say since she didn't actually invite me, but I was raised with manners that stick even when faced with a woman who I'm sure could order my disappearance with a single nod. She takes the

arrangement with the kind of glance that tells me she knows the florist, the price point, and what I was trying to say with it.

"How thoughtful," she says, passing them to a staff member who materializes from nowhere. "Come, we'll have wine before dinner."

We follow her into a sitting room where everything feels curated for impact rather than comfort. The chairs are beautiful but offer no forgiveness to the body. The artwork lining the walls speaks of conquest and loyalty, bloodlines and sacrifice. A decanter of red wine awaits on a side table, alongside crystal glasses that catch the light like prisms.

"So, Piper," she begins once we're seated, her glass balanced between long, elegant fingers. "Tell me about yourself. Lorenzo has been very reticent about you."

I feel Enzo shift beside me, his thigh pressing against mine. "Or we could start lighter. Perhaps ask about the trip first," he deadpans, shooting his mom an unimpressed glare.

Taking his hand, I squeeze it. "Why?" I ask him. "We might as well get to it." My tone is all sugary and false bravado.

His mom tilts her head slightly and gives me a smile that almost looks real.

"I'm in my last year at Georgetown," I begin. Then I throw myself into a description of what I study, and the line of work I hope to end up in.

She listens thoughtfully, but for some reason, her lips thin with each word I speak. "Ah, a kingmaker in the making," she says, her eyes flicking to Enzo with something that might be amusement. "How fitting."

There's that word again—kingmaker. Something stirs in my chest, and I feel like I should have figured it out before he told me yesterday.

"And how did you meet my son?" she continues, her tone casual but her eyes sharp. "Did you hope to use his connections to further your own career ambitions?"

I could lie and craft a more palatable version of our beginning. But something tells me this woman would taste the falsehood like poison.

"He stalked me," I say simply, taking a sip of wine that burns pleasantly down my throat. "To answer your question, I didn't even know he existed until he offered me an interview at his company. And even then, I was blindfolded for said interview."

Enzo's mother freezes mid-sip, her eyes widening fractionally before darting to her son. Then, unexpectedly, she laughs—a sound like crystal breaking, beautiful and dangerous.

"Of course he did," she says, setting her glass down with deliberate care. "My son has always known exactly what he wants."

The tension in the room shifts, recalibrates. Where there was coolness, I now sense something like respect—or at least a willingness to reserve judgment. "And you stayed," she observes, studying me over

the rim of her glass. "Despite the… unconventional beginning."

"I did," I confirm, squeezing Enzo's hand again. "I know what I want too."

Something passes between us, a current of understanding that transcends words. She sees something in me that she recognizes—not a threat to her son, but a match.

Her eyes soften almost imperceptibly as she looks at Enzo. "Even as a child. He was always watching, always three steps ahead of everyone else." She shifts her gaze back to me. "It's rare that he lets anyone close enough to see the real him."

I feel the weight of her words; the test hidden within them. I hold her gaze. "I don't take the privilege lightly." Not because I'm brave. Because he's here. Because if I stumble, he'll catch me before I hit the ground.

Her lips curve into something more genuine than her earlier smiles. "No," she says quietly. "I don't believe you do."

The grandfather clock in the corner chimes softly, and she rises in one fluid motion. "I think it's time for dinner," she announces, smoothing invisible wrinkles from her dress. "Though I'm afraid I won't be joining you as I have a previous engagement."

I blink, surprise momentarily breaking through my composed façade. We came all this way for dinner, and she's ditching us?

Enzo doesn't seem surprised. "Give my regards to the host," he says, standing and helping me to my feet.

"Of course," she replies, then turns to me. "It was enlightening to meet you, Piper. I do hope we'll see more of each other."

With that, she glides from the room, leaving behind only the lingering scent of her perfume and the distinct impression that I've passed some crucial test.

"Come," Enzo murmurs, his lips brushing my ear. "The others are waiting."

The evening is only beginning, and I've already navigated my first trial by fire.

We move deeper into the estate until we reach another massive room, this one dominated by a long table of dark wood so polished I can see my reflection on its surface. Three men are already seated, their conversation cutting off abruptly as we enter.

The silence feels like a blade drawn across exposed skin—not painful yet, but the threat is there. The man at the head of the table rises first. He's younger than Enzo but cut from the same cloth—expensive suit, calculated movements, eyes that miss nothing.

"Lorenzo."

"Remus," Enzo replies, pulling me closer to his side.

Remus' gaze cuts to me; cold, calculating. Like he's weighing my value on a scale that could tip either way. It's as though he's calculating my value in a complex equation. "You must be Piper," he says. "I'm

Remus." The way he offers no last name tells me it's the same as Enzo's.

"A pleasure," I say, meeting his eyes directly. I feel Enzo's approval in the slight pressure of his fingers against my spine.

"Sit," Remus says, and it's more of a decree than an invitation. Authority runs thick in Russo blood.

As we move toward our seats, the man on Remus's right smiles at me. "Nice to see you again, Piper."

I pause, searching his face. I've never met him before.

"Rafe," he supplies, amusement dancing in his eyes. "Though we weren't formally introduced last time."

Before I can ask what he means, the third man sprawls in his chair with the lazy menace of someone who knows exactly how dangerous he is. He barks a short laugh. "Fuck, I barely recognized you without Lorenzo's cock in your mouth," he says, grinning wolfishly. "The blindfold was a nice touch, though."

Enzo goes rigid beside me, a current of lethal energy vibrating through him so strongly I can feel it against my skin. The temperature in the room seems to drop by ten degrees.

"Matteo," he growls. "Shut the fuck up."

Ahh… the penny drops; Rafe and Matteo, they were there at my interview. Yeah… not awkward at all. But I don't shrink. I laugh—deep, unapologetic, and just loud enough to make Matteo blink.

I slide into my designated chair and reach for the wine already poured. "I'm not sure why you're thinking about his cock when I was kneeling in only my underwear," I say, taking a sip. "But I don't judge."

Matteo's eyes widen for a fraction of a second before he bursts into laughter again. This time with real pleasure rather than mockery. "Fuck, Enzo, she's a keeper."

The tension bleeds from Enzo's body as he takes his seat beside me, his thigh pressing against mine beneath the table. His hand finds my knee, squeezing once—approval, gratitude, desire, all compressed into a single touch.

He doesn't need to speak to make his claim. The way he touches me—the way he lets them see he'll burn the world down if I'm harmed—is enough.

Dinner unfolds like a chess match in candlelight. Casual moves hiding sharp edges. Staff appear and disappear with silent efficiency, serving courses that would make Michelin-starred restaurants envious.

"That fire in Brighton Heights," Matteo says at one point, tearing into his steak with barely restrained violence. "Clean job. No trace."

"The insurance won't pay out," Rafe replies, his tone conversational. "Too many questions."

"That wasn't the point," Remus interjects, not looking up from his plate. "It was about the message. Why is Enzo the only one who can

deliver a message without violence?"

Matteo guffaws. "Yeah, say that to Senator Jacobs. That was a bloody message—"

"I swear to God, I'll fucking stab you," Enzo growls.

Rafe looks over at me, and the grimace he makes is enough to tell me he doesn't like what he sees on my face. "Guess you didn't know about that one," he says, and there's a lilt of apology in his tone.

I chew slowly, letting the weight of it settle in my gut like warm metal. Yet, all I can think is, I fucking knew it. I still remember seeing Senator Jacobs resign, and even then, it felt forced.

"Why did he resign?" I hear myself asking, catching Enzo's eyes.

"Jacobs brutalized several interns," he replies coldly. "It was needed."

Nodding, I take another bite of the food. "And you murdered him?"

Instead of being horrified, I find myself leaning forward slightly, intrigued by the power dynamics at play. By the casual way they wield influence that most people only dream about.

"Technically, Cy did," Enzo replies. "But yes, Senator Jacobs died for his transgressions."

I lean closer to Enzo and lower my voice as I ask, "Have you ever killed someone who didn't deserve it?"

"No." There's no hesitation in the answer. "And I rarely kill. It's not what I do."

Closing my eyes, I take a moment to contemplate everything I've learned. It's a lot to take in, but surprisingly, I'm not as appalled by it as I would have thought I'd be. I mean, politics is messy.

I was never one of those getting into it without knowing the stakes, and the dirty deals that sometimes take place. World leaders have to sacrifice people all the time, so is this really that different? No, I don't think so.

But… it all comes down to one simple thing. A burning question I need to ask. "Will I have to kill someone?" I whisper.

Enzo takes my hand, bringing it to his mouth and pressing a kiss to the palm. "No, Toy. Not unless you want to."

The answer takes me by surprise. That's definitely not something I want to do. Not even Ben, who I know Enzo still holds captured. Does he deserve death? Yeah, he needs to pay. I just don't want to be the one to do it.

"I don't want to kill," I murmur, stroking his cheek. "But I want to be there when you finish Ben. I want to see his face when he realizes it's too late, and you're the one who ends it with me at your side."

Enzo presses one last kiss to my hand before moving it under the table, interlacing our fingers, and I squeeze back—a silent affirmation. I'm not running. I'm not afraid. I'm already inside the fire—and I want to see how far it burns.

The snow falls like a confession outside the window—
relentless, accumulating, refusing to stop until everything is
buried in white. Cleveland disappears beneath it, the city
lights diffused into hazy halos that barely penetrate the thick curtain of
white.

Inside, the warmth of our apartment feels like another world
entirely—quiet, golden, sealed off from everything but each other. It's
Christmas Eve, and the world outside doesn't exist.

I watch her more than I watch the snow. She's curled into the
corner of my Italian leather sofa, those long legs stretched across my
lap.

She's wearing my shirt—white cotton, half-buttoned, draped like
sin across bare skin. The collar slips wide, teasing the slope of her
collarbone, the shadow between her tits. Her hair is a tousled mass of
dark waves, still bearing the impression of my fingers from earlier.

"Open yours first," she says, nudging the box on her lap toward me.
It's larger than the one I'm holding, wrapped in matte black paper with
a thin gold ribbon.

"No." I place my palm over her gift, pushing it back toward her.
"Mine first."

She smiles—that particular smile that comes after she's already
decided to let me win. "Fine. But it's too small to cause much trouble,
right?" She picks up the black velvet box I've placed on her thigh.

I don't answer. I just watch her fingers, the way they hesitate just a
fraction of a second before lifting the lid. There's always that moment
with my toy—that split second where she considers whether to keep
fighting me, even over the smallest things.

When she sees what's inside, the change is immediate. Her body
goes completely still. The box sits open in her palm, and inside it, a

sleek obsidian business card catches the low amber light from the lamp behind us. Her name is engraved in gold beside mine. Our title beneath it.

On the back, it reads:

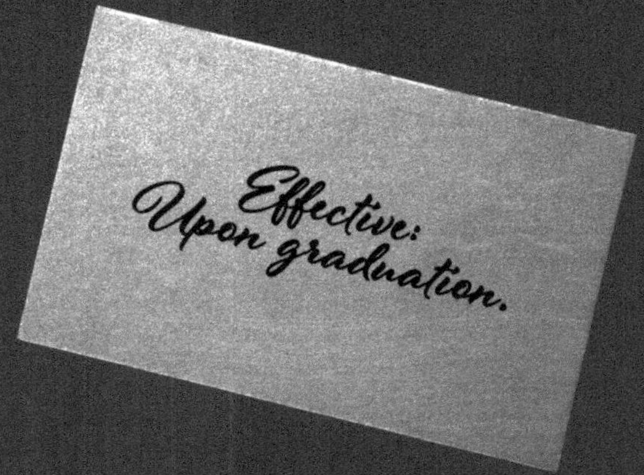

One fingertip traces the raised letters of her name—my name—as if testing whether they might vanish under her touch. Her lips part, but she doesn't speak.

"You and me, Toy. Forever." The words leave me like a vow, low and certain. Not a request. A declaration.

She finally looks up, those green eyes finding mine. "Are you proposing?"

I shake my head slowly, reaching to take the card from her. I hold it between us, turning it so the light catches the engraving. "It's not a proposal, Piper. It's a fact."

A tear spills over, tracking down her cheek. She doesn't brush it

away. Instead, she takes a shaky breath and sets the box aside, reaching for the package in her lap. Her hands aren't completely steady as she hands it to me.

"Your turn."

The weight of the box surprises me. It's heavier than it looks. I tear the paper away with less patience than I typically show, revealing a wooden case beneath. The lid opens on silent hinges to reveal a jigsaw puzzle.

The pieces are brutalist sculptures in miniature—stark, angular, uncompromising. I lift one of them, feeling its weight, the cold stone warming in my palm.

Then I see the paper with a print of what the finished puzzle looks like. It's of us; of me carrying her out of the secret hospital wing at Arlington Diagnostic & Preventive Services after Ben drugged her.

Piper shifts closer, her fingers brush against my wrist. "This is when I knew," she says, her voice barely above a whisper. "I'm yours, Lorenzo, and you're mine. I love you."

I can't speak. The puzzle piece is still in my hand, and I'm suddenly aware of how easily I could crush it. How fragile stone can be. How fragile everything is except what I feel for her.

She's watching me, waiting. Always gauging my reactions. But there's something else there too—a hunger for my approval that she would deny if I pointed it out.

"Say something," she demands, and I hear the smallest tremor in her voice.

I don't answer with words. I can't. Instead, I place the piece carefully back in the case, close it, and set it on the coffee table. Then I grasp her face between my hands and take her mouth in a kiss.

The sudden movement knocks the case. It topples, spilling pieces across the hardwood floor with sharp, decisive clicks. I hear them rolling, scattering, but I don't care. All I care about is the taste of her, the soft noise she makes as I bite her lower lip, the way her fingers curl into my hair.

Piper breaks the kiss first, her lips red and swollen from my teeth. Her palm flattens against my chest, not pushing me away but establishing her intent.

"I love you," she repeats.

"And I love you, my toy," I vow.

There's a glint in her eyes—that particular shine that means she's about to take what she wants. My body responds before my mind can catch up, blood rushing south as she presses me backward until I'm lying flat on the sofa.

"So," she says, straddling my thighs, "we should talk about the future." Her fingers trace idle patterns on my chest, dipping lower with each pass. "If I'm going to be a Russo, we need to make some plans."

I could flip her over, take control back in an instant. But watching

her hover above me, her skin flushed and her eyes bright with purpose, is everything.

"What kind of plans?" I keep my voice measured despite the heat building under my skin.

"I want us to move in together. For real." Her fingertips trace each muscle with deliberate slowness. "Not your place. Not mine. Somewhere new. Somewhere just for us."

Her nails scrape lightly across my skin as she says this, and my cock hardens beneath the thin fabric of my boxer briefs. She immediately shifts her weight so she's pressing against it.

"Whatever you want, Toy." I reach up to brush her hair back from her face. "Name the neighborhood. I'll have a place by morning."

She laughs, a soft, throaty sound that makes my heart contract. "So accommodating." Her fingers slip beneath the waistband of my boxers, tugging them down past my hips, and immediately reaching for my hardness.

"I aim to please," I groan.

"If I'm going to be your fiancée," she says, beginning a slow, steady stroke, "I need a ring."

I watch her face as she works me, the slight furrow of concentration between her brows, the way she wets her lips unconsciously. "Greedy girl."

Her hand twists on the upstroke, and it's exquisite torture. "Is that a yes?"

"Yes." I'd give her the fucking moon if she asked for it like this. "I already have it."

Her eyes widen fractionally, her rhythm faltering for just a moment. "You do?"

"It's safe at the estate. Custom. Six carats. The diamond is shaped like a puzzle." I reach for her free hand, pressing a kiss to her palm. "Black band."

"So that's the last piece." She smiles, and there's something almost tender in it before her expression shifts, becoming more calculating. Her grip on me tightens, her strokes quickening.

"And what about Ben?" she asks, and the name is a cold shock in the heated air between us.

But then her thumb circles the head, spreading the pre-cum that's gathered there, and cold turns to fire as I realize what she's doing— talking about killing a man while jerking me off like it's the most natural combination in the world.

"We can kill him whenever you want," I say, my voice rougher now. "Or I can have someone do it."

She shakes her head, her hair falling forward to frame her face. "After graduation," she says, her strokes becoming harder, more insistent. "I need to end one life before I start another."

Fuck. The casual way she says it—like she's discussing a haircut or

a dinner reservation. It shouldn't be so goddamn sexy. But it is. My hips rise to meet her hand, chasing the friction.

"Whatever you need." I'm close now, tension building at the base of my spine.

She leans down, her lips brushing my ear. "I want to watch the light leave his eyes," she whispers, and it's nearly my undoing. I grab her wrist, stilling her movements before I come too soon.

"Not yet," I growl, flipping us so she's beneath me. But she laughs, pushing against my chest again.

"No," she says, her eyes dark with desire and something else—something that looks like power. "Not like that. Not right now."

And I find myself yielding, letting her maneuver me back into position. This woman who speaks of murder with the same breath she uses to demand diamonds. This woman who arranges me like I'm one of her puzzle pieces—as if I haven't already surrendered every game to her.

I would burn cities for her smile. I would end bloodlines for her pleasure. But most of all—I would let her lead me, follow her onto whatever path she chooses, because the alternative is a world without her voice in my ear, telling me exactly how she plans to destroy a man who dared to touch her.

She pulls my shirt over her head in one fluid motion, her body unveiled like a secret I've already memorized but will never tire of reading.

Instead of straddling my hips as I expect, she crawls up my body with predatory grace, positioning her thighs on either side of my face. She's facing away from me, toward my dick, which strains upward as if seeking her heat.

The scent of her arousal fills my lungs—dark honey, salt, woman. Mine.

"Is this okay?" she asks, lowering herself until her sex hovers just above my mouth.

I answer by gripping her hips and pulling her down against my tongue. She gasps, her back arching as I lick a slow path through her folds.

She's already wet—slick and swollen from our earlier kisses, from the control she's been exercising. I feel her thighs tense on either side of my head as I circle her clit with the tip of my tongue.

With a moan, she bends forward, and the hot, wet suction of her mouth engulfs me. The sensation is electric, a current that arcs from my groin to the base of my skull.

We find a rhythm together—her lips sliding down my shaft as my tongue delves into her entrance, her hips rolling against my face as my hands grip her ass, spreading her wider. I slip one finger inside her cunt while my tongue focuses on her clit, feeling her inner walls clench around the intrusion.

A second finger joins the first, and I curve them upward, searching for that spot that makes her… there it is. She moans around me, the sound muffled but unmistakable. Her thighs begin to tremble.

"That's it," I moan against her folds. "Come for me like a good toy. Drench my face."

I increase the pressure, the speed, working her relentlessly toward her peak. Her movements become less coordinated as she loses herself in the sensation, but I don't mind. I'm too focused on her pleasure, on the way her body responds to me.

When she comes, it's with a sharp cry that she doesn't bother to suppress. "Yes. Right there. Fuck!"

Her entire body goes rigid, then shakes, her cunt clenching around my fingers as wave after wave of pleasure crashes through her. I keep licking, gentler now, drawing out her orgasm until she collapses forward, panting.

But she's not done. After just a moment's recovery, she takes me deep into her throat, swallowing around the head. The tight, rippling pressure is too much. I grip her hips hard enough to bruise as my own release builds rapidly.

When it hits, it's like being struck by lightning—white-hot pleasure that travels from my balls up through my dick as I empty myself down her throat. She swallows everything, not pulling away until she's milked me completely.

I expect her to roll off me, to collapse beside me on the couch. Instead, she slides down my body, still facing away from me, and grasps my softening cock. She strokes it against her slick folds, teasing us both until I begin to harden again.

"I want you inside me," she rasps, her voice rough with desire.

She positions herself over me, guiding my dick to her entrance, and sinks down in one slow, deliberate motion. The sight of her taking me, her back a graceful curve, her ass pressed against my hips, is almost enough to make me come again immediately.

I grip her waist, helping her establish a rhythm as she rides me reverse cowgirl style, her body rising and falling with increasing urgency.

"Look at you," I groan, watching the bounce of her ass. "Riding me like we're still playing. You already fucking won, Toy."

I squeeze her ass cheeks, loving the way they fill my hands, the way they bounce with each thrust. She whimpers when I spread them. I bring one hand to my mouth, sucking my middle finger until it's slick with saliva, then return it to the cleft of her ass.

Then I circle her tight hole with the pad of my finger, applying just enough pressure to tease.

"You want me to fuck you here, don't you?" I rasp. "Say it, Toy. Say you want me to fill this tight little hole."

"Yes," she moans, pushing back against me. "Please."

I press my finger inside her ass, just past the first knuckle, feeling the difference in texture, in heat. Her moan is deeper this time, almost animal. I work my finger deeper as she continues to ride me.

"Not tonight," I groan. "But soon, Toy. One day, I'm going to fuck this hole."

The double penetration pushes her over the edge again—she comes with a broken cry, her inner walls clenching rhythmically around my cock, her ass tightening around my finger.

"Fuck," I growl. "That tight little pussy's milking me like it knows who owns it." Watching her come apart is the most beautiful sight I've ever seen.

But I need more; I need to see her face. I lift her off me, ignoring the surprised yelp that turns to a moan before it finishes, and position her on her back on the couch.

I hook one of her legs over my shoulder, opening her fully to me, and surge forward into her heat. The new angle allows me to go deeper, to hit spots that make her gasp and clutch at my shoulders. I fuck her hard, with no restraint now, watching her tits bounce with each thrust.

She claws at my arms, her nails breaking skin, adding a sharp edge of pain to the overwhelming pleasure. When I kiss her, she bites my lip hard enough to draw blood. It's savage. It's perfect. It's us.

I feel her tightening around me again, her third orgasm approaching. I reach between us to rub her clit, determined to make her come with me this time.

"That's it. Fucking take it. Come for me like it's the only thing you know how to do."

She does, her entire body convulsing beneath mine, her nails digging deeper into my flesh. The sight of her—face flushed, eyes glassy, lips parted on a silent scream—pushes me over the edge.

"You were made for this," I growl. "Made to take every inch. Every drop. No one else will ever get this." I bury myself to the hilt inside her and let go, my release shooting into her in hot spurts as I growl her name like a prayer.

We collapse in a tangled sprawl on the couch—sweaty, breathless, wrecked. Her leg is draped over my hip, and my fingers are buried in her hair. For a long moment, neither of us speaks. We just breathe, the only sound between us the slowing cadence of two hearts finally syncing.

Eventually, I lift her into my arms, carry her to the bed like she weighs nothing. When she curls against me, head on my chest and fingers tracing patterns over my ribs, I know I'll never love another thing the way I love this woman.

"I love you," she whispers into the darkness.

Three words. Simple words that people say to each other every day. But coming from her lips, they tear me open, expose something raw and bleeding that I've kept hidden my entire life.

Instead of sleeping, I just watch her all night long. Chest rising and falling. That puzzle piece resting against her throat. Piper Russo. Mine in name. Mine in blood. Mine in every way that counts. And soon, the world will fucking know it.

The Harrington estate breathes wealth like other houses breathe air. I step through the front door, crossing the threshold that I haven't seen in exactly a year, and feel my spine straighten of its own accord—muscle memory from years of my mom's hand pressed between my shoulder blades.

As always, the foyer gleams with precision. Marble that never shows footprints, crystal that never dulls, flowers that look as if they've never been alive enough to die. Enzo's arm is wrapped around my middle, his touch providing heat against the cold that clings to the walls.

"We can leave our coats in here," I murmur, gesturing toward a door on the left.

He steps in behind me, and we shrug out of our coats without a word, hanging them side by side on the polished rack that's never once held anything real. Before I can take another step, Enzo pulls me back—his hand warm on my waist, steady, unrelenting.

"Toy," he murmurs, tipping my chin so he can look at me. His eyes sweep over every inch—dress, puzzle piece, the ring on my finger. His claim carved in gold and metal. "You sure about this?"

I nod once, sharp and certain. "Let's just get it over with."

He leans in, his mouth brushing mine—not a kiss, not yet. A warning. A promise. When it finally deepens, it's slow and consuming, one hand curled around my jaw like he's reminding me who I belong to.

"They'll see who you belong to the second you walk in," he says against my lips.

"That's the plan," I breathe.

His mouth ghosts over mine again. "Then kiss me like you mean it."

I do. And he takes it like it costs me something. Like it seals us.

When he finally pulls away, I almost chase him for more—but the air in this house makes my lungs feel too tight to breathe.

"I hate this place," I whisper, smoothing down the red silk clinging to my hips. My fingers drift to the puzzle piece resting just above my heart.

"I know," he murmurs, brushing my temple with his lips. "But I've got you."

He threads his fingers through mine, and together we move deeper into the house I used to call home—though I don't remember it ever feeling like one.

"Which room was yours?" he asks, voice low against my ear.

The question catches me off guard, but I answer anyway. "Second floor. Corner window."

"Want to show me?"

I laugh coldly. "I can't. The second I was kicked out, mommy and daddy dearest changed it into something else. Probably some kind of hobby room."

Taking a deep breath, I steel myself, and lead us into the main room of depressing festivities.

Waitstaff move like white-gloved ghosts between clusters of guests, their trays of champagne flutes catching light from chandeliers. I watch them navigate conversations in progress, appearing at elbows exactly when glasses are empty, vanishing before they can be thanked. It's a choreography I used to know by heart.

"Darling."

My mother's voice cuts through the room before I see her. Her heels strike a rhythm against the marble like a metronome counting down to something inevitable. She appears through a parting crowd, dressed in cream and diamonds, her smile fixed and brittle as she kisses the air beside each of my cheeks.

"You made it."

Not once does she look me in the eye. Her gaze skims over my shoulder, my earrings, the hemline of my dress—assessing, calculating, finding fault—before landing on Enzo with a smile that brightens to something theatrical.

"And you must be the…" The pause is so precisely placed it might as well be underlined in red.

Enzo's smile doesn't reach his eyes. "Lorenzo Russo," he says, voice calm as a loaded gun. He doesn't offer his hand or fake a smile, and I don't think I've ever loved him more.

My father materializes at her side like he's been summoned, a drink already in hand, ice cubes clinking against crystal with dissatisfaction. His gaze flicks over Enzo's tailored coat, the perfect cut of his suit, the subtle details that speak of money older than anything the Harringtons have touched.

"I didn't realize Piper was dating someone in security," he says, voice dry as gin, as if Enzo is the help who's wandered into the wrong room.

I want to vanish, to dissolve into the marble and re-form somewhere quieter, somewhere less cruel. Instead, I stand perfectly still, my face a porcelain mask.

"Actually," I say, clearing my throat and catching my mom's gaze. Then I lift my hand, the six-carat puzzle-cut diamond we picked up from the Russo estate before flying here catching the chandelier's light like it's throwing daggers. "Lorenzo's my—"

"I'm her fiancé," Enzo finishes smoothly, his voice absolute.

I watch my mom's lips twitch, the micro-expression of someone who's just been checkmated.

"Piper! Holy shit, you actually came."

Teddy appears like salvation, a whiskey tumbler in one hand and the kind of grin that's never been Harrington-approved. His tie is already loose, his hair a little mussed, his eyes clear despite the alcohol. He wraps me in a hug that smells like good whiskey and better intentions.

"You look like a revolution." He grins when he pulls back, hands still on my shoulders, eyes seeing all of me. Then he turns to Enzo, gives him a slow once-over that's neither threatening nor deferential. "So you must be war."

A laugh escapes me—the first real sound I've made since walking in. Enzo extends his hand, introduces himself properly. "Lorenzo Russo."

Teddy takes it with a firm grip. "Alright. Yeah. I see it." He nods, a private assessment completed. It's the only real introduction that happens in this house of performances.

We circulate for a full hour—sixty excruciating minutes. My mother finds me between conversations, her comments soft and steady, precision-guided missiles.

"Are you still at that internship? I thought it was only for… common people."

"Is that dress… yours? The cut is so interesting."

"Your lipstick is a little bold, darling. Remember what we discussed about first impressions."

With each question, each subtle criticism, I feel the weight of it building—every inch of distance between the daughter they want and the woman I've become. My shoulders tighten beneath my dress.

The room seems to contract, the air growing thinner as I breathe it. Enzo stays close, his presence steady, his eyes tracking every microscopic flinch I try to hide.

His thumb moves against my back, slow and deliberate. "Do you want to leave?" he murmurs, just for me. Rather than coaxing me, he's reminding me of the option.

I shake my head once.

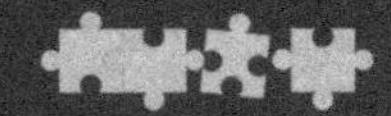

"You run this," he adds. "We go when you say."

The room fills with people who know a version of me that hasn't existed for years. Former classmates, family friends, business associates—they ask about charity organizations I don't know about, congratulate me on achievements I've never claimed, speak to me in the language of a future I rejected.

"This place doesn't deserve you," Enzo murmurs near my temple. "They look, but they don't see. And still you stand taller than all of them."

My father corners us near the library doors, martini in hand, his eyes slightly narrowed—the look he gets when he's about to deliver what he thinks is wisdom.

"Well, let's hope this one works out better than your last boyfriend," he says, glancing at Enzo with the idle disinterest of a man evaluating livestock. "That campaign manager nearly ruined your mother's summer."

I feel Enzo inhale beside me—sharp and slow. The kind of breath people take before court rulings or executions. One tilt of his head, one unreadable smile, and my father steps back like he's heard a threat no one else can.

"How tragic," Enzo drawls, eyeing my dad. "But I guess that's what happens when you try to pawn your daughter off on someone unworthy."

Yeah, I've told him all about the guys my parents tried to set me up with, and how it was always about how it affected them, how it looked for them.

Something inside me goes quiet at my dad's words. Not breaking— nothing so dramatic. Just a simple, clean silence, like a circuit being cut. The insult of comparing Enzo to someone who was most definitely not a boyfriend hits hard.

After placing my untouched champagne on a passing silver tray, I smooth my dress with hands that don't tremble, and I look my father directly in the eyes for the first time today.

I don't wait for Enzo to defend me. I don't need him to. But I feel him behind me—still, coiled, ready. Not a shield, a sword. And if I said one word, he'd burn this house down and salt the earth. But this is my fight.

"We're leaving," I say. "And I'm not coming back."

"You can't leave now," my father insists. "It would embarrass your mother."

I scoff.

"You had one chance to love her. You used it to measure her instead." Enzo's voice is quiet, brutal. "You have no idea what you lost," he finishes, still not raising his voice.

Then his hand finds mine like we've rehearsed this exit a hundred times—and maybe, without saying it, we have. Without another word,

we leave. And with each step, I begin feeling weightless. As if I've set down something heavy I'd forgotten I was carrying.

The front door clicks shut behind us with the soft finality of a safe deposit box. Outside, the air is sharp with winter, honest in a way the heated rooms behind us never were. I breathe it in, feeling my lungs expand for what seems like the first time in hours.

Enzo stands beside me. He's not pushing. Just there—solid as the ground beneath my feet.

"Fuck!" I scream, startling the parking attendants that are still busy outside. "Fuck! Fuck! Fuck!"

"Piper! Wait!"

Teddy bursts through the door behind us, coat half-buttoned. He moves with the loose energy of whiskey and absolute conviction, more alive than anyone inside that house has been in years.

"Christ, I didn't think you'd actually do it," he says, but there's something like wonder beneath the rasp, something like pride.

I cross the distance between us before I can think about it, wrapping my arms around him and holding tighter than I mean to. I press my face against the only part of my family that ever felt real.

"Thank you," I whisper, my throat suddenly tight, the words smaller than I want them to be. "For every time you saw me. For never looking away."

His arms tighten around me, one hand coming up to cup the back of my head. We stand like that for a moment that stretches. Behind us, I feel Enzo retreating, giving us space. Or maybe he's asking for his vehicle.

Teddy pulls back first. He cups my face in both hands, his palms warm against the winter air, and looks at me like he's memorizing something important. "You don't owe them a goddamn thing," he murmurs, voice low enough that only I can hear it. "You never did." He kisses my forehead.

"I know," I say, and for the first time, I think I might actually believe it.

Teddy turns me so I'm at his side, his arm around my shoulders as he looks at Enzo. "You," Teddy says to him. "You see her."

It's not really a question, but Enzo answers anyway. "Always," he says, the single word carrying weight beyond its syllables.

A soft purr sounds as one of the parking attendants drives Enzo's car up to us, leaving it idling as he gets out and hands over the keys. "Nice ride," the attendant observes before walking away.

Teddy steps back, giving my shoulder one last squeeze before releasing me entirely. "Go. Be free. Fly, Piper, fly."

Enzo moves then, opening the passenger door for me with the fluid grace that comes second nature to him. I get into the car without looking back at the house, at its windows glowing with a light that's anything but welcome.

I watch Teddy through the window. For a moment, backlit by the glow from the house, he looks like something out of a painting; the solitary figure, half in and half out of the world behind him. Then he turns and disappears back into the noise.

Enzo slides into the driver's seat like he's switching roles—from shadow to executioner. Every move precise, every breath measured, as though violence would've been easier than restraint.

"I was ready to drag you the fuck out of there," he seethes. "Fucking parasites."

When I look over at him, his jaw is tight, but there's pride in the set of it.

"I wanted to hurt them," he adds. "God, Toy, I wanted to rip them apart."

He reaches across the console and takes my hand, his thumb brushing once across my knuckles—a gesture so small it shouldn't matter, but it does.

Then, without a word, he leans across the space between us and kisses me again—this time slow, worshipful. Like he needs my taste to erase the stench of everything we just left behind. I kiss him back just as fiercely. Because he didn't just stand beside me in there. He let me fight. And he stood ready to burn it down if I'd asked him to.

"I almost wish you had," I whisper against his lips. "Almost."

Pulling back, he arches an eyebrow. "Airport?" he asks, and there's a universe of understanding in the single word.

"God yes," I nod, feeling the last threads of tension unravel from my shoulders. "Let's go home."

5 months later.

Graduation morning unfolds beneath a sky too blue to feel real. By the time I'm standing in line at Georgetown's commencement, the late May sun is already high and sharp overhead, pressing down on the black gown draped over my shoulders.

I can barely believe how quickly the last five months have flown by. Each day, week, and month has been swallowed by deadlines, duties, and Enzo.

After Cleveland, we found our new home fast; a ground-floor luxury apartment in the West End. In many ways, that move felt like the final step into becoming the new me. I'm no longer unsure of my place, or doubting my worth.

The cap feels too tight against my temples, its edge digging into my scalp with each slight movement. Or maybe I'm just impatient. Since the names are being called alphabetically, it would have been nice to have a last name beginning with A.

The dean's voice cuts across the quad, sharp and practiced. "Piper Harrington."

I step forward, feeling hundreds of eyes track my movement. My heart thumps once, hard, against my ribcage, and then steadies. I scan the sea of already-graduated students, finding Lena immediately.

When our eyes meet, she wipes at her eyes dramatically and makes a finger gun, pointing it straight at me. I laugh despite myself. Even today, in this moment that should feel heavy with ceremony, she refuses to let me take myself too seriously.

My gaze shifts, drawn inevitably to the spectators, quickly finding the two men who are always there for me.

Enzo stands tall and imposing in a charcoal suit, hands tucked into his pockets, eyes fixed on me like I'm the only person in the entire stadium. Beside him, Teddy sways slightly, beaming with unmistakable pride.

One is my anchor, the other my cheerleader—and together they form my new definition of family.

Something shifts in my chest as I cross the stage. For one electric second, I feel completely weightless. Free. Invincible. The diploma is heavy in my hand, unexpectedly substantial, as if they've somehow condensed all my late nights and panic attacks and victories into this single object.

The applause sounds distant, like it's happening underwater or in another room entirely, but when I toss my cap into the air with everyone else, I swear I hear Enzo's voice louder than anyone's—a deep, resonant voice that cuts through the chaos.

It takes forever to find Lena in the chaos. Between people angling for photos, and three different champagne toasts on the lawn, the ceremony's momentum spins out into messy, joyful pockets of farewell.

When I finally reach her, she throws her arms around me, and I hold her so tightly it hurts, breathing in the familiar scent of her perfume. She's moving to Europe tonight—her new job at a PR firm in Paris starts in a week.

"I can't believe we actually made it," she murmurs against my hair.

When she pulls away, I don't cry. I won't give her that weight to carry across the ocean. I just nod, swallowing hard against the tightness in my throat.

"Paris won't know what hit it," I say, forcing a grin. "And you better send me daily selfies."

We hug again, both of us softening, her fingers digging into my shoulders like she's trying to memorize the shape of me.

"I will," she promises. Then, always pushing, always refusing to let a moment collapse under its own importance, she adds, "I'm looking forward to my first European dicking."

I laugh. "I'm going to miss you," I breathe.

She rolls her eyes theatrically. "It'll be August before you know it, and then you're coming to visit."

The clog in my throat grows as I nod, confirming the plans we've laid. "I'll be there with bells on," I half-sob, half-laugh.

"Laters, bitch." She hugs me one last time, and I let her go.

I find Enzo and Teddy waiting for me at the edge of the ceremony grounds, both of them beaming with a pride that feels almost embarrassing in its sincerity. Teddy's clapping has evolved into full-body enthusiasm, his arms sweeping wide as he spots me approaching.

In contrast, Enzo's stillness is its own kind of intensity—he doesn't need movement to command attention. His eyes track me through the crowd, and the slight curve of his lips says more than Teddy's elaborate

gestures ever could.

I'm still getting used to how well those two get along. Somewhere between Christmas and Valentine's Day, they went from knowing each other because of me, to actually talking on their own.

Though, when Matteo visited in March, it quickly became clear who Teddy's favorite Russo is. The two of them got on like… I don't even know. I laugh softly to myself as I recall them nearly burning down a restaurant when Matteo claimed he knew a flambé trick that would surprise everyone.

And, well, he delivered. When he set fire to the tablecloth, everyone was truly surprised. That's not what got us kicked out, though. Nope, that was Teddy when he poured the contents of his flask onto the fire to douse it.

"There she is!" Teddy announces, loud enough to make nearby parents turn. "The most brilliant Harrington in three generations." He pulls me into a hug that smells like expensive cologne and the unmistakable bite of whiskey. The flask in his breast pocket presses against my shoulder, hard and warm.

When Teddy finally releases me, Enzo pulls me to him. He fuses our lips together in a kiss that makes the entire day fall away, even if it doesn't last nearly long enough.

"Congratulations," he rasps against my lips. "You looked amazing up there."

"Thank you," I murmur, pulling back.

"Are you ready to leave?" Teddy asks, taking another sip from the silver flask.

I spot Lena over Teddy's shoulder, gathering her things and saying goodbye to her parents. "Yeah," I reply, already moving toward my best friend.

When I reach her, I wordlessly link my arm through hers, an echo of our first day at Georgetown when we walked onto campus together, terrified and trying not to show it. Now we walk out the same way, past the historic buildings and manicured lawns that shaped the years of our lives.

"I can't say goodbye to you again," she says, her voice catching.

"It's not goodbye," I correct her. "It's 'see you in August after you've probably banged half of Paris.'"

She laughs, eyes bright with unshed tears. "A third at most. I have standards."

Behind us, Enzo and Teddy follow at a respectful distance, and I wonder if Enzo can sense the significance of this moment—how I'm walking the line between who I was and who I've become.

When we reach the gates, Lena hugs me one final time. "Be happy," she whispers. And then she leaves without looking back. I stare after her for several moments, not turning until she's disappeared from sight.

Teddy clears his throat. "Right then. Who's ready for the best

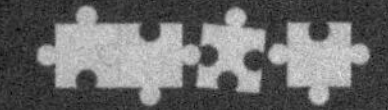

graduation dinner in D.C. history?"

By the time we pile into the car, the sun is beginning to dip behind the skyline, casting long shadows between the buildings. Georgetown's campus shrinks in the rearview mirror as the city shifts around us, dappled in gold.

As soon as we step inside, I realize Teddy hasn't just made a reservation—he's closed down the entire place. The host greets us with practiced deference, leading us to the center table where a champagne fountain bubbles gently beside arrangements of white roses and eucalyptus.

"You're insane," I tell my uncle as we sit. "This is way too much."

"Nonsense," he says, waving away my protest. "My favorite niece only graduates from Georgetown once."

"I'm your only niece," I remind him as always.

"Details," he dismisses, then launches into a story about his own graduation, which apparently involved a stolen mascot costume and the dean's personal golf cart.

The food arrives in elegant waves—delicate appetizers, perfectly cooked steaks, sides I can't even name. Teddy keeps the conversation flowing, occasionally drawing even Enzo into his ridiculous stories.

By the time dessert arrives—some elaborate confection involving chocolate and gold leaves—I feel properly sated and genuinely happy. This moment, suspended between my academic accomplishment and whatever comes next, feels perfect in its simplicity.

Teddy checks his watch and grimaces dramatically. "Much as I hate to break up this party, I've got an early flight tomorrow." He rises, dropping a kiss on the top of my head. "I'll swing by Blackwood next week when you're officially installed in your new office. Want to see my girl in her natural habitat."

He shakes Enzo's hand with genuine warmth, then winks at me before sauntering toward the exit, leaving a generous tip on the bar as he passes.

In his absence, the atmosphere shifts subtly. Enzo's arm drapes around my shoulders, his fingers brushing the side of my neck in a touch so light it might be accidental if I didn't know better. Every nerve ending in my body seems to realign toward him, like iron filings to a magnet.

"Are you ready to leave?" he asks, voice low and patient, but there's an undercurrent there that makes my thighs clench. I nod, not trusting my voice.

Outside, the city has surrendered to night. The glass walls of the restaurant glow from within like a jewel box. I check the time—well past nine.

He leads me to the car without elaborating, and I don't need to ask where we're going. I just slide into the passenger seat and let the city drift past the windows, streetlights blurring into streaks of gold against

the deepening blue of evening.

Every time his fingers brush the back of my hand where it rests on the console, I forget how to breathe. He hasn't really kissed me since we arrived at the ceremony this morning, and the absence of his mouth against mine has become a physical ache.

I thought we were going home, but the car doesn't turn toward the West End. Instead, Enzo drives us directly to Blackwood, the massive glass and steel building that houses his empire.

The streets are nearly empty this late, and the building looms against the night sky like a monument to everything he's built. Everything I'm now part of. The security guard nods to us as we enter, his eyes carefully averted—he knows better than to look too long at what belongs to Lorenzo Russo.

"I want to show you your new office," Enzo says, his hand finding the small of my back as we step into the elevator. His palm radiates heat through the thin fabric of my dress, and I fight the urge to arch against him like a cat.

He says nothing more as we ascend, the soft hum of the elevator the only sound between us. The tension is physical now, something I could reach out and touch if I dared.

When the doors slide open, he guides me through the dimly lit executive floor, his fingers possessive against my spine. Our footsteps echo on the marble, his steady and measured, mine a staccato click that feels too loud in the emptiness.

We stop at the end of the hall, and my breath catches. There, etched in gold on frosted glass, is my name: Piper Russo. Not Harrington. Russo. It's more than just a nameplate—it's a statement. A declaration.

"Your kingdom," Enzo murmurs, reaching past me to push the door open.

The moment we step inside, the scent of wine and leather hits me. My office. Clean lines, sharp corners, and a matte-black desk big enough to stretch out across. There are no flowers or frames yet. Those are things I wanted to pick myself.

On the desk is a crystal decanter of wine, a single silver cloche, and no glasses.

"So—" I begin, but before I can finish, Enzo shuts the office door.

"Strip," he commands, voice low and steady. "Now."

I hesitate, but not out of resistance. It's because the word hits me like impact play. My breath snags, and heat floods low and fast. My thighs press together instinctively. I'm already wet, slick just from the

tone of his voice.

He steps closer, slow and precise, like he's savoring the hesitation, then finds the zipper at my back. "I want to play with my toy," he says against my ear, and something inside me unravels.

"Yes," I breathe.

I kick off my heels, the muffled thud on the carpet absurdly loud in the quiet. My feet throb, but the ache between my legs is louder. I reach behind me to help, but his fingers meet mine, and I shudder.

The zipper gives. My dress slides over my hips, pooling at my feet like an offering I quickly step out of. My bra follows, leaving me naked in the cool air of the office. I'm not wearing panties. I haven't since Christmas in Cleveland, when Enzo accidentally-on-purpose didn't pack any.

He circles me in silence, and with every pass the air thickens. My nipples tighten, and my breath shortens. When he watches me like this, I feel seen in a way no one else has ever seen me. It's a high I can't describe, but one I crave.

Then he reaches into his pocket and pulls out a length of black silk. "Close your eyes," he instructs, and I obey eagerly. I've missed this game.

The silk slides over my eyes, and the moment I'm cast in darkness, my body stops belonging to me. I'm no longer Piper; I'm his. His toy, his possession, his everything. The transformation is immediate and total, a chemical reaction I can't control.

He lifts me like I weigh nothing and sets me on the desk. The polished surface is cool against my fevered skin. The contrast makes me gasp.

There's a soft clink of metal just moments before the rich scent of chocolate fills the air, dark and decadent.

"Open your mouth," he says, and I part my lips without hesitation.

Something smooth and slightly bitter touches my tongue—a piece of chocolate. But before I can close my mouth around it, his lips are on mine, his tongue pushing the chocolate deeper, melting it between us.

The taste explodes, mingling with the unique flavor of him, and I moan into his mouth. He pulls back, and I feel bereft until his mouth finds my neck, then my collarbone, then the curve of my breast.

I feel the sticky trail he's dragging over my skin, followed immediately by the wet heat of his tongue. He circles my nipple with the melting sweet, then sucks it clean, drawing a desperate whimper from my throat.

"Patience," he murmurs against my skin, and I feel him reach for something.

Only seconds later, he presses his lips to mine again, letting the wine from his mouth spill in a controlled flood. Some of it escapes, running down my chin and onto my chest in warm rivulets.

"Messy little thing," he growls, his voice like gravel. He chases

every drop with his tongue, lapping at the hollow of my throat, the valley between my breasts, the sensitive skin beneath them.

"Enzo," I cry.

My back hits the desk as he presses me down. The surface is cold against my shoulder blades, and already wet from the wine that's pooled beneath me. I don't care. I'm panting and exposed, my legs parted and trembling before he even touches me with intent.

He uses his mouth first—slow, reverent as he kisses his way down my body. Every touch is unhurried. He licks and bites at my hip bones, my inner thighs, everywhere but where I need him most.

By the time his tongue finally slides through my folds, I'm practically sobbing with want.

"Please," I gasp, my hips jerking upward, chasing contact like I'm starved.

Then his fingers are there, two of them sliding into me, deep and merciless, curling just right against that spot that makes me see stars behind the blindfold.

"Whose pussy is this?" he demands, his fingers never stilling.

"Yours," I gasp. "It's yours, Enzo."

He rewards me with his mouth again, sucking hard on my clit while his fingers work inside me. The dual sensation is overwhelming, and I come with a broken cry, my body clenching around him, my hands gripping the edges of the desk like it's the only solid thing in the universe.

Before I can recover, he's making me come again, his mouth relentless, his fingers knowing exactly how to push me over the edge a second time. I'm trembling, oversensitive, my skin slick with sweat and wine and saliva.

"Please," I moan, writhing. "I need you inside me. Please, Enzo. Please."

He chuckles, the sound dark and promising, and pulls back entirely. The moment he pulls away, I flinch. My body keens like it's been denied oxygen.

"You didn't beg prettily enough yet," he says, his voice closer to my ear now. "Try again."

In between my begging, I hear the rustle of fabric as he undresses, each soft sound magnified by my blindfolded state.

My other senses strain to compensate for my lack of vision—the scent of his cologne mixed with the musk of arousal, the lingering taste of wine and chocolate on my tongue.

Then I feel it, the blunt head of his dick nudging against my entrance, and my body responds instantly, a fresh flood of wetness welcoming him.

"Yes. Give it to me," I pant as I wrap my legs around his waist, digging my heels into the sculpted muscle of his ass, trying to pull him deeper.

But Enzo is never rushed. He controls this like he controls everything else. "You'll take every fucking inch," he groans against my mouth, "at the pace I decide."

He pushes inside me so slowly I whimper, my inner walls stretching to accommodate his size. I'm soaked, ruined, unraveling, and he knows it. I love it. His hands grip my hips, pinning me to the desk as he works himself deeper, denying my attempts to quicken the pace.

When he's fully seated inside me, he pauses. "Mine," he growls, not a question but a statement of fact.

I cry out. My back bows off the desk, hips chasing him. He moves like I'm his to ruin, and God, I am. He draws almost all the way out before slamming back in, setting a punishing rhythm that has the desk creaking beneath us.

Each thrust hits something deep and primal inside me, and I'm clawing at his shoulders, at the desk, at anything I can reach. "Enzo," I gasp, my voice not sounding like my own. "I'm going to—"

"Come," he commands, his thumb finding my clit and pressing down with unerring precision. "Come on my fucking cock, Piper."

My orgasm crashes over me like a breaking wave, my body clenching around him as I scream his name. I'm floating, drowning, completely at his mercy as pleasure ripples through me.

But Enzo doesn't stop. As I'm still trembling from the aftershocks, he withdraws completely. Then he lifts me off the table and flips me over in one fluid motion. He bends me forward with one hand flat between my shoulder blades, positioning me so my chest is pressed against the desk, my ass raised.

He spreads me open like a secret only he gets to read. "Stay still," he commands, his voice like steel wrapped in velvet. "Or I'll stop."

I freeze, muscles taut with anticipation. I burn with the need for him to touch me again. I tremble with the effort of keeping still when every instinct screams at me to push back against him.

His tongue finds my pussy again, lapping at my sensitive flesh while one slicked finger—when did he get lube?—circles my ass. The touch is slow, teasing, deliberate. A gentle pressure that doesn't quite breach me, just promises what's to come.

"Tell me," he rasps, his breath hot against my core. "Tell me you want me to fuck you here."

I gasp, the request sending another jolt of arousal through me despite my recent orgasm. "Yes," I manage, then, when his finger stills entirely, I add, "Please."

He rewards me by pressing that finger inside me, just to the first knuckle. The intrusion burns slightly, but there's pleasure there too, a fullness that makes me want more.

"Louder," he demands. "Tell me exactly what you want."

"I want you to fuck my ass," I sob, beyond anything but the desperate need for him to fill me completely. "Please, Enzo. I need it."

He slides his finger deeper, still licking and sucking at my clit, the sensation making me dizzy with pleasure. When he adds a second finger, stretching me wider, I moan his name like a prayer.

The stretch burns more now, a delicious pain that borders on too much but never quite crosses the line. He works me open methodically, scissoring his fingers, preparing me for his dick.

When he adds a third finger, I come again, unexpectedly and violently, my entire body shaking with the force of it. "Enzo. Lorenzo. Enzo." I moan his name over and over.

Before the orgasm even fades, the head of his cock presses against my ass. It's bigger than his fingers, much bigger, and for a moment I tense involuntarily.

"Relax," he murmurs, one hand stroking down my spine. "Breathe for me, Toy."

I force myself to exhale slowly, to relax my muscles, and he pushes forward. The burning sensation is immediate and intense—glorious and punishing at once. He feeds his length into me inch by agonizing inch, giving me time to adjust to each new stretch.

It fucking hurts. I'm gasping, white-knuckling the edge of the desk, tears leaking from beneath my blindfold. But I don't want him to stop. I want all of him.

"Such a good toy," he croons, and the praise washes over me like warm honey.

Once he's fully seated inside me, he pauses, letting me adjust to the fullness. Then he begins to move, shallow thrusts at first that gradually deepen as my body accommodates him. One hand grips my hip with bruising force, the other wraps around my throat, keeping me grounded as he fucks me harder, faster.

The pain doesn't fade. It transforms, sharp into sweet, fire into hunger. My body shakes with how much I want more. I'm coming again, but it's different this time. A deep, full-body spasm that seems to originate from my very core.

I come like it's being pulled from me, like it belongs to him, my body clenching around his hardness. "Enzo!" I moan. "Yes. Just like that."

His pace grows erratic, his breathing harsh and ragged against my back. When he finally comes, his cock buried to the hilt in my ass, his growl vibrates against my spine, a primal sound I'm getting high off.

"Mine," he snarls as he fills me. "Forever."

I don't just fall apart. I fucking rapture. "Yes," I cry out. "Yours, Lorenzo. Always yours. Fuck!"

We stay connected for several long moments, both of us breathing hard, sweat-slicked skin cooling in the air-conditioned office. When he finally withdraws, I whimper at the sudden emptiness, at the feeling of his release sliding down my thigh.

He lifts me carefully, cradling me against his chest as he carries me

to the leather couch along the wall. I'm in a blissful state, sated and perfect, floating somewhere beyond the reach of words.

Then he removes my blindfold with gentle fingers, and I blink as his face comes into focus, his blue eyes dark with something that looks almost like reverence.

I look down at our bodies, noting the chocolate that's smeared across my breasts and stomach, the wine that stains my thighs like bruises. The whole room smells like sex and power.

"You're not just mine," he says, his voice rough as he strokes my hair back from my face. "You're my equal. My partner. My fucking match."

And when I look up at him, bone-deep exhaustion mingling with a satisfaction so complete it borders on religious, I believe every word.

"You're my birthday wish," I whisper. "Last week, I realized that you're exactly what I asked for. When I blew out that candle, I wished to be wanted. To feel… fulfilled."

He makes a low, rumbling sound and strokes my hair, slow and reverent.

"That's you, Lorenzo Russo," I murmur, nuzzling closer. "You made my wish come true."

1 month later.

I watch the silver key slide into the lock, metal against metal—the sound of finality.

This compound isn't just a place; it's the terminus I designed for the man who dared touch what's mine.

For seven months, I've kept Ben Jacks alive when every cell in my body demanded his blood. I didn't do it for mercy, but for her. My everything.

The fluorescent lights overhead cast no shadows, leaving nowhere to hide from what's about to happen. My fingers twitch with the desire to wrap around his throat, but I control the impulse.

Tonight isn't about my vengeance. It's about hers.

"Piper." Her name tastes sacred on my tongue. "Are you ready?"

She stands beside me in that black dress I selected—plunging neckline, barely covering her delicious ass. It's perfect for an execution. Her hair falls in a dark curtain down her back, and when she turns to me, her green eyes show nothing but resolve.

"Yes." One word. No hesitation.

Pride swells so sharp it feels like devotion. Seven months ago, she would have flinched at the thought of this. Now she stands tall, unflinching. Mine.

I lead her through the labyrinth of sterile hallways, our footsteps echoing against concrete. Every inch of this place bears my fingerprints—the ventilation system Cy installed to my exact specifications, the surveillance cameras angled just so, the reinforced steel doors thick enough to swallow screams.

We stop at the final door, a seamless panel of brushed steel. Before I unlock it, I turn to her, cup her face in my hands, and kiss her—hard, possessive, declarative. Not for tenderness, but for the man waiting inside to see. I want him to know exactly who she belongs to before he dies.

Then I unlock the door.

The cell is exactly as I left it; stark white and coldly lit. The only furniture is a chair he can't reach or use. And then there's him; Ben Jacks, the man who drugged my toy. It's almost poetic that he's now chained by his wrists and ankles, hanging like meat.

His hair is matted with sweat, his skin color turned a sickly pallor. He looks up when we enter, and I see the moment recognition hits him—his pupils dilate, his breath quickens, his body jerks against the restraints.

"What the fuck is this?" he croaks, his voice hoarse.

My muscles coil with the urge to lunge, to tear, to break. I imagine my hands around his throat, squeezing until his eyes bulge. I picture driving my knife into his stomach and twisting, slow enough that he feels every millimeter of steel.

Fuck, I want to hear him beg, want to make him suffer like he made her suffer. Like I fucking suffered when I waited for her to wake up.

Instead, I lean against the wall, cross my arms, and force my face into impassivity. This is her show.

Piper walks toward the chair with measured steps, heels clicking against concrete like bullets. She sits, crosses her legs, adjusts the hem of her dress. A business meeting. Nothing more.

"Do you know why you're here, Ben?" Her voice is soft, conversational.

He tries to speak, but his voice comes out cracked. "Piper, please… I'm sorry—"

"That's not why you're here." She cuts him off, tilting her head. "You're not here because you drugged me. Did you think that's what this was about?"

My jaw clenches so hard my teeth might crack. Every fiber of my being wants to interrupt, to tell him that yes, that's exactly why he's here—because he put his hands on what's mine. But I hold my tongue. There's cruelty in her strategy, I know this.

"You're here because you've been doing it for years." She reaches into the slim folder she brought and lays out photographs on the floor, one by one.

"Alice Brown."

The third intern.

"Elise Porter."

Brunette, glasses, serious expression.

"Mallory Weiss."

Red hair, wide smile.

"Jennifer Gill, Tara Ellis, Sarah Alk."

With each name, each face, I feel my focus narrowing, my breathing

shallowing. These are the women he drugged before Piper. The ones who never got justice. The ones whose cases were buried, forgotten, dismissed.

Ben's eyes dart from photo to photo, his forehead beading with sweat. I watch him twitch, catalog every sign of his degradation. The tremor in his lips, the way his shoulders slump, then tense, the yellowish tinge to his skin after months of captivity.

I've kept him healthy enough to face this moment. Nothing more.

"Every woman you drugged. Every drink you spiked. Every 'party favor' you slipped to a classmate." She stands, walks a slow circle around him. "Did you think Georgetown would protect you forever? That your father's money would keep burying the complaints?" Piper continues, her tone clinical.

Ben's sobbing now, broken sounds that scratch against my ears. "I'm sorry, I'm so sorry, please—"

"You're not sorry you did it." Piper stops directly in front of him. "You're sorry you got caught."

I push off from the wall, taking a single step forward. The movement draws Ben's eyes to me, and I see raw terror bloom across his face. Good. He should know what waits for him when she's done.

Piper turns to me, and in that moment, she isn't just beautiful; she's transcendent. Power radiates from her like heat, and I want nothing more than to kneel at her feet.

"You're not dying because you hurt me, Ben," she says, turning back to him. "You're dying because you've poisoned the air too long."

My queen. My judge. And I am her sword.

The rustle of my toy's dress as she walks away from him is like a blade being unsheathed. She doesn't look at Ben a final time—doesn't give him that dignity.

Behind her, he collapses against his chains, a marionette with severed strings. Pathetic sounds spill from his throat; pleas, prayers, promises. I've heard them all before. Men always find religion when facing their end.

I step forward, my movements deliberate, each footfall a punctuation in his death sentence. "You don't get her tears," I tell him, voice flat as the concrete beneath us. "You don't even get her hate." My eyes hold his, forcing him to see the death waiting in them. "You get erased."

Ben thrashes harder, chains rattling like distant thunder. "Please," he sobs, "I'll do anything I can—"

"This was her mercy," I interrupt, the words burning low in my throat. "I would've taken you apart."

And I would have. For months, I've imagined peeling his skin in strips, breaking each finger joint by joint, cutting out his tongue for daring to speak her name. I would have kept him alive for weeks, a masterpiece of agony.

But my toy wanted a clean death. At first, I was against it. But when I realized it was for her and not him, I agreed to her plan.

I offer her my arm, palm up—a gesture from another century, formal and possessive. She takes it like it's her birthright, fingers cool against my forearm. We walk toward the door together, in perfect step. I don't look back at Ben. His existence has already begun to fade, a photograph left too long in sunlight.

At the threshold, I pause. My free hand brushes the reinforced steel of the door one last time before I pull it shut behind us, the latch engaging with a soft, definitive click. The sound of a period placed at the end of Ben Jacks' life.

Piper steps to the control panel mounted on the wall—sleek black glass, reflecting her face in fragments. Her finger hovers over the button for just a moment, not hesitation but contemplation. Then she presses it, firm and sure.

The hiss of gas is barely audible—a whisper, a sigh. Through the observation window, we watch as the colorless cloud floods the room. Carbon monoxide. Odorless. Painless, mostly. I didn't choose it for the mercy of it, but for the quiet. For her.

I reach for the tablet on the table, checking the levels. The numbers climb steadily, parts per million rising in precise increments. I've timed it perfectly, calculated the volume of the room against the density of the gas against the weight of a human body.

Three minutes to unconsciousness. Five to death. Seven to certainty.

Beside me, Piper leans against my side, her head coming to rest on my shoulder. Her eyes remain fixed on the window. Not on Ben writhing in his chains, but on the glass itself, as though watching static on an old television.

"Thank you," she says softly, the words almost lost beneath the mechanical hum of the ventilation system. "For waiting. For letting me have this."

I wrap my arm around her waist and pull her closer, feeling the heat of her through the fabric of her dress. "All you had to do was decide when," I tell her, lips against her temple.

The words settle between us, heavy with the weight of truth. I would have waited another six months, another year, another decade if she'd needed it. Time means nothing when measured against her justice.

Through the glass, Ben's struggles weaken, his body sagging against the restraints. His head lolls forward, chin to chest. The end comes not with violence but with surrender—a quiet slipping away, like snow melting in spring.

I watch without blinking, memorizing the moment. Not because I need the satisfaction, though it burns sweet in my blood. But because someone should bear witness to the consequences he earned.

My toy turns away before it's finished, already moving beyond this

chapter. I stay until the tablet confirms zero life signs, then power down the system. In death, Ben Jacks looks smaller than he did in life. Just a body in an empty room that will be scrubbed clean by morning.

Once it's over, we leave together. Piper doesn't speak, and there's a stiffness in her movements that I don't like.

When we're back in the car, she curls into me the way she always does after something sacred has passed between us. Her head finds the hollow of my shoulder, and her hand rests over my heart.

Piper's breathing grows deeper, more even. Not sleep, but the peaceful rhythm that comes after long-held tension finally releases. "It's done," she whispers against my collar. I feel it—the quiet ache still clinging to her. Justice is not peace. And peace was never the point.

I press my lips to her hair, breathing in the scent of her. "Yes." My hand tightens around hers. "It's done."

Epilogue 3
Lorenzo

1 year later.

The pale glow of morning light carves delicate shadows across Piper's bare back, illuminating the skin. "It's time," I whisper, though I know she's already awake, my mind already racing toward today's conquest.

One month ago exactly, she signed her new name beside mine on our marriage certificate. Piper Russo. Fuck, I love the sound of that. We've spent the last month on our honeymoon, but today, we're back at the office.

While we get ready, she memorizes talking points, and asks last minute questions she already knows the answers to. She's so busy preparing that she barely looks up from her tablet, her mind already in that place she goes to when she has empires to shape.

When she emerges from our closet, she's wearing a pale gray sheath dress that hugs her body like a promise. Her puzzle piece necklace rests against her throat, and it's still making me fucking hard to see her wear it.

I don't kiss her before we leave. I've learned better than to interrupt her when she's transforming into this—the woman who terrifies lesser men and arouses me in ways I can barely describe.

The car ride to Blackwood is silent. She still reviews notes I know she doesn't need. Her mind is a steel trap, and once something enters, it never escapes. I watch her fingers tap against her thigh, a subtle tell that makes my cock twitch.

We enter through the private entrance, her heels clicking a steady rhythm against the floors. I let her lead. Today, this is her domain. And my role isn't to guide but to witness, to ensure, to own the stillness behind her storm.

The boardroom door opens, and inside, Senator Lake and two other people await. He's young, ambitious, and reeks of desperation. I take my seat beside Piper, not across from her. Never above her. I position myself as her equal in the eyes of the Senator.

The Senator looks at me once, uncertain, like he's debating whether to address me. I tilt my head, barely. Enough to remind him he's not speaking to me unless I allow it. Piper is the voice. But I am the blade.

"Senator," she begins, her voice cool water over steel. "Let's not waste time. You need us more than we need you."

I watch her as she speaks, laying out statistics, polls, financial projections. Her data is razor sharp, her delivery flawless. Every word cuts with surgical precision. I feel myself hardening just watching her dismantle this man's resistance piece by piece.

My hand moves without conscious command, slipping under the table, finding the smooth heat of her thigh. She doesn't pause in her explanation of voting patterns in his district, doesn't flinch when my fingers brush higher. In fact, my naughty toy spreads her legs more.

"The numbers don't lie, Senator," she continues, not even a tremor in her voice as my fingers trace her slit. "Your base is eroding. Without our backing, you'll be forgotten by next term."

My dick throbs, thick and aching behind my zipper. I shift in my seat, as I dip two fingers through her folds, finding her already wet. I nearly groan at the discovery; she's aroused by her own power, by the man she's systematically destroying with nothing but words and intellect.

I begin to stroke her, my thumb circling her clit with precision.

She doesn't miss a beat. "Our backing comes with expectations, of course. Very specific expectations."

My balls are tight, straining. The friction of my pants is torture, every stroke of her cunt around my fingers sending zips through my cock like she's squeezing it instead. My thighs are tense, locked to keep from thrusting into nothing. My jaw aches from clenching. God, I could come right here just from her composure.

I push my fingers inside her wet heat, curling them inside her while maintaining perfect stillness in my face, my shoulders, my breathing. No one in this room knows that my fingers are buried inside the most powerful woman in Washington. The true First Lady.

No one sees how she tightens around me when she makes her key points. This is our secret language.

I feel her inner walls clench, a telltale flutter that announces her approaching orgasm. She's close, so close, yet her expression remains impassive, her voice steady as she lays out terms that will ensure this senator becomes our puppet.

When she comes, it's with such disciplined silence that I nearly come in my pants from the sheer control she demonstrates. Her thighs tense minutely, a small catch in her breath that only I would recognize, and then a flood of wetness coating my fingers as she continues speaking without pause.

"These terms are non-negotiable," she finishes, while I slowly withdraw my hand, keeping it hidden beneath the table. "So, what's your answer?"

"Can I think on it?" the Senator asks, looking shaken.

"No," Piper replies, shaking her head. "This is a take it or leave it deal."

His expression tells me that he knows he's been gutted, his political future now resting entirely in my toy's hands. And he doesn't even realize the woman who just executed him climaxed during the killing stroke.

The Senator accepts the deal, and Piper beams at him and his party as they shuffle out. He glances at me on his way out. This time, I let him see it; the death I've kept at bay for her sake. One misstep, and no one will ever find him. My mercy is conditional. My protection, absolute.

I get up and shut the door, the sound of the lock engaging is like a starting pistol to my restraint. Then I lean against the cool wood for a moment, just watching her.

Still seated, her legs are now crossed elegantly, one heel tapping a slow rhythm against the floor.

The boardroom still carries the scent of her power and something sharp and clean that makes my mouth water. Her victory hangs in the air between us, tangible as smoke.

"I think I like this chair," she murmurs, running her fingers along the leather armrests like she's considering purchasing it. Her eyes meet mine; green fire, unblinking, daring.

Every step I take toward her thunders in my ears. I've been hard since she first opened her mouth to speak, since I felt her come around my fingers while threatening a United States senator. The restraint I've maintained fractures with each footfall.

I reach her in four strides, cup her face in my hands, and kiss her. It's not gentle, not slow, but with the savagery I've been swallowing since dawn. My tongue invades her mouth the way I want to invade every part of her.

"That chair's yours," I tell her when we break apart, my thumb brushing against her jaw, feeling the delicate hinge where all her cutting words originate. "Everything in this building is yours now. But for now…" I slide my still wet fingers across her bottom lip, "… I want you to soak it with your juices."

"I have a better idea," she says, rising from the seat in one fluid motion. Her hands find the hem of her dress, dragging it up over her hips in a slow reveal of skin I've memorized but never tire of seeing. "Fuck me, Lorenzo. Fuck me as hard as I just gutted that senator."

My name in her mouth is a prayer and a command. I don't waste time with niceties or complete undressing. My hands find my belt, my zipper, freeing my dick with economical movements while my eyes never leave her face. I want to see every micro expression, every flutter

of her eyelids, every parting of her lips.

Lowering to my knees, I position her at the edge of the chair and grip her hips with force. In one brutal thrust, I bury myself inside her, feeling her body yield and clench around me in perfect counterpoint.

"Fuck," she gasps, her back arching, head tipping back to expose the long line of her throat.

My left hand finds her tit through the fabric of her dress, palm rubbing over her nipple until it hardens against my touch. My right hand moves lower, fingers finding her clit and circling it with the same deliberate pressure I used beneath the table—only now I don't need to hide my intentions.

"So fucking tight," I growl against her ear. "Do you know how close I came to coming in my pants when you told him 'You'll do what we tell you to do'?"

Her inner walls flutter around me at the reminder, her breathing growing ragged. I increase my pace, driving into her with enough force to make the chair creak beneath us. Her hands find purchase on my shoulders.

"Everyone in that room thought they were looking at a brilliant strategist," I continue, each word punctuated by a thrust. "But only I know what you really are. A fucking goddess."

"Enzo," she moans, her voice cracking around my name as her body tightens, thighs beginning to tremble with her approaching climax.

I see the exact moment she begins to lose control; her pupils dilate, and her breathing stutters. My hand moves from her breast to her throat, applying just enough pressure to make her eyes widen, to remind her who she belongs to even as she rules the world.

"Come for me," I command, pressing my thumb more firmly against her clit. "Come for me like you did when no one was watching, when you were breaking a man with just your words."

She shatters around me, her orgasm violent and encompassing. Her cunt grips me like a vise, milking me so hard it nearly breaks my control. Her moans are feral, animal sounds punched from deep in her chest, half-caught in her throat where my hand still rests. I release just enough pressure for her to gasp, to draw the air she needs to sustain the pleasure wracking through her.

I continue fucking her through it, relentless and precise, watching her eyes roll, her lips part, her body surrender to what only I can give her. The sight of her—my powerful, untouchable wife coming undone on my cock—pushes me past the edge of restraint.

"You are fucking magnificent," I tell her as my rhythm falters, as heat builds at the base of my spine. "My perfect fucking toy."

There's no restraint left—just possession. Just her name in my mouth and her cunt clenched around me. I come with a growl buried in her neck and her power carved into my blood.

When I can form thoughts again, I find her watching me, a satisfied

half-smile playing at the corners of her mouth. Her legs are still wrapped around my waist, her body still connected to mine.

"I think I definitely like this chair," she says, her voice husky and pleased.

I laugh against her neck, pressing my lips to her pulse point. "The chair, the table, the building. It's all yours now." I lift my head to meet her eyes. "Just like I am."

She raises an eyebrow, challenge sparking in her gaze. "Are you mine, Lorenzo Russo?"

I don't answer right away. I let her see it—everything that's passed between us. The secrets. The shadows. The choices. "I was always yours," I say, brushing my thumb across her lips. "The certificate just made it official."

B. Lybaek

9 781917 740098